Can't Stand the Heat

Also by Peggy Jaeger

A Shot at Love
Cooking with Kandy

Can't Stand the Heat

Peggy Jaeger

LYRICAL SHINE
Kensington Publishing Corp.
www.kensingtonbooks.com

LYRICAL SHINE BOOKS are published by

Kensington Publishing Corp.
119 West 40th Street
New York, NY 10018

All Kensington titles, imprints, and distributed lines are available at special quantity discounts for bulk purchases for sales promotion, premiums, fund-raising, educational, or institutional use.

Special book excerpts or customized printings can also be created to fit specific needs. For details, write or phone the office of the Kensington Sales Manager: Kensington Publishing Corp., 119 West 40th Street, New York, NY 10018. Attn. Sales Department. Phone: 1-800-221-2647.

Lyrical Shine and Lyrical Shine logo Reg. U.S. Pat. & TM Off.

First Electronic Edition: April 2018
eISBN-13: 978-1-5161-0109-2
eISBN-10: 1-5161-0109-X

First Print Edition: April 2018
ISBN-13: 978-1-5161-0112-2
ISBN-10: 1-5161-0112-X

Printed in the United States of America

For all the men who grill...and the women who let them.

Chapter One

"I can't believe I let Teddy Davis talk me into this," Stacy Peters mumbled as she riffled through her underwear drawer. "I could be on a tropical beach right now, sipping some exotic, fruity drink, instead of packing for a trip to Hell." She tossed two bras into the open suitcase on her bed.

"I wouldn't classify where you're going as Hell," her cousin, Kandy, said from her perch on the bed. While Stacy threw a few panties haphazardly into the suitcase, Kandy removed and neatly folded them.

"What do you call being stuck on a sweltering, smelly cattle ranch in July with a director who has the temper of an erupting volcano?" Stacy flung open the doors to her closet.

"A strategic career move?"

Stacy's hands stopped in the middle of hauling out a blouse, turned, and frowned at her cousin. "This isn't funny, Kan."

"I know, sweetie, but just think how much Teddy will owe you if you do this for him."

"Oh, he owes me, all right. Big-time. Before I left his office he green-lighted *Family Dinners.*"

One of Kandy's perfectly sculpted eyebrows rose a fraction. "Really? That was fast. I hope you got it in writing."

Stacy moved from her closet back to her dresser and dug through her humongous work purse. "You bet your sweet ass, I did."

She pulled a folded piece of paper from her wallet, opened it, and said, "I had him write and sign this before I agreed to go and had his personal assistant witness and date it. She had a conniption fit. Here," she handed it to her cousin. "Read it."

"I, Theodore Davis, network programming chef for EBS, agree to green-light Family Dinners *for Stacy Peters to develop and produce, and give her carte blanche for the hiring of a series director, star, and staff, after she acts as executive producer for the upcoming* Beef Battles *contest for EBS, under the directorship of Dominick Stamp."* Kandy set the paper down on her lap. "Wow. He really does want you in Montana. Director *and* star choice is yours. That's unheard of even with the most senior of executive producers."

"I know. His assistant was hyperventilating when she read that part, but I pushed hard for it and said I wouldn't go if he didn't agree to it." She rolled a pair of socks, but stopped before throwing them into the suitcase when she spied the folded pile Kandy had made.

Drawing a huge breath, Stacy plopped down next to her cousin. "Tell me I'm not absolutely crazy to be doing this. Please?"

Kandy took the socks and tucked them into the suitcase, then tossed an arm around her cousin's shoulders and squeezed. "You're not crazy, Stace. I think I'd classify what you're doing as a huge step, career-wise."

"Kinda feels like professional suicide to me." She stared down at her empty hands.

With another squeeze, Kandy rubbed her free hand along the younger woman's forearm. "You *have* been a primary producer before. It's not like you don't know what you're doing. Your track record is exceptional. Teddy knows that and is banking on you. Trust me, it won't be so bad."

"You're not the one who's going to be stuck on some godforsaken prairie for two months with a director who eats television producers as an appetizer, Kandace Sophia."

Ever since Teddy Davis had called her into his office that morning, his cryptic summons telling her he had something that needed her immediate attention, Stacy's stomach had been rolling.

Just a week ago she'd sent him her proposal for a new reality food series she wanted to create and produce called *Family Dinners*, and had been waiting anxiously for his answer. Her concept, she knew, was sound, had the potential to be a big hit for the network, and was a show that required relatively little in the way of funding. The budget she'd proposed was minor, something she knew the money-conscious programming chief would appreciate.

When Teddy's assistant had called requesting her presence, Stacy had been filled with equal parts joy and dread. To respond to a production idea in such a short time frame meant he was either thrilled with the concept or hated it. When she'd arrived at his office and then been told what he wanted from her first, Stacy had spent a long moment in panicked fear, and then a quick second on devising a plan that would benefit them both.

She hadn't grown up with a successful businessman for a father or a cousin who managed a multimillion-dollar cooking empire and not learned a thing or two about negotiation. When presented with her ultimatum—because that's what it had been—Teddy had, at first, been reluctant to agree. When Stacy insisted, he'd finally acquiesced. She knew it wasn't standard protocol for a show producer to have such a high level of control, especially for a program that hadn't been test-marketed yet. In all honesty, she'd thought he'd tell her to forget it, he would find someone else to go to Montana, and then shove her proposal back into his *to be determined* box. Stacy couldn't tell who was more surprised when he agreed to her demands: his assistant or her.

"I know Dominick Stamp has a volatile reputation when it comes to his work," Kandy said, "but he really is a top-notch technical director. You're going to learn an awful lot from him."

"If I survive." Stacy sighed.

Kandy laughed again. "You will. Guaranteed."

"How can you be so sure?"

"Because, Estella Elizabeth"—Kandy grabbed her hand—"you're a natural survivor. Of all of us, you're the strongest of Sophie's grandkids."

Stacy's mouth flew open in shock.

"You know you are," Kandy said with a nod. "No one. *No one* I know could have survived what you did and still grown into the amazing, smart, and wonderful woman you are. No one. Of us all, you're the most like Sophie."

Tears threatened behind her eyes. "I can't believe you think that. I've always thought you were the one who was the most like Grandma. In every way."

"I may have gotten the cooking gene," Kandy said, "but you got the backbone. Believe it. Just be your usual efficient, calm, and totally kick-ass self and all will be well in Montana. Now, let's get you packed. What time does your flight leave?"

"Five-thirty. I've got a car coming at four," she added with a swipe at her eyes. "How you get up every day at that god-awful hour is beyond me."

"Years of practice."

An hour and three packed, oversized suitcases later, Kandy gave her cousin a hug and a kiss on the cheek. "Text me if you need to vent or be talked off a ledge," she said with a grin. "Use our code word."

"Leech?"

With a laugh, Kandy nodded. "Anytime, okay? I'm always available for you."

"I know it, cuz." Stacy squeezed back. "Thanks for everything."

Alone in her apartment, Stacy dragged a hand through her hair. From her mental to-do list she ran through what she needed to still get done before she could crawl into bed so she'd be able to get up and out the door on time.

After throwing out all the food in her refrigerator that stood to spoil for the next eight-plus weeks she'd be gone, she paid her rent online, notified the post office to hold her mail, and emailed her parents to tell them where she'd be for the foreseeable future.

She crawled into bed at 8:30 with the two-inch-thick binder Teddy had given her, detailing all the information she needed to come up to speed on the show she was now in charge of producing.

Beef Battles was slotted as a headliner for the upcoming midseason schedule and the network was betting on it winning its slated Wednesday-night time slot. Ratings were the name of the game in television broadcasting and the EBS network had been slowly growing in popularity ever since Stacy's cousin's show, *Cooking with Kandy*, had soared to the top of the Nielsen ratings and stayed there three consecutive years. When it ended, Stacy, who'd been Kandy's assistant throughout the run, had been approached by Teddy Davis to act as assistant producer for another of the network's reality shows. That program had been having internal troubles, but with Stacy on board, it had turned around and after one season had climbed up in the ratings.

Knowing he had someone who could get along with any personality and who could remain calm during the most trying of times, Davis had given her another opportunity, this time to executive produce one of the network's most challenging programs, *Bake Off*. The hosts of the show were continually at personal and professional odds and the series was in danger of being cancelled due to overtime costs. Stacy came in, evaluated and identified the problems, and then turned the once combatant cohosts into on-air besties, pulling the show out of its dull ratings and into the top twenty.

It was during this time Stacy had come up with her own idea for a show and had researched and written her proposal. Now, with confirmation her idea would take off, she snuggled down under the covers and opened the binder.

Within two minutes she bolted upright in bed, fury heating her cheeks. *"That bastard!"*

She reached across her nightstand for her cell phone and was all set to call Teddy and back out of the job when her brain cooled down her emotions, forcing her to take a few deep, cleansing breaths and calm down. He hadn't told her that two producers had already quit before filming even began, citing personality conflicts with the director, or that Dominick Stamp's list of requests had already thrown the proposed budget to hell. And he'd failed to mention, or even hint at, the unusual living arrangements agreed to by the ranch's host in an effort to cut production costs.

Stacy fell back onto her pillows and closed her eyes. Pulling in air through her nose and gently blowing it out through her lips, her pulse slowed, and when her body relaxed again, she opened her eyes.

Grandma Sophie always said if you made a deal with the Devil, there'd be a heavy toll to pay. That statement had just been proven true. If she wanted her own show she had to dance with the Devil, or in this case, Dominick Stamp in Lucifer's guise.

With another heavy sigh, Stacy reopened the binder and read it from beginning to end.

Eighteen hours and two planes later, Stacy exited the jetway at Billings Logan International Airport, tired and cranky. And if the email she'd received from Teddy's assistant was to be believed, she still had a two-hour car ride to get to the ranch. Add in the time-zone difference and Stacy could feel her internal clock begging to be turned off.

A quick escalator ride down to baggage claim found her waiting for the carousel to spit out her luggage.

Stacy positioned herself as close to the metal carousel as she could and was just about to close her dry and tired eyes for a moment when she felt a tap on her shoulder. Turning, she found herself looking into an opened-collared, sun-drenched neck covered by a deep copper colored, long-sleeved shirt. She took a step back and lifted her chin.

"Miss Peters, ma'am?"

Stacy nodded as she stared up into the face of a man a few birthdays younger than her own twenty-nine. A broad and open smile lit the tanned face shaded under a white Stetson. Eyes so pale, Stacy blinked twice before she realized they were blue.

He stuck out his hand and said, "I'm Beau Dixon, Amos's son. I was sent to bring you back to the ranch."

Stacy took the proffered hand, and despite her sudden exhaustion, found enough energy to respond to his open and friendly smile with one of her own. "It's nice to meet you, Mr. Dixon."

"Just call me Beau, ma'am. 'Bout everyone does."

Nodding, she said, "And I'm Stacy. *Ma'am* makes me feel like my grandmother."

His smile widened and he shook his head. "Well, we can't have a pretty little thing like you feeling like that, now, can we?"

The carousel alarm beeped and the metal rotors started their accordion movements, various luggage pieces suddenly rotating around them.

"I've got three bags," she told him.

With a nod, he said, "You just point 'em out and I'll grab 'em."

"I was told it's a two-hour drive from here to your ranch," Stacy said, while he lifted the first piece she indicated.

"Probably more like two and half, three, with this midday traffic. Once we get out of the city proper, though, it'll go fast. Don't you worry."

As soon as all three pieces of her luggage had been obtained—Beau carrying two of them as if they weighed no more than a piece of paper each—he led her out of the building. Dry, hot, and arid air slapped her in the face as soon as they came through the revolving doors.

Get used to it, she told herself. This is what you're stuck with for the next two months.

A luxury town car waited at the curb, its hazard lights flashing.

"I didn't expect to see a car like this out here," she said while he stowed the baggage. Realizing a moment later how elitist that sounded, she added, "I mean, I just figured a truck would be the standard vehicle."

"I left the pickup at the ranch," Beau said, opening her door so she could slip in. He'd left the car running and the cool, refreshing air-conditioning blasting through the dashboard vents was refreshing and welcome. "Daddy thought this would be a more comfortable ride for you than in the cab of my truck."

He pulled them out into traffic and turned to grin at her. "Besides, he never lets me drive this beauty and I leaped at the chance when he offered."

Stacy grinned back. For several minutes he wove them through the busy traffic until they were onto the highway. "If you're tired, you can just lay your head back and take a little snooze," he told her. "I expect with the time difference and the travelin' you're about bushed."

"In all honesty I am, but if I take a nap now, I'll never sleep through the night and tomorrow I'll be even worse. Why don't you tell me about your ranch? I've only been given the basics about it."

There was unmistakable pride in his deep voice when he launched into a speech about the cattle ranch. The cursory description Teddy's assistant had slipped into her binder was adequate enough for her to get a picture of the business. But Beau was a wealth of knowledge about the intricacies involved in running it day to day.

"Now since we're almost into July," he told her after speaking almost nonstop for an hour, "most of our herd is out grazing, getting fat, and just waiting to either be sold or bred."

"Who makes that determination?" Stacy asked, her tired brain now spinning with all the facts and figures he spewed as if he were merely reciting the alphabet.

"My father and our veterinarian, Doc Burns." Beau tossed her a grin she was coming to think he was never without. "He's quite the character. Him and Daddy have been friends since they were boys."

"That's sweet."

A sound remarkably like a foghorn blasted from him. "Don't know that anyone has ever had the notion to call Cal Burns sweet, but he sure is entertaining."

"My notes say you've got two older brothers and their wives, plus you and your father all living at the main house."

He nodded. "Hopefully pretty soon that number will increase by one."

"Oh?"

Something moved across his face while she watched him drive; something eager, expectant, slightly bashful.

"Well, you see, I've been planning—" He stopped and snuck a quick sidelong glance at her before turning his attention back to the empty highway.

"Yes?"

He took in a huge breath, pregnant with anticipation and then, after he expelled it, said, "There's this girl. Jessie. Jessica. She's...we've... well, she's my girl, see? We've been together since grade school."

"Again, that's just sweet."

"Yeah, well, I'm gonna ask her to marry me."

"Oh! Congratulations."

"Thanks, but it's not a done deal yet. I need a ring. I need to ask her daddy, 'cause she's old-fashioned that way, you know?"

"I do." Stacy smiled. Her heart sighed at the thought of being young, in love, and having a shared future in front of you. Not that she considered herself old, but love wasn't something she'd ever felt for a man. Instead, she'd concentrated on moving in and out of every day, secure in the knowledge she'd made it through another twenty-four hours without the dark and miserable thoughts of her younger years breaking through and overtaking her once again.

It had been a long, hard-fought internal battle against her many demons to get where she was today emotionally, spiritually, and physically and she'd come to terms with the fact a lasting, happily-ever-after wasn't in the cards for her.

Beau pulled the car off the highway.

"We should be at the main house in about fifteen minutes. All this land you see is Dixon land."

Stacy's view of the empty and never-ending stretch of highway they'd just exited morphed into a length of road in front of them equally as vast, surrounded on both sides by fenced-in fields of verdant, wind-blowing grass.

"We've got just shy of thirty thousand acres," he told her.

True to his word, not more than fifteen minutes later Stacy got her first peek at the Dixon Ranch, or as Beau called it, the main house.

In her mind she'd pictured the house as resembling the one from the 1980s show *Dallas* she'd seen a few times on disc. The Dixon house was nothing like that iconic structure.

Three stories high and filled from side to side with gabled windows, the house was composed of multicolored gray slab in a patchwork design, Ionic columns shooting up from the wraparound porch to the second story across the front of the building, and a set of double front doors made of solid, unstained oak.

Several American-model trucks and cars littered the gravel road up to the house, but Stacy's gaze zeroed in on three huge box vans parked off to one side with the initials *EBS* blazoned across them. Satellite dishes covered most of the three vehicles' roofs. Several smaller box trucks surrounded them, all belonging to the network.

"The television trucks and crew arrived a couple weeks ago," Beau said.

"Did Mr. Stamp arrive with them?" she asked.

"No, ma'am—uh, I mean, Stacy."

She was charmed when his cheeks reddened.

"Got here three days ago. He's been out with Daddy, scouting locales for filming. They've been gone most of every day since."

When his lips pulled back into a dry grin, she asked, "What's funny about that?"

"Not funny, like you mean, ma—Stacy. It's just Daddy's been as ornery as a hungry mountain cat. He likes to order people around, does Mr. Stamp. Daddy doesn't take kindly to following other people's commands."

Great. Now she not only had to try and control her dictatorial director, but she probably had to smooth the waters with their host as well.

The rumbling sound of a large vehicle coming up the drive had them both turning to the sound.

"Here they come now, in fact."

Stacy's gaze tracked the truck as it pulled in and parked. The driver's door pushed open and she got her first view of the ranch's owner, Amos Dixon. Put thirty years and fifty pounds on Beau and you had his father, right down to the Stetson on his head and the well-lived-in jeans covering the yards of leg.

Dixon's eyes zeroed in on his son and then trailed to Stacy. A slow, steady, and welcoming smile drifted across his mouth as he boldly stared at her. She was about to return it when the passenger door slammed, its occupant pushing around from the front of the truck.

His height mimicked the man next to him at about six-one. The similarities ended there. Where Amos Dixon was stockily built and barrel chested, his physique laying claim to the fact he labored hard for his living, Dominick Stamp was lithe and athletic, narrow hipped, but broad-shouldered. Clad in jeans and a pure-white collared shirt, the last thing anyone would take him for was a rancher.

His eyes were hidden behind dark aviator sunglasses, his head hatless. Thick and wavy jet-black hair tinged with white at the temples and hairline framed a face that could never be called soft. Angular planes cut into his high cheekbones, deep corrugations running down from the corners of his thick lips to his chin. Even though she couldn't see his eyes, she knew they were locked on her, just as she knew behind those sunglasses, heated antagonism was staring at her face.

Stacy had prepared what she was going to say when they finally met. Her little rehearsed speech died a horrible death before she was ever able to utter it when the director stomped toward her, his mile-long legs eating up the dust and gravel beneath his feet, an angry scowl darkening his features. The hostility blowing from him sliced through her the closer he came.

Stacy took a deep mental and a physical breath. She'd known his reputation before agreeing to take this job and had decided to take it anyway. Working under his command was going to be difficult and the biggest professional challenge she'd ever set herself up for, but if there was one thing Stacy knew about herself it was she was determined to never quit. Anything. No matter what—or who—the challenge was.

With her mouth pulled into a determined line and her spine as straight and hard as a steel forged rod, she moved toward the director, one hand extended.

Chapter Two

This couldn't be the new executive producer.

She looked like an intern, barely out of college, not the seasoned television producer Teddy Davis had emailed him about.

The one he'd emailed back saying he neither wanted nor needed.

Hair the color of champagne fell just below her shoulders in a soft cascade of waves and ripples. Even in the heat and humidity engulfing them, it looked fresh. Her face was a perfect heart, a tiny dip in the center of the hairline bifurcating her brow into two perfectly aligned sections, her flawless chin falling into a delicate point. She had one hand out to shake his, the other shading her eyes from the strong and harsh afternoon sun, but underneath her fingers he was able to make out a pair of sloe-shaped eyes in a deep, forest green.

Taller than average but small boned, her legs took up most of her lissome body. With her lips held together in a tight line, she reached him.

"I'm Stacy Peters, Mr. Stamp."

He stopped and planted his feet, his gaze shifting to her outstretched hand and then back up to her face without taking it. Her eyes narrowed into a determined glare and it looked as if she wasn't going to back down until he shook it. With reluctance, he did.

Like the rest of her, her fingers were narrow and thin as they coiled around his.

A blast of heat instantly warmed and calmed his entire body like a few shots of his favorite Irish whiskey did after a rough and painful day. The subtle aroma of vanilla floated to him, filling his senses with the sweet fragrance. The persistent, throbbing ache in his left leg the liquor helped chase away was momentarily forgotten with his hand rooted in hers.

As soon as she pressed her fingers firmly against his palm once, she pulled her hand back.

For a split second, Nikko missed the touch.

In the next, he found his anger again.

"Look, Miss Peters—"

"Stacy is fine."

He ignored her. "I told Davis I didn't need an executive producer. I don't need anyone telling me how to run this show, what's going to make it a hit, how to rip the best from the concept. The show will be fine without someone questioning every decision I make and counting every dollar I spend."

Stacy nodded and folded her hands together in front of her, her gaze staying locked on his as he spoke.

"Those last two he sent me were worthless and more trouble than I could stand."

"Yes. I know there were…problems with the previous EPs—"

"Problems?" His scornful bark of a laugh was loud and harsh as he cut her off. "Two of the most annoying, incompetent people I've ever had the misfortune of meeting. One was worse than the other. They had no knowledge of how to run a television production. Knew nothing about costs, location shots, or even how to set up food service for the crew. Between the two of them together, I don't think they had a full brain."

Surprised was too tame a word to describe his reaction when she laughed out loud. The sound hit him square in the chest like a bullet ripping through his rib cage.

Christ, was she laughing at him?

His eyes narrowed and he took a step closer, forcing her head to lift so she could meet his gaze. If he'd thought to intimidate her with his height, he knew he'd failed when she stood her ground, her gaze never wavering from his, her shoulders staying square.

A tiny bit of respect warred with the irritation churning inside him.

"They never even made it out here, one of them quitting an hour after she arrived at the studio. I don't need incompetents like that around me or this production."

"I agree."

Her words didn't stop him. "Davis promised me creative control when I signed on to this show. That included managing the budget and costs as I saw fit. He gave me his word no one would bother me about piddling things like the price of airfare, how many damn cups we use for coffee or how much it would cost to film at night."

He took another half step closer, so close now his body almost came in contact with hers.

"What he didn't promise me was annoying paper pushers who don't know a thing about running a television show, so you can get right back in that car and have Dixon take you back to the airport, because you're not needed or wanted here."

From the side of his vision Nikko saw a small crowd had formed around them. Set technicians, a few of the ranch hands Dixon employed, even the food-service people. He knew he should get a leash on his temper, but the annoyance of being saddled with yet another producer—and one who didn't even look old enough to vote—had him unable to curtail his fury. Added in was the throbbing mess his leg had turned into from sitting in Dixon's truck for so many hours.

She'd been nodding at everything he'd said and hadn't interrupted him once. When he finally stopped, she came to life.

"I can assure you, Mr. Stamp," she said, her gaze slicing through him with its intensity, "I have no intention of taking any control away from you. This show is yours. Your name is on it, not mine. It's your baby. And unlike my two predecessors, I *do* know what I'm doing." She took a breath, snaked a side-glance at the gathering group of people, and added, "This isn't my first rodeo."

The crew laughed.

Before Nikko could form a response, she shot her gaze to the senior rancher. She moved toward him, saying, "Mr. Dixon? I'm Stacy Peters, from EBS. Thank you so much for allowing us to film our competition here, for putting us all up, and putting up with us all."

Nikko watched a free and easy smile grow on her face, one with twin dimples winking at the corners of her mouth, as she slipped her hand into the rancher's.

"Well, aren't you just the prettiest thing I've seen around here all day," Amos Dixon said, shaking her hand and wrapping the other one around it to cocoon it between his. "And it's my pleasure, young lady. My pleasure."

Stacy giggled at the rancher, her nose crinkling. Nikko's stomach muscles contracted at the adorable expression on her face.

"I was familiarizing myself with your ranch on the flight and I have to tell you how impressed I am with your business, and how I'm a little in awe of the scope of everything I've seen so far. I can't imagine living here, seeing all this beauty everyday. It's breathtaking."

Dixon's barrel chest puffed out at the praise.

"I'd be delighted to take you on a tour around the ranch anytime, darlin'—you just say the word."

"I'd love that."

"Well, you must be tired from the long trip," Dixon said, keeping her hand tucked in his. "And I imagine you're getting hungry too. Little thing like you needs a good, hot meal in her and I've got the best cook in the state."

She laughed and said, "I can always eat, Mr. Dixon—"

"Call me Amos, darlin'. Everyone does."

She nodded. "And a hot meal sounds great right now, but I've got some things I need to see to first before I take you up on your offer."

Turning her attention back to Nikko, she was all professional polish once again, the smile gone, a blank, unreadable look on her face when she said, "Why don't I drop off all my stuff, and then I can meet with you privately, Mr. Stamp? I know filming starts the day after tomorrow and there's probably a million things that need to get done before that. I've been brought up to speed on everything, but I'd like to hear from you what you need, when you need it, how I can help you get it, and how I can make everything easier for you. Would fifteen minutes be good?"

Dumbfounded, Nikko just nodded.

"Great." She turned to Dixon's son. "Beau, can you show me to my room?"

Nikko watched father and son jockey for her attention as Dixon senior said, "Boy, you get the little lady's bags. I'll show her up. Shall we?" He held a cocked elbow for her to take, while his son pulled luggage from the trunk of the car.

As the trio walked up the drive and then the porch steps, Nikko's gaze lasered on the slim back and long legs of his new executive producer as she smiled and listened to the senior rancher wax on and on about his "family's spread."

What the fuck had just happened?

Nikko turned to see a battery of eyes staring at him.

"Don't you have things to do?" he bellowed. "This isn't vacation camp."

Like lemmings, they all turned as a unit and scurried away.

Nikko rubbed his throbbing thigh, the unceasing pain careening through him. He needed to sit down, put his leg up, and relax for a while.

Maybe more than a while.

Unfortunately, the demands of his job weren't going to allow him that time, not now and not in the foreseeable future. Add in the fact he now had to meet with his new executive producer and listen to a load of network bullshit, and he knew it would be a long, long time before he could sit back and just rest.

* * * *

Stacy's gaze ran around the perimeter of the spacious and brightly decorated rooms she was given. A large bedroom, complete with a walk-in closet, an attached full bath, and its own veranda with wrought-iron table and chairs—the space she'd be calling home for the next eight weeks was almost as large as her Manhattan apartment.

"My late wife had these rooms done-up for my mother-in-law when she came to live with us," Amos told her, dropping one of her bags at the edge of the bed.

"Grandma moved in the day before I was born and stayed with us until she died, two years ago," Beau added.

"I'd read you'd lost your wife Caroline several years ago," Stacy told Amos. "I'm so sorry."

"When Beau was ten," he said. "Luckily Ruth, Caro's mother, stayed with us. Don't know how I'd have raised my kids without her." He shook his head, his Stetson gripped tightly in one hand. "Woman had the patience of a saint, that's the truth."

Beau chuckled. "She needed it, what with me and my older brothers always getting into mischief."

"Up to no good is more like it," Amos said. There was no real heat behind the statement, only paternal love and understanding.

"Well, we'd better let you get all settled," Amos told her, cocking his head at his youngest son. "Dinner's at seven, if you'd care to join us. Although the television people have mostly been staying to themselves. Heading into town to eat and such."

"Mr. Stamp as well?"

The subtle pursing of the rancher's lips was an indication of how he felt about the director.

It was Beau who answered. "Stamp and his daughter have their own place just off the stables. It's the old foreman's cabin. They usually stay there for meals."

"His daughter? I didn't know he'd brought any family with him."

She thought back to the bio she'd glanced at the night before. Stamp was divorced and his ex-wife had died, tragically, in an automobile accident a little under two years ago.

In a car Stamp had been driving.

Beau's mouth split into a huge grin. "Name's Melora and from everything I've seen so far, she's not thrilled about being here. Seems like a good kid, though. Just"—he shrugged—"not a happy camper. Cute, but teen-moody, y'know?"

She nodded, knowing exactly what he meant.

Been there. Been that.

Amos gave her directions to Stamp's bungalow and then the two left her alone.

Hands on her hips, Stacy mentally listed what she needed to do.

First things first. She pulled her cell phone from her bag and smiled when she saw she had full service at the out-of-the-way ranch. She hit a speed-dial number and was immediately connected with her mother's cell. Her parents were currently on a vacation junket in China, and the time difference, plus the availability of good service, was questionable. She left a message saying she'd arrived and would email during the week. Then she plugged in her laptop and sent an arrival email to Teddy Davis. She noticed she had several messages, including one from Kandy she decided to open.

Hey cuz. Hope you arrived safe and sound. Meet any cute, available and willing cowboys yet? LOL. Send pictures!! Check in when you can and remember to just be your awesome, efficient, and calm self, and everyone— including Dominick Stamp—will adore you. Love and miss you, K.

After her brief first meeting with the testy director, Stacy was pretty sure her cousin's words wouldn't prove true.

With a quick glance in the full-length cheval mirror, Stacy grabbed her e-notebook, her cell phone, and the room key Amos had given her, and set off to find the man she'd be working under for the next two months.

* * * *

The sound of shouting met her ears a full twenty feet before she got to the front door of the cabin.

Although *cabin* was a totally inaccurate word for the sprawling two-level structure. Her overactive imagination had conjured a small, single-leveled log home complete with a porch and maybe even a rocking chair, gingham curtains on a lone window, and smoke spewing out of the chimney from a cast-iron woodstove. This was Montana, after all, not Manhattan.

Her imagination did a 180 as she walked up the front steps to land on a porch—yeah, she got that one right—but in every other way she was way off base. The cabin was...well, *a house*. Not made of logs, but solid, firm brick, the porch wrapping around three sides. Two stories high, it looked like it belonged back in a New England town, not in the center of a cattle ranch. The front door was solid oak, the windows wide and curtained, although not in the red gingham she'd pictured.

The yelling was louder at the front door. Two distinct voices. A man, who sounded just like Dominick Stamp, and a female, younger and shrill. Obviously, the moody teenaged daughter. Stacy cringed at the anger in the young voice, recognizing the tone. She'd sounded much the same way during her teen years.

Should she knock and interrupt the fight, or leave?

The choice was made for her when the door flew open and a blast of cold, air-conditioned air from its interior blew out at her.

The girl was looking over her shoulder and not where she was heading.

Which was right into Stacy.

She avoided getting trampled by quickly shifting to one side.

The girl stopped short, her hand still on the doorknob.

"Oh!"

"Sorry," Stacy said, giving her an embarrassed grin. "I was just about to knock."

"Who are you?"

Suspicion curled around the girl's heavily made-up and lined eyes, her crimson lips pressing into a tight line as she flicked her gaze up and down Stacy.

Not a happy camper, Beau had said. Stacy could add another description based solely on the way the girl was staring at her right now and from the expression in her eyes: Pain. Deep, internal pain.

Been there. Felt that.

Stacy took a small breath and said, "I'm Stacy Peters, the new executive producer. I'm supposed to meet Mr. Stamp to go over a few things. If this is a bad time, I can come back."

"No, it's a perfect time, because you can, like, *deal* with him now instead of me." The girl cocked her thumb over her shoulder and added, "He's in his ogre's lair."

She didn't wait for a reply, simply shot past Stacy and jogged down the walkway.

Just as she disappeared around a corner, Stamp roared, "Melora? Where are you?"

This time, Stacy took a deeper, fuller breath and told herself to be calm.

She came into the house, shutting the door gently behind her. It wasn't difficult to locate Stamp. She just followed his booming voice.

"You get in here, young lady, right now. We're not done."

He was sitting behind a massive desk, foraging through several papers on top of it. Stacy took a moment before announcing herself to study the man.

Even from a seated position, his torso overshadowed the top of the desk, a testament to his height. He must have been raking his hands through the sides of his thick hair, because the ends were stuck at odd angles, proving the man hadn't seen a barber in some time. The deep corrugations bracketing the corners of his mouth told Stacy a few things. One, he was angry— but she knew that from the sound of his voice. Two, he was tired. Seriously sleep-deprived tired. Like a man who hadn't known the benefits of a relaxing slumber in quite some time. And three, as she'd seen in his daughter, he was filled with pain. His type, though, clearly signaled a physical kind.

"Dammit, Melora, get in—"

When his gaze connected with hers, Stacy had to remind herself to take a breath. Before, his eyes had been hidden behind his sunglasses. Nothing barred them from her now and when they settled on her, widening right before narrowing, Stacy was reminded of the color of her father's favorite cognac: Rich, bright sepia with tiny flecks of amber shooting out from where they surrounded the pupils, filled eyes tilted upward at the corners.

"What are you doing here? Where's my daughter?" He looked over Stacy's shoulder. *"Melora!"*

"She said she was going for a walk." Stacy braced herself and, unbidden, moved into the room, directly into his line of sight. "And we agreed I'd come and meet with you privately—"

"I never agreed. I believe I told you I didn't need or want you here."

Stacy nodded. "Yes. You did."

"So why are you still here?" He glanced down at his papers again, dismissing her.

Stacy longed to tell this annoying, arrogant man the real reason she was going to tolerate him for the next few months, but knew the benefit of keeping her mouth shut. Instead, she pointed to the chair in front of the desk, said, "May I?" and held her breath.

He lifted his head and, with what looked like a great deal of unwillingness, swiped a hand in the air.

When she was settled, notebook on her lap, her hands folded over it, she looked across the span of the desk at him.

"Thank you."

She was surprised when a deep sigh burst from him.

"Don't thank me," he said, gruffly, his gaze moving to hers again. "Just say what you need to say. I've got a shitload of work to do before filming starts and this is wasting what little free time I have." He leaned back in the chair, his hand dropping to his thigh, where he gripped it with his fingers.

Stacy ignored the jibe. "Yes, well, that's one of things I wanted to talk to you about. Time management."

Before she could say another word, he righted himself again and glared at her. "Excuse me?"

With just those two words Stacy knew immediately why the other producers had quit before production ever got underway. A lesser-willed person would never stand a chance against Dominick Stamp's forceful, intimidating personality. She could imagine grown men shaking when he settled that dark-eyed, frosted, and piercing stare on them.

Good thing she wasn't weak-willed and was used to dealing with tyrants and egotistical television personalities.

She clasped her fingers a little more tightly. "It's my job to see that you have everything you need—including enough time—for the show to run to your specifications."

"My specifications?"

"Yes. As I said before, this show is yours. You're in charge. Of everything."

"Everything, is it?" His sonorous chortle echoed in the room. "That's a new one."

"*Everything.* Budget, timetables, chef challenges, all decisions that need to be made. The bottom line. I've worked on and produced enough shows—"

"How many?"

Confused, she asked, "How many what? Shows have I worked on?"

"Yes. You don't look old enough to have worked on, much less produced, anything."

Okay, so it was obvious he'd never read the bio Teddy Davis assured her he'd sent before she arrived. She didn't like tooting her own horn, never had, but had to in order to get this odious man to see her as worthy.

"Three, to date. I was the executive producer of *Cooking with Kandy* for five seasons. When *Kandy* ended I produced the Dolly Cardson show, *Hello Dolly.* When that finished production, Teddy Davis brought me in to executive produce *Bake Off* after initial production began and the show started having…problems."

Stamp continued to stare across his desk at her, his expression contemplative.

"I finished with *Bake Off* last month. It did well in the ratings too."

Well? Hell, the ratings for the final two episodes had been through the roof, but she didn't say that.

"You actually worked with Dolly Cardson and lived to tell about it?" he asked after a moment. "Without any battle scars?"

A free and easy smile broke from her at his choice of words and she giggled. His face went expressionless, a fact she didn't miss.

"They're well hidden," she told him, shaking her head, her face becoming a mask of professionalism once again.

He stayed silent, his gaze trained on her.

"Look, Mr. Stamp. I'm not a green kid, looking to make my bones in the business. I'm twenty-nine and have been working steadily for EBS without a break since I graduated from college at twenty-one. Yes, I worked for my cousin in the beginning, but if you know anything about Kandy's program you know what a high-stress, fast-paced show it was. I know what I'm doing. Now, may I finish?"

Wordlessly, he nodded.

She took a calming breath. "There is only one person who should ultimately be responsible for making all the necessary decisions when it comes to a show, and it's not the executive producer. It's the technical director. You, in other words. Not me. My job is to make your job as easy and as worry-free as possible."

Stacy knew she had his attention when his eyebrows rose. Before he could ask the question she knew was coming, she beat him to it.

"And in order to do that I need to know what you want."

"What I...want?"

The heat in his eyes had her squirming just a tiny bit in her chair.

"Yes." She swallowed. "Like I said, *my job* is to make sure *your job* is worry-free, so I need to know details, like what food to go with what challenge? What times do you want to film? When do you want the sets prepped? The food ready? The chefs primed to go? All those things are important factors to time perfectly and any one of them can go off the rails for any reason, preventing you from proceeding. It's my job to see that the trains stay on the proverbial tracks. So, yes, what you want is important for me to know to ensure that everything happens the way you want it to."

Stacy stopped and took a breath. He'd interrupted her so many times before, she'd wanted to get everything out before giving him the chance to do so once again. She knew she sounded breathless and maybe a little nervous to boot, but at least she had his attention.

"Did Davis tell you how different this competition is from all the others on the network? I can assure you, you've never worked on a show like this one before, no matter how many credits you have," he said after silently staring at her for a few seconds.

"He didn't personally, but he gave me the show bible, which I read twice, so I could get up to speed. The concept is intriguing."

"Intriguing? That's an interesting word choice."

Why did he have to make everything she said sound as if she was foolish or immature? Well, two could play at this semantics game.

"How would you describe it?"

He leaned forward again, resting his elbows on his desk. "I guess *intriguing* is as good a word as any," he said after considering.

It was Stacy's turn to nod. "As I understand the format, there's an afternoon of prep once the challenge is given to the chefs, then the cook-off. Correct?"

"Yes."

"Then the meal is served to the judges and the ranch employees? The cowboys?"

"Right. The cowboys cast votes, secretly, while the judges mull over the food, which we film. No winner is announced until the final challenge is complete. The chef with the highest number of votes, plus the numerical scores assigned by the judges after each challenge, will be declared the champion."

When she'd read the show bible the night before, Stacy had seen immediately how such a format could be a ratings powerhouse. Without declaring a winner or voting off a chef after each challenge, and the audience never knowing anything other than the judges' musings on the meals, the viewers would want to watch each episode until the finale to see if their favorite chef walked away with the prize.

"It's a great premise," she told him. "Did you come up with it?"

For a split second she thought he looked embarrassed at the question. "It's been something I've been mulling around for a while," he told her, casting his eyes back down at the papers on his desk.

When he didn't elaborate, she didn't push. Keeping it professional with this man, she knew, was the key to keeping the peace—on set and with her.

"So, again," she said, opening her e-notebook. "Tell me what you need me to do before filming starts."

* * * *

Stacy tossed her room key on the dresser and let the yawn that had been threatening to break free for an hour, go.

After her meeting with Stamp, she'd come back to the main house, where she was met by the Dixons, who'd just finished dinner. Amos had introduced her to the rest of his family, asking if she was hungry—she wasn't—and then she'd asked for directions to the crew quarters. She needed to meet with them, introduce herself, and get the schedule for the next few days done.

Since the ranch was a working one, the property was littered with bunkhouses for the cowboys and ranch hands who helped keep it productive to live in. One such cabin, she was told, housed the technical crew and the rest of the individual producers who'd be personally assigned to the chefs.

Stacy found her way to the single-story building, the sound of raised voices and free laughter drawing her.

The front door was ajar, so she slipped in and got her first view of the people she'd be, for the most part, in charge of.

Her lips split into a huge grin when she recognized several crew members she'd worked with on other shows, one who spotted her and came rushing forward.

Stacy laughed as she was lifted in the air and spun around before being gently settled back on her feet.

"I heard you got here safe and sound," Peter Luccassi told her, pulling her into a side hug and guiding her into the house. "Long-ass trip from New York, isn't it?"

She grinned up at the man in charge of the sound and recording crew. "I don't think I'm in Kansas anymore, Toto," she said back.

"Not even close, kiddo. Hey, look who I found," he announced as he brought her into the fold. They were immediately engulfed by the crew. Stacy greeted some old friends and was introduced to several new faces, all of whom welcomed her with open arms.

After working on such diverse reality shows, Stacy knew the benefits of having good relationships with the staff, who would do the daily scut work necessary to keep the show moving. A happy crew, her cousin Kandy had told her more times than she could remember, was a productive and hardworking crew. Treat them fairly and with respect, and they'd do anything for you. When she'd worked on *Hello Dolly*, the main reason she'd been able to turn the show around to the ratings hit it became was because she'd demonstrated to the crew how much they were valued. Something Dolly Cardson had never even thought to show them.

Two hours later Stacy was finally allowed to plead exhaustion and escape to her rooms.

Forgoing a shower, she quickly washed and then rubbed lotion all over her face and body. After changing into her usual sleepwear T-shirt she opened the doors to the veranda and then climbed into bed. She snuggled under the down comforter, loving the cool, crisp air that filtered in from the land surrounding the ranch.

Her mind played over her meeting with her new director. Dominick Stamp, she'd discovered, was a minutia man, and one used to calling the shots, doing everything that needed to be done, and arranging for everything that needed arranging.

Control freak danced through her head numerous times when she'd questioned him about something an executive producer should have been responsible for, only to find out he'd already done what needed doing.

There were still a great many details and tasks that needed to be seen to before filming ever started, though, and she was going to make sure they were fulfilled. And to Dominick Stamp's specifications.

The analog clock sitting on the bedside table told her it was way past time for bed. Her body was still on East Coast time and screaming for her to get some sleep.

Tomorrow was going to be a time crunch, with the chefs all arriving on the same flight, needing to be picked up and then apprised of what was in store for them for the next few weeks.

Stacy'd told Stamp she'd go to the airport and round them up. His face had registered surprise, but after a moment he'd nodded.

Score one point, she'd thought at the time.

Stamp's reputation for being a perfectionist didn't intimidate Stacy in the least. *Perfection*, she'd often joked, was cousin Kandy's middle name and Stacy knew the value of paying attention to details. It wasn't going to be an easy job to wrestle some of that perfectionistic control away from Stamp and allow her to deal with the aspects of the show that were her job. He was famous—or was it infamous?—for dressing down staff in front of the entire production team and he wasn't discriminatory in who he screamed at. Everyone from the food-service delivery person to the directors of the various technical teams had been shown his wrath.

Some of the crew she'd just met alerted her to a few tense situations Stamp had already created with his outbursts and they hadn't even begun filming yet.

Stacy knew the job ahead of her was going to be arduous. Before allowing her mind to finally succumb to exhaustion, she said a silent prayer, invoking her grandmother's name and asking the woman to help keep her focused and calm during the show's production.

Chapter Three

Stacy woke just as dawn broke through the open veranda doors. Although the time she'd slept wasn't long, the quality of the sleep had been restorative and she woke fresh and charged for the day.

As she had for almost every day of the past fourteen years, Stacy slipped into yoga pants and a long-sleeved exercise shirt. The evening before, one of the tech staff had told her there was a natural spring about a quarter of a mile from the main house. Deciding that her morning workout would benefit from the fresh air, Stacy grabbed her mat and made her way from her room.

The smells of morning breakfast wafted up the central staircase as she came down to find Amos Dixon just entering the foyer.

"Well, you're certainly a pleasant sight early in the morning," he told her with a grin that encompassed his whole face.

It was impossible not to be pleased by the compliment. With a string of heat creeping up her neck and cheeks, she said, "Good morning. You're an early riser."

"Ranch life starts before dawn and ends when night blackens the sky."

"Kinda like a television production," she said, grinning back at him.

His gaze flicked to the mat she carried. "Was the bed not comfortable enough? You need to sneak a nap in someplace else?"

"What? Oh, no." She shook her head. "The bed was beyond wonderful. I fell asleep before my head hit the pillow. This is my yoga mat. I never leave home without it. I was just on my way out to find your stream. I heard it's a great place to—that is, it has a beautiful view in the morning."

Stacy knew the quizzical reaction she'd be met with if she'd said what she originally thought to: stretch and meditate. Too many times over the years she'd been on the receiving end of quizzical and questioning stares at the mention of her practice of yoga. Some people were naturally curious, asking questions to increase their knowledge. Some were condescending, scoffing at the notion, while others had been downright rude and laughed at the practice that had brought her such peace and calm and made it possible for her to get through each and every day.

She wondered how Amos Dixon would respond. Before he could, Beau barreled down the stairs and stopped short in front of them.

"Hey. Morning," he said, nodding at his father and gracing her with a smile.

"Morning. It seems your whole family rises with the sun," she said to Amos.

"Some earlier than others," he replied. "Where's Caleb? Hungover and sleeping in again?"

"In the shower. Said he'll be down in five and to save him some coffee."

Amos's lips thinned. Stacy had met the older Dixon son, Caleb, the night before. She'd have known he was Beau's brother anywhere; they almost looked like twins. Each movie-star handsome, they had that easy, laconic way about them that just drew people in.

A little family drama drifted around her and she wanted nothing to do with it. She had drama enough just keeping on her toes around Dominick Stamp.

"Well, I'd better get going." To Beau, she asked, "We need to leave for the airport by eleven, right?"

"Yup. I'll be ready, don't you worry none."

She tossed him a nod as he moved into the dining room, his father with him.

The cool, fresh morning air tingled her skin while she made her way to the stream.

The description she'd been given of its beauty was a totally inaccurate one. Words, she thought, simply couldn't do justice to the exquisite, natural splendor surrounding her.

About a half-mile wide, the sparkling, clear water swam slowly by her, surrounded on both sides by towering trees and rock-strewn terrain. Turning one way, mountains in the distance showed her the stream's origination point. Turning the other, she watched the water flow for as far as she could see. The sun was more than peeking above the horizon now, and the sky above her was rapidly lightening. The only sound she heard was the water as it cascaded over and across the rocks lining its path.

Stacy found a flat spot close to the water's edge and rolled open her mat. Facing the rising sun, she began the first of her exercises with the sun salutation.

With her feet together, hands at her sides, palms forward, she took a deep breath and then swept her arms over her head in a wide arc. Pressing her palms together, she tilted her head back and looked up at them.

Exhaling, she arced her arms downward and fell forward, bringing her nose to her knees and placing her palms flat on the mat, alongside her feet.

She went through the rest of the exercise, ending it in a downward-facing dog position, before beginning the sequence again and repeating it two more times.

With each move and breath she took, Stacy felt the calm and peace she needed to guide her through the day flow up from within her. When she'd moved out of the final position, she came back to center, standing flat-footed once again, and brought her palms together in front of her, prayer-like. With a final breath, she dropped to the mat, crossed one leg over the other, and closed her eyes, allowing all her senses but sight, to tune in to her surroundings.

She heard the water swishing down the stream, bubbling as it tripped over the rocks; felt the tiny breeze on her face. The subtle smell of smoke spewing from the ranch's kitchen chimney, followed by the unmistakable aroma of bacon frying, had Stacy's empty stomach bouncing and her taste buds standing at attention with craving.

Movement behind her forced her eyes open. Turning, she spotted the girl who had flown out Stamp's front door the night before.

"I'm sorry," the girl said, her bottom lip shooting under her top teeth. "I didn't see you and then, when I did, I tried to be, like, quiet. I'm...sorry."

Last night, the girl's thin and heavily made-up face had been pinched in anger, her lips furled back in a snarl as she flew from the house and her father.

This morning her youthful skin was clean and makeup-free, the anger replaced by anxiety. She looked less than the fifteen years Stacy knew her to be. Spiky black hair was pulled back from her face by a cloth headband, the ends flaming around the band at odd angles.

"It's okay. I was pretty much done." Stacy gave the girl an open smile, then unfolded from her cross-legged position and stretched her body upward.

"I'm Stacy," she said, while she rolled her mat. "We met very briefly last night, when I came to see your dad."

"I remember. I'm Melora. Sorry I was such a schizo then. Nikko was being a total tool."

Stacy lowered her head and kept her grin hidden. A very apt description of the man, but *Nikko*? *Really?* Had she missed the memo that it was cool to call fathers by their first names?

"I just had to get out of there, you know?" Melora came toward her, her apparent anxiety about interrupting Stacy now flown. "One more minute listening to him flay me and I'd have gone savage."

It was the tone and not the words that gave Stacy an insight to what the girl meant.

Good Lord, was I ever this young?

"But..." Melora shrugged her thin shoulders. "A good walk always sets me straight. When I got back I was chill again."

With a nod, Stacy started on her way back to the house. Melora fell in step. "So you're Nikko's new EP?"

"Yes."

"Hope you stick around longer than the last two, who, btw, were total incomps."

Surprised, Stacy asked, "You met them?"

Melora nodded and it was then Stacy noticed the camera slung around the girl's thin neck.

"Like, for a breath," she said with a dramatic roll of eyes that matched her father's for color and shape. "One of them showed up at the house and left screaming after an hour, like she'd been stabbed by a serial psycho. Real mature." Eye roll again. "I met the other one at the studio one afternoon when school let out. I thought she had a chance, but when Nikko lit into her in *that tone"*—her eyebrows rose almost to her hairline—"she started wailing like a diaper wearer and then bolted. When we got here I figured Nikko would be producer-less. He likes it better that way. But then you showed up."

Stacy nodded again, unsure if Melora thought that was a good thing.

"Major plus," the girl said, skirting around a tree stump, "you're still here the next morning. Props offered."

"Thanks." *I think.*

"Don't thank me yet. He woke up this morning right back in bear mode. That's why I was out walking again. If I keep this up I could walk back home in no time. And believe me, I've thought about it."

"Any particular reason why he's upset?" Stacy asked.

Melora shrugged again. "Nikko's not the biggest sharer in the universe. He's been under a boatload of pressure lately."

"Starting a new show is trying," Stacy said. "On so many levels. Physically. Mentally. And your father's a top-notch director. Some say he's a genius when it comes to what he does."

"Yeah, with the soul of the Dark Lord."

Stacy grinned. "I think that goes with the job."

Melora cocked her head and bit down on her lip again. "I don't know if it's so much this new show making him so volcanic. If I had to guess why he's ready to spew at an eyeblink, I'd say his leg has been bothering him."

"His leg?"

"Yeah. The one he tore up in the accident."

The subtle slip in Melora's tone from snarky and affected-teen to flat and adult-tinged sent a blast of awareness through Stacy. As soon as the girl put a period on her sentence, Stacy remembered reading about the crash. The accident had been a little under eighteen months ago.

"He's still in pain?"

Melora shrugged almost as much as she talked.

"He never says, but it's hard to miss." She lifted her gaze back to Stacy's face.

The internal ache she'd recognized the evening before was burning bright in the young girl. She'd physically lost her mother in the accident, and it seemed she might have lost a part of her father as well.

"Especially when you look."

Stacy stopped walking and regarded her. Behind the—at times—incomprehensible teen-speak, the ragged T-shirt with an 80s heavy metal band emblazoned across its front, and the distressed, torn, and naturally faded jeans covering her legs, this girl wasn't a typical spoiled and silly fifteen-year-old.

"Do you know if he's taking anything or doing anything to ease the pain?"

The shrug wasn't as careless this time. "Not during the day. He wants to stay sharp and focused, you know? Dad's all about being a professional."

Stacy nodded. So. It was *Dad* now, a change she didn't think the teen realized she'd made.

"But at night, sometimes...well..." She gazed over Stacy's shoulder at the lake, her lips pulling down. "He likes a drink or two. Or three. I guess it helps."

"No physical therapy? No exercise routine? Nothing like that?"

"When he first got...home, yeah. Now? Not so much."

Stacy knew the torment of constant physical pain. Pain that never eased, never quit, no matter what treatment or pill was used. It had been her constant companion for too many years to remember. To have Nikko's body ravaged to the point where he needed alcohol to help him deal with it wasn't a situation beneficial to his directing the show.

What could she do to help him?

"Look," Melora said, biting down on her bottom lip again, a habit Stacy recognized as the girl's emotional tell. "Nikko's really good at his job, and he totally wants this show to succeed."

"As do I."

"Well, that's good, then. So, you won't say anything, like, to him, will you? That I told you...well, about what I said?"

Because Stacy was a natural comforter, she reached out and rubbed the girl's bony forearm. "I won't, Melora. It's my job to make sure he has everything he needs and that this production runs smoothly. I take my job seriously. Whatever I can do, I will."

The girl sighed heavily and then nodded. "Thanks."

She suddenly looked a lot less like an intractable teenager and a lot more like a lost little girl.

"So, do you, like, do yoga every day?"

Stacy nodded. "I try to. It keeps me limber, mentally charged, and focused for the day when I do."

"Do you, like, meditate and stuff too? I mean, I heard somewhere that they kind of go together, you know? Like macaroni and cheese."

Stacy laughed. "Yes, you're right. They do. And yes, I do too."

"Meditation like, calms you, right? Helps take your mind off things? Stuff clogging it? I heard that too."

"If it's done correctly, it does. I've been practicing yoga since I was about your age."

"Wow. That's a long time."

Stacy's brow rose and her lips curved. "Thanks."

"Oh, no, no. I didn't mean, like, *you're* old. Because you're not." She flapped her hands back and forth in the air as she talked, as if she were erasing the words. "I just mean...well, doing anything for any amount of time is, you know, cool."

This time Stacy smiled outright. "No worries. I knew what you meant."

They were silent for a few moments when they approached the house.

"Do you think, like, maybe, I could... I don't know...join you? Like tomorrow? And give it a try? See if it...works for me?"

Stacy stopped and turned to the girl. Her unlined brow was grooved, her eyebrows practically kissing together above her nose. The way she held her thin body, bony shoulders slightly cowed in, fingers twisting together, told her there was a story there, one Stacy recognized as more than just usual teen angst. The girl was lonely and probably feeling left out since her father was involved in the production. Because Stacy knew precisely how that felt, she wanted to help.

"I'd love that."

Melora's mouth pulled into a wide grin and Stacy got a glimpse of the beauty she'd be when she reached maturity.

"Can you meet me at the spot I was at today by six tomorrow morning? I need to start my day early."

"Sure. I don't sleep much anyway. I'm never really tired since there's, like, *nothing* to do here. Oh, but I don't have something to sit on like that." She pointed to the mat in Stacy's hand.

"Just bring a towel. That'll be enough. Now, I've gotta get ready for the day," Stacy said, as she jogged up the porch steps. "The chefs and the judges arrive today and I'm meeting them at the airport."

A sudden thought blew into her mind. Turning, she asked, "What are your plans for today?"

That eye roll should be patented.

"Same thing as every day since I got here. A whole lot of nothing. Nikko confiscated my phone and my laptop for a week because he said I was mouthy and acting like a brat about having to be stuck out here in cowville for the duration instead of back home actually enjoying my summer, so I was just gonna hang at the house. Maybe go for another walk. Take some pictures. Lame, I know, but there's no one in my decade here, so..." She lifted her shoulders again. "Why?"

"Want to come to the airport with me? At least you'd get off the ranch for a while. Plus, you'll get to meet the chefs before all the chaos starts."

Several emotions scrambled across her young face. Surprise was covered by joy that instantly turned to wariness. "Nikko might not approve. I don't exactly have a long leash."

It was Stacy's turn to toss the girl a shrug. "You won't know unless you ask him. Want me to?"

"No, I will. If you hear, like, a nuclear explosion, you'll know his answer."

With a chuckle, Stacy ran into the house and said, "Meet me here at a little before eleven if he says you can go."

* * * *

Christ! This leg was going to kill him.

Nikko took his time walking from his cabin to the specialty kitchen EBS had constructed for the competition, cursing the stabbing pain shooting from his knee up his thigh and straight to his core.

Amos Dixon had allowed the production to use an old, badly-in-need-of-repair barn, and the construction crew and set technicians had worked their magic to turn it into a functioning area for the chefs to do the prep work for their meal challenges, and as a storage kitchen for the thousands of food items, appliances, and gadgets they would need.

Nikko had been so wrapped up in preproduction decisions and location scouting, he'd forgotten to verify everything was ready to go to his specifications with the remodeled space.

Trying to walk so he didn't limp—and broadcast to everyone what kind of miserable shape he was in—it took him longer than it should have to make his way from the cabin to the barn. He was sweating like a packhorse from the mounting heat and breathing hard when he finally arrived.

The moment he walked through the refurbished oak doors, a blast of ice-cold air- conditioning and the scene before him shocked him to a standstill.

The crew had done an outstanding job with the rehab. The barn officially resembled a high-end, professional restaurant kitchen.

Two long and wide stainless-steel prep counters jutted down the center of the space. The counters had been cordoned off into individual chef stations, each complete with a functioning dual sink. Surrounding the counters on the outer perimeter were eight ranges with four burners each for stovetop cooking. Industrial refrigerators lined one entire wall, three walk-in freezers the next. A six-pack of double-door ovens were built into another wall. A pantry stocked from ceiling to floor with bakers' racks filled with spices, condiments, starches, and baking items was set off to the side in a separate section. Across from it was the appliance room, complete with at least twenty KitchenAid mixers in a chaos of colors, pots and pans of every conceivable size and shape, more utensils than could ever be used—even at a state dinner—and every other kitchen item that could be bought.

When Teddy Davis had green-lighted the show, Nikko had insisted on buying every item new and he wanted them all professional grade and top-of-the-line. Teddy agreed after procuring a number of corporate sponsors who were more than willing to furnish the show with their wares, made more so with the frequent mentions the items and their manufacturers would receive on each episode.

Nikko took in the scene, pleasure swelling within him at how the crew had brought his vision to reality.

A sudden giggle had his gaze shooting to the pantry. He knew that giggle. He'd dreamed about it the night before when sleep had finally overtaken him and allowed him some respite from his aching leg. Those perfect coral-colored lips pulled back, revealing perfectly aligned white teeth; the way the corners of the mouth had tipped upward, a small dimple popping up around them while she smiled at Amos Dixon and his son.

But not, he remembered, at him. She'd laughed at something he'd said, twice, then with the next breath dissolved into the cool, professional, in-control woman she'd been when they first met.

While his new executive producer sat across from him in his study, he'd imagined running his tongue into and around those two little grooves, wondering what she'd taste like; how soft her skin would be.

And how much he'd like to erase that professional mien from her face and see the real woman buried underneath it.

Carefully he sauntered, with much more ease and nonchalance than he felt, toward the pantry.

Her back was to him. A simple, classic, and elegant long-sleeved white blouse that seemed ridiculous when the temperature outside was fast approaching ninety covered her torso, along with dark-fitted trousers ending just where black-and-white Converse sneakers graced her feet. That champagne cloud of hair was pulled off her neck into a messy bun on top of her head, secured with what looked like a pencil shoved through its center. Remembering how those soft waves had reflected the afternoon sunlight, Nikko had a sudden urge to come up behind her and pull the pencil out, allowing those curls to cascade to her shoulders. He went so far as to envision himself wrapping his fingers through the tresses and yanking her head back to his, where he could put his mouth all over her.

He blinked a few times and then, like a wet dog trying to divest itself of water, gave his head and shoulders a violent shake.

He wasn't going to put his mouth *anywhere* on his new executive producer, that was a fact. Her presence here was as a thorn in his side, not as a potential mate for his bed.

When she turned and giggled again at something the set technician said, he had a hard time remembering that.

Her eyes widened a bit when her gaze lit on his and in a fraction of a second, her smile disappeared, the laughter dimmed, and her lips pulled into flat line. She turned back to the tech, said something, and put her hand on his upper arm. The man nodded and smiled at her, while she squeezed his bicep.

With her e-notebook clasped in the other hand, Nikko swore she took a calming breath before she moved to him. The thought she needed it in order to speak to him sent a blast of anger through his system.

"Good morning," she said. "I'm glad I got a chance to see you before I leave."

"You're leaving? Dare I hope that means you're going back home so I can run my show in peace?"

He had to give her credit—again. Her gaze never flickered from his, her face never lost its poised expression. If anything, he was afraid she might be laughing at him behind those cool and composed eyes.

With a tiny head tilt she actually made him feel small and petty without ever saying a word. There was only one other person who'd ever been able to do that: his mother.

"I meant before I leave for the airport to pick up the chefs and judges."

"I forgot you're going to get them," he said.

"There's a twenty-passenger van scheduled to meet us at the airport." She glanced down at her tablet. "An empty bunkhouse is set up for the chefs to stay in and Mr. Dixon's housekeeper told me she's got the judges' rooms ready as well. But that's not what I wanted to speak to you about."

She glanced down at the device in her hand again, tapped it a few times, and then said, "All the proteins for the first three challenges have arrived and have been stored. Bryan was just telling me—"

"Bryan?"

She looked back up at him. "Bryan Sinclair? The supply manager?"

Nikko had forgotten the man's name, but did remember blowing him off a few days ago when he'd approached him about a problem. With his leg throbbing like a bitch, all he'd wanted to do was sit down, so he'd gruffly told Sinclair to take care of whatever the problem was on his own. Apparently, he had.

He nodded and waved his hand for her to continue.

"He only ordered enough for the first three challenges because he figured you'd like all the ingredients to be fresh and not frozen. The first three challenges should take up the entire first week according to what I read in the show bible, correct?"

Nikko nodded again.

"Good. Then I'll tell him that was okay to do. He wanted to make sure it met with your approval—"

"Then why didn't he ask me, himself? Why ask you? I'm in charge. Not you."

He knew he was behaving like a total jerk, but at the moment he didn't care. He wanted to see just how far he could push her before she pushed back. *If* she pushed back.

Disappointment filtered through him when she replied. "Yes, you are. There's no question about that. But as your EP, the crew knows to use me as a go-between for information and not bother you at every turn so you can concentrate on running the show as a whole. Remember what I said last evening?" Her gaze stayed on his face, never wavering, her expression staying calm. "My job is to make your job easier? By coming to me with individual issues, that allows you to do what you do best."

He was almost afraid to hear what she thought that was.

"Run the show," she said after a moment.

Dixon's son shot up to them before he could reply.

"Hey, Stacy. You just about ready to go? Hey, Mr. Stamp." The cowboy tipped a finger to the brim of his Stetson.

"Just about," she told him, a wide smile blooming.

"Okay, I'll meet you out by the truck." With a nod to Nikko, he was gone again.

"One more thing before I go," she said, turning her face—her professional face—back to him. "I'm going to assume you want to have a production meeting this evening once everyone has arrived and is settled in. I ask because with the schedule you've set up there doesn't seem to be a lot of leeway to have one before filming starts. Tonight is probably going to be the best time to round everyone up."

He kept his surprise to himself. He'd been planning on calling everyone—cast and crew—together before dinner to do just that. That she'd anticipated it proved what she'd said before was true: This wasn't her first rodeo. The girl knew how a show should be run.

"Fine," he said after a few seconds to organize his thoughts. "I'll do it before dinner."

"Whatever you want," she said. "I'll let the crew and everyone else know."

"You do that."

"Before I leave, is there anything I can get you, or do you need me to do anything for you?"

This time he didn't try to hide his surprise. Not one person on any other show he'd ever been connected with, had asked him that question.

"No," he said when he could find his voice. "No. Not now."

"Okay, then. I'll see you in a few hours." Before she left him, she snapped her fingers and pulled a piece of paper out of her pants pocket. "I meant to give this to you last night."

He reached out a hand and glanced down at the paper. "What is it?"

"My cell phone number."

His head whipped back up.

"I've found it's the easiest way to get in touch with me when I'm not readily accessible. Like now, when I have to leave the ranch. One of the sound techs told me the walkie-talkies don't have great range outside of the compound, so this makes more sense to use if you need me. Okay?"

Nikko simply nodded. He tucked the paper into his pocket.

"I'll see you later." When he didn't respond, she pursed her lips and walked away.

Nikko's gaze followed her through the building and out the door.

Chapter Four

The headache brewing behind her eyes after her impromptu meeting with Dominick Stamp was now blasting like a jackhammer: steady, loud, and pounding. With a silent curse she realized she hadn't taken her allergy medication after her shower and the sinus pressure she routinely was able to stave off had seeped through, making her feel like she was both underwater and stuffed.

Her allergies had routinely been a topic of amusement among her family, since she never suffered while living in the congested, pollution-filled city, but only when exposed to fresh air and open spaces.

"Just another weird physical thing about me," she'd said more times than she could remember.

The fact she was riding in a crowded, cramped van along with Melora and the contestant chefs, who were all speaking at once, their excitement and animation loud and nonstop, increased the drubbing tenfold.

Melora had been waiting by Beau's truck after Stacy said good-bye to Stamp. The girl had changed into a black summer dress with tiny straps that showcased her thin arms and delicate frame.

Too thin and too delicate. Did the teen have an issue with food? Stacy hoped not, drawing from unfortunate experience on how devastating an eating disorder could be, especially for a teenaged girl on the brink of womanhood.

"So your dad's okay with you going with us?" Stacy asked as she climbed into the cab with Beau's assistance.

"Everything's cool," the girl said while adjusting her seat belt.

Beau helped the time pass quickly by telling them amusing anecdotes about life on the ranch. He was a natural storyteller, and Stacy suspected he embellished a few of the stories to make them funnier. She didn't mind, though, because when she sneaked a look at Melora, the anxiety she'd previously seen in the girl's eyes had flown, replaced by a childish pleasure.

At the airport the van stood waiting, while the trio made their way to the baggage-claim area.

The preproduction crew had arranged for all the chefs and the two judges to arrive at the same time to make travel to the ranch easy. After reviewing the cast-info sheets, Stacy memorized all the faces she needed to find. Her eyes darted over the throng of travelers all waiting for the luggage carousel to begin spitting out their bags. She approached them, got their attention, and introduced herself.

A chorus of happy responses came back to her. Referring to her notebook, she called out the names of chefs and all were present, as was one of the judges. There was one glaring absence, though.

Stacy pulled out her phone and connected immediately to EBS headquarters. After a ten-minute wait she was told Jade Quartemaine, the second judge, had, at the last minute, opted to fly on her own and would be arriving later that afternoon.

After getting everyone's luggage stowed, Dan Roth, the second judge, asked if he could ride back with Beau, stating with a laconic grin, "I've been stuck with this rowdy bunch since before dawn and I need a break. Do you mind?"

Stacy told him she didn't, and she and Melora got into the van after making sure everyone else was situated.

Dan Roth had been right: This *was* a rowdy bunch.

Twelve of the country's best and brightest chefs had been chosen from a selection process that included over six hundred applicants. Dominick Stamp, Teddy Davis, and a selection committee comprised of top EBS network chiefs whittled the number down to fifty, and then twelve. Ten men and two women made the final cut, and while the number might heavily favor the male side, Stacy knew the women selected were the tops in their areas of expertise.

"No egos in this bunch," Melora whispered and then rolled her eyes. *"Not!"*

Stacy stifled a laugh. One thing she'd learned from being around world-class chefs and reality-television stars was there was never a shortage of egos of every size, shape, and gender.

"So, EP," Clayton Burbank, one of the more seasoned and louder of the chefs called from across the van, "what's the 411? We gonna start as soon as we get there, or is Nitro Nikko gonna give us a break and let us get settled first?"

Stacy heard Melora's swift inhale, felt the air shift as the girl touched her chin to her chest.

Just because her father had a reputation for being...volatile, it didn't mean his child had to be embarrassed by it.

"Clay," Stacy said, planting a smile on her face and leveling a forceful glare at the chef, "did you meet Melora? She's Mr. Stamp's daughter. She'll be staying at the ranch with us while we film."

She was pleased when the man had the grace to look embarrassed.

"Um, no. Hey, kid," he said with a wobbly smile. "Nice to meet you. I've worked with your old man before."

Melora lifted her head and nailed the chef with a level gaze of her own. "Yeah, I remember. *Kitchen Cook-Off.*" She pursed her lips and cocked her head. "You lost, right? Never even made it to the finals?"

If Stacy had been pleased when Clay looked repentant for his flippant remark, she was downright delighted with Melora's.

She knew she should have been upset at the girl's rude question. She was, after all, being disrespectful. But it gave her a tiny sense of pride to know the girl had a bit of a backbone and wasn't afraid of showing it.

Clayton Burbank's neck flushed a cherry red, and as the other cooks teased him about the loss, he nodded once, then turned his attention out the window.

Stacy happened to notice one of the other competitors—the youngest, in fact, at just barely nineteen—Riley MacNeill, slant a glance at Melora, a tiny smile pulling on his mouth. Melora noticed the look too. She slid her gaze up, then down again, her upper teeth clamping down on her bottom lip, a delicate blush coloring her cheeks.

MacNeill was not only the youngest of the chefs to win a spot in the competition—and with that came a world of worry in Stacy's mind to begin with—he was also the only chef to have never competed professionally before. At under twenty-one, he wasn't legally allowed to drink alcohol and if he did while on the show, legal issues could develop, potentially prompting sponsors to quit their association with the network.

All the other chefs were experienced in the food business, some major industry award winners. The closest in age to MacNeill was Dorinda Katay, at thirty. Stacy's concern was for the boy's emotional well-being more than anything else. Would he be able to keep up with the unyielding pace of a food competition, the wearing strain of long hours with little restorative sleep?

His bio told her he was a graduate from a prestigious cordon bleu cooking school and already had an impressive professional CV. But the rigors and demands of a cooking competition, when up against some of the most famous—and infamous—chefs in the country was very different from day-to-day cooking. She made a mental note to make sure she checked in with the young chef and his producer, often.

Stacy stood, swaying a little as the van continued speeding toward the ranch. It was a perfect time to address Clayton Burbank's question. She set her feet hip-distance apart and found her balance. "If I could have everyone's attention."

With all eyes focused on her, she said, "You've all signed the mandatory confidentiality clauses in your contracts, and once we get to the ranch, you'll need to surrender your phones and any devices you brought with you, including tablets, e-notebooks, and laptops."

"But my recipes are all saved on my tablet," Donovan O'Mara called out.

With a shake of her head, Stacy said, "Don, you know you're not allowed to refer to recipes anyway during the competition. Everything you do has to come organically or from memory."

"Tough break, O'Mara," Chesney Folds said with a laugh. "Your memory sucks on a good day."

The chefs all broke into laughter, a chorus of good-natured banter and ribbing exploding among them. Most of them knew one another in some capacity, either having a history of working together in restaurants, or competing on other cooking-challenge shows.

"Your items will be locked away so you can't be tempted to use them. I'll have the key and all your families have our production information, so if any one needs to get in touch with you, I'll let you know."

She went on to tell them they'd be meeting their individual producers once everyone was settled at the ranch.

"Dominick Stamp has thought of some amazing challenges, so you'll be working hard to win that two-hundred-and-fifty-thousand-dollar first prize."

The amount sent a cheer throughout the van.

A few minutes later they stopped at the main house.

Stacy was the first one to hop out, Melora at her side. She'd planned on waiting for the chefs to each alight and then escort them down to the bunkhouse Dixon had set up for them.

Before she could even plant her feet on the ground Nikko Stamp was on her.

"Just who the hell do you think you are?" he thundered, the force of his anger pushing her flat against the side of the van. Her tablet slipped from her grip and fell to the ground as her whole body startled at the rage in his voice.

"What—?"

"Where do you get off taking my daughter off this ranch without asking me? You had no right. She's not your responsibility."

Stacy's gaze flew to Melora's as the girl, terror written across her face, jumped from the van. When she tried to grab her father's arm, screaming, "Daddy, no!" at him, he grabbed her wrist instead. "And you," he roared. "How could you sneak off without telling me where you were going? Didn't you think I was going to be worried when I couldn't find you? Hmm? Were you thinking at all, Melora, or just doing whatever the hell you wanted, like you always do?"

Most of the occupants of the van had by now evacuated it and were watching Stamp's tirade, as were most of the production crew who'd come to greet the chefs.

"Dammit, girl, you know you're supposed to let me know where you are at all times. That's the one rule, the one thing I demand of you. You can't go off on a whim."

Before she could reply, Stacy pushed forward.

"Let me exp—" she said, trying to get between him and his daughter.

Ignoring her, Stamp told his daughter, "Get back to the house, Melora. Now. And don't argue with me. I'm in no mood."

The girl, tears in her eyes, face flushed, turned and ran from the scene.

"And you," Stamp turned his ire back on Stacy.

"Please, Mr. Stamp—"

"Don't *Mr. Stamp* me. Do you have any idea how frantic I was when I couldn't find her? Do you?"

She opened her mouth to reply.

He never gave her the chance. Looming over her, his face contorted with anger and something else that tugged at Stacy's heart, he spat, "I don't want you here. I don't need you here, interfering. But it looks like it doesn't matter to the network what I want or need, so I'm stuck with you. Fine. Just do your job. And only your job. Stay away from my daughter. She's no concern of yours. Do you understand me?"

"But—"

"Do. You. Understand. Me?"

Nothing she could say would make the situation any less volatile, so she simply nodded.

Without a glance at the throng of people staring at him, or another word to her, Stamp stomped off in the same direction as his daughter.

For a few brief seconds the silence surrounding her was deafening.

A sick wad of bile churned its way up from her empty stomach, threatening to fly free. Stacy bit back the acrid taste and tried to breathe. She hated raised voices and heated confrontations—with anyone and of any kind—and to be castigated so loudly and so publicly was mortifying.

Obviously, Melora had never asked her father's permission to accompany her to the airport. The girl's "everything's cool" statement had made it seem as if Stamp was fine with her going. Stacy should have been angry, but she remembered all too vividly what she'd been like at the same age and couldn't fault the teen for her actions. Melora was bored with her surroundings, robbed of her social media devices, and, having no one near her age to hang out with and simply be a teenager with, must have prompted her decision to omit asking her controlling father's permission.

Stacy got it. In spades.

She just wished she didn't have to suffer the wrath of that controlling father.

Something shoved at her hands, pulling her out of her thoughts. Riley MacNeill was attempting to hand her back her device.

"You dropped this," he said, his voice low and to her hearing, tinged with shyness. "I don't think it's broken."

"Thanks." She took it from him and managed a small smile. "It's not the first time this thing has found its way to the ground. Probably won't be the last, either. I think by now it's indestructible."

His return smile was just as shy as the inflection in his voice.

"So I guess, unlike a good wine, Nitro Nikko hasn't mellowed with age," Clayton Burbank said from behind her.

The tension of the moment broke, and, along with everyone else, Stacy chuckled.

"Okay, folks," she said. She knew how she dealt with Stamp's outburst, how she let it affect her in front of the crew, was important. They needed to know she could stand on her own and not fall apart whenever he had one of his famous outbursts. She had to be the proverbial calm in the storm that was Nikko Stamp so they could have someone to rely on, if need be. "Time is money in these parts. Let's get you all settled and then fitted with your jackets."

* * * *

By the time he got back to the house, Nikko had been able to tamp down his anger. Just knowing Melora was okay and not harmed or injured or, God forbid, anything else, had him breathing easier.

But it didn't get her out of being held accountable for going off without telling him.

Christ.

He'd never forget a moment of the blade-sharpened panic that had sliced through him when he couldn't find her for lunch. The agreement the therapist had come up with for them was Melora would eat three meals every day with her father. No matter what. So far, the plan had worked. She didn't eat much of what he cooked for her, but she did eat. And he made sure she didn't run off and try to throw everything up when they were done.

Things between them had been strained for the past few days, though, due to the unexpected flare-up of his leg pain and his irritation with being given another executive producer to deal with. Added in was Melora's continued harping on—as she so colorfully put it—being forcibly dragged by her teeth all the way out to loser-land with no friends or anyone her age.

Nikko realized she was smart enough to know he wasn't going to leave her in Manhattan while he was two thousand miles away. She was too young to be left to her own devices for two months and too old for a nanny to watch over her. Her eating patterns needed to be monitored and she needed an adult's presence to ensure she took care of herself.

He cursed again, the limp in his leg growing more pronounced the closer he got to the house.

If her mother hadn't died, Melora would be with her right now. The eating disorder she was currently battling wouldn't have formed, and she'd be a typical spoiled and obnoxious teenager instead of one hell-bent on destroying herself.

But her mother had died, and it was his fault. The joint custody they'd agreed on during their bitter divorce was null and void now, with him as the sole living, responsible parent. And being the parent of a moody, mouthy fifteen-year-old girl with a devastating eating disorder she could lay directly at his door was just about the toughest job he'd ever had, hands down.

"Melora!" he shouted as soon as he came through the front door. "Where are you?"

He wasn't surprised when she stalked from the kitchen, arms folded defiantly over her small chest, a look of absolute hatred crossing her thin face.

"Where I'm supposed to be. Chained, like a mad dog, in the kitchen, dutifully waiting for you to watch every crumb that goes in my mouth."

He winced at the hurt and anguish laced through her words.

"Melly, please. Don't talk like that."

"It's true."

Nikko crossed the room, his leg hurting almost to the point he thought he might pass out, and crumpled into a cushioned chair. His hand immediately flew to his thigh. He rubbed it, praying now that his weight was off it the pain would dissipate.

"No, it isn't. Now please, can you come sit with me? We need to talk."

"I know what you're gonna say." She stomped to the chair opposite him and collapsed into it, slouching to the point it looked as if her butt would fall off the edge. "I should never have left the ranch without telling you first."

Nikko shook his head. "That's not what I was going to say."

"Oh? *Shocking.*"

He bit back his temper. "I was going to say you should never have left the ranch without *asking* me first."

"I tried to find you," she said, scooting back up the chair and into a more comfortable-looking position. "You were, like, *nowhere,* and it was time to leave. If I'd had my phone I could have shot you a text, but I don't have my phone, do I?"

"For a very good reason, Melora, and if you think I'm going to give it back to you now, after this little stunt, you're dead wrong."

"Typical!" She bolted up from the chair, but before she could run from him again, he said, "Sit down. I'm not finished."

"Of course you're not." She slammed her body back down and onto the edge of the chair again.

"Do you have any idea how worried I was when I couldn't find you?" he asked. "I thought something happened, that you were injured, maybe all alone somewhere where you couldn't call for help."

"Oh, come on. That's just too dramatic, even for you." Her eyes rolled up and around. "Where would I go where I couldn't be found out here? And what could possibly happen? There's nothing to do around here that I'd get hurt doing."

"Oh, no? You like walking in the wooded area down by the water, right? Taking pictures?"

Her bony shoulders pulled up, then fell again.

"And did you know that bobcats, grizzly bears, and coyotes are indigenous to Montana? That Amos Dixon and the rest of the ranch hands drive around with shotguns in their trucks because they've seen these animals roaming a time or two around the property lines?"

This time the shrug wasn't as emphatic.

"Well, maybe you'd like to know, then, that a coyote was spotted close by the main stock barn a week before we got here. They still haven't captured it. Dixon isn't sure it's still in the vicinity, waiting to attack the livestock, but they're all prepared just in case one of them sees it."

He had her total attention now. Her light whiskey-colored eyes, twins to his own, had widened to half dollars, and despite the nonchalant way she was sprawled in the chair, he could see her hands were tensed on the tops of her thighs, her chest was moving in and out a little more rapidly than it had, and her mouth was slowly forming an open O.

His voice softened. "So I'm not really being as dramatic as you think."

He reached across and pulled her hand into his own, his pulse jumping at how cold her fingers were.

"I know you're unhappy being stuck out here for the summer, Melly. You miss your home. You miss going out and doing things in the city. I get that. But I couldn't leave you alone for two months. I just couldn't. Not only would I be unbearably lonely and missing you, I'd be worried constantly."

"I'm here and you're still worried," she shot back, but her voice had gentled from the antagonistic timbre of a few moments before.

"True, but at least here I can still check up on you and make sure you're okay. Until this morning, that is."

Her bottom lip disappeared under the top one. "Sorry I left without telling you—*asking* you. Stacy told me to make sure I had permission."

"I find that hard to believe."

"She did. Honestly. She wanted to make sure you were okay with it."

"And yet she still took you even though she knew I hadn't given my permission."

"She didn't." Melora shook her head. "Know, I mean. I... well... I kinda—you know, I didn't." She took a deep breath and avoided his eyes. "I told her it was okay. With you. For me to, you know, *go*."

He waited a beat. "So, you lied to her?"

"Not exactly"

"Melora Penelope Stamp."

"Uh-oh." Her neck disappeared as she scrunched her shoulders up.

"Did you or did you not tell Miss Peters that I gave you permission to leave the ranch?"

"Well, what I said when she asked was that everything was cool. I never said, exactly, that it was cool with *you*. Just... cool. You know?"

"So she assumed you'd spoken to me?"

"Yeah."

"Wrap it up any way you want, kid. What you did was lie."

Nikko dragged his hands down his face. And because his daughter had lied, he'd exploded, taking his wrath and worry out on Stacy. Publicly.

Even through his fury he'd seen the sympathetic looks and nervous side glances she was being given by the chefs as they alighted from the van to witness his outburst.

But the look that had the most impact on him was the one on her face as he'd towered over her.

Fear. Stark, white, bold fear.

Of him.

Nikko absently rubbed his thigh and shook his head. So far, he'd blown up at her two separate times, both in front of other people, and she'd taken it. She hadn't stormed off, or cried, or even given it back to him, as he'd expected. Every other underling he'd dealt with had, and had then quit, refusing to ever work with him again.

As far as he knew, Stacy Peters hadn't quit. Yet.

At this moment, he couldn't decide if that was a good sign or a bad omen.

First things first. He'd think about his EP later. Right now, he had a daughter who needed to eat and he needed to get prepped for the production meeting.

"Come on, Melly." He rose and winced once when the impact of his foot touching the floor shot straight up to his thigh.

Melora's eyes tracked his movements as he tested his balance, but she stayed silent.

"Time to eat," he said.

"The highlight of my existence," the teen muttered as she too rose, arms crossed over her chest, that perpetually dour teenaged pout on her face he was coming to detest.

Chapter Five

Nikko glanced down at the text from Stacy.

Chefs all settled in. Wardrobe fitting complete. What time do you want everyone gathered for production meeting?

Professional and succinct, just like the woman herself.

A quick glance at his cell phone's clock and he texted back:

One hour. Main dining hall. Arrange it. No one exempt.

Commanding and arrogant, he thought.

Her response was immediate. *Will do.*

He wouldn't have been surprised if she'd answered him with a *yes, sir* and then an emoji for a military salute.

He sat with his leg propped up on an adjoining chair in the room he'd turned into his makeshift production office, his hand squeezing his thigh every few seconds. The hammering pain had quieted, to be replaced by a subtle, continual ache from his groin straight to his knee. He could tolerate this much more than the pounding. The pain had become a constant companion since the series of surgeries he'd undergone to repair the multiple breaks, and he was able to ignore it most of the time.

Since the long plane ride, then the unending car trek to the ranch, and the added hours he'd spent on location scouting, his *friend* had made her presence known more and more over the past year. And yes, he realized he was being a jerk thinking of the pain as female in gender, but at the end of the day, after harping on him without end and invading his almost every thought, the reference was more than an accurate one to his mind.

Nikko adjusted his notes and shifted back in his chair. He could see Melora through the doorway in the next room, lounging on the couch and reading. Surprisingly, she'd eaten the late lunch of grilled salmon salad he'd put together for her without any of her usual arguments or stall tactics.

Granted, she only ate about a third of it, but it was 100 percent more that what she'd been eating a few months ago.

As the therapist he'd consulted had told him to, he'd praised what she had eaten and then made sure he kept her in his line of sight for at least an hour after. He'd been so wrapped up in his battle against his leg pain after the accident, he hadn't noticed his daughter's declining weight until it was almost too late to do anything to correct it.

While he'd been overwhelmed with trying to heal from numerous surgeries and deal with his professional life as well as settling his ex-wife's tangled estate, Melora had been battling a psychological war. Father and daughter were abruptly thrown together full-time and neither knew how to deal with the other's demons, let alone their own.

Melora had always been an exceptionally smart, intuitive, mature child, and Nikko had thanked God more than once after the crash that she'd handled her mother's death as well as she had.

But she'd been adept at hiding her starvation and purging behaviors from him while he'd been recuperating. It was only after she fainted in school after not eating for three days that he'd realized how blind he'd been to what she'd been doing. When he saw her lying in the hospital bed, her skeletal shoulders and sternal bones peeking out from underneath the johnny gown, her face pale, the deep circles under her eyes she'd hidden well with concealer, did he realize how close he'd come to losing the one person who mattered to him more than life itself.

When she'd tearfully confessed what she'd been doing to herself, the anorexia coupled with bouts of bingeing and then purging through vomiting and laxative use, Nikko'd had to choke back tears at what she'd been going through, both physically and mentally. He'd thought she'd handled her mother's death well. The truth was as far from that as possible.

She'd literally been starving herself to death.

Why she'd resorted to such a profound technique to cope with her mother's loss was heartbreaking. Nikko still struggled daily with trying to identify how much of her emotions and behavior were normal and age appropriate, and how much were a factor of her eating disorder.

Watching her now, carelessly flipping through the pages of the book, a look of complete boredom across her face, he wished for nothing more than to go back a few years in time and have everything be the way it was before the accident.

Knowing wishes were for fools, he went back to the papers on his desk.

* * * *

After making sure all the chefs were assigned to their individual show producers and handlers and that everyone was fitted with their chef jackets, Stacy snuck back to her room for a few minutes of reprieve.

The headache that had been threatening on the way to the airport had fully grown and was pounding like a heavy metal-drummer on acid behind her eyes. After taking twice the dose of over-the-counter pain reliever recommended, she removed her contact lenses, opting to wear her glasses to give her eyes a rest. The dry air on the ranch made wearing them for more than a few hours uncomfortable and she didn't want to be seen with red and watery eyes by the crew. Especially since they might interpret it to mean she'd been crying—which she hadn't.

For the second time since coming back from the airport, Stacy looked down at the sheet of paper Teddy Davis had signed.

When Stamp had backed her against the van and screamed at her in front of the entire production team, she'd been tempted to quit on the spot, run to her room, pack, and then have Beau bring her straight back to the airport. One of the reasons she hadn't was this piece of paper.

She'd agreed to work on this show to guarantee she'd be given her own in the end.

Nitro Nikko, Clay Burbank had called the director, and it seemed almost everyone she'd met today agreed it was an appropriate moniker for the man, herself included.

But underneath that explosive personality, Stacy saw two things she'd never thought to see in so vital, vibrant, and successful a man: vulnerability and pain.

The pain she could easily attribute to his leg. She'd watched him rub it the night before, as if trying to ease a chronic ache. He'd been trying not to limp when he'd stormed away from her today, and he'd probably been successful in his subterfuge with everyone else. But she was an expert at what to look for. No one was more attuned to what raw, punishing pain did to a person, their abilities, their body stance. Nikko was in a great deal of it and trying his best not to let it show.

As for his vulnerability...well, that could be laid right at his daughter's door. His out-of-control anger broadcast plainly as stark fear to Stacy. She couldn't begin to understand what lay behind it, but, as she'd thought before, there was a story there between father and daughter.

Dominick Stamp was a brilliant technical director, a bear to work with, and one of the most intriguing, captivating men she'd ever met, a thought that had her laughingly questioning her own sanity.

From the moment her hand had shot to his in introduction, to the first time she'd actually been able to see him, eye to eye and not hidden behind sunglasses, she'd been enthralled by the force of his personality and his rugged, all-male looks. His emotions were mercurial, his temper trigger-primed to unleash at a second's prompting. In essence, her personality opposite in every way.

Where she'd be a negotiator, he'd be a fighter. She'd approach a problem calmly and attempt to find a peaceful, effective resolution, while she imagined he'd face one head-on, make a quick decision and then implement it, brokering no one else's opinion. He was a yeller; she spoke quietly and firmly, as her grandmother had taught her to.

Even physically they were polar opposites, Dominick, dark and olive complected, his Italian heritage obvious, to her fair and light Polish and Irish–blended genes.

All in all, a fascinating, powerful man and one—she knew if she wasn't working with—she'd like to know on a more personal level. But she *was* working with him and one thing Stacy never mixed was business and her private life. She'd learned the hard way it never worked out, and when it ended—as it always did—she was the one holding the baggage left in its wake.

Besides, even though she found him intriguing, everything he'd said and done to her since she'd arrived told her he hated her guts.

Okay, maybe that was a little harsh. He didn't really know her enough to hate her, but he certainly despised her presence and the reason she was here.

So, despite the subtle physical attraction she felt for the man, keeping it cool and professional between them was the way to cope.

Stacy made a quick call to the airport to ensure the luxury car she'd ordered for Jade Quartermaine had picked up the overdue judge. It wasn't fair Beau should have to trek all the way back there. And she didn't want to tell Dominick the star of his show was arriving late, knowing the kind of response she'd get if she did. After saying a silent prayer to the Gods of Traffic the car would arrive at the ranch on time, Stacy took a final glance at the signed note, folded it, then stuck it in her top dresser drawer.

Armed with her e-notebook and the walkie-talkie that was now all but glued to her hip, she walked toward the dining hall.

Since the ranch was a large and vast working establishment, and the hands Amos Dixon employed were required to be on site at all times, a large structure built to house them during meals had been constructed five years ago when Amos had expanded his business. The Feedbag, as it was commonly called by the cowboys, was located upwind of the livestock buildings, almost directly behind the main house.

It took Stacy less than five minutes to walk there from her room. After speaking with the cooking crew Dixon employed, she knew tonight's meal for the production crew and the chefs was a ranch favorite: barbequed ribs, baked beans, and grilled corn on the cob, served banquet style. The head cook, a wizened, sun-leathered man with cornflower-blue eyes and a twinkle in them—whose name Stacy was enchanted to learn was Cookie—had informed her there was no alcohol allowed on the ranch or served with meals. Amos Dixon's orders.

Stacy thought about the fifty-five cases of California harvested red and white wines she'd seen listed on the supply manifest and made a mental note to discuss the alcohol's intended use just in cooking with Amos before shooting began. She could just imagine the shit storm Nikko would kick up if Amos forbade it. As long as the alcohol was kept away from the workers and used solely in cooking, there shouldn't be any problem.

She took a seat at the picnic-style benches a few minutes before the meeting was due to start and appreciated the silence surrounding her as she went over a few last-minute details. So engrossed was she in reading, she never realized anyone had come into the hall until a gentle tap on her shoulder had her startling.

"Sorry," Riley MacNeill said. "I didn't mean to scare you."

She smiled at the young man, charmed once again by his sweet shyness.

"Not scared," she said, patting the bench. "Have a seat." While he did, she added, "I'm actually glad to see you before all the others arrive. We didn't get a chance to speak a lot when you were being fitted for your jacket."

At a hair under six-foot, Riley folded his long legs under the table and Stacy took the moment to take stock of him.

His face still possessed a thin layer of baby fat in the jowls, a darkening shadow of afternoon stubble beginning to bloom on his square jaw. Eyes the color of blue Wedgwood had just enough guardedness in them to summon up the natural comforter in Stacy.

"Are you all settled in?" she asked.

"Yeah. It's gonna be a little weird, sleeping in bunk beds, sharing space, you know? One bathroom for ten guys. I'm used to living alone."

She nodded.

"I'm not complaining," he added with a head shake. "It's just...weird. I haven't had to share a room with anyone in a long time."

"I know. But it's not forever. And when the show wraps, just think how happy you'll be to get back to your own place. You'll appreciate it even more. You live in Manhattan, right?"

He nodded. "Tribeca. It's close to the restaurant so I can walk to work every day."

They chatted for a few minutes about the upscale New York eatery where he was, as he put it, second-in-command, until more of the chefs and crew started ambling in.

Stacy was struck once again by the noise level, but her headache had subsided courtesy of the pain meds. A beep from her walkie-talkie signaled someone wanted her. She connected and said, "This is Stacy."

Carrie James, one of the cast producers spoke back. "Jade Quartermaine just arrived and I'm on my way to pick her up and bring her to the meeting."

"Ten-four." Stacy disconnected.

Riley was quietly laughing at her side.

"What?"

"You sound like a cop. *Ten-four.* Cop-speak."

Stacy glanced around at the growing throng of chefs and crew and sighed. "I have to admit, I feel like a cop sometimes on a show like this. Trying to keep everyone focused and out of trouble. It's not easy with chefs of this caliber. You're all used to calling the shots, being in charge, and not listening to directions." She turned to face him. "You're like a bunch of toddlers who require discipline and a good spanking every now and then to keep you in line."

"I wouldn't mind being spanked by you," Clay Burbank said from behind her.

She looked up and burst out laughing at the lecherous—yet humorous—way he lifted his bushy eyebrows as he leered down at her. Dan Roth and two other chefs were with him and joined in the good-natured banter.

* * * *

All of Nikko's senses went on alert when he entered the dining hall. His gaze found Stacy in an instant, surrounded by a few of the male chefs, laughing and smiling easily at them. It was as if he was attuned to the sound of her voice. As if he could pick her out of a crowd without any trouble. As if he'd be able to find her anywhere he looked.

A momentary vision of Scarlett O'Hara surrounded by her numerous fawning beaux in a scene from *Gone with the Wind* played in his mind. While she didn't resemble a spoiled Southern belle, flirting and simpering, she did have the complete attention of all the men around her. Her lips pursed into the most kissable of pouts, and his blood started to pound in his ears as he watched Clay Burbank bend and kiss her cheek.

The twin stains of pink that immediately popped out on her skin made his breath catch. In that moment she lifted her head, caught him staring, and her cheerful smile vanished. She said something to the group, stood, and made her way over to him, the entire time her gaze staying locked to his.

He hadn't known she wore glasses.

"Almost everyone is here," she said as an opening.

If she was upset at the way he'd treated her just hours before, she was good at hiding it. Her features were calm and relaxed, her voice that smooth professional pitch again.

He was about to reply when he heard his name called from the doorway. Jade Quartermaine sauntered up to them.

"I just arrived and was told to report here immediately," she said, stretching up to him in expectation of a kiss. "Don't pass go. Don't collect two hundred dollars." Her lips pulled back in the faintest of grins. "Just get down to the dining hall."

Nikko bussed both her cheeks. "I wasn't aware you hadn't arrived with everyone else, Jade," he said, sliding a look at Stacy.

"I had to meet with my agent this morning," she said, wrapping her arm into the crook of his elbow and pressing her body in close to his.

Too close. He'd forgotten how clingy she was.

"Luckily, my assistant was able to reschedule my flight. I was so hurried, though. I haven't even been to my room yet. I must look a fright."

She ran her free hand down the length of a body-hugging green sheath from waist to thigh, then patted her perfectly coiffed red hair.

Nikko refrained from responding that she looked as if she'd stepped off a photo shoot, knowing that's what she wanted him to say.

"What have I missed?" she asked.

"Nothing, yet. I was just about to start."

Because it looked like she had no intention of letting go of his arm, Nikko walked toward the tables, now filled with the cast and crew, taking her along with him.

"Have a seat," he said, unwinding her arm from his.

Like a cat stretching in the midday sun, Jade lowered her body slowly, one vertebra at a time, with every male eye focused on her movements. Which, since he knew her so well, was exactly what she'd planned.

Stacy went back to where she'd been sitting when he arrived, wedging herself between Burbank and MacNeill, who both looked more than happy to make room for her.

"Okay, folks," he shouted, garnering everyone in the room's attention. "Let's get started."

Ten minutes into his rundown, he lost the thin thread of control he'd been hanging on to.

Between the numerous interruptions by the chefs, calling out questions at him, and then the joking responses they tossed at one another, Nikko had had it.

His leg hurt, the chefs were being assholes, and he needed to get back and get dinner started for Melora.

When the noise level crescendoed, Nikko slammed his palm down on the table.

"Enough!"

Like schoolchildren being reprimanded by an at-wit's-end-teacher, they all quieted in an instant.

"I know you're all excited to start this competition," he said, digging deep down for a semblance of control, "but let me get through this first and then you can all go do whatever you want for the rest of the night. Okay?"

A sea of nodding heads filled his vision.

"Now, as far as the filming schedule goes—"

He got no further.

"We know about the schedule, Nikko," Davey Crimes called from the back of the room. "No worries. Your EP filled us in on the way here."

Before he could stop it, Nikko saw a flash of red cross his eyeline and he spun to where Stacy was seated. "Oh she did, did she?" It took every ounce of willpower not to scream the words as he glowered at her. Her face turned three different shades of crimson under his scrutiny. "Well, let me remind you all, Miss Peters isn't in charge of this production. *I am.* So if you want to know what's really going to happen, you'd better listen up. That includes the crew, as well," he added, running his gaze around the room.

He went on to tell them that he'd changed the times they were going to be needed for the first day of shooting, and that the challenge he'd originally planned he'd scrapped for a different one.

He'd done no such thing, but as soon as he'd heard Stacy Peters had already spoken to them, he wanted to punish her. She needed to be reminded who was in charge on this show, who *she* reported to.

A few heads turned to her, sorry and embarrassed glances tossing her way. She didn't get up and run from the room, which, he admitted, he'd hoped for, but opened her notebook and began typing while he spoke.

When he finished, he tossed her another heated glare and reminded them, "This is a competition. I expect you all to conduct yourselves as professionals. No juvenile pranks, no ridiculous alliances. This isn't *Survivor*. You're all on your own. Act like grown-ups." He told them to get a good night's sleep in order to be at their brightest and best in the morning. Groans and grumbles came back at him.

"I see your dinner is being brought out," Nikko said when he spied the ranch kitchen staff bringing in pots of food through the hall's kitchen-entrance doors. "Enjoy your meal and I'll see you all tomorrow."

When he saw Stacy rise and go in the opposite direction of the food line, he called out, "Miss Peters, I'd like a word with you. Now."

Stacy stopped short. Clutching her notebook, the bulky walkie-talkie secured to a band at her hip, she followed him through the double entrance doors. Once they were closed behind them, he turned.

"Let's get something straight right now." He was substantially taller than she was and it gave him a little petty pleasure that the closer he came to her the more she had to dip her head back to maintain eye contact.

But she did, her gaze never once wavering, her body staying rooted, not retreating.

"It's not your job to tell the cast and crew anything unless I instruct you to. It's my responsibility to go over the shooting schedule, the production schedule—hell, even their sleeping schedule—with them. Not you. Do you understand me?"

Stacy nodded, her eyes trained on his.

"I thought I made myself clear last night about what I expect from you."

"You did."

"Then why the hell did you take it upon yourself to brief them all"—he swiped his hand in the direction of the hall—"about the shooting schedule?"

"I'm sorry I did," she told him. "I realize now I shouldn't have. I'm...I'm sorry. It won't happen again."

Was that a slight a warble in her voice? He wasn't sure, but it didn't get by him she offered no reason why she had.

They continued to stare at one another.

Why didn't she fight back? Why didn't she rail at him? Scream at him? Tell him he was a jerk and then storm off? Why the hell didn't she defend herself?

"It better not," he found himself saying.

She nodded. "Do you need me to do anything in preparation for the change in the challenge?"

He squinted at her, not remembering at first what he'd told the room. *Shit.* Now he'd put his foot in it. He had to come up with something quick.

"Not at the moment," he said quickly. "I'll text you the particulars in a little while. I need to get back to my daughter first."

Stacy opened her mouth and then just as quick shut it again.

"Yes?"

It took her a moment before she replied. He hadn't noticed until then how her hands were clenched around her notebook, her knuckles almost white with the exertion.

"I just wanted to apologize for this afternoon as well. For taking Melora with me to the airport. I'm sorry you were so worried, so...concerned."

He waited for her to tell him Melora had lied to her, but the words never came.

Intrigued, he wondered why not. He was about to tell her the fault was with his daughter's deception, but before he could, the doors opened and Jade Quartermaine came through them.

"Oh, good, you haven't left yet." She ambled up to them, cast a quick, dismissive glance at Stacy, and then wound her arm through his again. "I hope I'm not interrupting."

Nikko knew her well enough to know she didn't care if she was.

"No. We're finished," he said, flicking a quick look at Stacy. She was staring down at her shoes, her cheeks once again pink.

"Good." The smile on Jade's face was pure feline. "I'm not in the mood for the barbequed ribs they're serving in there." She cocked her head behind her. "Why don't you walk me back to the house and tell me where a girl can get a decent salad around here."

Without a glance at Stacy, she started walking, this time forcing Nikko along with her.

Chapter Six

Stacy closed her eyes and took a few deep breaths. She'd bet next month's rent Nikko'd only changed the shooting schedule and the first challenge just to make her look incompetent in front of the crew.

She'd worked with control freaks before. You couldn't avoid it if you worked in television. But Stamp stood head and shoulders and every part she could name above all the other technical directors she'd worked alongside.

He'd made plain his feelings on not wanting her here, about not wanting or needing any executive producer, not specifically her. Why, then, did she feel the animosity rolling off him in waves was about her, specifically, and not merely about her job and title?

She'd done nothing but be civil to him. Hadn't challenged anything he'd told her, carried out all his commands. Why, then, did he seem to dislike her so much?

The noise level coming from the dining hall was raucous, the cast and crew all laughing and enjoying their meal and one another. For a hot second she thought to march right back through the doors and join them.

But...she had work to do, especially now that Stamp was intent on making changes.

As she made her way back to the main house, Stacy promised herself one thing: She'd see this through. No matter how difficult and downright obnoxious Dominick Stamp was, she'd agreed to this job and had to remember what waited for her on the other side of it.

She'd just turned into the gravel walkway surrounding the house when she heard her named called. She stopped and turned to see Clay Burbank jogging toward her.

"Hey," he said by way of greeting. "You didn't get anything to eat."

"Typical chef," she said, summoning up a smile. "Always worried if someone's—God forbid—not eating."

He grinned at her and shot his hands into the back pockets of his worn jeans, the movement tugging his already snug T-shirt tighter and accentuating his pecs.

"I'm not hungry," she said. "I've got a ton of work to do before tomorrow. Plus, I'm fairly certain I'll be sick and tired of barbeque before too long."

"Oh? Is that a reference to the challenges?"

No one who looked like he did—buff to the bone with a heavy dose of badass—was ever able to pull off the innocent, angelic look he was trying for. Before she could stop herself, Stacy laughed.

"Oh, no you don't, Clay Burbank." She wagged a finger at him. "I may be tired but I'm not tired *and* stupid. You'll find out what the challenges are the same way and at the same time as every other contestant. Don't try to worm anything out of me, because my lips are glued. Tight. With super-glue."

The flick of his gaze from her eyes to her mouth and then back again was hot enough to singe. But Stacy was immune to the heat pouring off Burbank like water.

He cocked his head. "Not even a hint? A tiny one?" He held his thumb and index finger an inch apart.

"No. And you should know better. This isn't your first competition."

When his substantial muscles flexed as he shrugged, Stacy pitied any other woman who would try to resist his charm.

"Okay, point taken. But I want to ask you a question."

"As long as it's not about the challenges or anything else competition related, go for it."

"Why didn't you set Nikko straight? Back at the dining hall. Why'd you let him make a fool of you?"

Stacy sucked in a deep breath.

"You could have told him I was the one who pestered you about the schedule when we were all in the van. It was my fault you clued us in; you didn't just volunteer the info."

Stacy bobbed her head. "I know. It's true I wasn't going to say anything about the shooting schedule until you asked. I'd planned on just telling you all a little about the ranch, where you'd all be staying. Give you a heads up on your individual producers."

"So, again, why didn't you tell him that when he went off on his tirade?"

"Because he was right. I shouldn't have said anything. I'm not the person in charge of this production. He is. He wanted to go over everything with all of you, make sure you understood his concept, his direction. I don't want him to think I'm trying to wrestle any of his authority away, which, unfortunately, is what he does think. I don't work that way."

"None of us thought—or think—you're trying to step on his toes, Stacy. That's a fact. Most of us know you either from Kandy's show or from your rep on *Bake Off.* We know your style tends to be more peacemaker and problem-solver, not shit-stirrer."

He said it with a grin, and Stacy couldn't help but return it. "Yup. That's me. Switzerland." She sighed and glanced down at her hands. "Listen," she said when she lifted her gaze again, "I appreciate the support, I really do. But I made a mistake. One that I won't make again. Remember, on a shoot the technical director is God. The be-all end-all. For the purpose of this show that's Dominick Stamp. And he's an amazing director. You know that. You've worked with him."

"He may be God on this little show, but he's also a hothead, a know-it-all, and a bully."

Stacy stared up at him, remembering she'd been thinking almost the same thing just a few moments ago. For some reason, she didn't like hearing the words come out of Burbank's mouth.

"I prefer to think of it as being passionate and perfectionistic. Two qualities I'm more than used to dealing with since Kandy was—and is—both. If he's demanding, it's because he expects the best of everyone involved in the show, himself included, I'd imagine."

It was Burbank's turn to stare at her. Kindness mixed with concern filled his gaze.

"Look, I could tell him the truth on the q.t., that it was me who asked about the schedule. All you did was answer."

"Don't." She reached out and wrapped a hand around his forearm. "Please, Clay. Just let it be."

"He really shouldn't speak to you like that, Stacy."

"It's fine. Really."

He glanced down at where her hand lay against his bare arm, and then back up at her face. When he made to move closer to her, she jerked her hand away and retreated back a few steps, widening the space between them.

"Now go back and relax with everyone else," she said, planting a smile on her face that she hoped didn't look as forced as it felt. "You've got a busy day tomorrow and you want to bring your A game. This is, after all, a cooking competition."

His brows pulled together above his eyes, then smoothed over again. "No worries 'bout that, babe. My middle name is *winner.*"

He shot her a cocky grin and a cheeky wink that coaxed a real smile from her. "Really? I thought it was Peter."

With a shake of his head and a flip of his hand he said, "Nah. Nasty rumor, that. Don't spread it, okay?"

Laughing, she nodded, then turned toward the house. "See you in the morning," she called over her shoulder.

* * * *

Nikko pulled back into the shadows cast by the fading light. From his hidden position, he watched Clay Burbank wait until Stacy was no longer visible, and then take his time to turn and go back down the drive.

Nikko let out the breath he'd been holding.

After escorting Jade up to the house and then refusing to join her for a private dinner, he'd been on his way back to the cabin to start dinner for himself and Melora when he'd heard Burbank and Stacy speaking. He'd been surprised at the content of their conversation, and intrigued when Stacy asked Clay not tell him that he'd been the one to ask about the schedule.

That made two times now she hadn't pleaded in her own defense. Why didn't she want him to know the truth? Why did she allow him to think the worst of her and never jump to her own defense?

And when she'd called him passionate and perfectionistic, he'd almost gasped out loud and given away his position. Of all the things she could have said about him, he never imagined it would be anything so positive.

Or dead-on.

Nikko took his time going down the steps, his thigh screaming.

By the time he got back to the cabin, he decided he was going to make his daughter apologize to Stacy for lying and she was going to make that apology in front of him. That way he'd, one, know she'd really carried through with it, and two, it would allow him to offer his own apology for accusing her without knowing all the facts.

Nikko might have an almost impossible ego—he'd fully agree with anyone who claimed he did—but one thing he always did was admit when he was wrong.

After a simple, yet delicious dinner of grilled chicken, asparagus, and a light spinach salad that Nikko ate all of and Melora managed several bites of each, they retreated to the living room. Recognizing how bored his daughter was, he reconsidered his previous punishment and allowed her to have her laptop so she could watch a movie. But he kept his directive of no email or any social media connections.

His daughter scowled, but settled on the couch, the computer on her lap while he did some more preliminary work. He emailed the head of the camera crew and outlined how he wanted the kitchen cameras set up. That done, he did the same to the rest of the technical crew heads with instructions about the first day's filming.

Several hours passed when he felt his phone buzz in his pants pocket. He looked over at his daughter, now sound asleep with the laptop cuddled between her arms.

A text from Stacy. *Have you decided what you want to change the first challenge to?*

Dammit.

He'd forgotten he needed to come up with something new. He scrubbed his hands down his face, trying to devise some way to save face without looking like a total jerk.

He texted back: *After considering it, will stick to original plan.*

There. A perfect excuse, especially because it was true.

The phone vibrated again.

Chefs have head shots beginning at 8 am. Preliminary filming at 10. Are you still thinking of changing the start time? I can notify the crew.

He was tempted to, if for no other reason than to prove he could. Two hours for head shots should be enough. More than enough, actually.

Have everyone ready to go at 9:30.

Knowing chefs as well as he did, he'd be lucky if they all arrived by eleven.

Nikko leaned back in the chair and closed his eyes. Almost immediately the phone buzzed again.

Anything else you need me to do before tomorrow?

Yeah, you can stop being so nice and accommodating. Instead of typing that, he simply wrote *No.*

Staring at his laptop, his email still open, he sighed and forwarded all the conversations he'd been having for the past few hours to Stacy, after finding her email address in the note Teddy Davis had sent him. Then, he texted *Check your inbox.* Grudgingly, he realized she needed to know what he wanted to happen the next day so there would be no screwups. He could have been a prick and just let her muddle through, find out on her own, but he suspected she'd have no problem doing that. The crew liked her, and if he could take Burbank's words as true, they knew the type of worker she was.

When his phone buzzed, he swiped to the incoming text.

Thank you. I'll make sure everything is exactly as you want it in the morning.

Why didn't that surprise him?

Chapter Seven

Stacy bent from her waist and placed her hands, palms flat, on the mat. She squatted, then, in one swift move, vaulted her legs back to balance on the tips of her toes, her body weight all in her hands. She settled into the plank pose and tried to rid her mind of the chaos of last evening.

Once back in her room, her phone had started beeping every few minutes with texts from Carrie James relaying concerns, demands, and complaints from Jade Quartermaine. Stacy had thought the veteran producer would be able to handle the judge. Unfortunately, that hadn't proven true and Stacy had been forced to extinguish several potential fires.

Incensed to discover the ranch was alcohol-free, Jade ordered Carrie to drive back into town to purchase a case of wine and bill it to EBS. Carrie refused and Jade exploded. The girl barely had enough time to text an *SOS* to Stacy before the diva began criticizing the inadequacy of the rooms she'd been provided. When Stacy arrived, she'd calmly explained the suite had been used by the late Mrs. Dixon and Amos had opened and refurbished it just for Jade.

This appeared to appease the woman for a few moments. The lack of alcohol was brought to the forefront next, and after that Jade then questioned the time schedule for filming, her wardrobe choices, the exclusive use of a makeup artist. Anything and everything, it seemed, that she could find to complain about, she did.

Two hours of listening, explaining, and cajoling later and Stacy's headache had returned and morphed into a college marching-band drum line.

When she finally made it back to her room, she collapsed on her bed, fully clothed.

Her phone beeped within seconds with messages from the technical crew chiefs about the first day of shooting. She dealt with them all, barely able to keep her eyes open.

Right before falling asleep she remembered Stamp's desire to change things for the next day, so she texted him.

Staggered didn't begin to describe how she felt when she saw the emails he'd forwarded.

What was he up to? Was he trying to trip her up again, telling her what to expect the next day, and then—perhaps—planning to change it all without her knowing so she could look foolish in front of the crew? She wouldn't put it past him.

Before finally getting into bed to actually sleep, she made several notes in her tablet, highlighting events and the times he'd given for them.

Now, Stacy inhaled, then lowered her body to the mat, keeping it in a straight, secure line, and bending her elbows out at her sides, in push-up position. Right before she exhaled and began to move into downward dog, she heard a familiar rustling behind her, something drop to the ground, and then a muffled, "Crap-on-a-stick!"

Slowly, Stacy rose to a flat-footed stance and took a breath.

"I'm sorry. *Again*." Melora came through the trees, a rolled-up beach towel hugged to her chest, a plastic water bottle in her hand. Her spiky hair was held back from her face by a wide headband; a too-large black T-shirt that looked like it might fit her father slid off her shoulders. Black capri-length exercise pants hugged her skinny legs, and Stacy knew then what she'd only suspected: The girl had an issue with food. And from the tiny width of her skeletal calves and knobbiness of her knees, a big issue.

"I tried to get here earlier," Melora said, flicking the towel out and spreading it on a flat batch of grass, "but since I don't have my phone because I'm still being, like, *persecuted* for being bored and mouthy by *he who rules the world,* I had to rely on my mental powers to wake me up on time and they major failed. Then I had to, like, *sneak out* before his lordship woke up and grilled me like a steak about where I was going."

She stopped and her bottom lip disappeared as she sucked it into her mouth. "I'm sorry."

"Stop." Stacy smiled. "I haven't been here long myself, really; just getting started."

Melora's shoulders relaxed, one arm of the tee slipping down. She yanked it back in place only to have the opposite shoulder fall in response.

"Do you know any poses?" Stacy asked.

"Zippity-zilch."

"Okay, then. Let's start with some easy ones."

"Before we do, can I, like, say something to you?"

"Anything."

"About yesterday? When Nikko went nuclear?"

Stacy waited.

"I just wanted to say, to tell you... well..." She hung her head, then lifted her gaze back to Stacy and nodded as if fortifying herself. "I, like, *lied* to you. About him saying it was cool to go. He didn't. I never got a chance to ask him before we had to leave."

"I realized that when we got back."

"I'm so, so, so, sorry he went apeshit. Really. Nikko's a 'scream now, ask for deets' *later* kinda guy."

Stacy kept it to herself she'd figured that out too.

"I just wanted to get out of here, you know? Even for a little while. I was hoping he wouldn't notice I was gone."

"No chance of that, apparently."

With a headshake, she said, "Zero. I did tell him that I lied to you."

"Really? Wow."

"Yeah, well, don't be too impressed. I did it because he made me boil, thinking you were to blame. I was getting punished anyway, but I wanted things to be cool between the two of you."

No chance of that happening. Ever.

"Anyway," the girl said, "I'm sorry. For like, everything."

Because Stacy remembered so well what it was like to be a teenager, she smiled. "Not even a thought. Now, come on. Let me show you how this is done."

For the next several minutes, Stacy took the girl through a simple sun salutation, going slowly, and explaining how and when to breathe through each move.

Melora was a quick and astute student.

"And then," Stacy instructed, "move out of downward-facing dog into a final *savasana*. Raise your arms above your head slowly, bringing your palms together, drop your head back, and gaze up at your joined thumbs. Breathe, and bring your touching hands down to center."

With a side-glance, she monitored Melora's progress.

"Breathe. Bow. And that's it. Your first sun salutation. Great job."

The free and open smile on Melora's face touched her heart.

"Intense!"

Stacy laughed. After a quick glance at the clock on her phone, she began rolling up her mat, Melora mimicking her movements with the towel. "It should be. Especially if you do it right."

"Can we do this, like, again? Tomorrow? I promise I'll find a way to get here on time."

"Of course. Every day you practice, you get better and more comfortable with the movements, with knowing the progression of what comes next. When you feel up to it, we can do a full meditation at the end. That's my favorite part."

Together, they walked through the tree line and out onto the road.

"Why?"

Stacy considered how to explain what she considered such an important part of her life.

"It clears my mind," she said at last. "There's so much going on in here"—she tapped her temple with her index finger—"most of the time, and I'm so busy with a million things running at once, that just letting it all go and being quiet and still and calm is an amazing process. It took me a long time before I was able to do it properly."

"Like, what do you mean, *properly*? Don't you just sit, close your eyes, and, like, *breathe*?"

Stacy grinned. "I used to think it was that easy. Until I had to do it. The person I studied with told me to simply free my mind of all thoughts. To focus on breathing in and out. Five seconds in and I'd be thinking of what I wanted to have for lunch, or did I remember to hand in my math homework? How many calories were in the bag of chips I had last night? Did I look like a total alien in the new eyeliner I bought?"

Melora giggled, the sound echoing along the quiet walkway.

"It took me about three months before I got it, and was just able to...be. No thoughts, no internal chatter, no unending noise. Just...quiet."

She turned and was surprised to see Melora's cheerful mien had shifted. Gone was the easy and childlike smile, replaced now by lips pressed tight together in a flat line. Stacy stopped and reached out a hand.

"Melora, what's wrong? Did I say something to upset you?"

With the towel hugged against her slight frame, Melora shook her head. "No. It's just..."

"Sweetie, what?"

The teen's head shot up, tears pooling in the corners of her eyes. "My mom used to call me that."

"I'm sorry. I shouldn't have—"

"No. Please." She wrapped her hand around Stacy's arm. "I—I don't mind. I liked it. It made me think of her before she, you know...*died.*"

Through countless counseling sessions and years of personal introspection and professional therapy, Stacy had come to learn sometimes the best response in any emotional situation was to stay silent.

She reached her other hand up and placed it over the one on her arm.

"Sorry to make like a fountain." Melora swiped at her dripping nose with the back of her free hand. "When you said meditating helped you find, like, quiet?"

"Yes?"

"Do you, I mean, would you...do you think I could learn that? Learn to quiet all the"—she swiped her hand in the air—"crap and stuff? Do you think I might be able to learn how to do that?"

"I know you could."

"Would you—?" She bit down on her bottom lip. "I mean, could you, like...teach me?"

Stacy had it on the tip of her tongue to say no, she was too busy, she didn't have enough time to instruct Melora in the ways and nuances of deep meditation. Now that the show was ready to begin filming, her free time would be almost nil, and teaching such an involved process to a teenager wasn't how she wanted to spend her downtime.

One look at Melora's troubled face, though, and a rush of familiarity in her childlike expression sluiced through Stacy, and she experienced a stab of kinship so intense that she found herself acquiescing before she could pull the words back in.

They parted when the path did the same, one fork leading back to the main house, the other to the cabin.

A quick shower, dressed comfortably, and sans her contact lenses because she knew what a long day it was going to be, and Stacy trotted down to the barn that housed the set kitchen, sending off a text as she did.

A makeshift photographer's studio was set up in one of the refurbished kitchen rooms, several of the chefs, clad in their newly fitted white jackets with the show's logo stitched over the left breast pocket, waiting to get their head shots.

Stacy had liked the logo—a steer stomping on a fork—the first time she'd seen it, secretly rooting for the steer.

Clay Burbank was seated on a stool, his background a baker's rack filled with pots and pans. Armed with her ever-present notebook, she flipped open to the photography schedule, saw what time Riley was listed, and knew there were six chefs left after him to have their studio shots taken before they were all due in the set kitchen for their introductions and first official challenge.

Stacy questioned the few producers who were present and was assured everything was running smoothly. Just as she was leaving the area, Riley MacNeill came through the door.

"Right on time."

He smiled at her. He really was a good-looking boy with high, arched cheekbones and deep-set eyes that for some reason she thought missed nothing. In a few years, with some age-related weight and muscle, he would be the total package of a sexy chef.

"I packed it in early like you suggested," he told her.

"Good. You've got a busy day in front of you and on a fast-paced show like this it pays to be well rested. Keeps you sharp mentally and physically."

"Yeah, Clay said the same thing."

Stacy nodded. "He's been through a few of these competitions, so he knows."

Her name was called over the walkie-talkie, and with a quick squeeze to Riley's shoulder, she told him, "See you later," while she moved through the set and answered the call.

* * * *

Nikko took a moment to inspect the set kitchen and the camera placements from the production truck he was going to be calling home for the next few weeks.

Nine flat television screens were situated on one side, cued to various areas of the kitchen, which would stream continuous feeds of the chefs throughout the challenge. There wasn't an inch of the kitchen that couldn't be viewed from one—or more—of the cameras. Four techs would use body cameras to film up close and during the tasting portions of the challenge with the two judges.

The editing process would, as always, be tedious, culling from each camera the best shot to film the *story* of the competition.

His attention was diverted when Stacy moved into one of the camera shots to speak with a crew member. The sound wasn't on, so all he could do was watch.

As he'd noticed the night before, she wore glasses today, her hair pulled back into a tiny ponytail at her neck, making her look no older than his daughter. She had a communication headset secured around her head, the

Peggy Jaeger

microphone pointed downward as she spoke. Her ever-present notebook was crooked in one arm, a walkie-talkie secured to a waist harness.

The director in him noticed the way she gave her total attention to the man speaking, nodding at intervals, cocking her head as if questioning something. She didn't interrupt or speak until he was finished, something Nikko found fascinating, since so many people he dealt with day to day had a habit of doing just the opposite.

He still had trouble believing she was close to thirty. Skin unlined and clear, again reminding him of someone his daughter's age, glowed with health. She was thin, but not in a sickly way, more along the lines of someone who took care of her body. Once again, she was garbed in trousers, not jeans, as was the rest of the production team, himself included, and a long-sleeved blue blouse that shimmered under the studio lights. Silk.

Would her skin be as soft as the material? With a jolt, he realized he wanted to discover for himself just how soft she was under her clothes.

In all, Stacy Peters looked professional, primed, and prepared for production to begin.

The memory of how she'd smelled like vanilla, warm, sweet, and soothing, ran through him when her smiled broadened and her nose wrinkled, laughing with the tech. She reached a hand up, squeezed his shoulder, and nodded.

When she turned to move from the frame, the pensive scrutiny in the tech's eyes trailing her sent a hot slice of inexplicable irritation through him.

Like a moving slide show, her image walked from television to television, each camera tracking her movement across the kitchen. She walked with purpose, her strides long and determined.

He shouldn't be remembering the scent she wore, shouldn't be fantasizing about how soft her skin might be. And he certainly shouldn't be annoyed another man looked at her with thoughtful lust in his eyes.

He had a show to run. A career to get back on track. A daughter to keep a close and watchful eye on.

Why, then, did this woman, one he didn't professionally or personally need, want or care about, keep worming her way into his thoughts?

When Stacy finally moved out of the camera's range, Nikko shook his head.

Chapter Eight

Stacy was a master at remembering little nuggets of information that could be useful if needed, so when she poured herself a cup of herbal tea from the crew's food table, she poured another cup filled with coffee for Nikko. She'd watched the evening before in the dining hall when he'd poured himself one before starting his speech.

Full high-test caffeine with one sugar packet. How anyone could get to sleep at night drinking that stuff all day mystified her.

She made it the same way now, covered it with a plastic top, and brought it with her. Nikko had walked out of the production trailer a few moments ago, headed for the set. She found him conferring with the head cameraman, Todd Griffin, at one of the chef stations.

As he had yesterday, he looked tired and tense. Worry lines were etched deep along the side of his face from the corners of his nose to his jaw. Purple half-moons smudged under his eyes and his color, despite the perpetual, blazing sun of their surroundings, was pale. He was leaning against the countertop and it wasn't difficult to ascertain he was bearing his weight on one side more than the other.

Without interrupting, she waited while he finished speaking and then noticed her.

It didn't take long.

"Morning," she said to both of them when his gaze connected with hers.

"Hey, Stacy." Todd tossed her an open smile, which she returned.

Nikko did not.

She calmed her features and offered him the cup. His brows pulled together when he stared down at it and then back up at her. For a moment she was afraid he wasn't going to accept it and just leave her standing there with the cup grasped in her hand.

A smidgeon of satisfaction warmed through her when he took it, brought it to his lips, and took a sip. When surprise shot across his face as he tasted it, she wanted to do a happy jig.

"Are you blocking?" she asked before he could say anything.

It was Todd who answered.

"Yeah. Since this is the first challenge, Nikko wants to make sure the cameras get a clear view of each station while the guys cook."

She nodded and opened her notebook, ready to take down any information or direction given.

The two men walked from table to table, Todd gripping a handheld camera and aligning the shots the way Nikko instructed, Stacy following close behind.

The stiff, slow way he moved confirmed her previous suspicion. *Definitely favoring that left leg.*

Melora had alluded to the lingering pain from the accident. Standing so much must be adding to the discomfort, if not complicating his recovery. As director, Nikko wouldn't be afforded the luxury of resting his leg. She could offer him some suggestions to deal with the pain, but nixed the idea as soon as it came to her. There was no way a man so strong-willed and domineering would ever admit to being in pain, much less accept help in dealing with it.

The noise level rose on the quiet set when the chefs and their individual producers all arrived at the same time a heartbeat later.

The corners of Nikko's mouth pulled down at the unruly interruption.

"Want me to move them all to the stew room until you're ready?" she asked.

She was treated to a look of annoyance.

When would he stop resenting her presence? Why couldn't he see how useful she could be to him? She'd thought she'd done the right thing in asking first, instead of just going ahead and moving the chefs out of the kitchen. Asking his permission should have helped alleviate his concern she didn't feel he was in charge, but obviously not.

"Yeah," he said after a moment, shocking her to her core. "Get them out of here. We need a few more minutes to finish this. Then I'll go talk to them."

Once she had the entire cast and their handlers ensconced in the waiting room, euphemistically called the "stew room," Stacy spotted Jade Quartermaine and Dan Roth enter the building. Jade was surrounded by her producer and two other, younger women Stacy didn't recognize, one of whom held a wide umbrella over the star as they walked. She shut it once they were inside the building.

Stacy detoured to them.

"Miss Quartermaine, Mr. Roth," she said.

"Call me Dan, honey." He grinned at her and adjusted his tie. "'Mr. Roth' sounds too stuffy and makes me sound old."

"You *are* old," Jade quipped.

He threw her a side-glance and then rolled his eyes. "I've been going over the intros for the past hour," Dan told her. "I think I'm good to go. Is everything set in the kitchen?"

"Almost. Mr. Stamp is finishing up blocking and then we should be ready to start. Why don't I take you to the stew room? The chefs are already there."

"No," Jade said, the serious tone in the command giving no room for discussion. "I don't want to be in the same room with them."

"Why not?" Roth asked.

"I just don't." To Stacy she said, "Find us someplace else, preferably with air-conditioning. I'm boiling in this heat."

Stacy knew just the spot. She saw them comfortably settled in a small, extra pantry and motioned for Carrie to follow her into the hallway.

"Who are the those two with Jade?" she asked the moment they were out of hearing.

"Her personal makeup artist and wardrobe assistant. They arrived at five this morning. Drove themselves all the way from the airport after she called them last night and ordered them to get here. She doesn't want the studio people, quote—doing her—unquote. She doesn't trust them to make her look her best."

The girl took a huge breath and rolled her neck. "She's the most spoiled person I've ever worked with, Stacy. After you left last night she started harping on the no-booze-allowed rule again. I swear, she probably had those two"—she cocked her thumb behind her—"smuggle her in a couple cases."

"I hope not." If Amos Dixon got wind of that he'd be furious and she'd be the one charged with calming the waters.

"Ask them when she's not around," Stacy said. "Find out for sure. That's breaking the rules, big-time, and we can't allow anything or anyone to jeopardize this production."

Carrie assured her she'd get to the truth.

The earpiece Stacy had placed prior to leaving the set blared her name. She tapped it once and said, "Peters."

"You're wanted on set," one of the sound crew said.

"On my way."

"Nikko's ready to start," Todd told her when she arrived at the kitchen. The technical and film crew were all present now, adjusting lights, cameras, overhead booms to record any extraneous sound.

"The chefs are getting miked-up. Nikko just left to talk to them."

Stacy nodded and jogged down the hallway connecting the set with the waiting room. She arrived just as he began speaking. The only acknowledgement he gave her was a quick flick of his eyes in her direction and then back to the group. Several sound techs were moving among the chefs, securing battery-packed body microphones under uniform jackets.

With meticulous precision, Nikko went over every aspect of the introduction scene. "The judges will issue the challenge," he told them, "then they'll start the clock and you all get moving. At the appropriate minute marker we'll call time and you all stop what you're doing, whether you're finished or not. Hands in the air so the cameras can see them. Understood?"

A sea of nodding heads waved around the room.

"Can we have a hint about the challenge, Nikko?" Clay Burbank asked. "I mean, obviously it concerns something with beef. But it would be nice to know what we're up against."

"No. You know the rules, Burbank."

"Come on, man. Throw us a...bone."

The room exploded in laughter.

Stacy's own grin widened when she saw the corners of the director's lips curve up ever so slightly. He had the coffee cup she'd given him in his hand, and when he took a sip of it, his gaze connected with hers.

The subtle, lighthearted amusement floating in his expression turned serious as his gaze lingered on hers for a beat, then slowly drifted down to her mouth. The heat from his stare turned scalding, his pupils dilating, all but obliterating the color surrounding them. When his stare reconnected with her own, her breath clogged in the back of her throat as a waterfall of warm sensations cascaded down her insides. Strong, powerful, and resolute, he was the type of man she'd always secretly dreamed about having in her life, but the kind she knew wouldn't give her a second glance.

She wasn't tall and gorgeous like her cousins, with strong, bold features and arresting coloring. She was willowy and pale, a result of a lifetime spent avoiding the sun. *Sexy* was a word she knew would never be used to describe her.

She wasn't an icon like Kandy or an artist like Gemma. She wasn't healing the sick like Eleanor or fighting for the disenfranchised like Abby. Stacy was merely the person people thought of when they needed someone reliable, organized, and efficient. A problem-solver. A people-pleaser.

Men didn't fall for women with those qualities.

Her thoughts ran rampant as Nikko held her hostage with his stare.

If she didn't know better, she'd mistake the bald, assessing look in his eyes as desire.

But she did know better. There was no possible way this man felt anything for her other than annoyance and irritation.

Her earpiece buzzed, breaking the moment. Pulling her gaze from his, she turned away.

After tapping the device, she listened and then said, "Got it. I'll be right there."

Without turning back, she exited the room and wondered if his eyes tracked her. She almost turned back to look over her shoulder but decided there was no need.

* * * *

Nikko took one last glance at all the chefs and judges, and nodded. "Everyone ready?"

When he was met with a chorus of "Yeahs," he moved to the production truck.

He found Stacy immediately. She was seated in the back, two rows behind the main control panel, her ever-present tablet opened and on the table, and holding a bottle of water.

"We're all set, Nikko," Todd said.

Pulling his gaze from his EP, he took his seat, donned his headset, and said, "Cue judges."

When they were in place and ready, he said, "Roll."

Jade and Dan smiled full-faced into the teleprompter camera and began their introductions of the chefs.

Nikko sat forward, his mind running through the next ten steps of commands he wanted to give when he noticed the fresh, capped coffee cup on the panel in front of him. His name was inscribed on the cover and when he reached out and touched it, the cup was warm. When he removed the cap, the strong, brisk aroma of the roasted coffee drifted up and filled his senses. Without thinking, he looked over his shoulder to find Stacy facing the monitors, the reflection of the screens on her glasses making it impossible for him to see her eyes.

He knew without a doubt she'd been the one to put the fresh cup at his place. He hadn't even thanked her for bringing him the first one earlier. The gesture was one relegated more to an intern, not an executive producer.

Why was she being so nice to him when all he'd been to her was rude and obnoxious?

And how had she known exactly how he liked his coffee?

"Dammit!" Jade's irritated voice blared through the camera.

"Cut!" Nikko called. "What's the matter, Jade?" he asked through the intercom.

With her crimson-colored lips pulled into a pout, she peered into the camera and said, "The teleprompter is scrolling faster than I can speak. I'm missing my lines. You need to slow it down."

"I told you to look over the script," Dan said, shooting his cuffs. "But you were too busy deciding which color lip gloss looked better for the camera."

"Shut up, you old fool." With her eyes narrowed to slits and her mouth pinched in anger, Nikko wondered how she'd feel if she saw herself the way others did.

He hadn't been thrilled with Teddy Davis's decision to use her as one of the judges, knowing her reputation for being difficult as he did. He'd tried to coax Davis into someone else for the second judge's spot, but the network chief had stood fast and insisted on the former culinary talk-show host, saying she was the best person for the job. Nikko wondered if there was something personal going on between them, because he could think of at least six other network hosts who'd do a better job—and be more cooperative—than Jade.

He turned to Todd. "Can you slow it down a little for her?"

"No problem."

"We're gonna slow down the feed, Jade," he said. "Start from the beginning when I give you the cue."

It took two more adjustments before she was able to read her part all the way through without stopping and complaining.

When the chef introductions were complete, along with the rules and premise of the contest, Nikko gave them the okay to issue the first challenge.

Dan Roth, professional through and through, recited his part to perfection on the first try.

Jade needed four attempts before she made it all the way through without a fumble or flub.

"Christ. At this rate we'll never get through the challenge by lunchtime,*"* Nikko chided.

Once the challenge clock started, pandemonium broke out in the kitchen. Nikko sat, his gaze moving from monitor to monitor, as he issued orders for the camera crew.

The chefs were given forty-five minutes to butcher a side of beef as their first challenge. When the clock stopped, they'd be assessed on precision and accuracy of the cuts and the amount they'd been able to accomplish in the allotted time.

Once the time was almost up, Nikko noticed Stacy leaving the control tent. The desire to know where she went warred with the need to stay focused on the screens and watch the drama unfolding.

Jade and Dan had exited the set during the challenge, since they weren't needed. He was just about the call them back when he spied them walking into camera range on one of the screens, a smiling Stacy ushering them in.

Dan called time a few moments later and Nikko instructed each cameraman to pan the contestants to make sure they all stopped at the same moment.

The tiny hairs at the nape of his neck tingled, a little frisson of electricity shooting down his spine, and just like that, he knew Stacy had returned to the van. Before issuing his next command he slid a glance over his shoulder. She was in her seat, her eyes aimed down at her tablet, typing.

He'd think later about why a sense of contentment bolted through him that she was back.

First, he had a show to direct.

Two of the techs manned walking cameras as the judges went from station to station, evaluating and commenting on the butchering.

While that was going on, Nikko called out commands for the various mounted cameras to record the reactions of the chefs. He was already deciding how he wanted to edit the pieces together.

When every chef had been assessed, Nikko called "Cut!" He needed to confer with the judges before they issued the next challenge.

When he rose from the chair, his knee abruptly locked, shooting a bullet of pain straight up along his thigh to his hip. If the control panel hadn't been within reach to grab, he'd have fallen flat on his ass.

Praying no one had seen the slight stumble, he leaned into the panel and, trying to control the agony from slipping into his voice, said, "Take fifteen minutes, everyone."

The area emptied quickly, leaving him alone as he attempted to get his breathing back to normal. He inhaled deeply, a shudder of sharp pain firing through him from head to toe. He'd sat too long, knew it the moment he stood upright. The physical therapists he'd been forced to deal with after the accident had insisted he move as often as possible to keep the leg from seizing up.

It was unfortunate for him that the majority of his job was spent seated or standing, and now he had firsthand knowledge of just how much trouble either could cause.

Sweat drenched his forehead, moisture slicked through his shirt and pooled in his armpits. For the thousandth time he cursed himself for not taking the pain meds he'd been given. And for the thousandth and first time he told himself there was a valid reason he hadn't.

He swiped his forearm across his brow and a sudden sound behind him had him whipping his head around to find Stacy, standing quietly by the door.

Mortification paralyzed him into stony silence. Of all the crew, she was the last person he wanted to witness his current state.

He watched as she swallowed, the movement of her neck and shoulders visible under her blouse, and moved around the chairs to him.

It was on the tip of his tongue to say something scathing, to make her want to run from him, to leave him alone. The last thing he wanted was compassion. Or worse: Pity.

Before he could form a sentence, Stacy said, in a voice devoid of emotion, "Miss Quartermaine and Mr. Roth are waiting on set for you to discuss the challenge results. I told them you'd just be a minute." She lifted a bottle of water to him. "It's wicked hot in here. I thought you might want this."

Under her glasses, her gaze never wavered from his as she offered him the bottle.

If he'd seen kindness or sympathy in her expression he would have reacted differently. Sliced her with a pithy retort, or even just rudely ignored her. But there was nothing. Her eyes were calm and cool, no hint of worry, no speck of concern. Her mouth was soft and relaxed, her shoulders and neck loose. Composed. She was completely composed and self-possessed. Unlike him.

He took the bottle from her hand, uncapped it and, without a word, chugged, his focus remaining on her face. He wasn't sure, but when he came up to take a breath, he thought he saw something shift in her eyes. Soften. His spine automatically stiffened.

"I'll see what I can do about getting the temperature in here turned down a little. It tends to get hot and sticky with so many bodies sequestered for

CAN'T STAND THE HEAT

such long periods in these kinds of production trucks. That's why I always have water on hand."

Relief tripped through him. She hadn't seen him wobble, hadn't noticed he was in agony. She'd merely assumed he was overheated.

"Yeah," he said, recapping the now-empty bottle. "It does. Good idea."

He wasn't sure who was more surprised by his remark.

"Okay. Should I let the judges know you're on your way?"

"Yeah. I'll be right out."

With a brisk nod, she turned.

Before she could leave, he said, "Hey?"

She turned back.

"Thanks. For the water."

A heartbeat passed. "No worries."

With that, she left him alone. It was only after she disappeared from sight he realized once again she'd never smiled at him the way she did everyone else.

Why it bothered him so much was a mystery.

Chapter Nine

Once outside, Stacy stopped, closed her eyes, and took a giant breath in an attempt to calm the earthquake seizing her insides.

It had taken everything in her not to bolt forward from her seat when she saw him stand and stagger. She'd had to physically restrain herself from her natural instinct to offer whatever kind of comfort she could, knowing if she did, he'd most likely explode at her.

It was obvious he was suffering. The death grip he had on the console proved it. How he managed to contain himself and not let anyone else see the torture he was going through was amazing, and proved to her once again just what a control freak he was.

She had to admit she admired him for it.

The offer of the water and the lie she'd told him to go along with it had served its purpose well. He'd have soon as bit off her head than accept anything that would help if it made him look weak in her eyes.

Proud man.

Too proud for his own good.

Considering how she could help him without him knowing it, she moved back to the set and informed the judges of Nikko's imminent arrival.

She made the rounds of each chef, saying a few encouraging words and speaking with their individual producers. The contestants were standing around in a cluster, talking over the first challenge and evaluating one another's prowess—or lack of it—with the butchering. All but Riley. He stood alone at his station, quietly cleaning it of the bones and detritus of the challenge.

"You don't have to do that," Stacy told him. "We have a cleanup crew who'll take care of setting everything to rights again."

With a careless shrug, Riley rinsed his knives in the attached sink. "I like cleaning up. Especially my knives. I don't like anyone else touching them."

Stacy's smile was quick and understanding. "I get that. My cousin Kandy has this knife set she bought when she was in China a few years ago. When she showed it off she wouldn't let anyone touch it." She laughed at the memory. "She told us that she wanted the knives only to recognize her juju and no one else's." With a shake of her head, she added, "Chefs and their knives. They're like an appendage for you guys."

"And some of us have bigger...knives than others," Clay Burbank said from behind her. "And we know how to use them to maximum potential."

"Yeah," Damon Rodriquez said, rubbing his hands together and winking at her. "My knife skills are legendary among my fans."

"Why do I get the feeling they're not really talking about knives?" Dorinda Katay asked.

Stacy rolled her eyes. When the laughter died down, she said, "Because they're not."

Nikko arrived on set and went directly to the judges, so she moved toward them.

"His was by far the best of the bunch," Jade was saying to the two men as Stacy silently sidled up to the trio.

"I agree. The kid has talent," Dan said. "For someone his age, it's impressive."

"So, MacNeill is your number-one pick?" Nikko asked.

When the judges nodded, Stacy felt a surge of pride swell through her. "Who's on the bottom?" he asked.

The least expert chef to perform the butchering task was open for a bit of debate between the judges. After parrying back and forth a few times, Nikko forced them to make a choice, telling them they were wasting time. They did, but neither looked altogether happy with the decision.

"Okay, so when they're back at their stations you divulge the next challenge. Got it?"

Roth nodded and Jade gave him a bored, "Yes, of course."

Nikko turned to move back to the tent, Stacy right behind him when he turned back, adding, "And try to get it all on the first take this time, Jade. The crew needs to break for lunch."

Stacy didn't know what she was more surprised at: Nikko's snide request of his star judge or the said judge's openmouthed, silent response.

When Dan Roth caught her eye and grinned widely behind his costar's back, Stacy lowered her head and bit down on the inside of her lip. If she hadn't been looking down, she would have noticed Nikko stop. But she hadn't been looking where she was going and, subsequently, barreled right into him.

She would have ricocheted back and fallen from connecting with the solid wall of his chest as she hit, if he hadn't thrust his hands forward and grabbed her upper arms to prevent it.

Like a blast from a stun gun—quick, sharp, and penetrating—she felt the heat of his touch burn through her blouse and sear straight through her skin.

Numbed, she dropped her tablet, her hands incapable of holding onto it. They splayed, open-palmed, and sought purchase by grasping his elbows and clutching.

"Steady," he commanded.

Stacy felt anything but. Words wouldn't form correctly in her mind. All logical, rational thought had flown the moment the warmth of his hands seeped through the fabric of her blouse. It was as if she'd walked into an oven, the temperature set to broil.

His long fingers squeezed once, twice, then tugged her in closer.

Stacy couldn't decide which was more intense: the heat in his eyes or the natural warmth radiating from his body.

"I'm—I'm sorry. I didn't—I wasn't…I—Sorry." She tried to pull from his grasp, but he wouldn't let go.

As earlier when she'd caught him staring at her, she once again felt the mesmerizing pull of his gaze and was powerless to look away.

And for some inexplicable reason found she didn't want to.

The little shards of amber floating among the cognac color of his irises were lighter and brighter than she remembered. They looked like a wolf's eyes, and, just like a wolf, their stare was predatory, alpha, and hypnotic.

"Nikko? We're all set to start up again," Todd called from the doorway of the production trailer.

Without looking away from her, he called back, "Be right in." He still hadn't let go of her arms.

From deep down, as deep as she could reach, Stacy grappled for calm. She watched him watch her while she took a solid, full breath in, then relaxed it out.

"I'm sorry," she said when she trusted her voice wouldn't betray her again. "I wasn't paying attention to where I was going."

She shifted back, away from him, but he kept his hands around her.

This close she could read the exhaustion floating in his eyes and his determination to ignore it.

This close she could see the fine, subtle lines fanning out from the corners of his eyes as he narrowed them at her.

This close she could reach out and smooth the corrugations grooving down from his mouth to his rock-solid jaw. That she wanted to do just that, to offer him any comfort she could, to soothe the pain he tried so valiantly to keep hidden, stunned her beyond all thought.

Nikko Stamp was not a man who would ever tolerate being comforted or coddled.

Why, then, did she think it was exactly what he needed?

"I'm okay now," she told him and tried to move back again.

This time he let her go.

The tablet had fallen between them and when she bent to retrieve it, she took in another deep breath.

Coming upright, she adjusted her glasses, which had gone askew when she bent over.

"Was there something you wanted me to do?" she asked, making her features as blank and as relaxed as she could.

Confusion crept across his face.

"You stopped and turned," she clarified. "I thought you wanted to tell me something."

His brows pulled tightly together, his eyes going flat and hard.

"Yeah." His voice dropped to the temperature of flash-frozen ice. "Make sure Jade's up to speed the next time we film. Light a fire under her producer or manage her yourself, if you have to. I don't care, but do whatever you have to do to ensure we don't waste time on piss-poor preparation again like we did this morning. Got it?"

With her insides shaking like just-set Jell-O, Stacy bit her tongue and nodded.

* * * *

"Melora?" Nikko called when he got back to the cabin. "Where are you?"

"Where I always am," the girl shouted back. "Purgatory. Or as you call it, your office."

He should have called her on the snippy response, but Nikko couldn't summon up enough parental discipline to do so.

The morning's filming had gone overtime into the lunch hour, mostly due to Jade Quartermaine's continued incompetence. She'd flubbed the next challenge guidelines three times before Nikko had exploded and ordered Dan Roth to read the teleprompter instead.

Jade had been furious and spitting nails, threatening to walk off the set if she weren't given another chance. With exhausted reluctance, Nikko had acquiesced and she'd finally gotten the lines timed perfectly.

At any other time during any other production he wouldn't have been as furious about the messed-up schedule. But this production was different. This time, he had Melora to think about.

As he told the crew to break for an hour and a half, he once again questioned his decision to be the one responsible for Melora's eating schedule. It would have been so much easier if he'd brought along a personal chef. Then, he'd have been able to just be Melora's watchdog.

The therapist had made point after point about how Melora was using her anorexia as a way of grieving over her mother's loss, as a way of establishing some kind of order in her chaotic life, and as a means to deal with her abandonment issues regarding her frequently absent father. If he'd assigned someone else to cook for her, the therapist felt it would distance father and daughter even more. By cooking for her, sharing the meal, and then spending the aftertime together, she'd felt Melora would come to realize how much Nikko truly loved her, wanted her healthy, and wanted her in his life.

But, *Jesus,* he was tired. Even though he'd shared custody with Flannery, Melora had spent the majority of her time with her mother because Nikko's filming schedules hadn't been conducive to having a child around. All that had changed the moment Flannery died and he'd been thrown into the quagmire of single parent to a damaged and grieving teenager.

A teenager who was looking at him with a murderous and mutinous glare in her eyes at the moment.

"You're late," she said, bony arms folded across her tiny chest. "I've been sitting here for, like *hours,* bored out of my gourd and withering away with"—she flapped a hand in the air with a dramatic flourish—"*ennui.*"

Nikko stopped walking toward the kitchen, turned, and cocked an eyebrow at her. "Ennui? That's a new word for you." He struggled to keep the humor from his voice. Melora had inherited more than just her looks from her actress-mother.

"It was a vocab word for one of the dumb books I've been assigned to read for the summer. The title of it should be *Dumb and Dull.*"

She followed him into the kitchen and plopped down into one of chairs.

"Did you do anything else this morning aside from read?" He pulled out whole-wheat bread, slices of cheese, and a tub of soft butter.

While he set some of the butter to melt in the frying pan, he spread some more on to one side of the bread, slipped a few pieces of cheese on the unoiled side, and then slapped another slice of bread over that.

"I started the report I'm being tortured to write for *Dumb and Dull*. I had to print it out, like, *in pen*, because, Hello! My laptop is still being held hostage. It would be, like, so much easier if I could, you know, *type*."

Nikko tucked his tongue into the side of his cheek. "I read somewhere that writing things out in longhand makes you remember them better."

"I so do not want to remember this book. Ever."

"Did you do anything else?"

"Took a walk," she said.

"Did you bring your camera? Take some pictures?"

"Yeah."

When she offered nothing further, he glanced over at her. She was slumped over the table, her head resting against one flattened palm, her lips pressed together. His heart sighed for her.

"I'm sorry I was late getting back." He flipped the sandwiches over. "Filming went over and it wasn't...prudent...to stop until we were done."

She lifted her head and nailed him with her own version of a steely-eyed stare. "Prudent? And you had the nerve to, like, diss *ennui*?"

His smile came quick and free as he pulled the grilled-cheese sandwiches onto plates.

"Feel free to use it in your report if it'll help."

She rose and pulled two bottles of water from the refrigerator. "The only thing that will help is if, like, I didn't *have* to read the book in the first place. It's so bad they didn't even, like, make a movie of it. It would have tanked, big-time, you know?"

Nikko watched as she took a large gulp of the water, swallowed, and then took another chug.

It was a control mechanism for getting full fast, without food. She could claim she wasn't hungry and refuse to eat. He knew as much from the therapist. What he didn't know was how to effectively address it without her getting upset. If he told her to eat, she'd rebel and refuse to. If he ignored her not eating, she'd continue to do so and starve herself.

He took a bite of his own sandwich, realizing for the first time how truly hungry he was.

"This is good," he said nonchalantly and took a sip of his own water. "Good old-fashioned comfort food."

She peered over the expanse of the table at him, a questioning look on her face. "What do you need to be comforted about?"

"You'd be surprised, kid."

"Try me."

Nikko shocked himself by considering it. She was neither a child nor an adult, and as such, her opinions on, and experiences with life, were still made mostly from an emotional basis. She'd never worked; never known what it was to deal with deadlines, unions, and project problems.

But she had lived with her mother and if there was one thing Nikko knew, Flannery, born actress that she was, had shown Melora firsthand what it was like living with a mercurial personality who worked in a fast-paced and often fickle industry, and all the drama that followed it.

So he took a step of faith and shared the morning problems.

"Mama always claimed Jade Quartermaine was a spoiled, self-absorbed bitch," Melora said.

Before Nikko thought to scold her, he stopped. After delivering her opinion, she'd picked up the sandwich and taken a huge bite. While she chewed with more enthusiasm than he'd seen in a while, she looked over at him and added, "She thought Jade was gonna, like, make a play for you a few years back when you were working on that totally lame food-travel show together. I told Mama if you hooked up with Jade I was gonna, like, spurn you 'til the end of time."

Nikko swallowed, surprised when he didn't choke on the bread and his daughter's perspicacious statement.

The program he'd directed Jade in *had* been trying. She'd been rude to the cast and crew, often showing up late without an excuse and, like today, unprepared. At one point Nikko had threatened to walk out if she didn't start acting like a professional and do her job.

Jade had tried—unsuccessfully— to seduce him after that and he'd always wondered if she'd done it because she truly wanted him as a lover or because she saw it as a way to wrangle herself out of the corner she'd painted herself into.

Melora finished half the sandwich before taking another chug of water from the bottle and finishing it.

"I'm full," she said, tapping the bottle down on the table and staring straight at him, as if waiting for him to argue with her about it.

Nikko wanted to. He wanted to point out she still had an entire other half to eat, but remembered what the therapist had said about choosing his battles wisely.

He wiped his mouth with his napkin and nodded instead. "I'll wrap that up for you and stick it in the fridge in case you want something before dinner—"

"I won't."

"—because dinner will be a little later than usual. Remember, we're dining in the mess hall along with the judges and the ranch hands tonight, for the first challenge."

Melora rolled her eyes and for a moment looked so much like her mother Nikko had to take a breath to steady himself. In a few more years, when maturity filled out her face and she settled into her features, Melora was going to be a beautiful woman, just like her mother. The thought caused him no small amount of worry.

"Do I have to, you know, *eat* everything the chefs serve? Because I won't." She shook her head in the defiant way he'd become used to, pushed back in the chair, and folded her arms across her torso again.

He reached deep for calm. "No, Melly, you don't. The only ones who really need to take a bite of everything are the judges and the ranch hands, because they'll be voting. You can eat whatever you want."

"Then why do I even have to go? Can't I just stay here, alone? Nothing will happen to me."

"We've been over this, kid." Nikko shook his head. "I'm in charge of the show and I need to be there. And since it's dinner, and we agreed we'd spend every meal together, that means you go where I go."

"I hate eating in front of other people."

The whine in her voice grated on his already frazzled nerves.

"It makes me feel so...so...ugh!" She threw up her hands.

"No one is going to be watching you eat."

Just me.

"Everyone's attention will be on the chefs and the judges' reactions to the dishes they're served," he told her.

"You don't know that. Not for sure. People stare at me all the time around here because they know I'm your daughter. I hate being on display."

"You won't be on display. Stop being so dramatic."

"I'm not. Listen, can't you let Stacy be in charge instead? Have her, like, *oversee* everything instead of you?"

"What? Where did that come from? No. No, she can't."

"Why not? Isn't she, like, your number two? Although that's a ridiculously gross thing to call someone. I think—"

"Melora—"

"Or let me sit with her, then. She's cool. She's nice. She's *normal*. She won't"—she flapped her hand in the air again—"*hover*, or watch and evaluate everything I put in my mouth. Let me stay with her while you work. She's—"

"*Enough.*"

Melora's mouth slammed shut and a pink tinge flushed down her face from the tips of her ears to her chin.

Nikko placed his hands, palms flat, on the table and counted to five in his head.

Stacy's name had brought the woman to mind when he'd been trying to forget her very existence. Forget the way her beautiful, bright eyes had dilated under her glasses when his hands went around her arms. Forget the way her naked mouth had turned wet and plump when she'd run her tongue across it as she'd stared up at him. Forget the way he'd gone as hard as stone in a heartbeat when he saw the pulse pounding at her neck and realized how close he'd come to putting his mouth over it.

Christ. When was the last time a woman had stirred his body and engaged his mind like this one had? Not since before the accident for sure, and even further back than that, if he was being truthful.

He'd been annoyed to have her thrust upon him by the network and had been purposefully rude and obnoxious in the hope of sending her packing. In the next breath, he remembered the sense of comfort he'd felt when she was nearby, as if having her around him somehow calmed and soothed his tension away.

Nikko shook his head to clear it. He had enough to worry about with the show and getting his daughter healthy, to stop and engage in frivolous thoughts about a woman who wouldn't even smile at him.

He looked across the table at his daughter. "She'll be working the same way I will, and she probably won't even sit down to eat."

The teen slumped back in the chair, her arms still crossed over her chest, and heaved a dramatic sigh.

Nikko took a moment before speaking. Yelling was the wrong way to deal with his daughter, he knew that. In a much more controlled tone, he said, "This is my job, Melora. It's my show and that means I need to be present during every facet of it. Working and overseeing everything. Me. Not a producer."

"But—"

"No. No buts. Or any other arguments. This subject is closed. Do you understand me? Closed."

He rose from the table, grabbed both their plates, and brought them to the sink. He hated that he couldn't just let her be and not have to worry that if left alone she'd spend the evening trying to purge the small amount she'd eaten.

"I'll wash them," Melora said in a soft voice shouting with contrition from behind him. "It's my turn."

He took a deep breath before shifting out of the way and turned around. One look at her sad and miserable expression and his heart shattered.

Again, that she was neither adult nor child, broke through him. With a gentle yank on her emaciated arm he pulled her into a hug, settling her head on his shoulder.

As his hands rubbed down her back and skimmed across the spiny protrusions of her spinal column, worry flooded through him.

"I love you, Melora. More than anything. You know that, right?"

"I know." She'd shifted her head, buried her face against his shoulder, her response muffled by his shirt. "Love you too."

"I just want you to be happy. And healthy," he added.

"I'm trying." He felt the sigh, deep and troubled, expel from her.

He kissed the top of her head. "I know, kid. I know you are. We'll figure it all out. You and me."

"Promise?" When she sniffed he hugged her a little tighter.

"Promise."

Chapter Ten

Stacy ignored the headache pounding behind her left eye while she watched the chefs' images sail across the multiple screens. Since lunch break had ended and the three-hour time frame to prepare the meal they'd serve that evening had been given, the noise level in the set kitchen had risen to the sound of a war zone, minus the bombs and mortar explosions. With various-sized pots in their hands, banging and clamoring against one another as they ran from the storeroom back to their stations, yelling out warnings to others in their way, the chefs had been in perpetual motion, prepping and cooking.

Nikko stood, calling out directions for the set cameramen about which contestant to follow and where to focus the camera's eye, without once sitting down or taking a break. She'd made sure to have a fresh bottle of water at his place when they'd started up again, and she'd noticed he'd taken several hits from it while directing.

No thanks or acknowledgement had come her way, but then, she hadn't really expected them to.

Her lunch break had been spent overseeing the filming of the individual interviews of each chef that would then be edited and interspersed within the footage about their first challenge and the subsequent dinner they were preparing. She'd given a list of questions to each producer and most of the responses had been typical of a first day. The chefs were pumped, primed, cocky, and confident.

Nikko had devised the dinner challenge to utilize the remnants of the morning's butchering. Each chef was charged with creating a main dish to feed the ranch hands, cowboys, and judges using their favorite cut of beef. From the descriptions the chefs gave of their proposed offerings in the interviews, the flavor profiles filled the spectrum from hot and spicy to savory and smoky.

Her attention was drawn to the man directing the challenge.

Everything she'd heard and read about him had proven true in the few short days since she'd met him. Nikko Stamp was arrogant, demanded perfection from those around him, and was stubborn to the point of obstinacy. She'd seen firsthand all of those qualities.

A few others she'd learned for herself.

He was fiercely protective of his daughter, an attribute she found disarming. Nikko loved Melora, of that there was no doubt. His outburst on the day of the airport run when he couldn't find her had proven it. And even though his daughter complained about her current situation, Stacy had been witness to the love and worry she felt for the man.

Nikko may have demanded perfection from others, but it was only because he commanded it first from himself.

One thing she'd been flabbergasted to discover, though, was how attracted she was to him as a man. A man who'd made her heart pound and her insides quake by just holding on to her arms.

Hours later, she could still feel the impression of his fingers burning into her skin, as if she'd been branded by his hands. The moment they'd circled around her arms, Stacy's entire body had been engulfed by warmth, as if an electric blanket had been tossed over her.

The sensation had been shocking and wildly arousing. Yes, he was handsome in a rugged, brooding, and arresting way. His features depicted his ancestry: an aquiline nose that sat squarely in the middle of his face and tapered down to a defined point. A nose she'd found herself being looked down upon several times, usually coupled with a scowl and narrowed eyes.

Thick, wavy midnight hair falling down his neck and flirting with the collar of his shirts was several weeks behind a trim and had her fingers buzzing to run through it.

Full, dense brows arched over watchful, expressive, and attentive eyes she found herself mesmerized by more than once when they were lit on her. His eyes held secrets, intellect, and pain mixed with wariness and caution. Stacy couldn't for the life of her determine why she wanted to rub his furrowed brow smooth, or kiss away the torment perpetually filling his eyes, but she did.

Her earpiece buzzed. After she'd put out a few administrative fires and fixed a few production problems a while later, she slipped quietly back into her seat.

Before her butt hit the chair, Nikko turned and sliced her with a steely glare, making her feel like a teenager caught sneaking in after curfew.

In the next instant, his attention was pulled back to the screens and he continued to bark out orders to the filming crew.

She took a deep breath, settled into her chair, and watched the king rule his realm.

* * * *

"Hey, Stacy?"

She turned and spotted Beau, his long legs eating up the wooden floor as he moved across the dining hall, a grin across his face.

Her own smile was fast and free.

"Whew." Beau stopped in front of her, pushed his Stetson back from his forehead, and glanced around the room. "It sure is loud in here."

"Isn't it always this way at mealtime?"

"I wouldn't know, since I'm usually up at the house with Daddy for dinner."

She cocked her head. "I assumed you all ate your meals together as a—well, as a ranch."

"Nope. We always ate as a family when Mama was alive. She insisted on it. Said she never got to see Daddy during the day, since he was out working the land. The least he could do was sit down to a civilized meal at the end of the day." He readjusted his hat. "Habit stuck even after she died. Anyway, that's why I came over. Daddy would be honored if you'd sit with us, since this is the first official challenge and all."

"Oh, I wish I could. I really do. But I've got work. I've got to deal with any problems and help make sure everything goes smoothly. I'm sorry. I really am."

"Don't you get time to eat at all? A break? Anything."

"When filming is done and there's anything left over, maybe."

"That just seems wrong." He shook his head.

"Nature of the beast. I really would like to try a few of the dishes you're going to be served." Remembering how mouthwatering some of them had looked and smelled during production had her smile growing. "They all look fantastic. I'm glad I don't have to vote for a favorite."

"Well, if you get a break or can spare a minute, stop by the table for a spell. I know Daddy would appreciate it and so would I. That lady judge is seated with us and she's not the most friendly female I've ever met."

Stacy kept her opinion of Jade Quartermaine to herself, although she silently agreed with him.

Nikko and Melora came into sight when she turned. The girl had her arms crossed in front of her, her shoulders bowed and was trying her hardest, it seemed, to be invisible.

When the teen glanced up and saw Stacy, her entire face changed from morose to happy as a smile branched across it. She said something to her father and Nikko's gaze immediately shifted to Stacy.

With a small nod in her direction, he reached down, took his daughter's hand, and led her across the room, his eyes staying focused on her.

Stacy's feet glued themselves to the floor.

Ranch hands, technical crew, cowboys all moved out of his way as he marched toward her, Melora clamped to his side. He never had to break stride once to angle around someone, or wait for someone to move out of his way. Like the Red Sea had for Moses, the throng of people in his path all parted for Nikko Stamp.

The moment he was in hearing distance, she didn't wait for him to speak, but jumped right in to tell him, "Everything is just about ready to go. Hi, Melora." She smiled at the girl.

"Hey."

Turning her focus back to Nikko, she smoothed her features and said, "The chefs are going to serve buffet-style, just as you ordered. Film crew is set and the judges are seated with Amos Dixon and his family."

Nikko nodded, his gaze shifting about the room and then back to her.

There was something in his eyes she couldn't read. His brows pulled together and he looked down at his hand, joined with his daughter's.

Stacy watched as the girl squeezed it and bumped her father with her shoulder.

Nikko's gaze shot back to hers and Stacy swore he was nervous about something.

He took a deep breath and she stared, fascinated, as he shifted in his stance and tilted his shoulders forward.

"Listen," he said, leaning down closer to her, so close she inhaled the scent of sandalwood. "I've gotta get to the operations truck."

Stacy nodded.

"Would you—I mean, could you..." He stopped, glanced down at Melora, and then nodded again when she shot her eyebrows up and pierced him with a bug-eyed glare.

"Melora needs to eat," he said, turning his attention back to her. "Can you walk her through the line and...get her settled? Maybe...stay with her? So she's not alone?"

Whatever she'd expected him to say, this wasn't even close.

Without hesitation, she answered, "Of course I will. Do you want to get something and bring it back to the trailer with you?" she asked the girl. To Nikko, she added, "I mean, if it's okay with you that she's there?"

Relief washed across his face. The lines in his brow disappeared and his shoulders squared and lifted.

He turned to his daughter and asked, "Is that okay? Being planted in the truck while I work?"

Melora's head nodded so vigorously, Stacy had to bite her lip from laughing. How could Nikko not see how much the girl wanted to be with him?

"Okay, but you've got to be quiet," he told her. "I need to focus and I can't be distracted with questions or chattering. Okay?"

"'K." She reached up and kissed his cheek. "Thanks."

Stacy's heart swelled when he looked down at his daughter's happy face, smiled, and pumped her hand again.

"I'll bring her down as soon as the food gets served. Do you want me to bring you back something as well? I can grab a plate with samples."

He shifted his gaze to hers and nailed her with a look so hot, so piercing, and so filled with...intent, her breath caught.

His eyes skirted down to her lips and Stacy swore she could all but feel his mouth pressed against hers. Her insides fluttered and her thighs quaked together with the effort it took to keep her upright.

In the next instant that fierce professional mask shot down his face. The moisture in his eyes froze over and his mouth pulled into the thin, hard line he'd first met her with.

"No need," he told her, turning back to his daughter, dismissing her.

"I'll see you in a little while." He bent, kissed Melora's cheek, and without another word to Stacy, walked away. As it had before, the crowd of people filling the hall moved to let him pass.

Stacy blinked a few times and tried to mentally will her heart to cease pounding like a jackhammer.

What the hell? She'd never been so overtaken with any man she'd ever worked with before, and certainly not one who so obviously disliked her. Stacy wasn't the kind of woman who developed crushes or sentimental feelings about the men she was surrounded by.

In truth, she knew and accepted her reputation as the go-to girl around a television production, valued for what she could do, liked because she was a likable person, and not lusted after because she was devastatingly alluring.

But she swore she saw desire when Nikko Stamp had just stared at her, just as she swore he was angry about feeling it.

"You okay?" Melora asked from her side. "You don't mind, like, letting me hang with you? I promise not to be a leech."

Stacy gave herself an internal shake. Smiling, she rubbed a hand along the teen's shoulder. "That was the nickname my cousins gave me when we were kids."

Melora's open smile warmed her.

"Come on," Stacy said. "Let's go see how the setup is coming along and then we can get you something to eat."

"I'm not really hungry." Melora pulled back on Stacy's grip. "And I don't like barbeque," she added. "At all. It's, like, *barbaric*. I told Nikko I wouldn't eat anything but he, like, *insisted* I come anyway."

A mulish tinge colored her words. Stacy was well acquainted with teenage obstinacy. "Okay. We'll find you something," she told her as they weaved through the crowd. "No worries."

* * * *

He knew immediately when they entered the truck. Although they didn't make a sound and the noise from the monitors and the crew all around him was loud and boisterous, the back of Nikko's neck tingled, the tiny hairs standing on edge like a static-electricity charge when he sensed their arrival.

He tried to tell himself he hadn't been waiting for them, worried they were taking so long.

He attempted to convince himself he hadn't been more tense than usual, unable to completely focus on the scenes in front of him without Stacy's calming presence behind him.

He flat-out lied, calling the crazy notion in his head that he was fiercely, totally attracted to her a gross untruth, his visceral reactions to her nothing more than his body reminding him he hadn't gotten laid in a long, long time.

His gaze flicked from one monitor to another as the cameras filmed the chefs serving their meals.

Nikko pushed a button on the control panel. "Camera five, move closer to the judges' table. Get me some visuals."

A shot of Amos Dixon smiling at Jade Quartemaine as the judge flirted with her host came on screen.

"Record sound," Nikko commanded. "Camera six, zoom in on Burbank's hands. I want to see that steak portion."

Each cameraman did as he bid. Satisfied, he reached a hand down to the console and grabbed his water bottle.

A fresh one sat in place.

Nikko spun around to see Melora seated next to Stacy, a plate half filled with—what was that, salad? *Where had she gotten a salad*? None of the chefs had prepared one. Stacy had a similarly filled plate. Two small bowls sat next to them, one with what Nikko knew was Riley MacNeill's stew, the other Dorinda Katay's shish kebab.

His eyes almost popped out of his head when his daughter took a whopping spoonful of the stew, rolled her eyes at Stacy, then swallowed and smiled. His EP said something in a low tone to his daughter and the girl actually giggled.

When was the last time his daughter had giggled? Or even laughed?

Melora happened to catch him staring and, looking sheepish, squinched up her nose and mouthed, "Sorry."

He gave her a small grin and winked at the exact moment Stacy looked over at him. The smile she'd had for his daughter was still on her mouth, but when their gazes connected, it disappeared.

For one fleeting moment, though, he'd been graced with her unguarded expression, and in that sparse second he'd been enchanted.

Loud laughter from the screens pulled his attention back to his job.

When all the meals had been served, the food eaten, and the pans emptied, the cowboys and ranchers began filling out ratings cards on each meal they'd sampled.

Nikko turned around and without even saying her name, Stacy snapped to attention.

"Who's collecting the scorecards?" he asked.

"I thought Melora and I could do it," she answered.

"Can I, Daddy? Can I help?"

It had been on the tip of his tongue to snap at Stacy and tell her his daughter wasn't involved in the production, but the unexpected and rare expression of happiness on the teen's face killed the words before he let them go.

He couldn't refuse Melora anything if it made her that happy.

"Go ahead," he told them. "Bring them straight back to me so I can tally them. And tell Jade and Roth to set up for the judges'-table filming. I want it done now."

"Can I dismiss the chefs for the night, or do you want to talk to them about tomorrow?"

He rubbed a hand down his leg. In reality he wanted nothing more than to get back to the cabin, put his aching leg up, and have a few shots of the whiskey waiting for him in the den.

"I'll meet them in the stew room in twenty minutes. After that they can call it a night."

Stacy rose, as did Melora. Both gathered up their plates and empty water bottles. Before leaving, Melora moved to her father, kissed him on the cheek, and said, "Thanks, Daddy."

Emotion choked in the back of his throat, making speech impossible. He nodded and kissed her back.

Chapter Eleven

While she'd been packing to leave for Montana, Stacy had told Kandy the trip would be like one to hell.

It wasn't a far-off description.

Stacy opened the top two buttons on her blouse and dragged the cool water bottle from the front of her neck to the back. Her body was dripping with sweat and she wasn't even doing something fun, like hot yoga.

The pop-up canopy she sat under with a few of the tech crew and Nikko helped keep the blazing sun off of their heads, but did nothing to prevent the morning heat from sweltering their bodies.

Befitting the weather, the majority of the crew was in shorts and T-shirts, baseball caps atop their heads with the show's logo, and sunglasses to ease the glare.

Stacy wore her usual long-sleeved shirt to cover her arms, although she had opted for a lighter cotton-blend mix and cotton trousers. She'd secured her hair into a ponytail, her logo cap in place over it. Having forgotten to pack her prescription sunglasses, she'd been forced to wear her contact lenses, plain sunglasses over them, and her eyes had begun to sting and water the moment they'd arrived at the dry and rocky location shoot.

If she was boiling like a lobster after being shoved into a waiting pot, the cooks had to be near the dropping point.

The truck's thermometer when they'd left the ranch at six a.m. had already read 85 degrees. Three hours later, with the sun exploding in a cloudless blue sky, it had to be at least 100—if not more—in the shade.

The chefs were offered no refuge from the scorching heat as they barreled through their challenge.

Nikko had taken them a mile from the main ranch, the property still held by Amos Dixon. Stationed atop a rise of rocks, the chefs were given supplies to cook with that the average cowboy would use on a cattle drive. A cowboy of the 1800s, that is.

Three large, period chuck wagons, bursting with cooking supplies, surrounded the chefs in a wagon-circle fashion. Each chef had been given a pit to cook over and the instruments to start a fire. The challenge was an interesting one: make breakfast using only the supplies and utensils available from the food wagons.

"Dorinda's having some trouble with her fire," Todd said as he, Nikko, Stacy, and a few other techs watched the three portable monitors they'd brought with them. Since they were on a location shoot, all the filming was done with handheld cameras.

Nikko ordered the camera to zoom in on Dorinda's struggle to light the coals under the metal fire-pit grate.

Stacy chugged the remnants in her water bottle, then rose to get another. The last thing she wanted to do was dehydrate in the blistering heat. A quick scan at the others and she took out a few bottles of water from the cooler, placing one at Todd's seat, then Nikko's.

The director never lifted his head to indicate that he'd noticed her remove his empty bottle and replace it with a full one.

Stacy decided to take a few minutes and see if there were any concerns she could attend to.

They'd driven out to the site in four humongous, air-conditioned, and fully stocked motor homes. Nikko and Melora had been in one with the sound and filming crew, the judges, Jade's entourage, and the producers in another and the final two were split between the chefs. Stacy had driven out with the chefs and producers in order to make sure everyone knew what was going to happen and to answer any questions. In all honesty, she should have ridden in Nikko's coach, but when she'd met up with him for a few short minutes prior to leaving, he hadn't asked her to and she hadn't wanted to push herself on him, especially when they'd appeared to have come to some kind of truce.

After she and Melora had gathered up the voting sheets from the first dinner challenge, she'd brought them back to Nikko as instructed. She was supposed to tally the results with him and then seal and store them so no one could find out who had won the challenge. Nikko had told her he didn't feel like doing it just then, that they would get to it after the next challenge, and that he would be responsible for making sure they were put in the safe.

She'd wanted to tell him that wasn't the way it was supposed to go, but stopped herself when she realized he wasn't being obnoxious or challenging her. He was simply exhausted and in a great deal of pain. His hand gripped his injured thigh and she could read torment along his grooved brow and pinched mouth. His chest rose and fell in a staccato rhythm and a very fine line of sweat covered his upper lip.

Every fiber in her being ached to help this man, but she knew any reference to his pain would only serve to make him dislike her more.

Nikko Stamp was one of the proudest, most stubborn, and intriguing men she'd ever had the pleasure—or displeasure—to meet. If she gave him the slightest indication she knew the agony coursing through him, he would have been mortified and furious.

So she did the one thing she hated more than any other: She ignored his suffering.

Stacy knocked on the judges' coach and entered.

"Are they ready for us?" Dan Roth asked.

He was lounging, feet up on a chair, a makeup girl applying foundation to his cheeks.

"Not yet." She looked down at her tablet. "The challenge has twenty minutes left. You're going to want to stay in here until the last second. It's miserable outside."

"Why Nikko had to drag us all the way out here is beyond comprehension." Jade reclined in a chair, eyes closed as one of her assistants rubbed lotion on her face.

Both judges were garbed in what Stacy termed cowboy dress, complete with boots, a bolero for Dan and a frilly, flirty skirt for Jade. Twin Stetsons sat on a tabletop, ready to be donned before filming.

"You both okay with your scripts?" she asked.

Dan nodded and gave her a thumbs-up. She'd expected nothing less. The man's behavior since arriving had proven he was a total professional. Always letter-perfect, on time, and in a good mood, ready to give a bravura performance.

Jade, on the other hand, was still proving to be a nightmare.

Carrie had cornered Stacy before leaving from the ranch and told her Jade had made a hasty retreat from judges' table once filming had been done the night before and raced back to her room. When Carrie had caught up with her to discuss today's shooting schedule—through the door of her room—Jade had told her to go away and let her be. She was tired and needed her sleep.

Carrie had acquiesced, but as she was turning to go she heard the distinctive sound of glass banging against something metal. This morning, she'd run back to the room once Jade had left it and found two empty wine bottles in the bathroom trash bin.

Stacy glanced over at the now-upright woman in the chair and noted the puffiness around her beautifully made-up eyes. The skin on her neck was slightly sallow and Stacy feared her face was probably the same color under the heavy foundation.

Stacy knew how she'd handle this potentially disastrous situation, but she couldn't do what she wanted. Nikko was, as he'd repeatedly mentioned, in charge. It was up to him to decide what to do about the worrisome judge.

"I'll call when they're ready for you," Stacy told them.

The interior of the coach had been a pleasant and cooling break. The moment she stepped back outside the heat slapped her in the face and she immediately began to sweat.

Back under the canopy, at least, she was out of direct sunlight.

"Get the judges cued," Nikko said. He wasn't looking at her, but she got the distinct impression he was addressing her, so she beeped Carrie on the walkie-talkie. They could hear Jade's shrill and complaining voice the moment she stepped from the coach. One of her assistants held an oversized umbrella over her body so not one speck of sunlight filtered through, the other carried an opened bottle of water with a straw floating in it.

Nikko's sigh was deep, loud, and annoyed.

"What are the chances we'll get this in one take?" he asked.

No one replied.

Four takes later, the intro was done.

Jade repeatedly flubbed her lines, then, due to her sweating, had needed her makeup reapplied after each stop.

"If we get out of here before we all fry to death, we'll be lucky," Nikko said. "Okay. Start the tastings."

Since the challenge had been to prepare breakfast using the rudimentary utensils over an open fire, and in under forty-five minutes, the chefs were limited in the flavor profiles they routinely used and had to settle for cooking the best-tasting dish they could without an array of spices and herbs. This challenge was designed to show how good their food could taste under substandard conditions.

Stacy thought the challenge was brilliant. These were world class chefs, spoiled by having the finest of everything at their fingertips. How would the best-of-the-best rise to such an elementary task?

The smell of eggs and bacon filled the air, tinged with the subtle aromas of flour and sugar. Half the chefs had created egg dishes, the other opting for pancakes, or as Clay Burbank smilingly called his, "floured orgasms."

Once the tasting was completed, done without a flub or flutter from Jade, the judges were excused back to their comfortably cool coach and the chefs, as a unit, all began to unbutton their uniform jackets and slip out of them.

"I'm sweating like a friggin' farm animal," Dorinda said with a laugh. "I need water to drink and a pool to dive into."

Stacy surrounded them and their individual producers, handing out bottled water and commenting on the meals they'd made.

"I think the kid took this one, hands down," Clay said, tipping his bottle at Riley MacNeill. "Whatever the hell he made smelled like heaven in a skillet."

Stacy glanced over at the youngest chef and, as she had before, saw him straightening up his workstation. She walked over to him.

"You don't have to do that." She handed him a water bottle. "Get your coat off and get cooled down. You must be dying in this heat."

He opened the bottle, took a long draught, and then spilled the remainder over his head. "Thanks," he said, shaking his head like a wet dog.

Stacy's laugh was quick and easy. He was such a kid.

"We should be leaving in a few minutes," she said to the group. "When we get back, you all can get started on tonight's challenge for dinner. You'll have three hours to prep."

"Hey, when are we gonna get a break, Stacy?" Lou Jiordino called out. "Two days. Four challenges. All these friggin' filmed interviews. Usually on a competition show we get a day in between, at least."

"Lou, you knew the schedule before you signed on," she said. "This production isn't like the others you've done. It's set up differently."

"Truth," the chef said, crossing his arms petulantly in front of him. "Other shows we get treated like pros. So far on this one, Stamp has been treating us like indentured servants."

From the corner of her eye Stacy saw Nikko, who'd been making his way toward his motor coach, turn and level the group with a stare even she could see from this distance was irritated. Before she could think of what to say, he started marching toward them.

Instinctively, her gaze shot to his injured leg, searching it for any signs that walking was causing him pain or discomfort.

She took a quick breath when she saw none.

"Something wrong, Jiordino? Something you need clarified?"

Stacy had to admit, the director certainly had a way of changing the atmosphere in a room. Or in this case, a canyon.

"Not wrong, Nikko, no. Not at all." The chef's smile looked perfunctory and forced. "Just wondering when we're gonna get a little downtime, you know? The trip out here from the East Coast was long, and then we started up right away with filming. I'm still a little...you know, jet-lagged."

It was petty how happy she felt not to be on the receiving end of Nikko's displeasure for once, when he answered the chef in a voice that sounded like ice cracking on such a blistering day.

"Got somewhere you need to be, Jiordino, other than here, honoring your contract? Competing for two hundred and fifty thousand dollars?"

"No, man, it's just..." Face already red from the heat, Jiordino's cheeks turned the color of overripe tomatoes.

Nikko's gaze raked the group from one end to the other. "Anyone else feeling tired? Jet-lagged? Unable or unwilling to fulfill their contract obligations?"

Many of the gathered chefs drank from water bottles, looked around at their surroundings, down at the ground—anywhere but at Nikko.

Their silence echoed.

"I didn't think so." Addressing Lou again, Nikko said, "You can sleep in the bus back to the ranch if you're so tired, Jiordino."

With that he turned, stopped, and winced. For a short second his color paled and he bit down on his bottom lip so hard, Stacy was surprised he didn't draw blood. Then, he took a quick breath and stalked away from them.

She didn't think anyone else had seen the subtle jerky movement, since the chefs were all doing their best to avoid looking at Nikko, but she couldn't be sure.

The urge to run after him was strong. But she realized it was the worst thing she could possibly do. Nikko was already mad at Jiordino's flippant complaint. Add the pain in his leg on top of that and it was a sure bet if she so much as asked him a question he'd eviscerate her with a response. It was best to just let him be.

Stacy tossed her contacts out the minute she'd got back to her room, rinsed her face and eyes with an ice-cold washcloth and then stuck on her glasses, thankful her eyes now had relief from the dry, hot air out on the location shoot.

The moment they all returned to the ranch, the chefs ran to the kitchen in order to prep for their challenge, while Stacy was immediately run ragged with production problems.

Nikko, occupied in the command center filming and directing the prepping, told her to take care of the problems herself when she approached him with them.

Surprised and *pleased* were too tame for how she'd felt at his words. Finally, he was allowing her to help him, to trust in her abilities. Finally, he was letting her do the job she'd been hired for; the one she was so good at. Finally, he was coming to see how valuable she could be.

In the next breath, when he'd said, "Try not to screw anything up," Stacy had to bite back a laugh.

So much for an ego boost.

The problems got solved without issue. The moment she entered the truck again, Nikko's eyes lit on her and one eyebrow inched its way up his forehead.

Without even thinking, she gave him a thumbs-up. When he simply nodded and then turned back to the monitors, she took her usual seat two rows behind the console monitors.

The past two days had given her a fairly good idea of how he liked to run one of his productions and now that she had a good bead on how to act around him, what to say, and how to conduct herself so that he'd at least let her do her job, Stacy started to relax and allowed herself a few moments to observe Nikko work.

And watching Nikko Stamp work was to observe a master at his craft.

His eyes seemed to be on every monitor at once. Clipped, concise, succinct commands flew from him, his head and hands in constant motion. He stood, his thick thighs leveraged against the console, leaning in for, Stacy knew, support.

No one who'd spoken to her in all the days of production had commented on his—what was so obvious to her—leg pain. No one except Melora.

Even if the girl hadn't clued Stacy into the ongoing problems her father was experiencing from the accident, Stacy was an astute enough observer she would have realized he was in tortuous pain before long.

With an unconscious graze of her fingers, she traced a trail along her sleeve, up her arm from wrist to elbow. The tiny breaks and bumps her fingertips stroked were a constant reminder of what she'd suffered through during her youth and the way she'd dealt with her own pain.

An oath split the air in the truck.

Stacy shook out of her thoughts to discover one of the chefs bleeding on screen.

"Get the nurse in there right now," Nikko barked to the room. "Keep filming. No one stops."

The chef's personal producer popped up on the monitor, wrapped a towel around the man's hand, and pulled the chef from camera range.

Before she could be told to, Stacy bolted from her chair and ran to the set. Accidents were common in any professional kitchen, with chefs used to working with cutlery and machinery made to slice and dice. Add in the added stress of working under a time clock and the chance for something to go wrong rose exponentially. A registered nurse was part of the production crew, present at all times on set just in case an injury occurred. Most were easily handled and fixed. There were times, though, when a trip to a local emergency room was warranted.

The moment Stacy saw the injured chef up close, she knew this was one of those times.

"My hands were wet and the fucking knife just slipped," chef Angel Ortego said.

Talia Davids, the fortyish traveling nurse Stacy'd met the first day of production, was supporting Angel's hand above his head and pressing down so hard her own hand was beginning to shake.

"He needs to get to an ER," Talia said. "The finger is hanging—literally hanging—by a thread of tendon. We need to get him to an OR ASAP so he doesn't loose it. As it is, he's pouring blood so fast I'm afraid he's gonna go out on me."

Stacy knew the nearest hospital was twenty miles away. Transporting him in a truck, no matter how fast it went, wasn't going to get him there in time.

In a moment of stark decisiveness, she made an executive decision, knowing she'd have to deal with Nikko's wrath about it. She'd worry about that later, because right now they didn't have any time to waste.

She called up to the main house, asked to speak with Amos Dixon, and was given the approval to use the ranch helicopter she'd seen her first night.

Less than a minute later Beau came barreling into the building.

"Daddy's pilot, Kent Wickers, is getting the chopper all set, Stacy. I'll take y'all over to the hanger in my jeep. It'll be faster."

Stacy, a profusely bleeding and increasingly paling Angel, Talia, and Angel's producer, Juan, all sprinted from the building.

Less than five minutes later, Beau drove Stacy away from the helicopter and watched as it lifted and left the property.

"They'll be there in no time," Beau told her when he brought her back to the production truck. "Quick thinkin' to use the chopper."

Stacy nodded. "I'm just glad it was available. Thank your father for me again and have him send me an itemized bill for the gas and the pilot's time. I'll make sure he gets reimbursed from the network."

Beau flipped a hand carelessly. "Don't worry about that. Daddy said he was happy it got some use instead of rusting away in the barn." He moved a little closer to her, bent his head, and lowered his voice. "Listen, do you have a minute? I'd like to get your opinion on something."

She couldn't help being captivated as this big, confident, cocky man suddenly became nervous and awkward, almost like a teenage boy asking out a girl for the first time. His cheeks had turned a charming shade of embarrassed pink and he tucked a corner of his mouth between his teeth.

She had million things running in her head production-wise, but she put them all to the side, nodded, and said, "Shoot."

"Well, see"—he cupped the back of his neck—"since you're a girl, and a city girl at that, you know about...girl things. What they like and such, so I thought I'd get your opinion." His bashful grin was adorable.

"On what?"

He reached into his back pocket and pulled out a small box. Stacy instantly knew what it held.

He popped the top open and she looked down at a beautifully cut, round diamond, the ring band a shiny gold. "Is it too big?" Beau asked. "Too small? Not—I don't know—*sparkly* enough? I've never bought a ring before. Do you think she'll like it?"

Stacy couldn't help the wide smile that broke out on her face. "Well, as a girl, and a city girl, I can tell you it's perfect. It's not only big enough and sparkly enough"—he grinned down at her—"but I think she's gonna love it as much as she loves you."

"Yeah?"

Stacy reached out a hand and squeezed his arm. "Yeah."

His entire face relaxed.

"She's a lucky girl," Stacy told him.

In the next instant, he grabbed her in a bear hug and lifted her off the ground. Stacy yelped, then laughed along with him.

"I'm the lucky one," he said, gently placing her back down. "Thanks. I'm heading into town right now to ask her."

Her heart skipped a beat at how happy he looked. She squeezed his upper arm again and said, "Go get 'er, cowboy."

Beau tipped his Stetson, said, "Yes, ma'am," and then jumped back into his jeep.

* * * *

He knew the second she came back. Not because of any extrasensory perception he'd developed, but because he'd been watching for her.

A niggle of anxiety sliced through him when he heard the whirr of the helicopter. Had she gone with them? She hadn't radioed in either way, so he wasn't sure.

Nikko rubbed a hand down his aching thigh.

From the corner of his eye he'd watched Beau Dixon drop her off and breathed a sigh of relief that she hadn't gone to the hospital with the others. Then, instead of leaving, Beau kept her a few minutes in conversation.

When he'd pulled the box from his pocket and then shown it to Stacy, for a brief moment Nikko panicked.

Jesus, was the cowboy asking her to marry him?

The panic gave way to an insane moment when intense jealousy galloped within him.

When it became obvious Beau wasn't proposing, just showing her the ring, Nikko took a deep, relieved breath.

"They've got ten minutes left to prep," Todd said from next to him. "Then an hour before they need to serve."

"Enough time for a few sound-bite interviews," he said.

Nikko turned his head. Stacy immediately snapped to attention without him even saying her name.

"Do you want me to set them up?" she asked.

"No. Let one of the producers handle it. I need to know about Ortego when we're finished here so I can update the others."

With a nod, Stacy rose and started speaking into her communication device.

When Nikko called time a few minutes later, the chefs had finished their prep work.

Stacy stopped speaking just as Nikko stepped out of the truck.

"I have an update on Angel," she told him.

"Save it until we get on set. You can tell everyone at once."

The walk to the kitchen building was a mere hundred feet, but to Nikko it felt as if he were crossing the length of five football fields. His leg was screaming and he knew he needed to rest it. His usual brisk walking pace had dropped dramatically in the past few days and he was worried the crew had noticed. They all moved like lightning, used to a fast-paced production.

As they silently crossed to the building, Stacy kept her pace even with his. Todd preceded them to the set, opened the door, and stepped back to allow them entry.

"They're all itching to get going, Nikko," he said.

With a nod, he replied, "This'll be quick."

Ten minutes later the chefs mobilized as a chaotic unit and brought their food to the dining hall on portable food carts and in coolers. The cleanup crew began on the kitchen once it was empty.

"I'll arrange to have Angel's belongings brought to the hospital," Stacy told him, "and get him set up with a flight for when he's discharged. It's a shame he can't finish the competition."

Nikko looked down at her and shrugged. "Accidents happen," he said, hearing how gruff his voice sounded on the vast set as it echoed back to them. If he didn't sit down soon, he was afraid his leg was going to collapse under his weight. Sweat drenched through his shirt and on his face. He swiped the back of his hand across a slick trail of it over his upper lip.

With a nod, Stacy closed her tablet. "I'll go make sure everything's set in the dining hall."

When she looked up at him through her glasses, her brows pinched inward.

She took a step closer, one hand reaching out. He swore he could see compassion mixed with a question on her face and in her gaze. Horrified she was going to ask him if he was okay— or worse, offer to help him— Nikko retreated a few steps and nodded. Stacy stopped, her hand slowly falling down to her side.

"Good. I'll be over shortly. I need to get Melora."

For a moment she stood, her eyes browsing his own. Then she stepped back and asked, "Will Melora be helping me with collecting the votes again?"

With a terse nod, he said, "Yeah." He hesitated as a spasm shot up from his knee to his hip. He swallowed the pain. It took every ounce of pride and fortitude he could summon not to collapse in front of her. "I think that's a good idea."

It was Stacy's turn to nod. She kept her eyes trained on him for a moment, then, with another quick headshake, said, "Okay. I'm off."

It wasn't until the set door closed behind her that Nikko allowed himself to breathe.

Chapter Twelve

The moment she walked into her darkened suite, Stacy kicked off her shoes, wiggled her toes, and tossed her tablet onto the bed.

In the next breath, she raised her arms high over her head to stretch her spine, then slowly lowered from her waist until her hands fell, palms flat to the floor.

The early-morning location shoot had robbed her of her usual yoga/meditation session and her body was now begging for release.

She flipped on the bedside light, stripped from her workday clothes and, in her underwear, went into a quick stress-shedding series of poses, starting with a few rounds of *savasana*..

The tension that had grown and settled in her shoulders and back during the grueling day began to fade away as she sat, cross-legged, and walked her hands forward on the rug, stretching her spine and hips.

Her thoughts uncluttered and cleared as she took deep, cleansing breaths between each movement, allowing her body, mind, and spirit to quiet.

If only she could do the same for Nikko Stamp.

One look in his eyes, at the tension around his mouth, at the beads of sweat wetting his face, had verified how much pain he was in. She didn't think he even noticed how frequently he rubbed his thigh or squeezed the muscles through his jeans.

She'd been about to offer him some help in the kitchen when he'd retreated from her, clamping down on the agony she'd seen cross his face. His movement told her he didn't want help, especially hers. Either pride or dislike of her—she couldn't discern which—made him pull away.

During the dinner filming and then after the votes were taken, he'd seemed to go out of his way to avoid her. Melora had once again joined her, first to bring some food back to the production truck, where she quietly sat with Stacy and ate while they both watched Nikko work, and then to help her gather the votes from the ranch workers. The girl seemed happy to accompany Stacy, interact with some of the cowboys and even the chefs as the two of them made their way along the individual buffet stations.

It didn't escape her attention that Melora's openness closed down a little when they arrived at Riley MacNeill's station. Both chef and teen had tossed quick glances at one another while Riley explained his dish and then gave them a sample, his gaze darting between them, but lighting on Melora for the majority of the time.

Riley and Nikko's daughter were the youngest ones on the ranch and it wasn't inconceivable that they'd check each other out in the typical fashion of teenagers—shyly and surreptitiously.

Melora, despite the choppy, spiky haircut and goth makeup, was a very pretty girl. Her skin was flawless, even under the pale pancake foundation she wore, her cheekbones high and rounded, eyelashes thick and long.

Blue-eyed Riley MacNeill was, Stacy imagined, the type of guy a fifteen-year-old-girl could crush on pretty easily. Tall, lithe, with an impressive pair of muscular arms, he had the brooding, silent kind of charisma and charm women of all ages fell for.

Her heart warmed a little at the thought the two of them, both such loners, could be friends.

After dinner service was complete, the chef interviews were finished and the votes were sealed in the safe. Just when she thought she was done, her communication device blared and she had to meet with one of the producers who was having a personal crisis.

That solved, she glanced down at her cell phone, noted the hour, and hoped her day was finally over.

Stacy pulled to a standing position, rolled her arms above her head, took a deep, deep breath in and then let it out while allowing her hands, pressed together at the palms, to drop in front of her chest.

With a shoulder roll, she went into the bathroom and washed her face.

As she was applying moisturizer to the puckered and dried skin on her arm, her cell phone pinged.

"Stacy?"

"Melora. What's wrong?"

The girl's whispered voice sounded tense and troubled.

"Can you come to the house? Like, right now?"

"Is everything okay?"

"N—no. It's not. Please. Can you come?"

"I'll be there in two minutes."

Stacy threw on a long-sleeved T-shirt and yoga pants and then bolted from the room.

Melora was waiting at the cabin front door when she came around the corner of the house and pulled it open wide to let her in.

"Thanks," the teen said. "I don't know, like, what to do for him? Who to call to help him?"

"Sweetie, what's wrong?" Stacy pulled the shaking girl into her arms, then rubbed a hand down her thin back.

"It's Daddy. He's—"

"He's what, Melora?"

"He's in so much pain." The tears pooling in her eyes spilled free and, like waterfalls, cascaded down her cheeks. Her black eye makeup streaked in their wake. "I don't know how to help him."

"Where is he?"

Melora nodded and said, "He's in his office. He went in there, like, the *minute* we got back from dinner, shut himself in."

"How do you know he's in pain and not just working? That he just doesn't want to be disturbed?"

Melora swiped at her face, smearing the dripping eyeliner across her cheeks. "I just do."

Stacy stifled a sigh. Should she trust an emotional teenager, rife with personal issues and all the idiosyncratic drama that went along with her age, to know when something was truly wrong with her father? Or should she simply try to calm and reassure the girl, noting her father was a difficult man who didn't want or need anyone's help, especially hers?

Remembering what it was like to be fifteen, Stacy decided to trust.

"Take me to him," she said.

Relief overflowed from Melora's eyes, competing with the tears.

Following behind her through the interior of the house, Stacy stopped when Melora did.

"He's in here," she whispered.

"Call him."

Melora nodded. With a gentle rap of her knuckles on the closed door, she said, "Daddy? Can I come in?"

When no response came back, Stacy knocked. "Mr. Stamp? It's Stacy Peters. I need a moment of your time."

Again, silence, then a muffled, "Go away."

"See? He doesn't sound...right," Melora said and swiped her sleeve under her nose. "He sounds, like, sick or something."

Stacy agreed the usual booming, caustic timbre she'd come to associate with the director was missing from the voice that came from within the room.

"Mr. Stamp? I'm coming in."

With that, she opened the door a crack and peeked in.

The room was in darkness, save for the dim desk light. Stacy remembered the layout from when she'd been in it the night she'd arrived. A large desk and chair sat across one windowed wall, a leather couch and love seat across another.

It took her eyes a moment to adjust.

"I thought…I told you…to…go away."

His voice was weak, groggy, and tinged with a spoonful of anger. Stacy moved into the room, Melora on her heels. They could barely make out his figure reclining on the couch.

Melora flipped the wall switch, instantly bathing the room in bright light from the ceiling fixture.

"*Christ.* Dim that damn light," Nikko roared, his hand shooting up to shield his eyes. Melora adjusted the dimmer.

He lay, supine, his feet propped up on one of the couch risers, a decorative pillow stuffed behind his head. The rank smell of alcohol, combined with sweat, filled the air around him, and as Stacy drew closer, she could feel the heat piping off his body.

"Daddy." Melora ran to her father and knelt down next to the couch. "Are you okay? What's wrong?"

Nikko stretched out a hand and swiped it along her cheek. "It's okay, Melly. I'm just…my leg hurts…is all. Too much standing."

The girl started crying again as she pushed up and away from him, a look of horror on her face. "*Oh. My. God.* You're drunk. That's so, like, *disgusting.*"

"I'm not, kid, I swear." His words weren't slurred, but his breathing was ragged. "I just had a few shots to try and…take the edge off."

Melora wasn't having any of his excuses. She bounded upright and peered down at her father. "I was so worried about you. I thought you were sick. Or worse. And all you've been doing is *drinking.* God!"

She turned, but her father reached out and grabbed her arm.

"Melly, please…" Before he could say more, a savage sound, like the howl of an injured animal, shot from his lips. He dropped her arm, then clasped both of his hands around his thigh and squeezed as the sweat on his brow started to drip down his temples.

"Daddy!" Melora all but fell on top of him, her tears starting again.

"Melora, move." Stacy gently tugged on the girl's arm. "Let me."

"Help him. *Please.*"

"I will." She squatted so she was eye level with him. Even in the subdued light, his pallor was stark, his pain palpable.

"Are the muscles in your leg cramping? Is that what's causing this?" she asked, her voice low and composed.

Nikko opened his eyes and stared at her. Raw, unfiltered agony filled them.

"I can help," she told him. "But I need to know the cause. Are you spasming or is it a different kind of pain?"

"Spasms." The word choked from the back of his throat.

"Okay. Will you let me help you?"

She didn't think he'd be so stubborn as to refuse when he was obviously in misery, but his pride was so monumental and his dislike of her so vast, she just wasn't sure.

She waited a few beats before he closed his eyes again and nodded once.

Sucking back the relieved breath she desperately wanted to expel, Stacy addressed Melora. "I need clean towels, a bucket of hot water, and some lotion. Do you guys have a microwave?"

A few minutes later, armed with several thick cotton towels soaking in steaming water, Stacy came back into the room. Nikko hadn't moved an inch since she'd left.

His fists were balled at his sides, eyes closed, his throat working frequently as he swallowed every few seconds.

"I'm all set," Stacy said softly. "I need to get at your leg, though. We need to get your pants off. Okay?"

Under lids that were hooded and distrustful, his eyes raked her face.

"I—I'm sorry. I need to work skin to skin. The towels are drenched and heated. They need to lay over your bare leg so the heat dilates and relaxes your muscles. Otherwise, this won't work and all you'll be is... well, wet."

Hating how scattered and unsure she sounded, Stacy took a mental breath. "If you could get in a Jacuzzi or something heated like a whirlpool bath, that would work the same way."

"There's no Jacuzzi here."

His deep, pain-tinged voiced reverberated in the air.

With a nod, Stacy said, "Then this is the best option available. Okay?"

"Melora?" His gaze never left her face.

"I asked her to wait outside. I figured you wouldn't want her to see you like this. She's okay, though. Really. Just worried about you."

Nikko nodded and drew in a deep breath. Without another word, his hands moved to his belt. He undid it, then opened the button on his pants and dragged the zipper down.

He lifted his hips, but the effort blasted an oath from his lips as his hand sailed back to grip his thigh.

"Let me," she said. "Please." Gently, she slid his pants down over his hips, his legs, and then off.

Heat soaked her face when she spied the black boxers covering him. Compassion replaced the embarrassment when her gaze caught the long, jagged scars tearing down the length of his thigh to his knee. Dozens of impressions from surgical staples followed the scars on both sides. His leg was pink, the skin appearing healthy, but the scars were long, roped, and thick. The thigh itself was swollen when she compared to its twin.

"This is going to be hot," she told him, pulling a dripping towel from the bucket. Steam shot up from the cotton blend. "I'm going to lay it on your thigh for a few minutes to dilate the muscles. This helps alleviate the cramping. Okay?"

He nodded, his eyes half-opened now, watching her.

Stacy wrung the excess water from the towel, flicked it open, and positioned it on his thigh.

A hiss spilled from between his barely parted lips and one hand shot out to grip the back of the couch.

"I'm sorry. I know it's hot. But it really has to be. I won't let you burn. I promise."

Nikko closed his eyes while she put another cloth alongside the first one.

Every minute or so she removed one of the towels and replaced it with a fresh one. She worked in silence, the only sound Nikko's deep inhalations.

Soon, his death grip on the couch back eased and she watched his shoulders begin to drop and relax from their frozen, lifted position.

She removed the towels and ran a hand across the fleshy part of his thigh, relieved to feel the muscles underneath were no longer bound tight.

At her touch, his eyes flew open, his gaze stabbing. Her insides quivered and she took a deep breath to settle them.

"Your muscles are starting to relax," she explained, her tongue wetting her dry lips. "They can be massaged now to fully unwind them, or else they'll just tense up again. Okay?"

"Is that why you asked Melora for lotion?" His voice sounded as if he'd gargled with sandpaper: harsh and coarse.

"Yes. It helps aid the massage. May I?"

"Go ahead."

She started at the top of his thigh, at the insertion point of the muscle, her hands slipping under the hem of his boxers. Keeping her gaze trained on his leg, she kneaded, rolled, and squeezed the skin and underlying structures between her strong fingers. She'd lathered up her hands with a generous amount of the sweet, rose-scented lotion and then rubbed her palms together to warm them before touching him. Back and forth, around, up and down, her fingers gripped, flexed, and caressed his skin.

When was the last time she'd touched a man's body so intimately? So sensually?

They weren't lovers—not even friends, truth be told—and here she was stroking his naked flesh, learning the feel of him, of his body, as if they were.

Stacy's gaze roamed down his injured leg, crossed to the other one.

Touch. It was such an intimate act between two people. Almost like making love. Coming to know the texture of the other person's skin; learning which stroke aroused and stirred; which one stimulated and shocked. It didn't escape her she was the only one doing the touching right now, and it couldn't in any way, shape, or thought be construed as sexual.

A soft moan escaped from him.

"I'm sorry," she said. "I'm sorry."

Stacy let her eyes drift close, her hands continuing their work. Focusing her mind on her actions, she was able to detect subtle changes under her fingers, actually feel the muscles begin to return to a static, slackened state.

Nikko stayed silent, accepting her ministrations without comment or complaint.

What would it be like to have him accept her the same way?

The knot of anxious tension that wound within her daily while in his presence, while waiting for him to slant an annoyed glance or say something condescending to her, was currently absent. Stacy was totally in charge of the situation and Nikko was mutely compliant.

Oh, to have things between them be the same during work hours.

It took a long while before she was satisfied the muscles had indeed unwound enough for her to stop. She glanced up at Nikko's face. Miraculously, he'd fallen asleep. The deep, even tempo of his breaths told her she'd been able to give him the relief his body and mind craved.

In sleep, the harsh, haggard ravages of his persistent pain were eradicated from his face. His brow was unfurrowed, the lines branching out from the corners of his eyes, smoother. The grooves dropping from his nose down to his jaw were less etched and rigid, the line of his mouth plump and soft.

Long, fat black eyelashes rested on the tops of his cheekbones. A fringe of hair had fallen across his forehead, sweeping across his brows to settle in the corner of one eye.

Stacy's fingers, throbbing from their exertions, itched with longing to brush the hair back in place.

He looked so peaceful—for once—his face and body calm, she didn't have the heart to wake him so he could move to his bed. A simple throw blanket was tossed over the back of the couch, so she gently placed it over him and tucked it under his feet.

At the door, she flicked the light switch off, the room bathed only in the tiny glow of the desk lamp's dim light, and closed the door without shutting it.

Melora sat on the floor outside the room, her back up against the wall, her arms crossed over her chest. She shot up when Stacy moved from the room.

"Is he...how is he?"

She looked so tired and overwhelmed, Stacy wanted to pull her into her arms and hug all the pain and worry away. The girl had enough to deal with, with her own health, never mind being wrapped up in her father's problems as well. Fifteen was too young to handle the adult issues she was being forced to.

Stacy put the bucket down and gave in to her emotions. The moment she opened her arms, Melora fell into them.

"He's better," Stacy told her, rubbing a hand down her back. She mentally winced at how frail and bony the girl's spine was. "He actually fell asleep while I was working on his thigh."

Melora pulled back and swiped a hand under her nose. "Should we, like, *leave* him there? Won't he be uncomfortable?"

"He needs the rest," she said. "Let him be. If he wakes, he might go to his own bed, but for now he's fine."

"Thank you so much." Melora threw her arms around Stacy's neck and squeezed. "I was so scared."

"Oh, sweetie, you're welcome." Stacy pulled back after a moment and held the girl at arm's length. "Can I ask you something?"

"Sure."

"Is this how he usually is in the evenings, after filming all day? In pain and..." She flipped her hand in the air.

"Drunk?"

Stacy sighed. "I really don't think he was, Melora. I think, like he said, he was just trying to take the edge off the pain the best way he knows how. Does he have a prescription for anything stronger?"

"Like Oxy or something?"

"Yeah."

"No. Nikko hates pills. He won't even take, like, an aspirin. I think it's 'cause his dad OD'd when he was a kid. And my mom, well...she used to get...high...sometimes."

Stacy let that settle for a moment. "Okay. But self-medicating with alcohol, even just a few shots, isn't going to help him in the long run to deal with this. His pain is real. He shouldn't have to suffer through it."

"What will help it?"

"I really don't know because I'm not his doctor—"

"He hates doctors. All medical people."

Stacy gaped at her. "Why?"

"I don't know for sure." She folded her arms over her chest. "I think it has, like, something to do with...you know. *The accident.*" Her eyebrows rose at the words, her mouth pulling down into a grimace. "Nikko signed himself out of the hospital before the doctor told him he could go. Before he was really ready to be out. Typical. Stubborn alpha behavior to the max."

Stacy squeezed her bottom lip between her index finger and thumb. "Did he ever have physical therapy that you know of?"

She shook her head. "A few times. In the hospital. He wouldn't do more."

"Nothing outpatient?"

"Nada. Why?"

"Because if he had, he would know how to deal with the cramping more effectively than just ignoring it, or trying to drink it away."

What he needed were exercises and tools to prevent the pain from occurring in the first place. How to convince him of that was the problem, especially if the information came from her.

Stacy wasn't sure Nikko would remember much of what she'd done for him tonight when he woke in the morning. Agreeing to her help when he was incapacitated, in agony, and had no choice, was one thing. Being told what to do so the pain could be controlled was quite another. Nikko Stamp was, as his daughter stated, a stubborn, obstinate man who needed to be in control of his world and his surroundings. He wouldn't willingly accept any help she could offer.

Standing there in the hallway, with his fragile and hurting daughter, Stacy realized she needed to devise a way to help him without him knowing she was.

Chapter Thirteen

Nikko looked down at the fresh cup of coffee Stacy had slipped into his cup holder. He hadn't seen her do it, but he knew she had, since no one else had ever bothered to bring him coffee while he worked.

She wasn't currently in the truck, having been called away by one of the producers just as filming started on the prep work for the day's challenge.

Nikko took a sip of the coffee and sighed. It tasted…good. A little different, for some reason, but good.

He'd woken on the couch in his office, a blanket covering him, and the smell of fresh coffee tickling his nose. For the first time in weeks he couldn't feel any pain or even the twinge of it in his thigh. He tossed off the blanket and was surprised for a moment that he wasn't wearing pants.

With his next breath, the evening before shot a clear bullet of memory across the front of his mind: Stacy's concerned face staring down at him; Melora's tears and anger; the heat from whatever Stacy had draped over his legs.

The memory that hit him the hardest, the one that made him drag his hands through his hair and fight for air, was the feel of Stacy's hands on his leg.

Strong and firm, yet gentle and soothing, he remembered watching her through slitted eyes as she bent over him, her bottom lip tucked under her top one as her hands wove their magic and slid him out of the torture the cramping leg had caused. She was so involved in her task he was able to watch her without her knowing.

The whiskey hadn't done its intended job to either slake the pain or help him pass out so he wouldn't feel it. He wasn't drunk, as Melora accused—not even close—but he'd been on the verge when they'd come into the room.

CAN'T STAND THE HEAT

He'd watched Stacy as she'd ministered to him, so composed, so coolly competent. It occurred to him while her fingers danced across his leg that he wanted nothing more than to see her lose that professional air, watch her come unglued, and know he was the cause. He wanted to see her in something other than the long-sleeved blouses she perpetually wore. He couldn't understand how she could wear clothes that added to the heat surrounding them every day.

As her hands rolled and kneaded his aching thigh muscles, a picture of her, naked and under him while he pounded into her, watching those gorgeous green eyes flash with heat, raced behind his closed ones. He bit back a moan, fearful she'd know what he was thinking. He'd almost told her the truth when she started apologizing, assuming she was hurting him.

She was, just not the way she thought. If he had told her, she'd probably have run from the room and hopped the next flight back to New York.

A week ago he'd have been thankful for that, would have done whatever he could to make sure she left.

Now, he couldn't stand to think of it.

Nikko dragged his hands across the stubble on his cheeks. She'd even asked his permission before touching him, as if frightened if she did so without his consent he'd snap at her. Or worse.

Christ. He was such an asshole.

He'd been nothing but a complete jerk to her the entire time they'd worked together, barking at her, acting condescending. It killed him to admit it, but Stacy Peters did an excellent job. None of the little, annoying problems that routinely came up on a shoot were too small or piddling for her to deal with, and she always did so in a quick, efficient manner. The crew adored her. As did the chefs. She had a ready smile and a kind word for each of them, helping in whatever way was needed. Was it any wonder she never smiled at him? She was probably scared if she did he'd give her a tongue-lashing for the effort.

And yet she'd ignored his arrogant stupidity and found it in herself to offer help when he needed it.

"Yeah," he said aloud, the sound of his voice thick with loathing and disgust in the quiet room, "you're an asshole, all right." He dragged his pants on.

Following the smell of coffee to the kitchen, he got his second surprise of the day when he found Melora standing at the stove, flipping pancakes on the griddle. The table was set and the coffeepot was filled to the top of the carafe.

"This is unexpected," he said, bending to kiss her cheek.

"Yuck." Her nose wrinkled, making her look all of five years old. "You reek like a bar."

"And how would you know what a bar smells like, young lady? You're only fifteen."

He had to bite back a smile when she blushed.

"What possessed you to make breakfast?" he asked, filling a mug.

She lifted a thin shoulder and concentrated on flipping the pancakes lining the grill. "I thought it would be, like, a nice gesture. You've been doing all the cooking, working, plus taking care of me." She shrugged again and dropped the pancakes onto two plates. "I figured I could, you know, pay it back a little. Give you a break for once."

A wealth of emotion exploded in his chest as he looked across the table at her.

The therapist had cautioned him against suggesting or pressuring her to cook or prepare any food. Her aversion to eating would manifest itself in difficulty with making sound choices and would increase her already high anxiety about having to eat, so Nikko had done all the meal prep. This was the first time since her mother's death the girl had shown any interest in cooking, something he knew she'd done often before the crash. Because of her mother's occasional erratic and out-of-control behavior, there were many times Melora had assumed the adult role in their relationship. She'd been the one who'd cooked, paid a bill, or done the laundry in order to keep the household contained and running smoothly.

Nikko hadn't known the extent of what the teen had had to deal with until the night of the crash, during the fight with Flannery that had led to it.

He wondered at the reason for the change now. Did she think she had to care for him as she'd done for her mother? Had last night's events proven in her mind she did? He didn't want to ask, worried she might interpret his question the wrong way. She was still an emotional, dramatic fifteen-year-old and he didn't want to say anything that would set her off.

But still...

"These look great," he said. She'd put four on his plate, one on her own. While he slathered them with the butter and syrup she'd put on the table, she cut her own pancake into small pieces and ate it without garnish, a glass of water at her side.

Nikko knew enough not to push, happy she was at least eating.

"Yeah, they do," she said.

"Mel, I want to talk about last night. Can we?"

She looked over at him and lifted a shoulder again. "'K."

Nikko took a deep breath, then a sip of coffee. "First of all, I'm sorry for yelling at you, for being such a... well, grouch. I was in a lot of pain from standing so much yesterday."

"I know."

"Still, I shouldn't have taken it out on you. I'm sorry."

Another shoulder lift. "'K."

"I'm wondering why you called Stacy Peters to come over here?"

Her eyes widened as she stared across at him.

"I'm not saying you did anything wrong. I just want to know why her."

After a huge sigh, she answered. "I was scared. You wouldn't answer the door and"—she flipped her hand in the air—"you sounded... I don't know. Like, weird and out of it."

Nikko nodded. "But why call her, specifically, and not someone else if you were so worried?"

"Like who?"

It was Nikko's turn to shrug. "Todd, maybe. You've known him for years. Or Jade Quartermaine. You've met her a million times."

Melora's snort had him biting back a smile. "Yeah, like that was ever gonna happen. Like, *never*."

She took a large chug of her water. "I called Stacy because she's nice. She gets me. She likes me, even though you cut her a new lung that day we went to the airport. And I knew she'd come. She's that kind of person, despite what you think."

"Okay," he said calmly, the warning signs for a dramatic showdown becoming evident in his daughter's rising voice. "I get that. Thank you."

Suspicion clouded her eyes. "For what?"

"For calling her. What she did helped. A lot, actually. I don't have any pain today."

"Then you need to thank her and not, like, *me*." She rose and put her empty dish in the sink, added the griddle, and started washing them.

"You should give her a chance," she said, flicking a glance over her shoulder at him. "She's wicked cool and nice."

Nikko nodded while he sipped his coffee.

Stacy Peters had obviously done something to make such a good impression on his daughter. Melora said Stacy "got her." He might have been far removed from being a teenager, but not so far that he didn't understand the meaning behind those words.

Either because she was just a naturally kind person—which he was beginning to think was really the case—or for some other unknown reason, Stacy had accomplished the one thing he'd been so desperately trying to do since his daughter had come to live with him: gain her trust. He knew she loved him, just as she knew he loved her; there was never a doubt of that. But there was some part of her Nikko felt didn't trust him to stick around.

When they'd split, he and Flannery had decided physical custody was best granted to her. He moved around from project to project, never staying long in one place. Melora needed, as every child did, a stable home base, a place to feel safe and secure.

Flannery's death had shattered that security for the teen and Nikko knew she was still uncertain whether he'd keep her with him once school started again or ship her off to boarding school while he was working. He was doing everything he could think of to make her see she could depend on him; trust him to stick around.

"I need my laptop for research I've gotta do for this stupid book report," she told him. "Can I have it until you leave?"

Knowing trust went both ways, he nodded.

"You can have it for as long as you need it, Mel. No more restrictions."

Surprise pulled at her mouth, while suspicion danced in her eyes again. "Why not? You were, like, *adamant* that I couldn't have unrestricted access. What's happened to change that?"

Nikko rose with his plate and dropped it into the sudsy water in the sink. With both arms, he pulled his daughter into a hug and kissed the top of her head.

With a chuckle, he said, "Unrestricted access, huh?"

"You know what I mean," she mumbled into his shoulder, her arms wrapping around his waist. "And you still stink."

He pushed her an arm's-length away, cocked an eyebrow, and tried not to laugh. "I'll go shower, since I'm disturbing your tender senses. You get your laptop and get to work."

Before he made it to the doorway, he stopped when Melora said, "Daddy?"

He turned around.

"Don't you need to, you know, *watch me* for an hour? We just ate."

Nikko's heart stuttered in his chest. He wanted to pull her into his arms again and tenderly kiss away all the bad things that had happened to her. Convince her she was cherished; loved.

God knows how she would react if he did, though.

Instead, he tossed her a smile and said, "Nah. I trust you, kid. I always have."

He wasn't certain, but he was pretty sure when he walked up the stairs to his room there had been a fine sheen of happy tears pooling in her eyes.

* * * *

The hot, dry air struck Stacy in the face when she stepped out of the makeup trailer, the sun's glare stinging her already dry eyes. A boulder-sized headache was banging behind her left eye, screaming for relief.

She needed a bottle of water, a fistful of aspirin, and a nap.

In the past two hours she'd dealt with a disgruntled supply manager and a missing order; two crying producers—one because she missed her boyfriend, the other because she had a personality conflict with the chef she was assigned to—and had been raked across the verbal coals and back by a demanding, obnoxious, and diva-channeling Jade Quartermaine, who'd complained about everything from the heat, to the lack of alcohol (again!), and her wardrobe choices.

Stacy'd been able to locate the missing produce order in the back of the supply room where someone had erroneously placed it; listened compassionately to one producer's personal woes and then gently told her to suck it up or leave; she'd switched the next producer to a different chef, and finally stood silently listening to Jade's harangue without offering her any consolation.

Lack of sleep, the heat, and the headache now pounding away had her wanting to just run from the ranch and escape.

Just as she started walking toward the main house to find some relief, her walkie-talkie signaled.

"This is Stacy." She turned her back to the blaring sun and shielded her eyes with the back of her free hand. She really needed to remember to wear a hat.

Sweat dripped down her back as she listened to the latest crisis that needed her immediate attention.

Twenty minutes later, she left the dining hall after making sure the leaking sinks in the kitchen were being seen to and would be fixed before the chefs were due back to start cooking in a little under an hour.

Her headache had intensified, pushed to the front of her head now because she was starving.

Why did she ever agree to this? Did she really want to have her own show so much that she was sacrificing her well-being, her sanity—hell, even the health of her eyes—just to ensure that Teddy Davis lived up to his end of their bargain if she did hers?

The answer, she silently reminded herself, was a resounding *yes*.

Thankfully, when she slipped through the front door, the main hall was empty. She just wasn't up to talking with anyone else right now. Her rooms were, blissfully, chilled from the central air that piped throughout the house. She tossed the walkie-talkie on the bed and in a heartbeat shed her drenched blouse, shrugged out of her equally sweaty bra and slacks, and ran the water in her bathroom sink to the coldest temperature she could get it, then splashed it over her face and neck.

Heaven.

She filled the bathroom glass with cold water and then chugged it down in one long draught.

Better. Another filled glass and she grabbed three aspirin from her stash in her toiletry bag.

She really needed to lie down for a few minutes and just allow the meds to do their magic, but lunch break was almost over and she hadn't been in the production truck since she'd left Nikko his morning coffee.

Wonder if he noticed it didn't have the full zing it usually did?

As she ran a towel across her wet face and neck, she flexed and extended her fingers. They'd gotten quite the workout last night, but it had been worth it to finally bring him some much-needed relief.

Melora told her he was still sleeping when she'd slipped out of the cabin for their early-morning yoga session. After thanking her again, the girl had admitted she'd been scared to her core when she'd called the night before that something truly had been wrong with him. It was plain to see she worried about Nikko, about his pain. But Stacy could see past the obvious worry and sensed Melora was terrified of what would happen should she lose the one parent she had left.

It didn't take a psychologist to discern that the girl's food issues were directly connected to her mother's loss. Stacy was smart enough to know anorexia was all about control after having witnessed it, firsthand, when her last hospital roommate had suffered through the disorder.

Melora needed as much help as her father did, and because Stacy hated to see anyone in pain, be it psychological or physical, she felt herself drawn to the two of them more with each passing day.

Her thoughts drifted to, and centered on, Nikko. She hadn't seen him during the morning session because of all the fires she'd had to put out around the set. Was he angry with her for having invaded his house, his preciously guarded privacy? He hadn't asked for her help—for anyone's, really. Would he even mention her assistance when she finally encountered him, or just ignore it? Ignore her?

Stacy was self-aware enough to know that something had changed within her these past few days. Being around Nikko, watching him work and interact with the crew, had been an eye-opening experience. She'd known he was famous for being a control freak on a set, but for the first time acknowledged behavior like his might be a good thing. Watching him give direction, actually seeing how involved he was with every aspect of the filming, showed her how much work was involved in being the head of a show.

And isn't that what she wanted?

She'd agreed to come here to get her chance at the show of her dreams. This side benefit of watching and learning from a master like Dominick Stamp was something she'd never considered.

And he certainly was pleasant to look at, which she did often while seated behind him in the production truck.

Nikko had the kind of features that when he aged would be described as distinguished and patrician. As her hands had moved up and down his leg, a little jolt of awareness of him as powerful and sexually attractive had pushed up from deep inside, heating her face and neck. She was glad his eyes had been closed so he couldn't witness how nervous she was.

Or how turned-on.

Thoughts of how it would feel to be trapped within those mighty thighs, imprisoned within their hold, had bolted through her. A few times she'd squeezed a little harder than she'd intended, caught up in the fantasy of how she would feel pressed against the long length of him, losing herself beneath him as he made love to her.

Those thoughts had wormed themselves into her head at various times throughout the morning as well.

Of all the people to have a stupid crush on, why did it have to be the one person who could barely tolerate being in her presence?

Stacy toweled off and was about to get dressed in fresh clothes when a knock sounded at her door.

"Just a sec," she called as she threw on her robe.

Surprised was too tame a word for what she felt when she opened the door and found Nikko standing in the hallway.

He looked...nervous.

"Mr. Stamp? What's wrong? Melora? Is—?"

The nerves turned to annoyance in a heartbeat. His brows pulled together over eyes that narrowed as they peered down at her. His mouth tightened at the corners and he inhaled deeply, his nostrils flaring with the effort.

"Nothing is wrong, I need to talk to you about something. Can I come in?"

"Um, sure." She glanced around the room, noting her clothes and underwear were scattered in a discarded trail that led to the bathroom.

She held the door wide for him.

"I was just changing before the afternoon prep started," she said, gathering up the items. She rolled them into a ball, threw them into the closet, and then swiftly closed it. "It's so hot out, you know? I've been all over the ranch this morning dealing with production problems and I needed to just freshen up a little."

Realizing she was dangerously close to babbling, she stopped and took a breath. Clasping her hands in front of her, she squared her shoulders, calmed her facial features, and said, "What did you need to speak to me about?"

Nikko took his own breath and for a moment she was fearful he was going to light into her about something.

"I know you've been busy all morning. You weren't in your usual spot when I arrived."

She was about to tell him about the misplaced produce, but before she could, he continued.

"First, thanks for the coffee. I'm assuming you were the one who put it at my place?"

She nodded.

"It tasted a little different today. Good, but different. Thanks."

What would he do if she'd told him it was the same blend of coffee, but she'd mixed together half-caffeinated, half-decaf portions so he'd cut back on his caffeine use? Research had told her too much caffeine could exacerbate muscle cramps, and from what she'd seen so far, Nikko was just this side of being a caffeine addict.

Better to keep that bit of info to herself.

"You're welcome," she said, simply.

When he ran a hand across the back of his neck and broke eye contact with her, the thought he was nervous again shot through her.

Why? was the question.

"I also want to thank you for what you did last night. For coming over when Melora called you."

"Oh. Well, she sounded upset, so…" She lifted her hands, palms up.

"She was. Thanks for helping to calm her down." He lifted his gaze back to hers, cocking his head while he continued to hold her gaze. "And thank you for…helping me. My leg"—he shook his head—"was awful yesterday. Too much standing; too much sitting. I don't know what, but yesterday was pure torture. By the time we were done I could barely stay upright."

Compassion poured through her.

"You probably know I was in a car crash? That my leg got pretty mangled?"

"Yes. I'm so sorry. You lost your ex-wife in the crash too, I know."

He sighed, deep and long. "Yeah."

Stacy felt saying she was sorry again sounded hollow.

"How does your leg feel today?"

"Amazing," he said without hesitation. He shook his head, a ghost of a grin trailing across his lips. "I haven't had a twinge all morning. What you did helped. Considerably, so thank you. Really. Thank you."

"I'm glad." Stacy nodded and bit her bottom lip. She weighed what she wanted to say next, not sure at all of what his response would be. "I don't usually give advice, primarily because I hate getting it. Especially unsolicited," she said, secretly pleased when his lips lifted, "but can I just offer some?"

He waited a moment before saying, "Go ahead."

"Please don't be mad at Melora, but she told me you didn't keep up with any kind of physical therapy after the accident."

His grin lessened just a bit. Before she lost her nerve, Stacy quickly added, "I'm not questioning your decision for doing so, believe me. That's none of my business. But I think part of the reason your leg cramps so much is because you're not doing anything to strengthen the muscle. You spend most of your time either sitting or standing. Muscles fatigue and start to atrophy when they're not used and strengthened. They basically give up. When that happens, any movement will cause the cramping and spasms to come back."

She stopped. From the blank look now settled on his face she couldn't decide if she'd crossed a line with him or not. She wanted to help, not alienate. Arrogance and stubborn male pride were such staunch blockades, though.

"You sound like you know what you're talking about," he said after a few seconds. "Firsthand."

"In this instance, I do," she told him. "The pain from muscle cramps is, like you said, torture. The best way to deal with them is to prevent them from happening. That's why physical therapy is so important."

After a few moments, he asked, "What do you suggest I do, then, to prevent them from coming back? I can't just call for a therapist to come out here. The production schedule is tight enough as it is. I can't make leeway in it just so I can get a massage."

"You wouldn't need to. The easiest answer would be to move around more during the day. You stand a lot of it, especially while we're filming, but you don't move much."

"So, what? I need to take a walk? That'll get rid of the pain?"

He looked so doubtful she wanted to laugh.

"That would be one of the ways," she said with a quick nod. "The other would be just to simply stretch out in the morning first thing when you wake up and then again right before you go to bed. And try not to stand still so much when you're directing. You can easily move around in the production space."

He stared at her, his eyes dark and guarded and filled with doubt.

"You used heat last night. Hot towels. You told me the heat would relax the muscles."

So, he did remember the particulars of what she'd done. She hadn't been sure he would.

With another nod, she said, "Warmth actually dilates the surrounding skin, muscles, and tendons. When they're dilated, they relax. The pain comes from constant flexion, extension, and contraction of the muscle all at the same time, with no relief. Adding warmth and massaging the area helps the muscles unwind and stay that way. Actually, if you had access to a Jacuzzi or hot tub, it would really help. There's nothing better for cramped muscles than a long, hot soak in pulsating water."

She gave him an open smile. "As decadent as it sounds, it's really beneficial. Physical massage is, as well."

Something in his eyes changed. Warmed. *Grew.*

He wasn't looking at her now with his usual aggravated glare, or even the doubtful one he'd given her just moments before. Nor was his expression simple curiosity at her expertise.

No, what was in his eyes was something she'd never expected to see from this man: need.

A stab of unexpected hunger, so piercing and swift, sliced right through her midsection and dropped lower, tickling the area between her thighs.

And the hunger had nothing to do with the fact she hadn't eaten anything in hours.

Nikko took a step forward, then another, until he stopped directly in front of her.

Stacy had to tip her head back to maintain eye contact with him. Hypnotized by the intensity in his eyes, she couldn't look away from it; didn't want to.

"Yes," he said, his breath drifting over her, making her insides flutter like a flimsy curtain battling a sudden breeze. "I remember that. I remember you massaging my leg for some time." He moved in closer, their torsos just a hair's width from her breasts scraping along his chest.

"I remember the feel of your hands on my leg. Kneading. Rubbing. Your fingers, gliding along my muscles, up and down. Helping me. Easing my pain."

"I—I..." She backed up a step and hit the dresser, her spine flattening against it. She braced her hands behind her, the tips of her fingers landing across one drawer. "I'm glad I did. Help, I mean."

Was that her voice? It sounded as if she'd just run a marathon.

Uphill.

In thin air.

Nikko's hands rose, slowly, purposefully, and came to rest on the top of the dresser, bracketing her between them, effectively imprisoning her.

With every breath she took now, her torso grazed his.

His knees bumped hers as his head lowered, his eyes never moving from her own.

"Easing my pain," he repeated softly, as if she'd hadn't spoken, "and making me...want." His lips floated a breath above hers, then touched hers once, just a brief buss; a sample; a promise. "Want...you."

In the next breath he fulfilled that promise by resting his mouth fully against hers. Soft yet powerful, seductive and masterful, his lips glided over hers. Pressed. Savored. *Asked.*

Stacy answered by relaxing against him, moving into the kiss without thought, without reservation, without worry.

He kissed like a man who knew what he was doing. He demanded nothing of her than to simply let him pleasure her mouth, and yet she poured everything inside her, offered every bit of herself into kissing him back without the slightest bit of hesitation or concern.

He shifted, changed the angle of his head, and lifted his hands from the dresser to cup her cheeks between them. Tipping her head back, her body arched as he deepened the kiss, greedily parting her lips with his tongue then forging between them, overwhelming her, claiming her.

Under the thin robe her nipples came to two hard points as his tongue tugged and wound with hers. He tasted like...nothing she could put a name to. Full-bodied, like the thirty-five-year-old port her father favored after dinner; sweet and refreshing like Grandma's orange sorbet, her favorite dessert; savory and woodsy like air in a forest after a quick, unexpected downpour.

A fleeting thought that maybe, just maybe, Nikko didn't dislike her as much as she'd believed flew through her mind.

Her hands developed a will of their own as they danced up his broad, rock-hard chest, and wound around his thick neck to grip his hair. Fisting it, she hung onto the ends as if her life depended on it. As if she'd crash back to earth if she let go.

His fingers drifted along the column of her throat, across her shoulders, down her back, to settle, through her robe, on her butt. Molding his hands to her rounded flesh, he pulled her in closer, folding her into him and letting her know just how much what he was feeling *wasn't* dislike.

Not even close.

Except for her thong, she was naked under the silk robe and as his hands glided over the material, whispered over her body, the luxurious feel of the fabric rubbing against her bare skin shot erotic flares all along her spine, straight down to her toes.

While his tongue mated with hers, his hands slipped under the hem of the short garment to cup the bare skin he found there.

As she'd massaged the muscles and sinew over his leg the night before, he returned the favor, squeezing and kneading her butt in his warm, firm grasp. For a heartbeat, Stacy tensed, her gluteal muscles instinctively tightening. The touch of a man's hands so intimately pressed against her flesh wasn't something she was used to.

In the next instant, spurred on by the gentle, thorough pressure of his fingers, she relaxed and pushed in even closer, nothing separating their bodies but their clothes.

Nikko slipped one finger under the strip of her thong, tugged it to the side, and with another traced a line down along the cleft between her cheeks.

Her knees buckled when he thrust a knee between her thighs, forcing them to open for him, pressing intimately against her. She could feel the soft denim of his jeans through the tiny wisp of the thong's lace panel and when he began rubbing his knee across her mound, her insides turned to melting gold.

Good Lord.

Every nerve fiber in the lower half of her body stood straight up at attention. Stacy widened her stance as much as she could. It was then she realized she was standing on the very tips of her toes. Nikko bore most of her weight as she leaned against him.

He shifted again, reached down, and dragged his finger along the heat pouring from her core, now separated and open to his touch.

A guttural moan, deep and filled with longing, escaped in the air as his lips left hers to trail down and nuzzle the sweet spot behind her ear. He tugged the lobe between his lips and bit down, while his wicked and persistent finger dared to dip into the long, wet length of her.

And she *was* wet.

Drenched, in fact.

His strong, steady finger glided from one end of her to the other, slipping across her flesh and through every defense she had.

A quick thought that nothing had ever felt so good, so god-blessed good as Nikko's hands on her skin, came to her.

She clutched the ends of his hair tighter, her breaths shallow and fast as his fingers dragged along her, their rhythm timed to perfection with the movement of his tongue in her mouth.

The air around her exploded with the echo of a deep, reverberating groan.

Just as she realized she'd been the one to make the sound, the room was shattered by a blare of static from her walkie-talkie.

"Stacy? Stacy? You copy?"

Nikko jerked his head back, surprise and anger mixing on his face as he heaved his gaze from her face to the device resting on the bed, and then back to her.

A well of boiling heat suffused his half-closed eyes as he gazed down at her. His lips were swollen and kiss-slick-wet, and when his tongue flicked out and ran across his top lip and then the bottom, as if savoring the taste of her, Stacy's breath caught.

He still had her pinioned against the dresser, one hand caressing the nape of her neck, the other burrowed between her legs.

"Stacy? You there?"

Reality washed over her like a tidal wave.

"I—I have to get that." She pushed against his chest, tried to slide from his hold.

The man was as solid as a fortress. He stood, stone-still and immobile. "Please."

Nikko shook his head a few times, blinked, and then with a jagged oath, slipped his hands from her body, stepped back, and set her free.

Stacy sprinted across the room on unsteady legs to the bed. Her hands were shaking so hard it took two tries before she could activate the *respond* button.

"This is Stacy."

She listened, carefully avoiding looking toward Nikko, as one of the set crew told her there were still problems in the dining-hall kitchen.

"I'll be right over," she said.

As she ended the transmission, she lifted her head.

Nikko was standing, as still as death, next to the dresser. He hadn't moved at all during her conversation, except to drop his hands into his trouser pockets.

Mortified beyond anything she could imagine, and more turned-on than she'd ever remembered being in her life, Stacy nervously twined her fingers into the collar of her robe and tugged it tighter across her bare chest where it had almost fallen open.

Jesus, had he seen—? *No.* She wouldn't think about that now.

"I need—" She swallowed and tried to slow her rapid breaths. "I need to get dressed," she declared, summoning up as much calm as she could.

Nikko continued to stare at her, his eyes skimming to where she grasped her robe together, then back up to her face.

"Stacy—"

She didn't give him a chance to speak. "You need to leave. Now. I have to see to this problem and you need to leave."

He scraped his hands through the hair at his temples, then dropped them to his thighs. "I—"

"No. *Please.* Don't say anything. Just…please. Go. I have to get dressed."

She bolted across the room, opened the door with more force than she intended, and held it for him.

"Please."

She was threateningly close to losing what little composure she had left. As it was, her hands were flapping they were shaking so hard, the sound of her knees knocking together, loud in the room.

It was a wonder she could stand upright.

Never in her entire life had she felt so many conflicting and unfamiliar emotions swimming inside of her at the same time, battling her thoughts and will.

Longing blended with confusion, which rammed up against desire and fear.

Thankfully, he heeded her request.

At the door, his eyes raked over her face. "Will you—" He stopped and cupped a hand along the back of his neck. "Are you coming back to the production truck?"

She nodded, staring at the buttons on his shirt. "As soon as I see to this problem."

His shoulders lifted as a breath hove out. "Okay then. I'll…I'll see you in a little while."

She swallowed and nodded again.

He dipped his head so she was forced to finally look at him. One quick glance at the question in his eyes, and she dropped her gaze again.

"Are you all right?"

"I'm fine," she told his collar, bobbing her head. "Fine."

With a deep, cavernous sigh, Nikko stood tall again and left her.

Stacy shoved the door closed and fell against it, her forehead slamming into the wood as she inhaled a huge gulp of air.

Jesus.

Jesus Christ.

Chapter Fourteen

Focused on the television monitors, chaotic sounds pouring from the kitchen set, Nikko felt the subtle shift in the air he'd come to recognize that told him she was moving to her seat.

He drummed his fingers absently along the console as he watched the chefs scurry about the kitchen, and let out a deep huff of air through his lips. His eyes may have been watching the chefs, but his brain was reliving every moment of what had happened in Stacy's room.

Every pulse-bounding, heart-stopping, scorching moment.

What the hell had possessed him to kiss her? One second he'd been listening to her go on and on about how to relax his muscles, his gaze centered on her plump lips while she spoke.

Then she smiled. Actually smiled. *At him.* And with the next breath he'd felt a familiar twinge in his lower back that shot straight to his dick and all he could think about was how those delicious-looking, smiling lips would taste.

Shit.

He could lie and say he hadn't realized what he was doing when he'd caged her between his arms and leaned down to brush his mouth over hers. That he was so exhausted, his mind running in a thousand different directions, he hadn't given a coherent thought to what he was doing, but had just reacted to the bolt of lust that popped through him.

But it *would* be a lie and as brazen and bold-faced a one as he'd ever told.

He'd known exactly what he was doing when he slid his hands down her arms, around her trim waist to settle on her back and pull her against him. And he'd never hesitated a second before molding his palms to her fabulous ass and grinding her body into his, letting her know exactly what she was doing to him.

The feel of her, slim and lithe and so incredibly soft, had silenced every bell and whistle in his head, screaming that what he was doing was as wrong as it could be.

Never, not once ever before in his entire career, had he crossed a line like that with a subordinate. And that's what Stacy was, in every sense of the word. She may have the title of executive producer and all the clout and power that went along with it, but it was his name, his professional reputation, his utmost responsibility that guided the show. He was, in the very purest, most simple definition of the word, her boss. And as such there was a clean, concise line of conduct that should never be crossed. No matter what.

Today he'd not only crossed that line, he'd obliterated it.

What truly shook him straight down to his marrow was he wanted to do it again—would in a heartbeat—if Stacy gave him any indication she wanted him as much as he did her.

Where in the hell had this longing; this deep, devouring need, come from? He could blame it on the fact he hadn't gotten laid in too long to even consider and anything with the necessary opposite-sexed parts was capable of turning him on.

But that wasn't it. Not by a long shot. He was surrounded by women all the time in the business, knew several who'd given him open invitations into their beds, and others who'd hinted they wouldn't mind a little mattress action.

He'd steered clear of them all.

Stacy had given him no clues—hinted or overt—that she was interested in him. Hell, she'd never even really smiled at him until an hour ago. She was continually on guard around him, tempering her responses, cooling her actions. Keeping her real self hidden. The thought she didn't like him, was merely tolerating him because she had to, had played in his head more than once. In that one fleeting moment, that one second she'd been unguarded in her response, he'd witnessed the true woman who lay beneath the professional mien and thoughtful replies.

And he'd been more turned on than he could ever remember being.

Her unbridled, quick response to his kiss knocked him back a few paces. He'd been braced for a hot face slap or a screaming recrimination.

Neither had come.

She'd simply slipped between his arms and hung on tight, matching him move for move as if she did it every day of her life.

Nikko took a chug from the bottled water he had on the console, hoping to quench the fire still burning in his belly. Her lowered voice floated up from behind him as she answered a question from one of the techs.

He'd thought of her as nothing other than a necessary pain in the ass when he'd first heard about her from Teddy Davis. Someone he was ready to battle against over every decision and idea he made or had. He was going to do everything he could think of to make her leave.

When had that changed? When had her presence become something he expected, looked forward to, even needed, around?

"Call time," he barked into his headset.

When the movement on set ceased, Nikko turned and landed on Stacy. She shot straight up to attention.

"Is the Feedbag kitchen problem solved now?"

She nodded. "Everything's back in working order."

Her voice sounded calm and composed, but the true depth of her nerves was obvious to him in the death grip she had on her notebook. Her knuckles had blanched to a milky white around the device's edges.

To Todd, Nikko said, "Have them cart everything over. Let the dining-hall film crew know they're on their way."

"You got it," Todd said, tapping his earpiece and then giving the order.

Nikko grabbed his water bottle and moved to where Stacy continued to stand, rock-still, her eyes huge behind her glasses. They tracked his movement as a wounded animal would an approaching predator.

She was terrified of him and trying her damnedest not to show it. He had to give her points for her resolve.

"Do me a favor?" he said, his voice low and for her ears only. Her eyes widened, but she simply nodded again.

"Melora wants to help out with the voting tallies again tonight." He swiped a hand through the side of his hair. "It gives her something to do and if I know she's with you I won't worry about her being alone. Can she eat with you again? Help you? Do you mind?"

"Not at all," was her immediate reply. In the next instant her shoulders relaxed and he spied her fingers loosen their grip on the ever-present notebook. A quick, fleeting grin pulled at her lips when she said, "She's actually a big help."

He huffed out a breath. "Thanks. I'll have her meet you over at the hall."

He knew he should leave her, just walk away and leave her alone. But his feet weren't complying.

"Listen—" he started.

"I wanted—" she said at the same moment.

They both came to a verbal halt, waited a beat, just looking at one another.

"Go ahead," Nikko said after a fashion.

She bit down on the corner of her lip, sending his already jittery insides rolling, lowered her gaze, and then brought it back up to him.

Christ. It took everything in him not to lean down and bite that plump, ripe mouth.

"I just wanted you to know I checked all the arrangements for the next location shoot. The flights are booked, as are the hotels. Jimmy Rodgers emailed me his staff have all been alerted about our arrival."

Nikko nodded and slid his hands into his back pockets. He'd almost forgotten that they'd be filming the next segment in Big Sky's newest hot spot, the Meat Rack, owned and operated by famed chef Jimmy Rodgers. Apparently, his executive producer hadn't.

"He says you have full takeover of the restaurant for the two-day challenge," Stacy continued, "and that he's looking forward to seeing what the contestants do with his menu. I copied and forwarded the note to you."

"Thanks. I'll look it over after we're done filming for the night."

Either she couldn't hear how tight and grating his voice sounded, or she chose to ignore it, because she tapped on her screen a few times, her eyes shifting back and forth under her glasses.

"The vans are scheduled to leave for the airport by eight. That should be enough time to get everyone out of bed and mobilized."

A swift image of her naked and panting in his own big bed blasted across his vision. The crotch on his pants grew uncomfortable as she continued rattling on about travel arrangements.

This needed to stop. *Had* to stop.

Now.

He cut her off her midsentence, his tone terse and gruff when he said, "I don't have time right now to go over every little detail. Just email me everything and I'll look it over later."

In his zeal to get past her he moved too quickly and felt his knee wrench, followed by a lightning bolt exploding up his thigh. Reaching out to grab the table to balance himself before he did something mortifying like fall on his ass in front of her, heat seeped into his system when her hand snaked around his upper arm. She'd dropped her tablet in her attempt to reach out to him and the echo of it crashing down reverberated through the now-empty space.

Her grip was like granite: hard, intractable, solid; so in opposition to how she'd felt when he'd been holding her in his arms. Then she'd been soft, compliant, liquid. The contrast had need shuddering through him, at war with the pain.

"Is your leg cramping?" she asked quietly, peering at him from behind her glasses, her eyes large and filled with concern.

He bit back an oath. "No. I moved wrong. Torqued it."

With a nod, she reached beyond him to grab a chair. A hint of orange and some tangy spice he couldn't place drifted from her. An impossible, ridiculous urge to bend his head and sniff behind her ear cascaded through him.

"Sit down," she gently commanded, guiding him into the chair.

When he was situated, she let go of his arm and crouched beside him.

Pressing her hands together like she was about to say a prayer, she looked up at him and asked, "May I?"

Confused about her intent, he nodded.

Later on, he would pick apart and analyze why, when her hands rested on his aching thigh, did the pain almost instantly ebb. She'd done nothing but touch him and lightly push down on his leg, but he'd felt an immediate rush of warmth and then, like magic, his muscles started to relax.

"You're right," she said, her hands kneading along the fabric of his pants, "you're not cramping." She grazed over his knee, pressing just a bit at the sides. Then, she cupped her fingers around opposite sides of his thigh and twisted in a rolling motion, manipulating the muscles. The move looked, somehow, erotic and wildly arousing.

For the first time he noticed how long and graceful her fingers were, the backs of her hands smooth and unlined, no hint of sun-kissed freckles or age pestering the skin.

His mind flashed back to how she'd looked in the thin excuse for a robe she'd greeted him in when he knocked on her door. Yards of creamy leg peeked out from under the hem and his imagination pulled them around his waist, settling all her heat and softness against him.

Pulsing against the zipper of his jeans at the thought, he was worried she'd notice what was happening just north of where her hands were positioned.

"It feels better now that I'm sitting," he said. "You don't have to do that." He circled one of her wrists to halt her movement.

Stacy turned statue-still, one hand fisted in his grip, the other remaining over his thigh. She lifted her gaze to his and in a split second, the pulse he felt under his fingertips quickened.

The long column of her throat bobbed when she swallowed. Her eyes trained on his face through the lenses of her glasses and when her lips parted in an unasked question and her tongue swiped against her bottom lip, Nikko had to dig to his toes for control. The need to lift her onto his lap, to crush his mouth down on hers, was almost too much for him to resist.

As the thought crossed his mind to do just that, he wondered what she was thinking because the beat drumming under his fingers increased.

The moment broke when she blinked hard several times and pushed upright to a standing position again.

"I'm—I'm sorry..." she said, tugging on the hand he still held.

When he released it, she took a few steps back, twining her fingers together. Just as she opened her mouth to say something else, Todd came over to them.

"The film crew's all set up in the dining hall," he told Nikko, his gaze bouncing to Stacy and then back, his brows almost kissing his forehead as he regarded them.

Stacy reached down to grab her forgotten device, her glasses shifting down on her nose as she rose back up. She shoved them back into place and said, "Right. I'll go over now and make sure things are set properly." With a quick glance at Todd, she skirted her eyes to Nikko, added "Have Melora come find me when she's ready," and then briskly exited the truck.

"Everything okay with Stacy?" Todd asked him once they were alone.

"Fine." He sat forward and lifted from the chair, bracing a hand on the tabletop just in case.

"She looked a little—I don't know—flustered, maybe?"

Nikko stood tall and was silently thankful when his leg responded without pain.

"I only mention it because Stacy's usually steady as a rock. Never loses her temper, never even gets upset."

"When did you turn into such a mother hen?" Nikko pushed through the door and was immediately overcome by the dry afternoon heat. "She's fine. Don't concern yourself with her. We have more pressing things to worry about." His voice was a little harsher than it needed to be, but he didn't feel like discussing his executive producer.

While he outlined how he wanted the evening's challenge filmed, she was never far from the front of his mind, though.

Chapter Fifteen

"I want to do a walk-through of the restaurant and kitchen with the production and film teams," Nikko said as they rode the elevator. "Make sure they're all there. No one is excused."

Stacy was in the process of inputting all the individual room numbers of the crew and cast into her notebook when she realized he was speaking to her. It was the most he'd let cross his lips in the past forty-eight hours. Ever since THE KISS. For now and the rest of her life she was going to refer to it just like that, in capital letters, the emphasis clear, meaningful, and memorable.

She'd had a hard time thinking of anything else but THE KISS for the past two days.

A quick glance at her watch and she asked, "Fifteen, twenty minutes okay?"

"Fine."

He didn't look at her, hadn't since that awkward moment when his leg had gone out on him.

And what a look it had been. She could still feel the power behind it, heating her insides to the temperature of slow-flowing lava. There had been so much meaning, so much intention, so much…possibility behind that potent stare.

Only now it appeared he was back to thinking of her as the lowliest of the low again, not worth more than a few cursory words, never mind any smoldering glances.

"I suppose you'll want me to, like, *disappear* down to the pool while you're working?" Melora asked, breaking the silence in the rapidly rising elevator. With a nonchalant glance at her fingernails, she sighed and added, "So I can be out of sight, out of mind?"

Stacy had to stifle a smile from the ultra-bored tone in the teen's voice and the look of utter weariness crossing through her rolling eyes and in her pursed lips. Stacy knew that tone and expression well, and what they were meant to convey. She'd used them many times herself when she was Melora's age. By giving the impression she really didn't want to go to the pool, she hoped Nikko would suddenly think what a good idea it was for her to be occupied while he was busy with the production, and make sure she did just that.

Unfortunately, as her own father had with her, Nikko saw right through his daughter's ploy.

"You can unpack and order us up some snacks from room service to keep in the room. We'll go down to the pool later and check it out together."

The huff of disgruntled air that filled the elevator was hot enough to scorch.

"Fine," Melora said, mimicking her father's tone.

When the elevator stopped at their designated floor, the trio alighted, Stacy turning to her left, the Stamps to the right.

Before she followed behind her father, Melora slipped something into Stacy's hand.

Once inside her room, Stacy tossed her overnight bag on the bed, perched on its edge, and unfolded the note Melora had surreptitiously given her.

Yoga in the morning? When had she written it? In the plane? Or on the van ride from the airport to the hotel?

It didn't matter. What did was that Stacy had promised to teach her how to meditate and the opportunity hadn't presented itself for very much instruction yet. With the three days they'd be staying on location, Stacy was determined to give the girl some definitive one-on-one guidance.

She wished she had a few spare moments right now to sit and just calm her mind. But she didn't. Nikko, ever punctual, would be waiting down in the restaurant. She shot off a group text to the production and film crews citing Nikko's command, took a second to splash some cold water on her face and, before taking the elevator down to the lobby, dug out the sheet of paper she'd had Teddy Davis sign and read it again, needing the reminder.

* * * *

Two hours later and seated in Nikko's luxurious suite, the beginnings of a headache tapped at her temples. She took a large chug of the bottled water she'd made sure everyone seated had, herself included, before they'd begun the actual meat-and-potatoes part of the production meeting.

Melora had been granted a respite from the adults and given access to the pool while the meeting took place. Stacy'd heard Nikko tell his daughter to keep her cell phone active so he could contact her when he was done. He'd given her a laundry list of dos and don'ts as well, and when the teen sauntered past Stacy on her way out the hotel-room door, she'd winked, her lips barely able to contain a grin.

As she was coming to expect of him, Nikko barked orders at the crew chiefs, demanded some changes to the filming sequences after getting a close-up look at the limited space they'd have to maneuver about in the kitchens, and generally looked much as she pictured Atlas did after a long day of carrying the weight of the world's problems over his head.

Filming in the restaurant's kitchen was going to be a nightmare for the camera crew and a tight squeeze for the chefs, who hadn't been involved in the walk-through.

Stacy rubbed two fingers along the side of her temple as she listened and took notes on all the salient points Nikko wanted addressed. A few times when she happened to glance up from her tablet, his gaze was trained on her while he spoke. The moment their eyes connected, though, he looked at someone else.

Was it her imagination—or just really wishful thinking—that he'd been staring at her with something more than just his usual irritation?

THE KISS was never far from her mind as she listened to him speak, his voice firm, authoritative, and filled with enough gravely rasp to light little fires along her nerve endings. In the shockingly few relationships she'd had, Stacy could never remember being kissed with such total dedication and possession before. If it were possible, Nikko's mouth had been hand forged by the Gods above as an instrument devoted to sheer pleasure.

Hers.

Stacy wasn't one given to fanciful thoughts or adolescent musings. She was cut from a pragmatic, logical cloth that rendered her the girl everyone wanted to be their friend and never the source of male fantasies. She knew this about herself and accepted it.

But in Nikko's arms, his mouth pulling every hot, sexy fantasy from the back of her mind, he'd made her feel like a desired woman.

She hadn't realized she'd been lost in her thoughts until he'd said her name twice.

Mortified, she bolted upright in the chair and found every eye at the table trained on her.

"Sorry." She shook her head. "What?"

Nikko's nostrils flared as he stared across at her and she braced herself for the verbal scolding to come.

"I asked," Nikko said, the sharp edge in his tone letting her know he didn't like repeating himself, "if Jimmy Rodgers was made aware of the filming schedule and when we'd need him on-site."

"Yes, he was." She tapped her device, brought up the email she'd received from him that morning, and read it aloud. "He's all set."

When Nikko nodded and went on to the next point on his list, Stacy felt as if she'd dodged a bullet. What did it mean that he hadn't chastised her for daydreaming? Just a few days ago he would have verbally flayed her.

Now he simply went on to another topic.

A few minutes later he ended the meeting. As everyone began filing from the room, Nikko motioned for her to wait.

When they were alone, he sat back down opposite her. Once again, she braced herself for a lashing, thinking he'd kept her behind to reprimand her for zoning out.

"Are you okay?" he asked.

Stunned was way too tame a word for what shot through her system.

"Um…yeah. Why?"

He stood, crossed to the bar, and took out two new bottles of water from the refrigerator. Offering one to her, he took his own and leaned a hip on the table. "You zoned out for a few minutes." He shrugged. "I just wondered if…something was bothering you."

How could she tell him *he* was the reason for her daydreaming? Or more specifically, the kiss they'd shared, that had her mind wandering?

The answer was she couldn't. Telling him he'd made it almost impossible to stop thinking about him wasn't the right thing to say. Not if she wanted to keep the subtle truce between them alive and flourishing.

"Sorry about that. I've got a lot going on and I was trying to categorize and prioritize everything. The schedule for the next few days is jam-packed. Honestly, I wish we could have an extra day here, just so we could catch up." She cupped the back of her neck, shrugging her shoulders to work out the kink. "And then we've got to film immediately when we get back to the ranch, so I've been texting the crew we left behind to ensure all the produce and everything else we need has been ordered and gets delivered on time. It's a lot to remember. Not that I can't remember it all, but, well... Having a lot on my mind is no excuse for not paying attention during a meeting, though, so I'm sorry."

She stopped, aware she'd not only started babbling again, but he hadn't said a word or tried to interrupt her the entire time.

His expression, when she glanced over at him, was inscrutable.

What made her more nervous? When she could read what he was thinking across his scowling brow and narrowed eyes, or when she couldn't figure out what was going on inside his mind?

An answer wouldn't come.

"Well." She stood. "I'd better go check on the chefs, make sure they're all behaving. A little freedom can make for a great deal of trouble with this bunch."

"You have producers for that, Stacy. Let them handle it."

He pushed off from the table and came to stand in front of her.

She nodded. "Normally I would, but some of these chefs can be bullies. Big babies *and* bullies. That's a terrible combination. I've already had to deal with some personal issues, reassign a few producers."

When the deep corrugation welled between his eyes, she knew she should have kept her mouth shut. This—*this* expression—she had no difficulty interpreting.

"I wasn't made aware of any personality conflicts."

"No. No, you weren't." Nervous now, she silently screamed at herself for being an idiot and divulging something she should have known would irritate him. But she had, so she might as well finish it.

"Again, I'm sorry," she said. "But that's my job, remember? Deal with the annoying minutia so you can deal with the whole shebang? Not be bothered by stuff that will take you away from running the show effectively, but deal with it before it becomes a problem?"

She tilted her head back a little so she could maintain eye contact. If she'd take a step back, she'd be able to see him more clearly, more comfortably. But Stacy knew doing that looked liked she was stepping back in retreat, and she didn't think that was the best way to deal with his anger.

"So that's what I've been doing. It's fine. Really," she told him. "It's all good. Don't worry."

"I'm not worried about the behavior of a group of self-absorbed, egotistical chefs."

"Oh? Well, good. Good, then."

Her stomach did a little jig when his hand came out and tucked a few wayward strands of her hair behind her ear. When his finger trailed a lazy line down her temple and cheek to settle on the tip of her jaw, the jig turned to a full-out clogging step dance, complete with jumps and leaps.

She swallowed, her gaze locked onto his. She wasn't sure, wouldn't have been able to say for certain if a gun was held to her head, but she thought—*hoped*—the deep, thoughtful gleam in his eyes wasn't anger, but something more along the lines of arousal.

Just when the thought hit her it very well might be, the sound of the Black Eyed Peas shattered the air.

Nikko blinked hard a few times, dropped his hand from her face, and then reached into his pocket for his cell phone.

"Melora?"

The girl's exaggerated sigh was loud enough for Stacy to hear through the speaker. "Is your meeting, like, *over* yet? A pack of annoying toddlers just arrived and they're, like, *screaming*, at the top of their little overinflated, underdeveloped lungs. *So rude.* What's with parents? Can I come back up now?"

A smile instantly bloomed on her face. When Nikko closed his eyes and shook his head, a sudden flash of her father doing the same thing many years ago came to her.

Teenaged daughters truly were the bane of a father's existence.

"Yeah, come on up," Nikko told her and disconnected the call, his eyes never wavering from her face.

"I'll let you two have some privacy," she said, her lips still pulled up. "It's almost dinnertime and I'm sure you've got plans."

"I wish you'd do that more often," he said, his hand circling her upper arm as he turned her, slowly, back to face him.

"What? Leave?"

He stared at her a beat, the line between his brows deepening. "Smile." Flabbergasted, she stood, rooted.

"More specifically," he added, "smile at me. You do at everyone else. From Dixon to his son; the crew. Even Melora. Everyone, but me."

"I—"

His grip tightened a little as he pulled her in closer, their torsos almost touching.

"Why? Why can you show everyone else that little piece of yourself, but not me?"

"I—I don't know how to answer that," she said. "I know I was thrust on you without you wanting me here. I know you don't like me. I—"

"That's not true. I didn't *want* to like you," he admitted. "There's a difference. You're a producer. A bottom-line watcher. An annoying necessity. Liking you goes against the grain."

At that she did smile, because she knew it was true.

"See now," he said, as he slid his other hand up her arm to settle on the back of her neck, fingers curling up into her hair to hold on. "When you do that? When you smile at me like that, so openly, so...freely? I can't think about anything else."

A gentle tug and he had her head pillowed in his spread palms as he bent his own down to hers.

Through her glasses she watched the fine whiskey in his eyes blend with the ink of his pupils as they dilated.

"I haven't been able to think clearly about anything for the past few days." His mouth was a whisper from hers. His gaze skimmed from her eyes to her mouth and back again in one slow string of heat. "Except for this."

She thought she'd be prepared for the feel of his lips on hers again. After all, she'd done little else but reminisce about their texture and taste for days. But she was wrong.

So wrong.

Nothing could have ever prepared her for the way the slight pressure he placed on the back of her neck as he brought her closer sent a shiver of such carnal delight down her spine she almost hummed. Or the way his breath, warm and full, felt as it washed over her cheeks. And she certainly wasn't prepared for the onslaught of emotions he released within her when he quite expertly parted her lips and deepened the kiss, pulling at her very soul.

No, nothing in her life had equipped her with how to deal with Nikko Stamp's kiss.

So she simply let go of all thought, fear, and concern, and surrendered to it.

Nikko snaked his hands down her back to settle just below her waist, while she sighed, felt her entire body relax into him, and wound her own hands up around his shoulders. She twined her fingers together at the back of his head, the spiky hairs on his neck jutting above his collar and pricking her fingertips as she rubbed them across his skin. She shifted, turned her head more to the side so she could fall even deeper into the kiss, and when the just-starting scratch of his jaw stubble chafed against her cheek, a solid ball of full-fledged lust dropped straight to her groin, making her wet, inside and out.

The full punch of his own mounting arousal hit her square in the midsection when he cupped her butt and ground her body against his.

As she had in her room at the ranch, Stacy lost the battle to keep from moaning aloud. Completely unabashed, she clung to him, her mouth becoming insistent and arrogant as she gave herself up to what had to be the best kiss she'd ever gotten—even better than the one they'd shared before.

Every suck and nip of his tongue sent little sparks of desire popping off inside her mouth.

Greedily, as if he needed to bring her even closer, he pushed the back of her neck with his widened hand. Their teeth scraped against swollen lips. She sighed, long and deep and heard him moan in response.

Good Lord. She could come just from that sound.

When his hand dawdled up from her butt and slid over one breast, cupping it and then rubbing his thumb along the rapidly hardening nipple poking through her bra and blouse, Stacy knew she was as close as she'd ever come to losing her mind. She arched her back, pushing her breast further into his hand, letting him know how much she liked what he was doing.

Understanding, Nikko tugged her blouse from her slacks and let his hands skim over the skin at her waist and lower back.

A warning bell went off in the back of her mind when his hand came dangerously close to her bra strap. As the thought to pull away, stop this now before it got completely out of control shot through her, it was Nikko who jerked back when the sound of the electronic door locks rang out.

"Melora. She's back."

Stacy's desire-drenched mind cleared in an instant. She pulled out of his arms, turned, and quickly righted her shirt.

She knew she was flushed, could feel the heat steeping her cheeks. Her one hope was Melora wouldn't notice.

They heard the teen before they saw her enter the room.

"God! I've never seen so many obnoxious three-year-olds in my entire existence. I swear, they brought, like, an entire preschool to the pool. What a pai—"

Stacy turned and placed a smile on her face, only to drop it a tad as she watched Melora's squinted gaze go from her father, to her, and then back to settle on Nikko.

"What's going on?" the teen asked, an accusation loud and crystal clear in her tone.

"Nothing," her father said, slipping his hands into his pants pockets. He tossed a quick chin thrust at Stacy and added, "We were just finishing up with the production meeting."

"I'll go make sure everything's set for the morning," Stacy said, moving past them to the door.

"Hold up a sec," Melora said, her gaze darting to her father.

Stacy stood at the door, her hand grasping the knob. She tried to calm her breathing, not wanting to give Melora any indication that something had happened between the girl's father and herself.

Melora laid a hand on her shoulder and walked with her through the doorway and into the hall. She closed the door slightly. "What time can we meet in the morning? The gym is open twenty-four-seven. I, like, checked, before I came back up here."

Relief poured through her at the question.

"We start production at nine, and I need to be on set about an hour and a half before that. Could you make it by six? That will give us enough time to do a complete morning workout."

"No probs. See you then."

Stacy nodded and made a quick getaway.

As soon as she locked the hotel-room door behind her, she let out the breath she'd been carefully holding since Melora had come back to the suite.

With her back flat against the door, Stacy closed her eyes and lifted a hand to her lips. Swiping her tongue across them, she could still taste Nikko. Her heart beat a fluttery tattoo at the memory of how he'd held her as if his life depended on it, kissed her with more passion than she'd ever felt from any other man.

Twice, now.

And both times she'd been stripped of any will to resist him.

Okay, let's be honest here. There was no way she'd wanted to resist him.

The moment he'd moved in closer, passion and intent in his eyes, all she could think was *Kiss me. Please, oh please God, kiss me.*

The buzz of her cell phone pried her eyes back open. A quick glance down and she saw a new text with Nikko's name assigned to it run across the screen.

She swiped right and read *Are you ok?*

A good question. Was she?

Fine, she typed back.

Well, that wasn't quite true. The knowledge she was in way over her head where Nikko Stamp was concerned shattered through her. She tossed her tablet on the bed and moved to unpack her suitcase.

Her cell buzzed again.

Okay. Good, he replied.

While she put the few clothing items she'd brought with her into the dresser and closet and placed her toiletries in the small adjoining bathroom, she tried to sort out what was going on between her and Nikko.

It was obvious they were physically attracted to one another. There were enough heat and hormones flying between them whenever they were in the same room. And anytime they touched, no matter how innocuous, something pinged inside her head.

He'd asked why she couldn't smile at him openly and freely like she did with everyone else connected to the show. What would he have done if she'd told him the truth? If she'd admitted that the only reason she was here at all was because she was being rewarded if she stuck it out until the end, helped the show and him succeed?

If he didn't like her now, he'd surely hate her after finding that out.

But...he did like her. He'd admitted it. Maybe not in those exact words, but he'd told her he didn't *want* to like her, the implication being he did.

What was almost as mind-boggling was she liked him too. More than liked, if truth be told.

Yes, he was arrogant, difficult, and could be the rudest person in any room.

But.

He was a brilliant director, smart, and so gosh-darn good-looking and sexy—like a fallen angel. Plus, he loved his daughter to no end.

So what if he was demanding and overbearing in his job? With the person he loved the most, he was a total mush. Nothing was more attractive to Stacy than a man who made no excuses for how much he loved his family.

When Melora had finally confided the reason she was with her father on the shoot instead of at home for the summer school vacation, Stacy's heart had softened for the man more than she could have ever thought it would. The not so-secret secret about the girl having an eating disorder and the hoops her father was jumping through to ensure she got well only solidified in Stacy's mind what a wonderful man he was.

Dealing with a teenaged daughter with emotional and physical issues was a topic Stacy knew more about than most people could ever dream of. Her intimate knowledge of just how devastating an illness like that could be to an entire family was something she could have written a book about.

Nikko loved and cherished his daughter. Of that there was no doubt.

And she was starting to realize what she felt about him was much more than a little workplace crush.

A lot more.

Chapter Sixteen

"Where are you going?"

Melora screeched, clamped a hand over her mouth and dropped her sneakers, all while spinning around from the hotel-room door.

"*Holy Christmas!* Don't go terrifying a person like that."

Nikko's gaze raked down her body, an eyebrow inching upward at the oversized T-shirt and skintight leggings covering her thin form. Her spiky black hair was pulled off her makeup-free face by a thick white headband. She looked all of ten years old, standing and snarling at him, shoeless and clad in white ankle socks, her hands fisted on her tiny hips.

He wanted to laugh out loud at the absolute scowl of indignation blasting across her mouth. Wanting to and doing so were two different things, though, so he shot his own fists to his hips, lowered his chin, and glared right back at her.

"I asked, where are you going, Melora? It's not even six a.m."

"Well, back at'cha, *Dad*. You're not exactly dressed for, you know, *sleeping*. Where are *you* going?"

Nikko dug deep for calm. Starting off the day with an argument wasn't what he wanted to do. Melora might look like a child standing right in front of him, and she certainly was behaving like one, but he'd made a promise to himself to start treating her more like a burgeoning adult and not always as if she was two years old.

Even if she acted like it.

He took a quick breath and said, "I was heading down to the gym to see if I could snag a treadmill for an hour or so before the day gets crazy."

His daughter's large eyes widened, the effect making her resemble an anime drawing.

"No lie?"

He frowned. "Why would I make something like that up, Melly? Stacy suggested it might help with the cramping in my leg if I moved more during the day. I figured," he shrugged, "since the hotel has a gym, I'd take advantage of it."

Tears lightened the corners of her eyes.

"Daddy."

She ran to him, threw her arms around his chest, stretched up on her toes, and squeezed tight.

At a total loss as how to interpret this sudden mood shift, he simply wrapped his arms around her thin frame and hugged her back.

Melora's loud sniff tore right through his heart.

"Why are you crying?"

"I'm not," she declared, indignation in the muffled words. A second sniff proved her a liar.

When she pulled back, she did a quick, nonchalant swipe at her cheeks and said, "I think this room is, like, toxic or something. Filled with mold. Maybe I'm asthmatic."

He might not have been the smartest man in a room, but he was savvy enough not to challenge her.

"Anyway." She stood tall and shook her head a few times, her gaze coming to rest on him. "I was heading down to the gym too, before you, like, gave me a heart attack."

A warning bell dinged in his head. A memory of the therapist telling him to watch for any signs Melora would try to overexercise in order to keep her weight down filled his head.

"Oh?" he said as nonchalantly as she had. "What were you planning on doing at this hour?"

The question mustn't have sounded as casual as he'd intended, because Melora narrowed her eyes and re-fisted her hands on her waist.

"That tone is so accusatory it practically reeks with condescension."

With a shake of his head, Nikko told her, "It's good to see those astronomical fees I pay for your schooling have paid off in your SAT-worthy vocabulary. Answer the question, Melora."

Her petulant pout and eye roll were old acquaintances, so he ignored them.

"I know what you're thinking," she said, dropping her shoulders and shaking her head. "I remember what the therapist said too, but it's not like that."

"What's not like what?"

She huffed a huge, theatrical breath and dropped her chin. "I'm meeting Stacy in the gym for a yoga lesson."

Whatever he'd expected her to say, it hadn't been this.

"Since when do you do yoga?"

While she rolled her eyes again, she said, "Since I met Stacy. She's like this uber-yogi and she's been teaching me in the mornings before you all start filming."

"You've been meeting her every morning at the ranch and you never told me?"

"Like, why would I?" She lifted her hands, open-palmed, at him. "You've made it crystal since day one, moment one, you loathe her. I figured if you knew I was, like, hanging out with her you'd pop an artery."

"I don't loathe Stacy, Melora." As far from loathe as he could get, actually, but he wasn't sharing that fact with her.

"You certainly don't like her."

"That's not true."

She stared at him, suspicion and skepticism dancing on her raised brows and pursed lips. "You didn't. When did that, like, change?"

Nikko swiped at his temples and sat on the couch. While he slipped into his sneakers, he said, "I never *didn't* like her. It was more the fact of her I didn't want around. Executive producers can be pains in the a—um, butt. She's not, though. She's actually very good at her job."

Melora, looking like a stork as she stood on one skinny leg to slip her feet into her own sneakers, cocked her head at him and said, "Then why is she still, like, *in terror* of you?"

"What do you mean?"

"Every time she's with you," she slipped her foot in her other shoe, "she looks like she's gonna do a Usain Bolt and make like the wind. You ask me, I think she's scared of you. And I don't blame her. You can be, like, so *gruesomely intimidating* at times."

He stared across the room at her, dumbfounded. Fear was the one emotion he'd remembered seeing in vivid detail after the airport incident.

A fat swell of self-disgust grew inside him at the memory that he'd been so harsh and critical when she'd been nothing but professional and just plain nice.

"If you don't, like, loathe her," Melora said as they walked to the elevator bank, "you should try being nicer. She really is fab. And super-smart about stuff."

As they got into the elevator, she added, "And everyone else likes her, so..." She shrugged as he hit the button for the gym level.

Nikko nodded, deciding it was the best way to answer her. He couldn't quite admit to his daughter, much less himself, that he was coming to more than just like Stacy Peters.

Way more.

The minute they walked into the gym, he found her. She stood off to one side, talking with Riley MacNeill and Clay Burbank. He noticed a few of the other chefs clad in workout gear, including the two female contestants, standing around waiting.

Melora said "See ya," and made her way over to the group. A broad, easy smile lit Stacy's face when she spotted his daughter. Melora tossed a hand over her shoulder and pointed to him while the two spoke. The moment Stacy's gaze connected with his, Nikko felt an unseen weight lift inside him.

His daughter's accusations blew back. Stacy didn't look terrified. In fact, judging from the easy smile she gave him and the tiny head nod of connection, she looked...pleased.

He acknowledged her smile with a quick head bob and then climbed onto an empty treadmill. From his position he had a clear and unobstructed view of Stacy and what appeared to be a yoga class. MacNeill, Burbank, and the others formed a few lines on mats, with Melora included, all facing Stacy, who appeared to be their leader.

While he started off at a slow pace just to loosen and warm up his stiff leg muscles, he kept close watch on his executive producer. Once again, while everyone around her was clad in muscle shirts or armless T-shirts, Stacy wore a full-sleeved bright-blue Henley and black yoga pants that skirted her bare ankles. He'd never seen her in anything but long-sleeved tops, even with the hot temperatures at the ranch. Either she was one of those people who were chronically cold, or she didn't like to bare her arms. Since he'd seen her flushed and sweating a few times on set, he assumed it was the latter.

Why?

Her frame was thin, her shoulders and hips slight, even though she was about five-seven or -eight. The way her well-fitting clothing currently caressed her skin, showing off the long, clean line of her body had his lower back twitching again. When she bent from her waist, knees locked and straight, and placed her palms flat on the mat in front of her, the twitch turned to a tingle.

As she raised her arms together high over her head, a small slip of perfect, fresh, cream-colored skin peeked out at him from where her shirt lifted at her waist, and the tingle turned to a quiver of prickly lust so fast and so unexpected, he almost missed a step on the foot pad rolling beneath him.

He reached out and grabbed the supporting bars on either side of the treadmill and took a deep, full breath.

Who in their right mind got turned on by an inch of skin?

For the next forty minutes, while he put his legs through a slight uphill climb, Nikko came to learn a few things about his executive producer.

And himself.

He already knew she was kind, having witnessed it firsthand with her treatment of his daughter and during the night she'd helped ease his leg pain.

That she was someone who remained calm and in control he'd realized early on, evidenced in all her dealings with him when he'd been at his worst, mood-wise.

He'd guessed she was a good leader from the way the crew all took their problems to her.

But what he hadn't known was how playful she could be or how irked he could become when other men, namely Clay Burbank, blatantly flirted with her.

It was obvious Burbank wasn't a yoga practitioner. Every movement, every pose he tried to adopt, he needed help achieving and every time it had been from Stacy he'd sought assistance.

The sight of her long, thin, deft fingers pressing against the chef's hips as she helped him adopt a pose sent a shiver of unexpected jealousy down his spine. He knew, intimately, what those fingers felt like against his own body.

When she'd gone on her knees behind Burbank and pressed into his back to help him stretch, that shiver turned to a full-body shake filled with possessiveness.

Burbank must have said something to annoy her, because before she stood back up, she swatted the chef on the shoulder and wagged a finger at him, setting the rest of the class to break out in laughter.

As his heart began to beat faster from the uphill climb, it warred with the deep breaths he took to try and calm his emotions. He had no right to feel possessive of Stacy, or jealous.

But he was, on both counts, and it not only irritated him, it made him nervous as hell. He hadn't felt so emotionally torn over a woman in...well, a long, long time. Not since he'd discovered Flannery's infidelity.

The program slowed, the treadmill automatically lowering down from the hill-climb pace.

It appeared Stacy was almost finished with the class as well. The group lay supine on their mats, eyes closed, as she walked among them, speaking.

From the little he knew about yoga—and it *was* little—she was guiding them through a breathing cycle to end the session.

Her face was peaceful and calm, a tiny smile pulling at the corners of her lips when she spied Riley winking one eye open at her. Nikko could read her lips when she told the boy to close his eyes, breath, and relax.

If life were only so simple.

The walking pace slowed, then stopped. Nikko swiped at his sweating face and neck with the gym-provided towel and took a large chug of the individual bottled water provided on each treadmill. The group rose and bowed to Stacy.

Her giggle floated on the air and sucker punched him straight in the abdomen. She laughed at something Riley said to her and Melora and crinkled her nose in the most enchanting way. When she found his gaze centered on her from across the room, Stacy dropped her chin and bit a corner of her bottom lip as she regarded him from under her lashes. It was a damned good thing the walking program had ended, because he'd have missed a lot more than one step if he'd still been moving.

Melora turned, called his name and asked if he was done.

When he nodded, she said something to Stacy and Riley and then jogged over to him.

"How's your leg?" she asked, grabbing the bottle from his hand and taking a long, deep swig.

"It's fine. Walking definitely helps. I didn't realize you were actually taking a class with Stacy. I thought it was just the two of you."

"It was," she told him, handing him back the bottle. "The others came down planning to just, like, work out, but when they saw Stacy and asked her what she was doing here, they, like, decided to join in."

"I was watching. You did pretty good, kid. Better than the others."

An eyebrow-grazing eye roll was accompanied by a huge grin. "I know. It was cool knowing so much more than the rest of them. Burbank, btw, is a huge tool. He was, like, *blatantly* hitting on Stacy. So lame."

The muscles in Nikko's stomach gnarled into knots. "What did he say to her that was so lame?" he asked, trying to keep the irritation from spilling into his voice.

They started walking to the elevator.

"Just really dumb comments about private yoga lessons, and if, like, doing yoga would make him more *limber* in certain departments." She snorted as they got in the elevator. "He said *that* really skanky and suggestive-like. Stacy hit him." She snorted again.

Nikko wanted to do more than hit the chef. The urge to hurt him flashed fast and furious across his mind.

He blinked, surprised at the sudden possessiveness rearing its head again. What to do about it was the question of the day.

* * * *

Stacy rubbed the back of her neck and sighed.

The day had started out perfectly with the early-morning yoga class—a class she'd been surprised to be asked to lead—but had deteriorated as quick as rapid gunfire right before filming was due to start.

As usual, Jade Quartermaine had been late to arrive on set, no excuse given. The red lines train-tracking the whites of her eyes and the sandy rasp in her voice told Stacy the woman had had a late night, obviously spent with a bottle of alcohol. The huge hickey on the side of her neck told everyone she hadn't been drinking alone.

When all the chefs were in place in the restaurant kitchen waiting for their first challenge to be issued, the film crew set to begin, it became apparent Jade was even more unprepared than usual.

While her words weren't slurred, they were garbled when she spoke and it was obvious she hadn't gone over her lines before coming to set. Nikko was forced to stop filming several times due to the woman's inability to get even one line of script correct.

"*Christ.* Jade, what the hell is the matter with you?" He stormed from off set where the production crew was situated and right up into her face. Stacy had to give the woman credit for not shrinking back from the accusatory and threatening scowl facing her.

With her own frown pulling at her crimson-colored mouth, Jade shot out a French-manicured, pointed fingernail and poked it squarely in his chest.

"Back off, Nikko. I'm not in the mood for one of your testosterone-fueled temper tantrums."

The noise level in the kitchen dropped to a silent hum. From next to her, Stacy heard Todd mumble, "*That* she can say, but not the easy words written in the script?"

"I wouldn't lose my temper if you did your job," Nikko roared.

Stacy flinched.

Jade wasn't a woman to be yelled at and not respond in kind. "Whoever wrote this drivel has no concept of the spoken word," she screeched. "These lines are ridiculous."

"It's you who are ridiculous," Nikko tossed back.

Within a heartbeat, the argument escalated to three times the volume, with both star and director screaming at the same time.

"Somebody needs to stop this before we get bloodshed," Clay Burbank said, loud enough to be heard above the din.

When no one else moved, Stacy did. Into the fire she strode, wedging herself between them. At her back she could feel the heat of Jade's breath on her neck as she continued to yell; from her front, the natural heat of Nikko's body bearing down on her.

"Both of you, please stop," she said loud enough to be heard, but not shouting. "*Please.*"

Maybe it was because they were both stunned someone had intervened, or that Stacy's presence between them acted as an obstacle; or perhaps they'd both come to their senses at the same moment, but for whatever reason, the commotion came to an abrupt halt. All eyes were trained on Stacy, breaths held, as she looked from Nikko to Jade and then back to the director.

"Thank you," she told him.

Something in his eyes changed as he stared down at her. She swore the hard, angry glare he'd thrown at Jade just seconds before, shifted now to a gentler, calmer one. His furrowed brow smoothed, his mouth softened from a tight, hard line, and his shoulders pulled down from their hunched position around his ears.

It was captivating to watch him gain control of himself. On any given day, Nikko Stamp was a force of nature. Volatile and unpredictable, like a threatening storm. And right now, with the echo of his anger floating around them as he valiantly warred to get his emotions under control, he was the most fascinating man she'd ever encountered.

Realizing she could have stood all day, just gazing up at him, hit her hard. He made her forget the reason she was standing there, lodged between himself and his obnoxious program host.

Stacy blinked, swallowed, and turned to face Jade.

"Why don't we go run through your lines a few times? Maybe"—she held her hand up, anticipating what the disgruntled star was about to say—"we can rework the text so the words flow more naturally."

Jade's mouth snapped shut. With a withering, narrow-eyed glare at Nikko, she nodded. "At least someone involved with this production understands what I've been saying."

She turned and strode from the set, a red-faced Carrie, who'd been standing on the sidelines nervously twisting her fingers together, following.

"There's nothing wrong with that intro," Nikko said when Stacy turned her attention back to him.

With a subtle nod, she moved a step closer and said, "I know. I just wanted to get her off set. Maybe get her a cup of coffee. She seems, well… not at her best right now."

Nikko snorted, sounding so much like his daughter Stacy bit down on her bottom lip to keep from laughing out loud.

"What she seems is either badly hungover or still soused." He shoved his hands into his pockets and shook his head in disgust.

Stacy didn't feel the need to respond.

"Okay." He blew out a breath. "Go and try to calm her down. Sober her up if she needs it. Whatever it takes. We can film around her for now."

With another nod, Stacy moved away from him.

"Okay, everyone," she heard him address the chefs and crew. "Show's over. Let's get this challenge underway. Dan? You good to go with your lines?"

She didn't hear his response, but knew what it was. At least one of the cohosts acted like a professional.

Outside an office abutting the kitchen that had been designated as the show makeup room, Stacy heard Jade's voice clear as a ringing bell, complaining about what had just happened.

Steeling herself, Stacy walked into the proverbial fire.

A half-hour later, with two cups of caffeinated coffee forced on her, a quick makeup refresh to hide the hickey, and her intro reworded ever so slightly, Jade was ready.

When she marched back to the kitchen, the challenge was already underway.

"Nikko says we can film your part when they're done and he'll edit it in," Dan told Jade when she came to stand next to him off set.

The diva pursed her lips and said nothing.

Stacy squeezed Carrie's shoulder, the producer's fingers still nervously tapping a rhythm against one another, and went to take her place behind Nikko.

The noise in the kitchen was cacophonic and it resounded in the area cordoned off for the direction team.

Stacy slid back into her chair, took a deep breath and, along with everyone else, turned her attention to the monitors.

Nikko tilted his chair back, slid his headset off one ear, and over his shoulder asked, "She good to go now?"

Stacy nodded. "She knows you're going to film her intro after the challenge tasting."

"How much did she change it?"

"Just a word or two. I think she'll be fine."

He called time two minutes later. While Dan and a now camera-ready, professional-acting Jade went through the tasting, Stacy snuck surreptitious glances at Nikko.

Had she noticed before how long and dexterous his fingers were, watching them snap in time to his commands to give the crew an editing beat? His timing was perfection in itself, and Stacy made a wish when she had her own show she could be as precise and on target as Nikko always was.

Noticing his fingers led her to remembering how they'd felt gliding along her face and then her body when he'd kissed her. His warm, gentle touch had sent her insides bouncing and her toes tingling.

Had a man's touch ever made her come so undone so swiftly before?

No, it hadn't. And the notion she wanted to feel his hands on her again was so uncanny, she shook her head a few times to clear it of the thought.

After Jade's intro was done—letter-perfect—they'd issued the challenge to rework one of the restaurant's signature dishes into something of their own conception. The chefs had been given twenty-four hours to devise their recipes. Stacy, Nikko, and the film crew then followed them to a local market to purchase ingredients they'd need that weren't supplied in Jimmy Rodgers's kitchen.

When the entire crew and cast had gotten back to the hotel, the chefs were left to their own devices for the evening. Several decided to take advantage of the free time and pair up to sightsee. Others spent the time lounging at the pool. Since they weren't allowed any contact with family or friends, several of them had formed friendly alliances, Riley MacNeill and Clay Burbank among them.

With none of the privacy constrictions placed on her, Stacy took the time to call and chat with Kandy.

"You didn't use the code word when I answered," her cousin said, making Stacy smile, "so that lets me know this isn't a distress call. You doing okay out there in God's country?"

"Yeah. Things are...good. Interesting, but good."

"Interesting, huh? What's that mean?"

Not having had a sister growing up, Stacy had looked toward her older girl cousins for guidance on questions or concerns she didn't want to address with her mother. Kandy, the oldest cousin and five years Stacy's senior, had typically been the one she turned to. Kandy was a sympathetic listener and a thoughtful advisor, two traits Stacy had come to treasure.

"It means I've changed my opinion about certain things since I've arrived."

"Things?" Kandy asked. "Or people? One person in particular, maybe?"

Stacy sighed, then chuckled. "How do you do that?"

"What?"

"Know exactly what I'm going to say, before I even say it? It's creepy sometimes."

Kandy's own deep chuckle tickled through the phone. "Grandpa said it was because I knew how to read a room, just like he did. Grandma disagreed and said it was because I was just naturally nosy."

"Either way, it's uncanny. But you're right. I have changed my mind about Dominick Stamp."

"For better or worse?"

"Definitely better. He's everything I'd heard he was: arrogant, rude, a perfectionist to his core."

"I hear a big *but* in there."

"But," Stacy stretched out in her comfortable hotel chair, "he's so much more." She told her about Melora, about the teen's struggles, and how Nikko was devoting himself to her recovery.

"He's a wonderful father and anyone can see how much he loves her," Stacy said. "He's got the filming schedule blocked so he can cook and spend time with her every day no matter what happens to wreck the schedule on set."

"How's he doing physically? I heard the accident really screwed up one of his legs."

Stacy told her of Nikko's struggles and how he'd allowed her to help him.

"And speaking of that, can you overnight something to me?"

"Sure. What?"

"I want to give him some of my medicated cream and there are no drugstores near the ranch I can have it shipped to or ordered from. I'm sure the menthol in it will help him with the cramping and the pain. There's a bunch of it in my apartment in the bathroom. I ordered a new batch of it about a month ago."

The silence that met her had her checking the cell screen to see if the call had been dropped.

"Kan?"

"I'm still here. You just caught me off guard. You never, ever, talk about...what happened. And none of us like to push."

"No, you don't. And I love you for that." Stacy bit down on a corner of her lip.

"So you still have pain?" Kandy asked, her voice filled with concern. "Enough to need to medicate it?"

With a sigh, Stacy said, "Sometimes. If I don't work out for a few days my arm tends to get stiff. When it does, the pain worms its way in, and I need the cream to help relax the muscles and tendons. It penetrates deep. That's why I think giving it to Nikko would help him."

Kandy waited a beat. "So it's Nikko, now, not Dominick?"

Even though her cousin couldn't see her face, Stacy blushed to the roots of her hair.

"Everyone calls him that," she said, trying for nonchalant and hoping she succeeded. She should have known better. Look who she was talking to, after all? Kandy Laine could have been a top-notch criminal interrogator, she was that skillful at worming things out of people. Things they never wanted to divulge.

"Maybe," Kandy said. "But I hear something in your voice that I don't hear when most people talk about him."

"What?" She was terrified to hear the answer.

"Why don't you tell me?" her cousin asked. "Because I think you know what it is I'm hearing."

She'd called Kandy's intuition uncanny. It was too tame a word.

Maybe if she told her cousin what she was feeling, the mixed-up jumble of emotions she was tethered with every time she and Nikko were alone together, maybe it would help her clarify and understand what was going on inside her head.

Or maybe it would just confuse her more.

Either way, Stacy did what she'd done for most of her life. Settling into the chair, she crossed her ankles together and told her cousin everything.

Chapter Seventeen

"Are we, like, eating here first?" Melora asked the next afternoon when Nikko came back to the suite for a few minutes during a break in filming. The chefs were all getting ready to serve the restaurant of packed patrons, and he had needed a few minutes to himself.

"I thought you might want to eat downstairs with Stacy again and help her with gathering the votes," he told her while he got a bottled water from the room's mini-fridge.

"Is it the same setup as at the ranch? Buffet and then people vote?"

"A little different. The challenge was for the chefs to modify and individualize one of the restaurant's beef dishes. The guests are going to order off the reimagined menus and each chef will serve them."

"So, I have to, like, *sit there* in the restaurant with all those strangers, and eat?"

Knowing how much his daughter despised eating in front of people she wasn't comfortable with, he'd already thought this through.

Melora had no trouble eating in front of him, but he needed to direct, so he couldn't watch her. But Stacy could. "I've arranged a table for you and Stacy just off the main dining area. You won't be seen or watched by anyone. When you're done, you can help Stacy gather the patron votes. Okay?"

The unexpected and rarely-seen smile that bloomed across her face had a little twinge twisting in his heart.

She looked...happy. Really happy. For the first time in more months than he could remember.

Melora threw her arms around his waist and squeezed tight, rubbing her cheek against his chest. "Wicked more than just okay. Thanks, Daddy."

"Anything for you, kid," he said, squeezing back. "Now we've got to get down there. Service starts in a little under a half hour and I've got to make sure everything is set."

He spotted Stacy the moment they walked into the kitchen. She was engaged in conversation with several of the producers. He took a moment to study her as he and Melora walked over. Her shoulder-length hair was tied up into a messy topknot, a stylus sticking out of its center. She wore her glasses and absently pushed them up over the bridge of her nose when she looked down and then back up again.

Another long-sleeved white blouse—silk, he'd bet on it—covered her, one button undone at the neck, giving him a subtle view of the unlined skin peeking through. Casual fawn-colored ankle-length trousers dropped down her legs, legs he knew were toned and trim after seeing them covered by body-hugging yoga pants. She looked polished, professional, and totally in control and all he could think about was yanking that stylus out and twining her freed hair around his fingers as he pulled her into his arms and gave vent to this irresistible, persistent craving to kiss her senseless.

After observing her in the gym, Nikko understood Stacy had become something more than just his executive producer, more than just an available, single woman. The thought solidified inside him when she stepped between him and Jade in the kitchen. Glancing down at her, hearing her plea, he'd instantly gone from royally pissed to a peaceful calm he'd forgotten he could possess. Just looking at her tranquil face and hearing her soft voice had turned his anger switch to silent. His entire body relaxed, and in that moment he knew she was the reason. The knot untangled from his gut and all he wanted to do was bend down and thank her with a kiss.

Well, maybe more than thank her. And maybe more than with just a kiss.

Definitely, more than just a kiss.

As they approached, she glanced up. That instantaneous smile he was beginning to dream about broke across her mouth as her gaze shifted from Melora to settle on him.

He didn't think it was imagination or wishful thinking when her eyes softened behind her glasses. Gone was the wary, guarded glare she typically gave him, replaced by something sweet and accepting.

"Everything's all set," she told them when the others scurried away. "Service is about to start." She looked around at the line of people waiting to be seated. "It's a full crowd and Jimmy Rodgers's maître d' just told me they're fully booked for three complete table turns. It's gonna be a late night," she said to Melora. "If you don't want to, you don't have to stay to help me with the votes."

"It's okay. I like helping you."

When Stacy's nose crinkled with her smile, Nikko had to clamp down hard as the desire to toss her over his shoulder and bring her back to his room, overwhelmed him.

"You're a big help too," she told the teen. Turning her attention to him, she said, "Todd's got the hand cameras all ready and Dan and Jade both said they'd be willing to walk among the diners and ask opinions of the food for you to use as B-roll."

Nodding, he said, "I don't want Rodgers involved, though, until Jade and Dan sit down after we're done with service. Does he know that?"

"Yes." Her lips twisted and she shook her head. "He's got the typical chef master-of-his-domain ego. When I told him you wanted him to stay away from the kitchen until after service was done, he got a little…testy. Said since we were using his restaurant, his food, and his menu, he had a right to be present during prep."

"No, he doesn't. I'll go find him and set him to rights."

She snaked out a hand and grabbed his forearm. He didn't know who was more surprised she'd touched him: Stacy, him, or Melora, whose eyes practically bugged from her head when she spotted the move.

"No need," she said, tugging her hand back, her face flushing in a wildfire of red from neck to temple. "I explained why you didn't want him around the chefs, about how intimidated and distracted they'd be to see him while they were preparing, and after thinking about it, he agreed. With a huge, self-satisfied and egotistical smirk, I'll add."

She could have told him the man had stormed away and cut off his nose for all Nikko cared. The feel of her hand circling his arm had sent a shower of warmth sluicing down his spine. When she removed it, he'd felt cold and abandoned.

He wanted that warmth touching his entire body, wanted to give it back to her in turn. The simple thought of pulling her away from everything and everyone galloped through his mind again. Without a notion of what he was doing, where he was, or who was around them, he took a step closer, one hand poised to grab hers back. He watched her eyes widen behind her glasses, and then dart a meaningful glimpse at his daughter.

That one small move shipped him off *Fantasy Island* and back to reality.

With a silent oath, he stepped back.

"This guy sounds like a major-league bonehead," Melora said, adding a careless hand flip.

"Melora." Disapproval settled deep in his tone.

The teen rolled her eyes and shook her head. "Sorry. *Dad.*"

When Stacy dropped her chin, he swore she was trying to hide a grin. Before he could say anything else, Todd called out from across the dining room, pointed a finger at his watch, and then cocked his head.

"I guess it's time to start. I've got to get situated. Come find me if you need me," he told Stacy.

"I've got my phone, so text me if you need me to do anything too," she said.

With a nod, he bussed Melora's temple, then pointed a finger at her and said, "Be good."

She threw him a speaking glance and chucked her hands on her trim hips.

With one last glance at Stacy, he moved into position.

Service did, indeed, go long.

It was well after eleven by the time Jade, Dan, and Jimmy Rodgers sat down in the now-empty restaurant to discuss the chefs' offerings. When Melora's head had begun to bob, Nikko sent her back to the suite after giving her his cell phone and requesting she text Stacy when she got there.

The teen gave him a tired kiss on the cheek and was then accompanied by Stacy to the elevator bank.

She retuned a few moments later and slipped into her chair behind him.

Nikko slipped his headset to one side and over his shoulder said, "Let me know when she texts."

Not ten seconds later she tapped his shoulder and leaned forward to show him her phone.

Home safe and sound. Copping z's now.

One side of his mouth twitched as he glanced from the phone to Stacy. She was so close, leaning forward as she held the phone for him; all he needed to do was shift a mere inch or so and he could kiss her like he'd wanted to do for hours.

He still had the taste of her swirling in his senses from the last time.

As if she somehow knew his intent, Stacy wet her bottom lip with her tongue as her gaze dropped to his mouth.

Anticipation whispered through him. Just a slight bend of his shoulders and that expectation would be fulfilled.

"Finally." Todd's exasperated, tired voice flooded around them.

Stacy blinked, shook her head a few times as if she'd just woken from a dream, and then fell back into her chair.

"They've decided on a winner," Todd said, tugging his headset off.

Nikko whistled out a breath, leaned forward while readjusting his headset over his ears, and listened to the conversation between the three judges.

From the flirtatious grin sliding across Jade's mouth to the intimate way she rubbed a well-manicured hand along Jimmy Rodgers's arm, Nikko confirmed what he'd suspected that morning during Jade's tired and nasty outburst. She'd been out drinking into the night, and since Jimmy was a legendary drinker and ladies' man it was obvious who she'd been with. He caught Dan Roth's quick and annoyed side-glance away from the two as their conversation turned from the competition results to a planned late-night drink.

"That's it," Nikko said, rising from the chair. "We're done."

He flicked on his communicator and announced the same to the crew.

"Call is nine a.m.," Todd added before removing his own headset. With a deep yawn, he tossed it on his chair. "I'm beat," he said to Nikko. "Do you need me for anything else right now? 'Cause if you don't, I've got a hot date with my pillow."

"No, we're good. Get some rest and I'll see you in the morning."

"My crew will be doing the last of the location shots tomorrow, then heading back to the ranch. You joining us?"

"No. I trust you to get great fill-in footage."

Before leaving the production area, Todd turned to Stacy. "I hear you lead a kick-ass yoga class. Any chance you're doing another one in the morning before we head out?"

Nikko's attention went on hyperalert while he waited for her response.

"That kind of just happened," she said. He could hear the smile in her voice. "I was there to practice and a few of the chefs were there at the same time with a similar idea, so I got volunteered into leading. But, yeah, in answer to your question, I plan on being in the gym by six. I try not to miss a day if I can help it and I thought I could get in a good, long workout before heading to the airport."

Todd nodded. "My wife got me hooked about a year ago when I had a little blip on a routine cardiogram. Said it would help me relax when the cardiologist said I needed to get rid of some of the stress in my life. Guy obviously didn't know what I do for a living. Stress is the major component of the job description. Anyway, my wife wasn't wrong. I started taking some instructional classes at a local studio and my repeat scan was way better. Lost some weight as a side bonus."

"All good things," Stacy replied.

"The wife's certainly happy. Okay, then. It'll be good to get in a workout with other people. I'll set my alarm and see you in the morning. 'K?"

"Sounds like a plan."

"'Night, Nikko," he said over his shoulder.

Nikko nodded.

Happy they were now alone, he turned his attention to her.

"Do you need me for anything else?" Stacy asked, stifling a yawn behind her hand.

It was on the tip of his tongue to say *Yeah, I need you in my bed, underneath me, easing away my own stress,* but knew saying it out loud would send her running.

"No," he said, instead. "But I do want to thank you, again, for what you've been doing for Melora. Letting her assist you, eating meals with her, even teaching her yoga, something I didn't know you were doing until this morning."

"I'm sorry she didn't tell you. Like the class this morning, it just kind of…happened." She flipped her hand in the air. "She was out walking one morning while I was just beginning a routine, and started asking me about it. One thing led to another and she asked if I'd teach her some moves. She's a very quick study, by the way. Show her something once and it takes root in here"—she tapped her temple—"for good."

Nikko shook his head, a ghost of grin popping on his lips. "Kid's always been inquisitive, even when she was little. And despite speaking like she's got the IQ of a Valley Girl lost in vague-land, she does great in school. She's very smart."

Stacy smiled and when she crinkled her nose, he forgot to breathe.

"I've witnessed that for myself."

He swallowed and blew out a quick burst of air between his lips. "I'm not surprised. Thanks, again, for taking the time with her. It's been a huge help to her. And me."

Her eyes softened, the skin at the corners creasing when she smiled. "You don't need to thank me for any of that. She's a great girl and it's been my pleasure. Truly." When her lips lifted and the smile went from sweet to wistful, he wondered at the cause. He was just about to ask when she offered: "I remember what it's like to be that age." With a shake of her head, she closed her tablet and rose from her chair. "Stuck between wanting to be treated like an adult, and a kid with none of the responsibilities of a grown-up and all the perks of childhood. It can be tough. She's been through a lot lately. A lot for a kid, no matter what her age."

Didn't he know it.

"She has," he agreed. "It's been…hard on her."

"On both of you, I think."

He slanted her a look and through lowered lashes said, "You're perceptive, that's for sure. I bet you were one of those kids that always walked the straight and narrow." He grinned, picturing her at Melora's age. "The kind the other kids turned to for advice. Never in trouble. Never grounded for doing something stupid and thoughtless."

"You'd be way wrong," she replied without a moment's hesitation. The next second, she lowered her gaze from his and bit down on her bottom lip.

His eyebrows crept up his forehead. So, his utterly dependable and consistent executive producer had a bit of a wayward past. That tiny tidbit, that little glimpse into her character, sent a decided thrill spiraling through him like a building tornado.

Before he could think not to, his hand shot out and wound around her forearm.

"Stacy."

The moment he said her name her body stilled. Her eyes grew huge behind her lenses as she regarded him. Huge and filled with a quiet expectation that had his hopes rising and his desire bounding.

He should let her go. Really. It was better all around if he just shut down this uncontrollable need to touch her, be with her, talk to her.

But he couldn't. Didn't want to, and in truth, wasn't sure he could if compelled to.

As if possessing a mind of its own, his hand slid up to her elbow, gently drawing her closer. She didn't resist. If she had, he might have reconsidered what he was about to do.

Her blouse prevented him from directly touching her skin, but when he pressed his fingers against the material, he could feel the tight muscles it covered.

"You always wear long sleeves," he said in a soft voice. "I noticed it at the ranch when we did that hellish location shoot. The temp was sweltering and yet you were covered up. Even this morning during your workout. You shield yourself, Stacy."

Her eyes opened a little wider, her pupils grew a little larger, obliterating some of the deep green.

"Makes me wonder why. What are you hiding? Why are you hiding?"

Inclining his body forward as he brought her in closer, he watched her lips part on the tiniest of sighs and her shoulders lift with the exertion. The subtle fragrance of peaches came to him, ripe and sweet; juicy and with enough candied sugar to make his taste buds swell in anticipation. Just when he knew she'd kiss him back if he pressed his lips to hers, he saw her eyes suddenly flick away from his and heard her breath catch. With a quick, awkward jerk, she wrenched back and out of his hold just as Jade's theatrically throaty and phony laugh shot from close behind.

Nikko whipped around and found her practically wearing Rodgers as the duo sauntered across the kitchen area toward them. One of Jade's arms was woven through the chef's, the fingers of her other hand trailing up and down his sleeve in a gesture that bespoke intimacy, possession, and expectation.

Jimmy's gaze slid from him, then beyond, to land on Stacy. When it settled back on him, Nikko had the strongest urge to punch the keen, arrogant smirk from the chef's face.

"Well, we're finally done," Jade said, her gaze hopscotching from Nikko to Stacy. "Jimmy and I were just heading out for a late...supper up to his private dining room." The hand that had been trailing up and down his arm squeezed his bicep, the little hesitation, Nikko knew, meant to imply food was the last thing on her mind.

"I would think you'd be full," he said, not bothering to hide his sarcasm, "after sampling all tonight's dishes."

The lines at the edges of her eyes deepened as she narrowed them at Nikko. "That was hours ago. And besides, we only had to taste them, not clean our plates."

Jimmy's lips twitched while he zeroed in on Stacy. "How's that beautiful cousin of yours doing, Stace?"

"She's good. Enjoying motherhood and throwing herself into the new restaurants."

"I hear Teddy Davis just signed her to three more spots for next year. I thought she was done with TV."

With a nod, she answered, "She is with prime-time programming. But she's still up for a few specials. Everyone loves a holiday cooking show, so she agreed to do an Easter-dinner special, Fourth of July beach barbeque, and a Christmas-cookie baking show."

"Gonna be like old times?" he asked. "You working with her on those like you used to do on her weekly show?"

"Not this time," she answered.

When she didn't elaborate as to why, Jimmy asked the question that had popped into his own mind.

"Is your schedule free, then, for the spring? 'Cuz I've got a programming meeting with Davis next week about a new show I've got coming up. I could use a top-notch EP like you on my team."

Nikko waited, holding his breath, for her response. He'd think later about why the request was as sharp and painful as a hard kick to his balls would have been.

"Oh, well, thanks," Stacy said, a swirl of red spinning up her neck and landing on her cheeks. "I've kind of...committed...to something for the spring. Sorry."

The chef's smile dropped a notch, but his good humor remained. "Well, listen, if whatever it is falls through, keep me in mind, will ya?"

"Thanks, I will."

She looked at each of them as she said, "It's been a long day. I'm heading up. Enjoy the rest of your night," she said, addressing Jimmy and Jade. "See you in the morning," she said to Nikko.

Nikko caught Jade's squinty-eyed glare as it followed Stacy from the area.

"You're lucky to have her on your team," Jimmy told him. "Gal's a workhorse and nothing fazes her. Anybody who can put up with Dolly Cardson's shit and turn a loser show like hers into a success is an asset you'd want to have on your side. Plus, she's pretty easy on the eyes," he added with a cocky grin that had Nikko's fingers curling into a fist.

"If you like the bland ingénue look," Jade said. With a pout, she squeezed Jimmy's arm again and turned his attention back on her.

Nikko watched the chef's grin broaden, his head cocked to one side. He laid a hand over the one still clinging to his arm and rubbed it suggestively. "Bland is boring. In cooking and in women. I happen to go for more exotic tastes, myself," he said.

Sickened by the both of them, Nikko pushed up from his chair. "I'll let you two get to dinner."

"We actually came over to see if you'd come for a drink with us," Jade said, easily. "I have a proposition for you. A directing one."

Nothing she could suggest would make him join them right now. Not when his mind was still occupied with Stacy.

"It's late," he said. "And it's been a long, tedious day," he added, pointedly looking at Jade. Her feeble attempt to blank her face fell flat.

"Why don't we grab a few minutes before you have to head back to the ranch tomorrow morning, then?" Jimmy asked. He glanced at Jade. "Say, breakfast in my office? About ten-ish?"

It was on the tip of his tongue to refuse, use any excuse he could. But Nikko was business-savvy enough to know when to listen to a proposal and when not to. Once *Beef Battles* wrapped and editing was completed, he didn't have anything lined up.

Deciding on the spot, he nodded. "See you in the morning." He turned back once before leaving to see the two of them, heads together, Jimmy cupping Jade's cheek as he said something into her ear that had her giggling like a girl Melora's age.

Chapter Eighteen

After a quick shower, Stacy washed and moisturized her face and body, and then shrugged into her makeshift pajamas of an oversized, long-sleeved EBS T-shirt that came down almost to her knees. Just when she started brushing out her hair, a knock on the door sounded.

She opened it without first checking, expecting it to be the extra pillows she'd called down to housekeeping for.

When she discovered Nikko Stamp standing there, his hands thrust in his pants pockets, her mind went blank.

Silently, she watched his eyes take their time gliding down her face to her torso, then lower. He angled his head and then his gaze drifted back up, a slow, heart-stopping, sexy smile tugging at his mouth until he landed back on her eyes.

She couldn't decide if the heated flush that instantly flamed up and engulfed her body from toe to scalp was due to embarrassment or desire at the way his eyes darkened and dilated as he stared at her.

Taking a quick guess, she thought it might be equal parts of both.

"I—I thought you were housekeeping," she said, gripping the doorknob with such intensity she felt it rattle against her hand at the strain. "I'm waiting for a delivery."

The elevator chimed and echoed in the distance.

"Sorry," he said with an amused shake of his head. "Not housekeeping."

When he said nothing further, she asked, "Is everything okay? Problems? Melora?"

"She's fine. Sound asleep when I checked two minutes ago."

"Then—"

Before she could finish, a rotund, uniformed housekeeper marched up to them, three enormous pillows in her arms.

"Miss Peters?" she addressed them both. "You called for these?"

"Yes. Thanks. Thanks, so much. That was quick." She took the offered pillows all at once, the weight more than she'd calculated.

"Can I do anything else for you, miss?"

"No. No. I'm good." She shuffled the pillows between her arms, awkwardly trying to not let them fall. "Thanks again."

With a fast smile, the maid bobbed her head and said, "Good night."

"'Night," Stacy said.

One pillow slipped from her grasp and as she tried to catch it before it hit the floor, Nikko did the same.

He was quicker.

"Here," he said, "give me these."

Without waiting for her to do so, he plucked them from her hands as if they weighed nothing more than a single feather and walked into her room. He tossed them on the bed, asking, "Why do you need so many? The bed already has two."

She stood at the threshold, the door wide open, memories of the last time they'd been alone together in her room at the ranch flooding back in a rush. She'd been unprepared, then, for the depth of her desire when he'd kissed her to distraction and caressed all her free will away. She still felt the same.

"Stacy?"

"Why are you here?" she blurted. "I thought we were done for the night. What's wrong?"

He let out a breath, then crossed back to her, reached a hand around and securely closed the door behind them, flipping the lock.

"Nothing's wrong," he said.

Towering over her, his body was so close she could hear his heart pounding as he stared down at her through eyes that had deepened to the color of tempered chocolate.

"And you and I are far from done."

The soft, sonorous timbre of his voice reverberated through her insides, settling deep in her pelvis. Instinctively, she pressed her thighs together. The motion made her gasp as her legs quivered.

Stacy had to tip her head back to maintain eye contact with him when he moved in closer. She'd thought his eyes were hot and piercing before. She wasn't prepared for the cavernous, endless depths of them right now.

One hand circled around her waist, the other slipping under her hair to cup her neck. With the pad of his thumb, he rubbed her cheek, his gentle touch firing off nerve endings all the way to her toes.

"I don't know what you mean." She was barely able to speak above a whisper.

"No?" His mouth pulled back into a wicked grin. "Then let me explain."

When he'd kissed her before, he'd started with just a gentle brush of his lips against hers, telling her without words what he wanted, patiently awaiting her response.

It seemed he had no patience for waiting this time around. From the first touch of his mouth against hers, Nikko took control.

Complete, total, and absolute control.

And Stacy was unable to fight against it. In truth, she craved the domination.

His lips were masterful as they glided over hers, stripping her of any will she still had— which wasn't much. He took possession of her tongue without waiting for permission, captured it, and claimed it for his own.

And once again, Stacy acquiesced without a thought.

While his mouth took ownership of her lips, his hands laid claim to her body, a body that now shuddered and quaked with every brush of his touch.

He nestled her butt in the span of his hands and then with one easy lift had her wrapping her legs around his waist as he walked her to the room's love seat, never breaking contact between their lips.

Falling back on to the cushions, he settled in with her straddling his lap, while his hands roamed under the bottom of her long sleep shirt and up her naked back.

The feel of him throbbing and pulsating underneath her, had Stacy offering up a silent thanks she'd put a new thong on after her shower. If she'd left it off, as she usually did while sleeping, she'd be naked and pressed against his pulsing length and he'd know just how much she wanted him.

Nikko kneaded the exposed skin over her butt, his strong fingers massaging and flexing against her skin. When he slipped one finger under the thin strip covering her, she startled. He removed his hands to rub up her back and along her sides, instead.

A brush of his knuckles over the sides of her breasts had her shifting back just enough for him to cup them both. Rubbing his thumbs over her swollen and hard-as-marble nipples, she heard herself groan from down deep in her chest while his fingers continued their amatory movements.

She should stop him, stop this. Right now. It couldn't go any further; shouldn't. Their relationship was supposed to be professional. She was here to help run the show, make sure it was produced without any problems, time or money concerns. She was supposed to be keeping Nikko's temper in check, his demands low, and get the show finished on schedule.

She wasn't here to be gloriously tortured by the feel of the man in whose lap she was nestled. That had never been part of the bargain with Teddy Davis.

None of those points mattered at the moment. All that did was how wonderful she felt being seduced by a man who knew what he was doing and had decided she was the one he wanted to do it with.

Stacy snaked her fingers down the front of his shirt, dexterously popping open each button on her trek until she was able to freely glide her hands over the concrete wall of his chest. With little circling and pinching motions she teased his nipples into pebbles, rewarded when she felt him flinch beneath her.

If she'd been paying full attention, she would have realized his intent before he lifted the hem of her shirt up her back and almost had it over her head. As he did, he brushed over her upper arm and the back of her shoulder and when his fingers felt the texture of the skin over her bicep, he stopped trying to get her shirt off.

As if she'd dropped into a lake of ice-covered water, Stacy froze.

Gently, Nikko pulled back from the kiss. Except for the loud drumming of both their hearts, silence surrounded them.

Stacy dropped her chin. She couldn't look at him, was terrified to. She already knew what she'd see in his eyes.

"Look at me," he said, his voice soft and warm.

She kept her chin down, shook her head.

Nikko swiped back the hair falling and shielding her face and tilted her chin up, forcing her to.

"Stacy."

"You should go," she said, darting a quick glance at him, and then settling on his shoulder. With a solid tug she yanked her shirt back down, willing herself not to come undone. "You shouldn't be here. This isn't…" She tried for a careless shrug, but couldn't pull it off.

Pushing against his chest, she tried to lift off his lap.

Nikko wouldn't let her. His hands wove themselves back around her waist, holding her in place.

"Stacy, look at me," he said again. "Look at me, sweetheart."

The endearment shattered through her. When she finally did, she felt the hot sting of tears drop down her cheeks.

Nikko reached out and swiped at them with the pads of his thumbs. Then, in a move so gentle it threatened to undo her even more, he pushed the sleeve of her shirt up to her shoulder to bare her entire arm. He made sure the loose sleeve didn't fall back by bunching it between his fingers and holding it in place. With his other hand, his fingers caressed the blanched, puckered, scarified skin covering her from wrist to shoulder.

Back and forth, up and down, he traced the line of the scars, his eyes following the trek of his hand.

From under her lashes, Stacy ventured a glance at him. Past experience with men had told her disgust—or worse, *pity*—would be in his eyes.

He had neither.

Nikko met her gaze with his own and wrapped his entire hand around her scarred upper arm.

Most of the nerve endings had long been destroyed and her perception of touch over the area was slight at the best of times. But she could feel when his hand hugged her arm, holding her firm.

"Tell me how this happened," he commanded. When she stayed silent, he asked again. "Tell me."

"I need a drink of water," she said, instead. "Let me up."

In answer, Nikko stretched to the mini-fridge next to the love seat and pulled two unopened bottles from it with his free hand.

He handed her one, took the other for himself.

"Drink," he said. "Then talk."

"You're as bossy as your reputation asserts," she said, then winced when she heard the nasty tinge in her voice.

He chuckled while she dragged her hand across her face to dry her cheeks and then took a long pull from the bottle.

He did the same and when he was done, settled his hands casually around her waist.

Stacy had never had to explain her accident to a man before. When intimacy occurred, she'd usually give a quick excuse and then convince the guy sex was better with the lights out. Feeling her skin was very different from seeing it and the guys usually acquiesced to her request.

Instinctively, she knew that wasn't going to work with Nikko Stamp, just as she knew he'd require—*demand*—a full explanation of what had happened to her.

"Talk to me," he said.

With a nod, she gathered her thoughts.

"When I was six, I had pneumonia. Pretty badly. At one point, the pediatrician advised my parents to call our parish priest because it looked like I was going to…die soon. As you can see," she looked up at him and shrugged, "I didn't. But I was in the hospital for over a month and then I recouped at home for a long, long time after that before I started to feel better. Be better. The doctor said my lungs had been scarred and the chance of getting sick again was increased more than usual because of it. My parents kind of lost their minds when they heard that."

"As a parent myself, I can understand why."

She nodded. "Yeah, you probably can." She sighed and repositioned herself. When his eyes crossed and a flash of pain zipped across his face, his hands bit into her waist.

"I'm sorry. I'm sorry," she said, close to tears again. "Let me up. I'm hurting you."

Nikko swallowed and let out a thready breath between his lips. In a tight voice, he said, "No. *Hurting* isn't the word."

Her face caught on fire from the heat rushing up from her neck.

"Just…sit still," he said, "and I'll be fine."

She watched him for a few moments until his breathing eased again. "Talk."

She swallowed. "Overnight my parents turned insanely overprotective. I wasn't allowed outside to play, especially in the fall and winter. I wasn't allowed to run around, get sweaty, get dirty like all the other kids did. I never learned how to ride a bike. They kept me indoors most of the time just to ensure I wouldn't catch so much as a cold. I grew up like some banished princess, secured from the world in a guarded castle."

She took another sip of water.

"When I turned fourteen… well, my father describes it to this day as the time his little princess turned to the dark side. I was sick of being the protected child. I wanted to be normal like everyone else."

"I can understand that as well."

"Maybe. But it's different for boys." She shook her head. "Really different. My brother skated through his teens. Anything he did wrong, like borrow the car without asking, or coming home with beer on his breath from an underage party, was chalked up to boys-will-be-boys behavior. A little slap on the wrist and he was free to go. I wasn't allowed the same freedom. It really sucked to be me."

"So is this when you went to the dark side?" His lips twisted up as he asked it, and the understanding in his tone warmed through her.

"Yeah. I started sneaking out after my parents went to bed. Found some friends—older friends—who thought nothing of corrupting a little Goody Two-shoes like me. I started drinking beer, then hard liquor if it was available. I was scared to try cigarettes or pot, though. One whiff of smoke in the surrounding area was enough to start me coughing and I was terrified my lungs were gonna fail, just like my pediatrician had predicted. Anyway, one night, I got into a car with an older boy who went to the same high school as me, for a ride."

"As the father of a teenaged girl, I can tell you those words strike abject fear in my heart and soul."

"They should." She sighed again and when Nikko rubbed his hands up her back to settle on her shoulders and began to knead, she leaned into him as if the move were as natural as breathing.

"I wanted to be cool, be liked by the older kids. When he asked me if I wanted to ride around with him, I knew—*I knew*—I shouldn't, especially since he'd had a couple of beers before he asked me."

"Strike that: Not just fear. Absolute terror. What happened?"

"People do stupid things when they've been drinking," she said. "When the people drinking are also wild teenage boys hell-bent on making themselves look cool, those stupid things expand exponentially." She took a sip of water again.

"He wanted to impress me by showing me how fast his car could go, so he sped up and started dragging down one of the neighborhood streets. When he tried to negotiate a tight turn, he lost control. The car swerved a few times, then hit a light pole head-on. We weren't wearing our seat belts because we were too cool, and the car didn't have airbags like they do now. There was nothing to restrain us or cushion us."

She stopped, reliving the moment as she had so many times before. No amount of therapy could ever fully remove it from her mind. The cringe-causing, spine-tingling sound of metal scraping against metal; the boy's screams when the door crushed into his side. After, when...

She felt his hands tighten as he continued to knead her neck. "Tell me the rest of it, Stacy, because I know there's more. These are burn scars, aren't they?"

She nodded again and took a deep breath. "From the impact, I got tossed onto the dash and knocked out for a few seconds. The engine exploded into flames and before I could be pulled to safety, my sleeve ignited. I was admitted to the hospital with deep second- and third-degree burns on my arm and upper back and I was in a coma from the head trauma for over a week. Just like when I was six, I was in the hospital again for another extended amount of time. Two necessary surgeries to set the broken bone in my upper arm; three painful, horrible skin-grafting procedures before my fifteenth birthday, and then enough excruciating physical therapy sessions to last me a lifetime, and here we are."

"When you told me you knew something about how to deal with pain, you were speaking from experience," he said after a few moments.

"Yeah. The surgeries were bad enough. The graftings hurt so much the docs medicated me into a zombie-state for most of the time. But it was the PT that almost did me in, pain-wise."

His brows pulled together in the middle of his forehead. "Why?"

She took another sip of water and looked down at her knees. "Muscle contractures. They're a by-product of severe burns and grafting. Everything stiffens as it heals. The bones knit together, the muscles, even the skin under the grafts. Moving makes it hurt more because it's all so raw, so you tend not to move to avoid the pain. But when muscles aren't used, they tighten up. Then it hurts even more to move them." She snuck a glance up at his face. "You get the idea."

"It's a vicious circle." He nodded. "Like you told me about my leg. Not using it, not exercising it, makes the pain worse."

"It does. I had six hours of PT every day for four months in the hospital and then another six months as an outpatient. When I was finally discharged from the service, my physical therapist told me she'd never had another patient so determined before. She didn't know the reason I was so determined was because I'd do anything so my arm wouldn't look freakish. Contractures aren't pretty and my arm already looked like it had been put through a meat grinder."

Nikko rubbed the scars with tips of his fingers again as she spoke. Then, in a move so uncharacteristic, Stacy had to blink a few times to ensure it really happened, Nikko bent to scrape his lips over the area.

His crooked grin, when he pulled back, filled her heart. "Melora was a big fan of kissing the hurt away when she was little."

"If only it was that easy." She swiped at her teary eyes again.

"This is why you never show your arms?"

She nodded.

"Because you're, what? Embarrassed by the scars?"

"Well, they're not exactly pleasant to look at. People usually react one of three ways when they see them." She ticked the ways off on her fingers. "One, they get all pop-eyed and want to know chapter, book, and verse about what happened." She looked pointedly at him when she said it. He looked back at her, his face blank. "Two, they get grossed out, wince, and ask me to cover them, hide them."

"And the third?"

"The worst one. They don't ask any questions, just look at me with pity, like I was a leper or scheduled to die at sunrise or something. I hate that one most of all."

Nikko brought one of her hands to his lips and kissed the knuckles. When his tongue grazed against them, she shifted her hips again. Tiny electrical pulses shot from her hand straight down to her groin.

He spun her hand and pressed his lips to her palm, his gaze never wavering from hers.

Running a hand over the scarified tissue again, he said, "You've seen the scars on my leg. They're raw and fresh and not very pleasant to look at. And yet..." he chucked her under the chin, forcing her to look at him again. "And yet I never saw an ounce of pity, or disgust, or fascination in your eyes the night you tended to me. All I saw was kindness."

"You were in pain," she said, carelessly flipping a hand in the air. "I knew I could help."

"Yeah. And you did." He pulled her in for a quick kiss. "Even though I'd been acting like a prick to you. Rude, nasty. Overbearing. You still showed me compassion when it would have been so easy to just forget about everything and walk away."

"No. No, I could never walk away from someone in pain. Especially if I could help ease it."

It was Nikko's turn to nod. "I realized that about you that night. You have a kind heart. You're generally a kind person."

"Not always," she admitted.

"From everything I've seen," he said. "And certainly if you use Melora as a yardstick."

"I told you before: I know what it's like being that age and being, well..."

"What? Say it."

"Angry. Powerless. Consumed."

He squeezed her neck and slid his fingers up to her face again, caressing her skin along the way. "Interesting word choices. Explain them."

She swallowed. Hard.

"At one point in my recovery I was so angry about everything. Angry at my parents because I blamed them for being overprotective. Angry at myself for being so stupid to get in that car. Angry with the boy—who was dead—for being so irresponsible as to drink and drive. I was even angry at my cousins because they got to have normal, pain-free lives while I had to spend most of what should have been my sophomore year in high school confined to a hospital bed. I was so angry I just wanted to die. Dying would get rid of the pain, on the inside and the outside. I just wanted the pain to go away."

Nikko took her chin between his hands and forced her to look back at him. "What happened?"

She debated with herself for a moment about whether or not to tell him the full story.

"Sweetheart, talk to me." Nikko kissed her lips so tenderly she wanted to cry again. "I want to know. Please."

She sniffed, then nodded. "I was still in the hospital after the last surgery to align the bone. The pain was beyond excruciating. Really, there needs to be a better word to describe it. Anyway. A new girl was admitted one night, my age. We... well, we hit it off. She was smart and funny in a totally snarky way, and I just adored her. We spent all the time we could together. We talked about everything. Held nothing back. She was supposed to be discharged over the weekend, but..." she stopped, tears springing up again.

Stacy dropped her chin to her chest and bit down on her bottom lip. Nikko said nothing, just kept his hands back on her waist, holding her, waiting.

"She, she...died. Before she could be discharged. Her heart gave out. When I saw what her death did to her parents, how destroyed they were, I stopped being angry. Stopped wanting to die, and started looking for ways to control the pain. To fight it. Through my physical therapist, I found a yoga teacher who helped me heal. Inside and out."

"I'm almost afraid to ask," he said, "but why did that girl's heart give out? She was, what? Fifteen?"

She nodded.

"Did she have a congenital heart defect or something that weakened it?"

Instead of answering him outright, she said, "Remember when I told you I understood how Melora felt? About the stressors of being a teenager, torn between wanting to be treated like an adult and yet still being a child?"

"Yeah."

"I know how she feels because my roommate, the one who died, was admitted in an advanced state of anorexia."

She heard and felt the breath push from between his lips.

"She hadn't eaten any real food in so long, her heart grew weak. So I do understand the challenges Melora has been facing."

He didn't say anything, just kept his hands on her waist and continued to stare at her.

She knew she'd overstepped. Stacy had no right, none at all, to call attention to so private a matter. Her only excuse was she cared for the girl, deeply, and she more than cared for the father.

"How long—" Nikko said, then stopped, pressing his lips together so tight the outer rims blanched.

"What?"

His throat bobbed as he swallowed. "How long had the girl been suffering from the eating disorder?"

"Since she was ten."

"Five years?"

Stacy nodded. "A third of her life devoted to intentional starvation."

"What...what triggered it? Do you know?"

"Yeah. Her mother had been a professional dancer and Kitty—that was her name—had been taking ballet lessons since she could walk. Her mom never made it big and had shoved all her plans for fame onto Kitty. When she turned ten, she started noticing the other girls in her ballet glass were a lot skinnier than she was, and were getting better and bigger dancing roles in shows and pageants. She asked her mom how she could look like they did."

"Don't tell me this kid's mother was the one who told her to stop eating."

"I wish I could, but she was."

"*Christ.*"

"Her dad didn't know about it until Kitty was well into the cycle of starving and purging. By then, too much damage had been done to her heart."

Nikko closed his eyes and leaned his head back on the sofa back. "Melora's eating issues started with the death of her mother."

"So, not too long ago."

"No. But I didn't notice it for a while. I was so busy trying to be a single, working dad. When she told me she'd already eaten when I got home from work, I believed her. When she said she'd grab breakfast at school with friends, I let it go."

"When did you find out?"

"When she passed out at school. The nurse called me and in the emergency room she told the resident she hadn't eaten anything—*anything*—in three days. And I'd never even noticed."

He shook his head so violently, Stacy's body shook.

The need to comfort was so strong in her, she instinctively reached out and took his face in her hands. With the slightest of movements, he burrowed a cheek into her palm.

"You know it's not your fault, right? You didn't cause this to happen to Melora."

On a sigh, he said, "Yeah. The therapist we've been seeing assured me of that. It's all about control, she said."

Stacy nodded.

Nikko slammed his eyes closed, squeezing so much the lines at the corners furrowed into deep grooves. "It's so damn hard," he said when he opened them again, "to know how to help her. Who to trust and believe. The therapist she saw in the hospital wanted her to be admitted for up to six months. The minute she said that and I saw how terrified Mel was of the thought, I started researching other therapists who specialize in eating disorders. The one we've been seeing came highly recommended. I've done everything she's suggested. I've adjusted my schedule so I can cook for her. Not balk if she only eats a fraction of what I make. Stay with her after she eats so she doesn't run off and get rid of it. But I'm still so damn scared something is gonna happen even after doing all that."

"For what it's worth, she's as concerned about you as you are about her. She worries about your leg and your pain level a lot. And," she added, "I'm sure she's just as scared that something is going to happen. But to you. She's already lost one parent. She's probably terrified of losing you, as well."

Nikko spit out an oath. "The two of us are some screwed-up pair."

"As an outsider looking in, I think you're a terrific pair," she said, honestly. "You love one another a great deal and it shows in everything you both say and do. Please believe that."

His hands were still around her, casually placed on her waist, holding her in position on his lap. She'd tried to ignore the tiny, unconscious circular motions he made with the pads of his fingers while they'd both been speaking, but was having a difficult time doing so. His fingers, like his hands and everything else about him, were long, strong, and thick.

As if realizing what he was doing for the first time, Nikko's glance dropped to where she was perched on top of him, her naked knees drawn up against the outside of his thighs.

His grip tightened when his looked back up at her.

Something shifted in his eyes as he stared at her. Warmed, then heated, then—she swore—turned molten.

Her mouth went desert-dry and she became acutely aware of her sitting position. Especially when she felt him pitch, roll, and lengthen beneath her.

"You know, I didn't come knocking on your door tonight looking for sympathy and understanding."

"No?" She had trouble getting the simple word out.

"No."

His lids went to half-mast, his mouth pulling up at one corner. With the merest press of his fingers against the small of her back, he moved her in closer, so close the heat of his breath warmed over her.

"If I'd had to wait another moment to do this, when it's all I've been able to think about for days, I don't know how I would have gotten through the night."

It was on the tip of her tongue to ask what he meant. Before she could, he showed her.

In the time it took her to form the question in her mind, Nikko had his mouth on hers, his arms pressing her body against his again, and her pulse jumping beneath her skin.

She didn't think. About anything but how good, how really good, it felt to be kissed by him.

The tips of her fingers scampered across his pecs and she swore they came away singed. Stacy had tasted desire before, but had never been consumed by it as she was right now. Every rake and slide of his hands on her body sent a million little fireballs exploding through her system.

She welcomed the inferno, ran headfirst into it.

The hottest, wettest part of her felt the long, long line of him throb along the heat hidden by her panties.

"Do you have any idea what I've been going through?" he rasped against her ear. "I'd welcome my leg pain back if it could take my mind off remembering what you taste like; feel like." His wet lips slid along the column of her throat. She threw back her head to give him full access.

"Knowing you were sitting right behind me every day and I couldn't touch you has been torture. Pure—" he sucked the skin at her collarbone, making her cry out—"torture."

Gathering her hair between his hands, a quick tug had her looking him in the eye.

She almost came undone just from the unbridled want on his face. Reaching up, she smoothed her finger along the grooves on his forehead, down the corners of his eyes to his chin. A quick nip at a corner of his chiseled jaw had him sucking in a breath.

He angled her face back to his, sought her lips, and laid claim to them.

"No woman has ever distracted me from working before," he said against her cheek.

Stacy didn't bite back her laugh quick enough.

"You're laughing at that?"

She stared him square in the eye and trailed a finger across his swollen mouth. Swollen from kissing her.

Good Lord.

"*I* distract *you* from your work?" she asked, her own kiss-slicked lips pressing together. "You don't have a clue what it's been like for me, do you? One minute you look as if you're going to throw something at me, in the next your eyes get so hot they scorch with just a passing glance. Do you have any idea what that's been doing to me?"

His slid his hand across her shoulder, pulling the T-shirt to the side, allowing the edges of the scarring to be seen.

He dipped his head and pressed the gentlest of kisses along the scar line. Stacy's heart tumbled and turned over and she had no will or power to stop it.

"You're so polished and perfect and prepared all the time," he said, punctuating each description with a kiss along the scars. "Tapping away on that damn notebook device. You make me want to ruffle your feathers just so I can see you lose that control."

"I'm far from perfect. Anytime." She tilted her head back so his mouth would have better access to her jawline. "Oh!"

His evil chuckle at her response sent a shock wave up her spine. One finger dipped down her back, across the thin strap of her thong and pulled it to the side.

"I want you, Stacy. Too much for my own good, I know it. But I want you. I've never slept with a coworker before, that's the truth. Too many potential problems, hurt feelings—*Christ*, even the threat of a sexual-harassment suit, have all been valid reasons not to."

He cupped her butt cheeks in his hands and ground up into her. The sensation of all his hard, long length meeting her wet heat sent her heart jackhammering.

"But I don't care about any of those reasons when I think about being with you. When I imagine what you'll feel like coming apart in my hands. You make me forget every single one of those excuses. And probably a half-dozen more," he added with what sounded like surprise.

Stacy laid her forehead against his and sighed. "I forget about all the rules and the reasons they're put there in the first place too, whenever I'm around you." She pulled back and laid her hands on his chest for support and felt his heart drumming. "But I'm afraid."

Nikko lifted one of her hands to his lips and kissed it. "Of?"

"So many things." With a dry laugh, she hung her head again.

"But not of me, right? You're not afraid of me, are you, sweetheart?"

A week ago she would have told him she was. Now? There was no way she could say that and have it not be a lie.

She laid a hand across his cheek and placed a kiss on the corner of his mouth. "I feel a great many things for you, Dominick Stamp, but fear isn't even on the list."

She moved, pressed her lips against his and in the time it took an old-fashioned clock to tick once, he changed the kiss.

Hunger and frenzied need rose up while his mouth took possession once again. A desire she'd never known before coiled deep, deep inside her, screaming to be unwound.

Nikko wrenched his mouth from hers just long enough to rip her shirt up and over her head before his lips circled around one breast and tugged the nipple between his teeth.

Fisting his hair between her fingers, Stacy arched and rose up, balanced on her knees, from Nikko's lap. She cried out in the next moment as his hand snaked down and cupped her.

"*Good Christ.* You're drenched." With slow, steady, and determined fingers, he stroked, front to back, over the thin wisp of material covering her skin. Stacy's hips began to rock to the same tempo. With a sound she could only describe as feral, Nikko ripped the material from her body in one swift move, allowing his hand free access now to her bare flesh.

His fingers glided along her length, then snuck one, two inside her. While he slowly pumped in and out, his thick thumb circled around her clitoris, pressing, easing, then pressing again, zeroing all her attention to that one spot.

A slow burn of liquid heat flamed down her spine. Her breathing turned coarse and shallow as his movements quickened. Blood pounded so loud in her temples, she was amazed it didn't deafen them both.

Nikko shifted and moved her to the sofa, flat on her back. He knelt and, with his hand never leaving her body, replaced his thumb with his mouth. Stacy's hips shot up, the orgasm ripping through her with no warning and no way to slow it down.

Her insides clenched around his fingers, her thighs imprisoning him as the quaking peaked higher and higher until she swore her body would burst. She had no idea how long she lay, suspended, floating on the crest. All concept of time ceased and all she could do was feel.

Nikko rode the storm out with her. When she opened her eyes, she took a ragged breath and found him staring at her, his own gaze hooded, but piercing right to her very soul.

"That was…" She couldn't find words descriptive enough.

"Just the beginning," he said.

A gentle tug and he lifted her in his arms and moved them to the turned down bed.

"Why am I the only one naked?" she asked, pushing up on her elbows after he laid her down and tossed the extra pillows to the floor. He stood at the foot of the bed, just watching her.

"Because you're prettier than I am."

Her skin blushed from toes to scalp, as his words warmed her insides.

He grinned, toed off his shoes, undid his pants, and let them drop to the floor. Stacy crept to her knees and popped the buttons she hadn't already opened on his shirt, then pushed it down his arms.

With her hands flattened on his chest, she nipped at his jaw and worked her way down his shoulders to his pecs. "You're built like a fortress," she said as she twined her fingers into the curly blue-black hair cloaking his torso. "Solid and hard."

"I'm hard, all right," he quipped. "Harder than I've been in a long time." She watched his eyes cross again, his jaw slack open as he flung his head back when she wound her hand over the hardest, hottest part of him.

She hummed her approval while her hand tugged up his length. Her gaze fell to the jagged, raw, and puckered skin traversing his thigh. As he'd done to her, Stacy pressed her lips against the scar and skimmed a gentle kiss over it.

When she glanced up to see him watching her, her thoughts turned wicked. With a subtle shift in position, she brought her filled hand to her mouth, flicked her tongue once across his tip—rewarded when he hissed, his stomach muscles going concave—and then filled her mouth with him.

Just as she was delighting in the hot, salty, *manly* taste of him, Nikko pushed back on her shoulder and lifted her.

"Sweetheart, I wasn't kidding when I said it's been a long time. You keep doing that and it's gonna be over way too fast."

Stacy giggled and scooted back up on the bed.

Nikko crawled over her, propped himself on his elbows, and nestled himself between her thighs. He scraped his hands along her temples and cupped her neck. "Do you have any idea what that sound does to me?"

"What sound?" She reached up and nipped at his chin.

His mouth captured hers, delightfully torturing her for a few moments.

"When you laugh like that, all free and easy, it settles me, calms me when I didn't even know I was tense. It's odd, but the happy sound you make makes me happy."

She filled his cheek with her palm. "That's one of the sweetest things I think anyone has ever said to me."

He cocked an eyebrow, his mouth pulling down at one corner. She almost giggled again, but he stopped her by saying, "I'll show you *sweet*," right before he laid claim to her lips.

After that, laughing was the last thing on her mind.

How was it possible for such a big, hard, and arrogant man to be so gentle and considerate a lover?

Stacy felt cherished with every caress of his hand along her bare skin; treasured when he trailed his lips across every inch of her body. And when he slid into her after donning a condom, slowly, gradually, filling her inch by inch, and then slipping out again in the same torpid tempo, she knew for the first time in her life what it truly meant to be made love to.

This wasn't just sex, simply two people slaking a need, giving in to a mutual desire.

This was different. It was...more.

Better.

When he trembled above her, she knew he was fighting for control. He wasn't joking when he'd told her he was hard and wanting. Stacy skimmed her hands down his sweat-slicked back, over the tight and corded muscles, to land on his butt. With flattened palms, she lifted up to him, and wrapped her legs around his waist to keep him secured.

"Stacy—"

"Don't hold back from me," she whispered. "I can feel you holding back." She eased up and kissed his lips, tasted salt, and licked it from him. "I want you to come inside me. Now. Right now."

Lifting her hips higher with his hands, he buried in deeper, a hot, ragged gasp pulling from his soul.

He exploded into her, his shoulders and arms shaking with the force of the effort it took not to collapse on top of her.

What would he think if he knew she craved just that?

"Come here," she said, placing a kiss on his cheek and pushing against his back with her hands. "Rest on me."

The pulse at his neck thrummed against her shoulder when he placed his head down next to hers.

With tiny feather strokes, she caressed his back, his shoulders, his waist; until his breathing eased.

One final, deep exhale against her neck and he rose up on his elbows again. Through eyes that were half closed and totally sated, he looked down at her.

"You're a bossy little thing when the spirit moves you, aren't you?"

She grinned, her pulse jumping again when he kissed her mouth.

He levered up and went into the bathroom. She heard him flush the condom, run the water in the tap. Before settling back next to her on the bed, he grabbed the two opened, forgotten water bottles, handed her one, and then took a long, full pull from his own.

"You look very thoughtful right now," she said, gazing at him from under her lashes. "Having regrets already?"

She'd kept her voice light. She didn't want him to worry she'd suddenly turn into some clawing, clingy coworker. She wasn't a child or naïve.

His head shot up, his eyebrows kissing. She'd purposefully kept her face soft, her lips tugging up at the corners.

"I am thoughtful, but it's not about regrets."

He reached over and grabbed her free hand, brought it to his lips, and kissed it. "It's about where we go from here."

Stacy was astonished she could keep herself in check. His words weren't what she'd thought to hear.

"Where would you like to go?" she asked, her heart jumping just a bit when he drew one of her knuckles into his mouth and lazily ran his tongue across it.

"If I had a say, we'd stay right here until we got kicked out," he said, shaking his head and grinning at her.

She pulled her hand from his, leaned forward while cupping his cheek, and kissed him. "Sounds like a plan. Unfortunately, we can't. You have a show to finish."

He settled down on his back and cuddled her next to him. With her head now on his shoulder, her fingers drew lazy circles on his chest.

He kissed her temple. "I wasn't lying before when I told you I've never been involved with someone while working on the same show together."

Stacy shifted and tossed her top leg over his, the gesture intimate and arousing. "I can't say the same because I did, once. When I was working on Kandy's show."

"Obviously, it didn't work out," he said, snaking a hooded glance at her, "because you're here. With me."

She kissed his pec and said, "Yeah, but not for any reasons you can come up with. I found out the guy was using me to get to Kandy."

It still stung to this day to admit she'd been so blind and naïve during that time.

When Nikko asked for details, because of course he wouldn't just let it go—no surprise there—she told him about the assistant director who'd stalked and terrified her cousin for weeks in a feeble attempt to get her show canceled so he could take advantage of a film-directing offer. Kandy's staff contracts were ironclad and anyone who wanted to leave the hit show had to pay out half to three quarters of their salaries for the time left on the contract. For an assistant director like Mark Begman, who'd made 90,000 a year, he had to come up with almost 200,000 dollars to be set free of his work obligation. Money he didn't have and couldn't get.

He'd started paying attention to Stacy over a course of a few weeks, wined and dined her, and then just as quickly let the relationship drift. Only after he'd been arrested did the private investigator hired to look into Kandy's stalker discover Begman had targeted Stacy because she was a direct link to her cousin. He wanted to get information to use in his campaign to drive the cooking-show host to a nervous breakdown, thereby canceling her show.

"Luckily, the PI I hired, Josh Keane, figured it all out before Kandy or anyone else could be seriously hurt."

"Wait...Keane? Isn't that Kandy's married name?"

Stacy smiled and nuzzled his neck. "Yeah. Josh proposed the second the case wrapped up."

He didn't say anything. After a few moments, Stacy rose up on her elbow. "Nikko?"

He turned his gaze to her. "That's the first time you've ever called me by my first name. I like the way it sounds on your lips." He gave the spot in a question a quick buss. "As if it belongs there. Call me that from now on. No more of this *Mr. Stamp* crap, or waiting until I look at you for you to speak to me."

Because that's exactly what she'd done, she couldn't help laughing. "Ah, there's the arrogant Dominick Stamp the world is used to."

One eyebrow crept up to his uncombed hairline. Mimicking her position, Nikko settled on one elbow and traced a finger from her temple to the point of her chin. "Here's some more arrogance for you," he said. "I don't want this to end when I leave this bed, Stacy. We started something tonight, something... I don't know. Special, maybe?" He shook his head. "Different? I can't find the right word, but I don't want it to end. I want to keep seeing you and not only when we're on the job. Off it too. How do you feel about that? Do you want to continue this?"

Without a moment's thought, she said, "Yes."

"Good." He kissed her again. "Good."

With a nimble move that belied his bulk, he had her pinned under him, his mouth doing wild and wicked things to hers. Against her thigh she felt him grow, her own desire drenching within her again.

She widened her hips and let him nestle in the cradle she'd made for him. Just as she could feel his desire pulsing against her, she knew he could feel hers as well.

As his mouth dragged a sweet line down her throat, she mumbled, "There's something to be said for arrogance."

He laughed against her skin and made her tremble.

Chapter Nineteen

Please God, deliver him from pain-in-the-ass chefs and their explosive personalities.

Nikko blew a thick stream of air out through his nostrils and crossed his arms over his chest as he watched two of the contestants shouting at one another on the monitor.

"What caused this blowup?" he asked Todd. "I was watching the MacNeill kid on the other screen when this started."

The camera chief shook his head. "Cayman wanted Chinese-five spice for his recipe and Burbank *allegedly* took the only sample we had in stock."

The sound of raised and heated voices blared through the tent.

"Should we stop rolling and get someone over there to break it up before it comes to blows?" Todd asked, his eyes nervously darting across the monitor as the two chefs stood, toe to toe, hands fisted at their sides, continuing to shout at one another.

Nikko considered for a half second before saying, "No. It won't come to that. Burbank's a dick, but he likes his pretty face too much to stick it out and potentially get it smashed."

A strangled giggle came from behind him. Nikko glanced over his shoulder at Stacy, who quickly bent her head, her gaze intently focusing on her notebook. A ghost of a smile played across her mouth.

It gave him a warm and calm sensation just knowing she was settled behind him.

"My bet is he'll charm his way out of this in about three more seconds," Nikko predicted, turning his attention back to the ruckus.

As predictions went, it was fairly accurate. The crew watched as Clay Burbank grinned and then handed something to Alonzo Cayman. Cayman took it, his mouth pulled tight and his body language still on the defensive. But he'd stopped yelling. When Clay held out his hand, the other chef took it, reluctantly if Nikko was to guess, pumped it once, and then stormed off back to his station. The camera stayed fixed on Burbank, his grin turning cocky as he went back to preparing his dish.

"See?" Nikko said. He leaned back in the chair and took a hit from the water bottle he knew Stacy had placed on the console. "Guy's a class-A chef, but a douche, just the same."

Stacy's walkie-talkie sounded. Nikko turned again to see her lift from her chair and move out of the truck. His gaze settled on her cute, tight butt as she left the area and for a hot moment he remembered how it had felt, naked and perfect, in his hands.

Since coming back from Big Sky three days ago, they'd gone back to their pre-intimacy professional relationship while production was underway. Stacy had assumed her executive producer role without pause, putting out fires when she had to and keeping him apprised of problems both real and potential along the way. He was sure no one in the crew or cast suspected anything had changed between them.

But it had.

After he was assured Melora was asleep each night, Nikko would leave the cabin and take the back path up to the main house. Amos Dixon never locked the front door, so he was able to sneak up the stairs and to Stacy's wing unseen. He felt like a teenager again, slipping out after curfew, exhilarated at the prospect of spending a few stolen hours with her.

A swift rap on her door and he'd have her in his arms within a heartbeat. Everything he'd fantasized about doing to her, and for her, during the hours they were enslaved with the production, he now gave free vent to. Stacy matched him, passion for passion, peak for peak, giving as good as she got.

Stacy Peters was a different woman from any and all he'd known before. She asked nothing of him and gave him everything. There was no hidden agenda with her, something common with so many other women he knew. *Unselfish* was the term he thought best to describe her. She never lost her temper in situations he knew would have caused him to explode. She was kind, but firm in her dealings with the producers and the other crew, and once she was brought into a situation, it was usually resolved to everyone's satisfaction.

After those all-too-swift hours alone together, where Stacy would fall asleep, cradled in his arms, Nikko, with a heavy heart, would leave her with a kiss on her brow and head back to his own bed.

In the morning, he would hear Melora trying her best to be quiet while getting ready for her dawn workouts with Stacy. They mutually decided to keep their relationship a secret from his daughter for a number of reasons. Since coming back from the production shoot, the teen seemed happier than she had in quite a while and he knew a big part of the reason was his executive producer. He didn't want anything to jeopardize her recovery—Stacy agreed—knowing that any little blip could send her off the deep end again emotionally, and the mutual agreement to keep their budding relationship from the girl seemed sound.

A sudden realization he too was happier than he'd been in years, radiated through him as he watched the chefs scramble to finish. And it wasn't just the fact he was getting laid, although the sex was phenomenal all by itself. For all her spit and polish, cool and controlled demeanor, Stacy Peters was an uninhibited and thoroughly sensual lover. He'd shown her that her physical scars in no way detracted from the fact that he desired her. Once she was convinced of his sincerity, she'd given herself completely to him without reserve.

No, it was the woman he was rapidly coming to view as important in more than just her professional capacity that he could claim made him happy.

He regretted treating her so horribly when she'd first arrived. The look of fear on her face when he'd railed at her the day she'd taken Melora to the airport still haunted him and he vowed he'd never make her frightened of him ever again.

"You lucked out, you know," Todd said from next to him, pulling him back to the production.

"What do you mean?"

Todd pointed his thumb over his shoulder and said, "Having Stacy Peters as your EP. You lucked out."

He knew it, but he was interested in why his camera chief thought as much, so he asked.

"Smart as they come and she's hard to ruffle. Plus, she's one of the nicest people I've ever known."

Nikko nodded.

"Having said that," Todd said, chuckling, "she's also kicking my ass into shape. Did you know she's now leading a yoga class at sunrise down by the lake?"

"I'd heard that. I saw it for myself when we were in Big Sky."

"Yeah, but the class has grown since word got out. She must have twenty people every day now. A few of my crew, and a bunch of the chefs, our wild child Burbank among them."

Shit.

The way Burbank had blatantly flirted with Stacy came back to him in a nanosecond. As did the conversation he'd overheard between them before filming began. The chef was obviously interested in her. Nikko recalled hearing of Burbank's man-whore rep prior to being chosen as one of the contestants. Back then he hadn't given it second thought.

That changed the moment he'd taken Stacy to bed.

"He's such a tool," Todd said with a droll grin and a shake of his head. "Drives Stacy nuts with all his questions and requests."

"Requests?"

"Mainly about how to get into some of the stances. 'How far do I spread my legs?' and 'This is gonna make my abs irresistibly touchable to the ladies.' Shit like that. Like I said, the guy's a tool."

Nikko bit down hard on his immediate response. So hard, he felt his back molars shift.

"Is it bothering Stacy? Making her uncomfortable?"

For the first time Todd turned, full face, to him. Nikko couldn't quite read the expression on the man's face.

"*No-oooo*," he drew the word out. "She can handle herself. Puts him in his place more times than not, making him look like the jerk he's acting. Nicely, of course, 'cause it's Stacy."

"Well, that's good."

His gaze flicked to the chef in question, who was currently putting the finishing garnish on his challenge dish. Nikko could feel Todd's gaze still on him. "What?"

A heartbeat passed before Todd asked, "I've known you, what? Eleven, twelve years?"

"About that. Why?"

"In all that time, through all the shows we've worked on together, you've never given one thought that wasn't a pissed-off one about any producer, executive or otherwise. Usually you just ignore them and act like they don't even exist."

Nikko knew the benefits of staying silent, so he did.

"And then, out of the blue, you ask me if I think Stacy Peters—an EP you screamed bloody murder about having out here—is feeling uncomfortable because of a few off-color comments from a guy she knows."

Nikko turned back to the screen after taking a quick look at the countdown clock. "What's your point, Todd?"

"I don't really have one. I just find your... well, *concern,* interesting."

"My concern is litigious in nature," he said, quickly thinking of something to satisfy the man's curiosity. "The last thing this production or the network needs is a sexual-harassment suit from her if Burbank is being inappropriate. Countdown in ten," he said into his microphone as Jade and Dan moved into the kitchen and took their places.

For the next few minutes both men were occupied with watching the monitors. Jade and Dan walked through the kitchen, sampling each dish and giving a quick commentary. For once, Nikko thought as he watched her, Jade Quartermaine was letter-perfect.

When the segment was finished, Nikko spied Stacy walk on set and speak to a few of the chefs and their individual producers who had gathered around. He tracked her as she moved from station to station, making comments and referring to her ever-present tablet as she did.

Her only concession to the deplorable dry heat engulfing the ranch was to pull her hair off her face and neck, held back by a wide scrunchie. The typical long-sleeved blouse she favored was a pale pink today, the color highlighting the gold in her hair. Tan trousers and tennis shoes finished the look. As usual, she was professional, proficient, and perfect and all Nikko could think was how much he longed to strip those polished clothes from her long, lean body and melt into her.

"Sexual harassment, my ass," he heard Todd mumble from behind. When he spun around, the camera chief began talking into his headset.

Nikko removed his own headset and finger-combed his hair.

It was time to make lunch for his daughter. The break was just what he needed.

While he walked from the trailer, he wondered what Stacy was doing for lunch.

* * * *

"This is, like, so cool," Melora said with a bright smile and childish glee in her voice. "I always have to eat lunch with just Daddy." Her eyes rolled 360 degrees. "It gets wicked boring, so it's nice to have someone else to talk to instead of just him."

It didn't get past her notice that the teen had called her father *Daddy*. It was at rare moments such as this, when Melora was open and free and not behaving like a typical, surly teenager, that Stacy could see the girl she'd probably been before her eating disorder, before her mother's death and her father's accident.

Nikko stopped pouring the iced tea he'd pulled from the refrigerator and slanted a squinty glare at his daughter. "I may be wrong, but I think you just tossed a boatload of shade at me, young lady."

Melora's eye roll was a thing of beauty, Stacy thought.

"It's, like, *amazeballs* you even know what throwing shade means, *old man.*"

Nikko placed the pitcher on the kitchen table and, in a speedy move which Stacy marveled at coming from such a big man, had Melora in a body lock, his arms circling her thin frame.

"Who you calling an old man?" He kissed her temple when she giggled. The sound touched Stacy's heart.

Nikko grinned at her over his daughter's head and then released his hold.

She'd been more than a little surprised when Nikko had found her in the set pantry going over the needed produce stock with one of the supply crew. Her tummy muscles did their usual giddyap when he entered the spacious room.

Not too long ago, those muscles would have tensed with nerves and worry whenever he sought her out. Now, the flutter was pure anticipation, laced with a sexual awareness that still stunned her.

Never in her wildest dreams would she have thought an affair with Dominick Stamp was in the cards when she agreed to work on the show.

Okay, well, maybe *affair* wasn't quite the right word. Stacy'd always considered it a tawdry and salacious way to describe a mature sexual liaison. Besides, they were two single and consenting adults, neither one in a marriage or a relationship, so *affair* really didn't do justice to the situation.

All semantics aside, she was unsure of exactly how to describe what she and Nikko were doing. Yes, they were having sex, and yes, they were keeping it a secret, both of them agreeing it was best for all concerned, mostly Melora. The last thing Stacy wanted was to compound the girl's precarious emotional state by admitting she and her father were involved, off set. And Stacy had her own reason for keeping her actions with Nikko a secret from his daughter: She didn't want anything to come between their own budding relationship.

Stacy truly loved being around the teen. Never having a sister of her own, Stacy had always been a little jealous of Kandy, her six sisters, and the unbreakable bond they shared.

True, Melora was over a decade younger, but the age difference didn't seem to matter much when they were together. Stacy sensed the girl needed a strong and supportive older woman in her life at the moment to act as a foil to her—at times—overbearing father.

"You *are* an old man," Melora said, slaking a glance at him under her lashes, "to me. No shade, just fact."

Stacy smiled into her glass.

"Todd told me you've got quite the yoga class going on in the mornings now," Nikko said to Stacy, forking in some of the rice pilaf he'd made to go with the leftover turkey Melora had cooked the day before.

She nodded and swallowed.

"I can't believe how it's grown since we've been back. I had no idea so much of our crew were practitioners."

"Well, I think it blows, big-time," Melora said. "It was way better when it was just, like, you and me."

Stacy had to agree. She'd never liked being the center of attention, much preferring to work on the sidelines or under the radar. But ever since word had gotten out that she was a master of the art, their quiet duo had expanded significantly.

Stacy cocked her head and watched as the girl cut her turkey into several smaller slices, all almost identical in size and shape, and then forked one into her mouth, chewing with rapid ferocity. As soon as the fork hit her plate, she raised her glass to her lips and chugged almost a third of the iced tea.

From everything Stacy remembered about eating disorders, she knew stress and negative emotions could trigger lapses. For some reason, Melora was stressed about the additions to their workouts. Maybe it was because she didn't like being watched by people as she exercised, much the same way she hated being observed when she ate. Whatever the reason, Stacy wanted to help.

"You know, I kind of feel the same. It *was* more fun when it was just you and me." Stacy turned her gaze to Nikko and then back to his daughter. "Why don't we try and find some free time during the day when just the two of us can practice? How does that sound?"

Stacy was doubly rewarded when Melora's smile bloomed once again, and when she caught the warm look of thanks Nikko threw her.

"Daddy always cooks lunch for us. It's his *thing*." She rolled her eyes and tried to suppress a grin when she looked over at her father. "Why don't we do it while he's cooking? Then, when we're done, you can, like, have lunch with us every day. How's that?"

The look of expectation on her face and swimming in her eyes was impossible to refuse. But Stacy looked to Nikko first for approval

"Is that okay?" Stacy asked him. "It won't cut into production time at all, since you allot ninety minutes for lunch break. Our workout takes just a teeny bit under thirty."

"Please, Daddy?" Melora reached over and laid a hand on his forearm. His gaze drifted from her hand, up to her face, and then over to Stacy's.

When he started to nod, Melora jumped up from her seat and threw her arms around his neck, just as he said, "Okay. I guess it's as easy to cook for three as it is for two."

While his daughter hugged him, Nikko's eyes found hers. The thanks in them just moments before had changed, deepened to something more, something...wanting.

Stacy squirmed in her seat and pressed her legs together. She had to quell the gasp that threatened to explode from the erotic tingle that flashed through her system and settled between her thighs. He could make her ache with just a glance. Make her want with just a flick of his eyes. Make her half blind with need just by being in the same room with him.

"You're like, *the best* father, ever!"

And when he smiled and tapped a finger to the tip of his daughter's nose, Stacy knew he could make her fall in love with him as well, without even trying.

"You two can start tomorrow, since we're almost done now," he told her. "Besides, I have some things I need to go over with Stacy before we head back. Think you can manage cleanup alone today, kid?"

"I'll try to, like, *muddle* my way through it," she told him.

"Muddle? Another five-star word."

"You are so lame."

"I thought I was, like, the best father, ever."

Stacy couldn't control the giggle that bubbled out of her at his dead-on imitation of his daughter's speech pattern, tone, and dramatic eye roll.

She almost burst out laughing again when Melora tossed her a haughty glare and said, "Traitor."

As soon as lunch was finished—Stacy happy when she saw how much Melora actually ate—Nikko excused them both to his office.

"Don't mind me," Melora said, waving them out of the room with a dramatic sigh. "I'll just be slaving away here, all by my lonely self. Just call me Cinderella. Is, like, dishpan hands a real thing?"

Nikko turned at the kitchen doorway and shot his index finger at her. "Knock it off, *Cindy*. I cook, you clean. When you cook, I clean. Those are the rules."

"Yeah, yeah." She filled the sink with running water.

"What did you need to go over with me?" Stacy asked when Nikko shut the study door behind them.

He leaned back against it, his hands out of sight behind him, just staring at her.

Good Lord, the man invented the smoldering stare!

When she heard him bolt the lock in place, her knees started to tremble and her hands started to shake; so much so, she had to place them in front of her, holding fast to the tablet so it wouldn't fall.

Nikko pushed off the door and in two, purposeful strides stood in front of her, his gaze locked on hers.

Without breaking eye contact, he grabbed her tablet and tossed it carelessly onto his desk. When his hands were free, he snaked one around her waist, pulling her in so she molded against him, the other cupping her neck, holding her in place as she arched her head back to look at him.

"I needed," he said, then placed a soft, swift kiss on her mouth, "to see you about this."

This time the kiss was neither swift nor soft. His mouth claimed, commanded, consumed.

With a none-too-gentle tug, he yanked the scrunchie from her hair and fisted the falling tresses, bowing her back to allow him to plunder even further into her mouth.

The trembling in her knees quivered all the way up her thighs to settle in the hot space between them when the hand at her waist rounded down and cupped her butt, pulling her up on her toes. Stacy wound her hands around his neck for purchase and held on tight.

In the next breath, he lifted her. With her legs twined around his hips, he walked them to the couch and fell back with her straddling him just like that first time in the hotel.

He never broke contact between their mouths this time, either.

They were needed back in the production truck for afternoon dinner-prep filming in just a few minutes.

She had at least ten to-do items that needed immediate attention, and probably another half dozen that had erupted since lunch.

Added to those facts, Melora was a mere room away and might at any time need to speak with her father.

None of that, it appeared, seemed to matter to either of them. Right now, the only thing that did was getting their hands on one another and sating the consuming hunger thrashing through them.

Weaving her hands into his hair, with an impatient tug filled with intent, she forced his head back to give her better access to his mouth. And his tongue.

Christ, she craved his tongue like it was some sort of lifesaving nourishment.

Nikko tugged her blouse from her pants and danced his fingers up her back while his mouth mated with hers.

If the taste of him was nourishment, the feel of his large, warm, and demanding hands on her naked skin was added sustenance. Manna from the Gods above.

"I want to be inside you. Right now," he whispered along the column of her throat, sliding his tongue down to where her blouse opened at her neck. "I've been thinking about having you underneath me all morning. Hell, since I left you last night."

His hands slid underneath the waistband of her pants to plump and pinch her butt cheeks.

Stacy opened her knees a little wider and lifted just a bit, just enough for him to snake his hand down further to slide two fingers inside her thong.

"I knew you'd be this wet," he growled. In a slow, steady stride he traced his fingers from the front all the way to the back and then did it again. Every nerve ending in Stacy's core exploded at his touch. His thick, long, and nimble fingers tortured her with pleasure as they rubbed against her swollen, wet flesh. Needing him to run his fingers along her most sensitive spot, she lifted even higher to give him access. Nikko bit down on her earlobe and pushed those two fingers inside her.

Stacy clamped her lips together to keep from screaming aloud and dug her nails into his neck. With her head thrown back and her eyes closed, she focused every ounce of attention on the feel of his fingers.

"You're gonna come right now, aren't you?" He captured her mouth again. "Right in my hands."

She answered him by pistoning her hips to the rhythm of his pumping fingers and clenching down when the orgasm barreled through her.

When she screamed this time, he swallowed the sound.

Nikko slid his fingers from her and then cradled her against his chest. While she floated back down, he kissed her forehead and rubbed her back. The sound of his heart thumping resounded against her ear.

When she could see clearly again, she pushed back to look at him. Thick, glossy hair where she'd clutched it stood out at odd angles from his head. His mouth was swollen and kiss-slicked and had her panting again just looking at it. But it was the expression floating in his half-closed eyes that undid her. Dark inkwells, so deep and warm she wanted to dive right into them, stared back at her filled with so much emotion, so much yearning she wanted to tell him what was rapidly growing in her heart.

Just as the words formed in her mind, the harsh blare of a cell phone exploded through the quiet room, silencing her declaration.

"That's you," Nikko said, glancing down at her lap.

With a nod, Stacy lifted up fully onto her knees to gain access to her pockets, her breasts now level with Nikko's mouth, and pulled the phone from where she'd stored it.

While she answered, Nikko leaned forward, undid a few buttons on her blouse, and then nipped her nipple through her silk bra cup. The move was so unexpected, along with the bullet of need that shot straight through her soul, Stacy arched and pressed forward.

Nikko needed no further encouragement. He snagged the breast from its cup and, after licking his lips and making her almost come again just from watching him do it, sucked the puckered point into his mouth.

Once again, Stacy went blind.

And apparently deaf, because the producer on the other end of the phone was repeating herself. "Are you there? Stacy? Can you hear me?"

"Y—yes. I'm here. I'm good. Um… what did you say?"

Nikko's shoulders shook with mirth. She clapped him on the collarbone. He glanced up, her breast plumped in his hand, his tongue swirling around her nipple, a grin of absolute devilry on his face and her heart simply turned over. Pursing her lips in a fake pout, she bent and kissed the top of his head while listening about the latest personality crisis.

"Okay, I'll be right down." She sat back down on Nikko's lap, almost impaling herself with the hard, pulsating rod pressed up against his trousers. His self-satisfied smile had her wicked-meter pulsing too, and for a subtle form of payback, she slid her pelvis back and forth along him.

Nikko's face went blank as his head dropped back. His hands shifted to her waist again, a silent plea to hold her in place.

"Give me five minutes," Stacy said into the phone. "And try to keep them separated, okay?"

A second later she ended the call.

"I have to get back." She glided off his lap to stand within the confines of his spread legs.

"Problem?"

While she tucked her breast back into her bra, then buttoned her shirt, she glanced around for her hair tie.

"Cayman and Burbank got into it again during lunch. Seems Cayman is on a tear about his spices going missing. He's blaming Clay."

She shoved her shirt back into her pants, still looking for her scrunchie.

"Here." Nikko picked it up from where he'd tossed it onto the sofa cushion. While she wound her hair back up, he said, "Speaking of Burbank..." then swiped his hands through his hair, finger-combing it back into place, and sat forward. "Todd told me he's been acting like an asshole during your morning yoga sessions."

Stacy smoothed down the front of her slacks. "He's just being his normal bad-boy self. He can't help but flirt." She sighed. "It's the way he's made."

"Is he bothering you with what he's saying and doing, though? Do I need to have a conversation with him, Stacy? To make him stop?"

Touched more than she realized she could be by his offer, she stepped back between his open thighs. Instantly, his hands wove around her waist, securing her, bringing her in closer.

With her palm against his cheek, she said, "Don't worry about him. He's a pain in the butt, but harmless. I've handled more obnoxious people than Clay"—she peered pointedly at him—"without any bloodshed. I find the best way to deal with guys who act like he does is to either ignore them or embarrass them."

While she'd been speaking, Nikko had been tracing circles along the small of her back. Every inch of her spine tingled at his touch.

He flatted his hands against her butt and pulled her in closer until his mouth was a whisper from hers.

"Stacy." He touched his forehead to hers. "I wish we didn't have to go back just yet."

She kissed the tip of his nose. "Me, either. But we do." Her sigh sounded heavy and forlorn even to her own ears.

With his hands tucked inside the back pockets of her trousers, he palmed her butt and squeezed. "Can I come to your room later?"

She smiled at him and kissed a corner of his mouth, then nodded. "Now, I need to go before there actually is bloodshed."

"Call me if you need any backup with those two. Otherwise, I'll see you back at the production trailer."

With a quick grin and nod, she unlocked the door and left.

Chapter Twenty

"Can I, like, ask you a personal question?"

Stacy swallowed the spoonful of Asian beef stew she'd taken from Alonzo Cayman's dinner challenge, the delectable, spicy meat going down in an uncomfortable bolus. Seated next to Melora in the tiny private area Amos Dixon had cordoned off for them in the Feedbag, she sat her spoon back down on the wooden table and waited a beat before nodding, praying the question wasn't one about her and Nikko.

For the past several minutes the teen had been cutting her meat into miniscule portions and then pushing them around her plate, alternately taking huge sips from a water glass she'd already refilled twice.

She's troubled about something, Stacy thought.

Since joining them at lunch every day over the past week and then eating dinner every night with Melora while the competition was filmed, Stacy had become very attuned to the girl's eating habits.

At lunch, she was usually happy, smiling, and ate most—but never all—of what her father prepared for the three of them. Stacy thought the prelunch yoga workout might have something to do with Melora's increased food intake, because she usually ended the mediation with an "I'm starving" comment. When Stacy mentioned it to Nikko, he'd replied, "She hasn't said those words in more months than I can remember."

Since Amos had provided them a quiet, private place to eat the challenge dinners, the girl had also been eating more.

And she looked good. Still way too thin for her lanky frame, her cheeks had filled out from their hollows, though, and the dark circles under her eyes had faded. Her beautiful smile came much more easily and Nikko had even commented that his daughter hadn't seemed so moody of late.

But right now she was exhibiting eating-avoidance tactics. Stacy didn't know if she should confront her about them or just let them slide.

Melora's question gave her an opening.

"You can ask me whatever you want, Melora." She reached across the small table and rubbed the girl's hand. "Is something wrong?"

Melora's bottom lip disappeared under her top one. "Not wrong. I'm just, you know, a little confused about…something."

The idea that she knew about Nikko and her pushed right back to Stacy's thoughts. She swallowed her own nerves and asked, "About what, sweetie?"

Melora looked down at her plate. "Well, how do you know when a guy, like, really likes you—for you, you know?—and isn't just giving you a line to get in your pants?"

Of all the things Melora could have asked, that wasn't even on Stacy's *maybe* list.

"Okay. Wow. Wasn't expecting that."

Melora's head shot up, her gaze worried and pleading.

Stacy flashed back to all the times she'd wished she'd had a sister to ask a question just like this one and Kandy's face came to mind. Her older cousin had been a good sounding board when Stacy wanted to avoid her mother, knowing anything she asked her mom would be picked apart and analyzed ad nauseam.

Channeling her older cousin's always sage advice, Stacy thought for a second.

"I have to ask first, Melora: Is anyone pressuring you to do something you don't want to do?"

Ink-colored brows, twins to her father's, folded in the midline over expressive eyes. "What, you mean, like, *have sex*? No. No. Ew."

Stacy's lungs expanded a little in relief when the girl's head starting swaying back and forth.

"Like, *double-ew.*"

"Okay… well, good. Sorry. I had to ask."

She composed herself mentally, thanking the heavens she didn't have to contend with teenage intimacy concerns.

"To answer your question then, I guess I have to know who you're talking about."

Melora's eyes flicked to the side of the room where the chefs were stationed. In that instant she got her answer.

"Is this about Riley MacNeill?"

The girl's pale and makeup-free cheeks turned an apple red. "Um. Yeah. Maybe." A jerky shoulder shrug accompanied the declaration.

"Tell me," Stacy said, giving her hand a squeeze before letting go of it. "We've been, you know, hanging out," she said after a moment. "Just talking."

"His schedule is fairly filled during the day. Aside from seeing him at morning yoga, I've barely gotten a glimpse of him in days. When have you been able to see him? To just talk?" she added.

Melora's gaze dropped back to her plate while her skinny shoulders slumped forward.

She's making herself look small and invisible.

Stacy's hospital roommate had done the same thing whenever her parents had visited. It was an avoidance behavior that went hand in hand with the eating disorder.

It was also a way to brace against any kind of verbal attack or outburst.

"Nikko sleeps like the dead," the teen said, hiding her upper lip again. "I've been…going out, like, at night, and meeting him down by where we do yoga."

Good Lord. All the nights Nikko had thought he was the one sneaking out to come to her room for a few hours of uninterrupted privacy, his daughter had been doing the same thing with a boy.

Well, hopefully not the same thing as she and Nikko. But still…

Apple, meet tree.

"Okay. Well, I don't think it's necessary to tell you that you shouldn't be sneaking out at anytime to meet anyone, Melora, because you know that for yourself."

"Thanks, but I, like, hear a big *but* in there."

"But you can get hurt with that kind of behavior. Let me finish," she added when Melora sat upright and appeared to want to argue. With Stacy's request, she clamped her mouth shut.

"By sneaking out, no one knows you're gone or where you are. You could fall, or trip on something in the dark and get hurt. Or worse. Amos Dixon has had two cows attacked by coyotes just this past week."

The girl's red cheeks went pale again.

"Safety concerns aside," Stacy continued, "You're only fifteen. Underage. Riley is nineteen. He's legally of age and subject to all the laws and consequences that go along with that. I know four years doesn't seem like a great deal of difference, age-wise, but it's a world of difference legally. Trust me on that."

"It's not like that between us," Melora said, her shoulders now going back, a pout of petulance forming on her naked lips. "All we've done is talk about stuff. We haven't, like, *done* anything that would get him or me in trouble."

"Stuff like what?"

"Just...stuff." She flipped her hand in the air.

Good Lord. Is this what her parents had gone through? She made a mental note to call her father when she had a few free minutes, tell him how much she loved and appreciated him, and apologize for everything she'd put him and her mother through when she was a teen.

It was the least she could do.

Stacy took a deep breath and dug deep for wisdom. She cocked her head and said, "You asked me how to tell if a guy really liked you or just pretended to in order to get in your pants, right?"

"Yeah?"

"Has Riley...done, or suggested anything to make you think that's all he wants? Said anything that would make you believe he was using you, or leading you on?"

Melora pondered that for a moment. "No. No, he hasn't. He's, like, *nice.* And sweet. He talks all the time about food and how he wants to open a restaurant one day. He's the first guy I've ever known other than Nikko who treats me like a person with a functioning brain and an opinion."

"Major pluses, there." Stacy smiled.

"Truth. I'm just... I guess *unsure* is the best word, about why."

"Why what?"

"Why me? I mean, he's crazy cute. Pure eye candy. He could be with, you know, *any* girl. Why me?"

Was I ever this young and insecure? Stacy thought. *Of course you were. Why else would you have behaved the way you did as a teen?*

"I agree he's a cutie," she said. "But so are you."

"No. I'm not. My mother was gorgeous. I'm...not."

"Stop it, sweetie." Stacy kept her voice low, but her tone was firm, much the way her grandmother's had been when speaking with her misbehaving grandchildren. "You're lovely. In fact, you've got the kind of looks and bone structure I've always envied."

"Get out."

Stacy gave her back her own words. "Truth. You've got those perfect cheekbones, pale skin, and dark hair my cousins have. They all inherited those genes from our grandparents. All but me. I got my father's dishwater coloring. Fair and boring."

"But you're, like, *beautiful.* Your hair's, like, sunshine and I'd maim for your eye color."

"Have you looked in a mirror lately, young lady?"

Melora dropped her gaze again.

"To answer your question, Riley—who I think is a really wonderful guy—likes you because you're you. Smart and snarky and cute."

When she raised her head again to stare right at Stacy, she'd lost some of the previous nerves.

"Really?"

"Really. I know you don't see it, but believe it, sweetie, because it's true. I never lie."

"I just..." She looked off, her brow crinkling again.

"What?"

Melora heaved a huge sigh and rolled her eyes when she looked back at her.

"I just wish...I don't know. That things could be easier, maybe? That people could be."

"Oh, God, I wish the same thing. Every single day," Stacy said with a shake of her head.

Melora's grin was quick to erupt. Just as quick, her mouth went flat again.

"I really wish things could be the way they were before my mom died."

Stacy's heart broke a little. To lose a parent, and so tragically, was bad enough. To lose her at an age when every girl needed her mother for guidance and insight was heart-shattering.

"You miss her very much, don't you?"

Tears swelled in eyes that had gone huge and sorrowful. When she nodded, one slipped down her cheek, followed by more.

Natural comforter that she was, Stacy leaned over and hugged her.

"I really miss her." She sniffed against Stacy's shoulder. "She was a major pain in the neck and batshit crazy at times, but I miss her. What does that say about me, that I miss the crazy parts? That I miss being the one to take care of her when she went off all wacky and unstable?"

With a rub down the girl's back, Stacy said, "It means you love her. All of her. And because you do, you miss her more than you ever thought you could. That, by the way"—she pulled back and looked at her tearstained face—"is one-hundred-percent normal."

And, she thought, it went a long way to understanding why Melora developed an eating disorder after the woman's untimely death.

Stacy felt her cell phone vibrate in her pocket.

"Sorry," she said. She read the message and typed a reply. "Your father says dinner service is done and we should start gathering the votes. Are you okay?"

She nodded, rose, and then picked up her plate. The food was macerated across it.

"Yeah, I'm okay. And I'm glad this is the last challenge before the finale." She glanced down at her plate. "I'll be happy if I never see another cow-inspired dish again."

Silently, Stacy agreed.

"Hey." Melora laid a hand across Stacy's arm. Shyly, the girl lowered her eyes, then looked back up at her. With a tiny smile, she said, "Thanks."

Stacy patted the hand.

"You won't, like, tell Nikko, will you? About the sneaking out. Or... anything?"

Stacy considered it. The girl was entitled to some privacy, some secrets of her own, such as having a huge crush on a boy, without her father hounding her about it. But sneaking out had almost cost her her own life at a similar age. Instead of agreeing or disagreeing, she tried a different tactic.

"You shouldn't sneak out, no matter what, Melora. You know that. If something happened to you, just think how devastated Nikko would be. Remember how he was the day you went to the airport with me and you hadn't told him you were going? Multiply that by a million and you'll get an idea of what it would be like for him if you got hurt, or worse, and he couldn't find you because you'd snuck off somewhere. Think about that."

While they deposited their dishes on the cleanup counter and then began giving out the ballots for the final dining-hall vote, Stacy said a prayer her words, and their meaning, got through to the teen.

* * * *

"So, is everything all set, production-wise, for the finale?" Nikko asked the assembled crew.

They were gathered around one of the large tables in the dining hall, an hour after filming ended.

"Location cameras are heading out at dawn tomorrow," Todd said from across the table. "We'll film the chefs as they wake up and get ready, then the travel footage while we're in the vans." He turned to Stacy. "You still need some final interviews, right?"

She nodded. "Half are done, the others will be done on-site," she said, referring to her notebook.

While she gave them a rundown of the times each chef would be required to give their final sit-down interview before the winner of the competition was declared, Nikko's eyes took a slow and steady walk across her face.

Principal production would wrap tomorrow after the finale and the announcement of the winner. The crew would start packing up all the equipment, the trucks would be loaded, and then they'd be on their way. Nikko had his and Melora's flights already booked and he was sure if he asked Stacy she'd be able to tell him to the minute when everyone else was scheduled to leave the ranch.

Then what?

Once they were back in New York, what would happen between them? What were her future plans? He'd never asked and they'd never discussed what would happen after they left the confines of the ranch and got back to their real lives. Had she scheduled a little break for herself before starting something new?

That sounded great. He could use a break himself, and it would be nice to take Melora some place where she'd actually enjoy her free time and get to see other people her age. Maybe they'd head out to his beach house in Malibu. He hadn't been back since before the accident, before his life had quite literally changed forever.

Melora loved the beach.

Did Stacy?

The sudden need to know exactly where she was going, what she was going to do, who she was going to see, once they were done, exploded through him.

He thought back to the proposal Jade had presented him with that last morning in Big Sky. It was a great idea and he was surprised someone at the network hadn't thought of it before now. It would mean traveling and he needed to consider what that would mean to Melora. He certainly didn't want to board her at school or leave her in the city with a professional minder. He'd hate that as much as she would. Maybe he could work it out so he could bring along a tutor if the show filmed during the school year.

He needed to give it more consideration, maybe even discuss it with Stacy. He'd need an EP for the program, and she'd proven her worth more times than he could count.

And wasn't that just a little bit of amazing? In all the years he'd directed, he'd bitched about executive producers and had never wanted one on set or in his eyesight. Not one.

Until Stacy.

One thing he did know for sure: He wanted to keep seeing her. He knew himself well enough to realize her calming presence, her soothing, professional personality on set was one thing. She was by far the best producer he'd ever worked with.

The connection they had as a man and a woman, though, was entirely something else.

He *needed* her at work.

He *wanted* her in his private life.

"The set team is already on site," Stacy said. "I got a text from Brian Moody about an hour ago saying everything's unpacked and in place. All that needs to be done in the morning is to set up the tents."

"The chefs have no idea what they're walking into for this last challenge?" Todd asked.

"No. My producers were all sworn to secrecy, as were the food and set crew. Our two cohosts don't even know what's in store for them."

"That ought to make for some interesting commentary from Jade," Todd said with a smirk. "I'll make sure I have a spare camera trained on her."

The table erupted in laughter. Stacy caught Nikko's eye, her broad and easy smile making his stomach muscles clench. Her gaze lingered on his just a fraction of a moment, but enough for a deep ache to shoot straight up from his core.

Christ, how he wanted her. He wished this stupid meeting would end so he could send everyone on their way and be alone with her.

It didn't look like that was going to happen anytime soon, since his production team was still in the thralls of discussing every aspect of the finale.

It was well after midnight before they were done. Stacy had been yawning into her hand for over an hour and he'd seen her eyes droop, then fly open, at least twice.

After everyone said their good nights, Nikko walked with her up toward the main house. The moon was a full, solid disc above them, shining bright against the blanket of stars surrounding it. The night air was warm, as the day had been scorching.

"Tomorrow should run smoothly from production's end," she said, tilting her head back and looking up at the sky.

"I'm not worried about the crew," Nikko said, shoving his hands in his pockets when all he really wanted to do was toss an arm around her shoulders and snuggle her next to him. They had to keep up the pretense they weren't personally involved for only one more day, he thought with a silent prayer of thanks. Once the show wrapped, they wouldn't have to deny they were together any longer. But first, he needed to tell Melora.

"It's our exhausted chefs and one pain-in-the-ass cohost that's making me nervous."

Stacy chuckled. The sound hit him—like a cheap shot—straight in the groin.

"It'll all be over tomorrow night," she said, stifling another yawn. "Sorry. It's been a long day. Long few weeks, actually."

"Do you know what your plans are when you get back to New York? What your next job is?"

He thought he sensed a subtle shift in her stance.

"I've got a few weeks before I need to worry about anything. Why?"

"I've got a line on something that sounds interesting. I thought, if you weren't already planning on your next assignment, you might like to hear about it. I'll tell you all about it tomorrow after the wrap party."

She was silent for a few beats and he wondered why.

The path veered, bringing them even with the copse of tall, bushy trees surrounding the main house. Nikko grabbed her arm and tugged her into an opening between them so they wouldn't be seen.

"Nikko?"

He wove his arms around her lithe frame, pressing her in as close as he could. Inhaling the sweet scent of fresh oranges in her hair, he took a deep breath, laid her head down on his shoulder, and just held her.

When he let out a breath and rubbed his hands down her back, she squeezed his waist and asked, "What's wrong?"

"Nothing. Now." He kissed her temple. "If I'd had to sit in that room another five minutes and not be allowed to hold you like this, I'd have gone crazy."

Her shoulders shook against him. "Why are we standing out here in the trees then, when we could be up in my room?" she asked, nuzzling his chest through his shirt.

"You have no idea how much I want that right now. But it's late and I can tell you're exhausted." He pulled back and scrubbed his hands down her arms. "Tomorrow is a long, long day and we all need some rest."

As if to underscore the point, another yawn broke from her.

"*Lord.* Sorry. I'm tired, that's the truth."

"As much as it pains me to say this—and I'm not kidding—I'm in some serious pain right now—"

"Your leg?" She glanced down and moved to massage it through his pants.

With a jagged groan, Nikko shook his head and said, "The pain's just north of your hand, sweetheart, and if you keep doing that it's gonna get worse."

With her hand clamped over her mouth to smother the giggle he felt swelling up in her, Stacy stared back up at him, her eyes crinkling, filled with moisture in the moonlight.

Nikko took a breath and yanked her back into his arms. "Stay here for a second," he whispered.

When she tucked her head under his chin and relaxed against him, Nikko experienced a peace he hadn't felt in quite some time.

"We're leaving early," he said into her hair, "and you need some sleep. So do I. If I came up to your room right now, neither one of us would get much, that's the truth."

"Promises, promises," she said against his chest.

He pinched her butt and swallowed her yelp with his mouth.

He could kiss her all night and never tire of it. Hell, all day and all night. And longer still.

With her chin cupped in his palms, her brushed her cheeks with the pads of his thumbs and kissed her one last time.

"Let's get you inside."

He peeked between the trees, gave a silent thanks the path was empty, and pulled her along with him up to the front steps.

"I'll see you in a few hours," he said and squeezed her hand.

With a quick nod, she went through the door.

Chapter Twenty-one

"I've never been so hot in my entire life. Why can't I go back to the trailer and cool off?"

Stacy glanced over at Jade from behind her sunglasses to where the woman sat under an umbrella, held by one of her minions. She was fanning herself frantically and Stacy had to admit, the diva looked drenched.

The temperature had already been an uncomfortable 80 degrees when they pulled into the location shoot by eight a.m. Now, at almost noon, it had to be 20 degrees hotter, the sun above them bright, blistering, and burning.

"Just a few minutes more, Jade, and then you can cool off," Nikko said, never once looking at her, but keeping his eyes trained on the portable monitors stationed under the canopy. "I just need you and Dan to tell the chefs good luck with the final presentation. Then we can all break for a while."

From her vantage point, Stacy could see the ring of sweat circling Nikko's neck. Unlike his whining cohost, though, he wasn't complaining about it. Stacy pulled a couple of bottles of cold water from the cooler next to her chair, handed one over to Jade, then Todd, and finally gave one to Nikko, dropping the bottle over his shoulder.

When he slaked his hand up and took it from her, his fingers lingered just a second on her own, wrapping around them in a silent thanks that had her insides heating as much as her outsides. As she settled back into her chair, she spotted Jade's intent gaze on her as she took a long, full drink from her bottle.

"Okay, Jade, Dan," Nikko said. "Get in place. Dan, call time when you're ready."

Jade was handed a pair of dark sunglasses by one of her assistants, then the same girl walked with her to her camera spot carrying the huge, opened umbrella over her head.

It didn't escape anyone's attention the girl had no protection of her own against the sun, either on her face or over her head.

Dan Roth called time and then the sound of utensils clattering down on the wooden slats they'd all used for counters echoed in the canyon.

While the camera panned each chef as the cohosts stopped by their stations, Stacy noticed a few of them were so red from the heat of cooking over an open pit and being out in the sweltering midday sun, that she quickly sent a group text to her producers, ordering them to stand by with bottles of water and towels.

Once the scene was finished and Nikko called "cut," her crew moved in.

"Hey, Nikko," Clay Burbank yelled from his station.

All eyes turned to the chef to watch him yank his sweat-doused uniform jacket over his head, leaving his muscled chest bare and glistening. He took the water bottle his producer handed him and poured it over his head, then grabbed another and swigged from it. "What stupid asshole decided it was a great idea to have us cook out here? It's a thousand-fucking-degrees."

"What's that saying, Burbank? If you can't stand the heat...?"

Stacy couldn't decide who was more surprised by Nikko's lighthearted comment and rare show of humor: the crew, the chefs, or Nikko himself.

"And I'm the stupid asshole who decided to put your final challenge out here. Deal with it."

He stood from his chair and swiped the bottle across the back of his neck, then down his temples.

"He's right about the temperature, though," he said to Todd.

Stacy watched Jade as the woman ambled under the canopy.

"Nikko," she said, "I need a few minutes of your time before you rush off. Meet me in my camper."

Without waiting for a response, she walked by Stacy without even a glance her way.

"What's that all about?" she heard Todd ask.

"Jade wants me to direct a new program she's developing." He glanced over at Stacy. "Are you free for a few minutes?"

Surprised, she nodded and waited for him to come to her.

"I'm pretty sure this is about what I mentioned last night," he said, lowering his voice. "Come with me so we can hear her out."

Nikko wrapped his fingers around her forearm and started walking. Stacy couldn't think of an excuse to beg off quick enough. Before she knew it, he opened the door to Jade's camper and went in.

The frigid air inside was such a stark contrast to the outside temperature, Stacy shuddered from the difference. The front of the camper was empty.

"It's like a freezer in here," Nikko mumbled when he climbed in behind her and closed the door. "Jade?"

"I'll be right out," she called. "I'm just getting changed."

"Make it quick," he called back, the irritation that had flown from him for the past few days back in his voice again. "I've got to get lunch ready for Melora."

"Your daughter won't starve to death if she has to wait five minutes for her lunch."

Stacy gasped and, turning to Nikko, saw his nostrils flare.

Was the woman so blind, selfish, and ill-mannered she didn't even realize the import of her words to the girl's father?

She reached out a hand and squeezed his forearm, turning his attention to her. Before Stacy could say anything, Jade pranced from the back of the camper dressed in a floor-length silk bathrobe. From the way her legs peeked out when she walked, it was obvious she had nothing on under it.

The seductive smile she'd planted on her freshly fixed, made-up face, died the moment she spotted Stacy.

"This is a private meeting," the diva told her, her pout pulling into a thin, crimson line.

"I asked her to come with me," Nikko said. "I assumed you wanted to talk about your program proposal. I want Stacy's take on it and it was just easier hearing it from you and not having to repeat everything later."

Bald annoyance filled Jade's glare, but after a moment it was replaced by something that had a nasty edge.

Jade moved to the built-in kitchen counter, pulled open the small refrigerator, and took a bottle of wine from its depths.

Nikko hissed in a breath. "You know Amos Dixon's ranch is dry, Jade."

With a flippant hand wave, the woman said, "He's nowhere in the vicinity and I want a glass of wine. I'll assume you don't, Nikko, since you're being such a prig about it."

She didn't bother to offer one to Stacy.

After taking a large sip—more a gulp, to Stacy's mind—the woman turned to them, skimmed her eyes over Stacy, then settled on Nikko. With a grin channeling a Cheshire cat, she asked, "What do you think of my little idea? Intriguing, no?"

"It could be. If done correctly. You'll need a lot of preproduction and research. Plus setting up the travel needed to each place. That's why I asked Stacy here. Organizing something like this is right up her alley."

"I'm sorry," Stacy said, her gaze settling on him. "What kind of show are you talking about? A new food contest?"

Jade set her wineglass down on the counter and folded her arms across her chest. The upswell of flesh pressing against the fold of the robe proved Stacy's suspicion the woman was naked underneath it.

"Not a contest, no," the woman said. "The idea has more depth than just a simple competition."

When she didn't elaborate, Stacy turned to Nikko.

"Jade has this idea to tour around the country, visiting old-fashioned mom-and-pop restaurants and diners off the beaten track. Sample good old Americana cuisine and promote the kind of family dinners we grew up having."

Stacy's heart tripled in speed as he went on to describe the logistics of the show.

Her show.

Her fingers started to tingle and she could hear her blood coursing through her body. Slowly, determinedly, she turned to Jade. It came to her the moment the woman's gaze met her own what she'd seen floating there just seconds before: a malicious glee.

How? How had Jade found out about her program concept?

As soon as she asked the question she answered it. Teddy Davis. She remembered the rumors claiming Jade was sleeping with Teddy. He'd either told her of Stacy's plan, or she'd found out another way.

Stacy wouldn't put it past the odious woman to have conspired with Teddy's assistant, Althea, against her. Stacy remembered exactly how horrified Althea had been when she'd had him sign her guarantee, claiming Stacy was blackmailing him. She hadn't wanted Teddy to sign it and made her thoughts known. Loudly.

"Stacy?"

She realized Nikko had been speaking to her. Brows furrowed together over his eyes, his head was cocked to one side.

"I'm sorry. What did you say?"

"I asked what you thought about the idea?"

Before she could reply, his cell phone pinged. After checking it, he told Jade, "Look, I've gotta go. We'll talk more about this after filming is completed." He moved to the door. "Are you coming?" he asked Stacy.

"You go on ahead, Nikko," Jade said. "I need to speak with Stacy for moment. A quick question about later on. Go on, though. She'll be right along."

He squinted at her and then Stacy. She gave him a subtle nod.

Once the door closed behind him, Stacy turned back to Jade.

With a simpering grin that bordered on cruel, Jade sipped her wine as she regarded Stacy over the rim of her glass.

"I'm not surprised you didn't say anything to him." Seething, Stacy did what she always did when anger lashed up inside her: called for calm.

"After all, how would it look to the man you've been sleeping with if he knew the real reason you were in his bed?"

"You're despicable." The words shook from her. Even though she was able to keep her voice low, it cracked with emotion.

"I'm despicable? That's a little like the pot calling out the kettle, dear. You're the one who blackmailed Teddy. The one who only agreed to work on this show so you'd get your own if you stuck it through to the end."

"Did he tell you that? That I'd blackmailed him? Because that's not what it was."

"I have my ways of knowing things. And you can call it whatever you like: The end result is the same."

"Why are you doing this? Why are you being so cruel? I've never done anything to you."

"Oh you poor, sweet, naïve little girl. It's not about you."

"Then what? You've basically laid claim to a show idea I've been developing for the past two years. An idea I've done the research on, I've sweated over the budget, the production value, the promotion. You've done nothing. Nothing but steal the idea."

"I have my reasons." She took another sip of wine.

Stacy took a step closer, her hands grasping her notebook so tight the tips of her fingers tingled.

"Your little idea would never even have been considered," Jade said, "if Teddy hadn't needed someone to keep the reins on Nikko. He only gave his consent in order to get you to agree to come out to this godforsaken place. He truly had no intention of going through with it."

Stacy felt as if she'd been punched in the stomach. "You don't know that."

"Oh, I do. When you backed him into a corner, he signed your little document—which, by the way, won't stand up in any court, especially when the network's lawyers destroy it."

"If that's true, then why did you present the idea to Nikko? Why bother?"

The malice on her beautiful face turned, hardening her soft features. For a brief moment, Stacy knew fear.

"Let's just say he needed to be punished and this was an easy way to do it?"

Stacy shook her head, the raw edge of a headache sharpening across the back of her neck. "You're not making any sense."

"No? Well, let me put it as plainly as I can." The smile dropped, her eyes darkened to two hard stones, and she fisted her hands on her tiny hips. "How do you think Nikko is going feel once he discovers the only reason his newest little bedmate is with him is because she believes she's getting a huge payout? I don't think he'll be too happy knowing that you're sleeping with him as a means to an end."

"It's not like that. You know it isn't."

"Do I?" She cocked her head and regarded Stacy as if she were a spider who's just found a fly trapped in her silken web. "Do you know the story of Nikko and his ex-wife? Of why he divorced her?"

"No." Stacy rubbed the back of her neck, trying to ease some of the tension coiled there.

"Flannery Adair was a minor bit player. A fair actress at the most, nothing certainly that would propel her to the stardom she so wanted. Nikko directed a small television movie she was in and she saw him for that proverbial meal ticket to success. She went after him like a heat-seeking missile, conveniently getting herself pregnant. Knowing the kind of man Nikko is, she knew he'd never ask her to get rid of it. After they were married, she badgered him endlessly to help her get roles in commercial movies. Which he did. Once she'd made a name for herself, she moved on to someone more influential in the business and blindsided Nikko with a divorce. Knowing he was used as a stepping-stone gave him a rather jaded view of the rest of our sex."

She stopped and took another drink. Stacy knew in that moment that Nikko had somehow, some way, hurt Jade and this was her way of getting even.

Stacy was just a pawn.

"What's to keep me from telling him you stole my idea?" she asked. Before she took her next breath, Stacy realized the trap she'd fallen into. Jade's smarmy smile confirmed it.

"Oh, I don't think you will, dear. If you do, we both know he'll come to confront me. I'll be forced to tell him about your little deal with Teddy. Your little quid pro quo. And, just like before, Nikko won't appreciate being used to further another woman's career. How do you think he'll feel knowing that? His ego is as big as this state, so I can imagine he won't like it one bit. He'll put an end to your torrid little romance and will never look back."

"And what do you get out of all of this?" Stacy knew the answer, but she needed to hear the odious woman say it.

"Me?" With a theatric air, she laid her hand in the space between her breasts. "Well, it's a win-win all around for me, isn't it? I get to star in a show with a very intriguing concept, plus, since I'll already have an award-winning director lined up, the network will surely be appreciative."

"It's more than that, though, isn't it? More than just professional kudos and garnering network favor. You want to hurt Nikko. For whatever sick and mean reason, you want him to suffer."

"Of course I do! He deserves to for the way he treated m—treats women. It's about time he had a comeuppance."

Stacy kept her tongue. She refused to allow Jade to see how truly devastated she was.

While the situation might have been a self-proclaimed win-win for Jade, it was a total loss for her. If she went to Nikko and tried to explain about the letter, it might confirm in his mind that she had used him to further her career, just as Jade stated. If she told him nothing, she'd see her dream stolen outright with little recourse. Jade was correct on that. Another valid point was that the note from Teddy was handwritten. It hadn't been drawn up by the network lawyers like every other legal document was. Even though he'd signed it and had his assistant witness it, EBS's legal team could very well fight its legitimate status. They could claim Teddy signed it under duress, which in truth, he had.

Jesus. This was a nightmare.

Her cell phone vibrated in her pocket. When she pulled it out, Melora's *where are you?* brought her back to the present.

"What are you going to do?" Jade asked, refilling her wine.

Stacy slipped the phone back into her trouser pocket and turned. There was no way she was going to let this bitch see how upset she was. She wouldn't give her the satisfaction.

Channeling Grandma Sophie's straight-as-a-steel-rod backbone, she opened the camper door and tossed over her shoulder, "Have lunch."

Chapter Twenty-two

For the third time, Nikko turned his head around to check on Stacy. Seated under the blaring late-afternoon heat pouring down on the tent canopy, sunglasses wrapped around her face, he couldn't get a bead on what was bothering her.

She'd been unusually quiet at lunch, and despite Melora's exuberant chatter, Stacy had seemed distracted. He figured the cause easily enough: Jade Quartermaine. The woman was a royal pain in the ass. She must have said something to Stacy that upset her after he left them.

But what?

At lunch he'd wanted to broach the subject of Jade's proposal, but had thought better of it when he sensed Stacy's mood. If Melora had suspected something was off, she'd never commented, continuing to chat away at how happy she was to be flying home soon. When the teen had asked Stacy when she planned on leaving the ranch, Stacy's reply had been wooden.

"My flight's in two days," she'd said. "I need to stick around to ensure that everything is shipped and returned without any snafus."

After that they finished quickly, due to getting a late start with Jade's interruption.

Stacy had pleaded an excuse to check on something, bolting from the Stamps' RV as soon as she'd cleared her plate. Nikko wanted to run after her, but a text from Todd about a camera issue prevented him.

Now, as the chefs prepared to serve their final challenge dish, Nikko had a thousand thoughts running through his head about production needs, but uppermost was his concern about Stacy.

With the end of production just a few short hours way, he knew his time with her was almost over from a professional standpoint. He'd be the one working on editing the footage for broadcast, along with the editing team. Her assistance would no longer be needed on a daily basis, and wasn't that a hoot? For all his bellyaching about never needing or wanting an executive producer, wasn't it just a kick in the nuts that now he'd come to rely on the one assigned to him?

He wanted Stacy in his life, there was no denying it. She'd come to mean more to him than any other woman he could recall, including his ex-wife. Flannery had been an obsession for him while they'd been together. Once he discovered how she'd manipulated and used him to further her career, coupled with her blatant infidelity, he'd never known such a personal low point. Flannery had been hauntingly beautiful, but all that beauty had hidden a cold, calculated, and manipulative heart.

Stacy's heart, he'd witnessed firsthand, was as open and sweet and as far from scheming as he could imagine.

He knew she had a home and a career to go back to, as did he. The knowledge he wanted her to share in his life was something he was going to tell her tonight, after the winner was announced, and the competition done.

"Service is in twenty minutes," Nikko called after checking the time stamp on his console. He turned around once more to Stacy and asked, "Is everything set up?"

With a nod, she held up her cell phone. "I just got a text that the guests are starting to take their seats in the tent. Everything appears to be functioning from a service standpoint."

"Okay, good. Have them start carting the food over," he said into his headset. On the portable screen they watched as the set producer gave the signal for the chefs to start walking with their filled food trolleys from the makeshift food-prep stations they'd been assigned over to a massive tent.

Amos Dixon, his family and all his ranch hands, in addition to twenty other invited guests, among them Jimmy Rodgers and several restaurateurs from the surrounding area, and five master chefs along with Jade and Dan, were all part of the final voting group.

Although Nikko already knew who had taken the top votes throughout the competition, tonight's overall winner could cause an upset. There were two chefs who'd come out on top equally through the weeks of filming and it truly was for either of them to win it all if tonight's offering held up to their past performances. Either way, in a little under five hours a *Beef Battles* champion would be announced.

"Okay, everyone," Nikko said, as he glanced around the group. "This is it." He noticed Stacy rise, tap her earpiece, and move from the canopy.

He spotted Melora making her way over to him. She looked so much better than she had when they'd first come out to the ranch. Gone was the city pallor made even worse by the stark white face powder she routinely wore. Her face was clean, makeup-free, and the color she now sported was a natural and healthy glow. Her cheeks had filled out and all the harsh angles and planes on her bony frame had softened. Today she was wearing calf-length blue-cotton pants with an oversized, paler blue T-shirt. For the first time in a while her clothes didn't look like they were hanging on a skeleton.

Nikko knew he had Stacy to thank almost as much as he did himself for the girl's recovery. Her calm, loving presence had helped guide his daughter back from an emotional brink that he'd been powerless to prevent. He was indebted to her for that and so much more.

"You're right on time," he told her, gathering her into a hug, an embrace she was quick to accept.

"Yeah, well, it's easy when you've got, like, *nothing, literally nothing,* to do to pass the time."

She said it with a free and easy smile and none of the teenaged disdain usually imbuing her tone.

"Where's Stacy?"

"Getting stuff seen to. Let's get over to the tent and we can find her and get you two settled."

"Stacy told me what this final challenge was a few days ago, but I forgot. Obviously"—she rolled her eyes—"it concerns cow of some kind, because, *hello,* what else?"

He laughed. "Yeah, but today it's also side dishes. They each had to prepare racks of ribs the old-west way of cooking them on a spit."

"Now there's a word that, like, just makes you want to eat everything in sight. Spit. *Not. Yuk.*"

"Plus, they had to make the side dishes using only a campfire. No frills. No fancy sauces or anything else. True ranch cooking."

As soon as they came to the tent, the aroma of the succulent meat hit them hard. Banquet tables were aligned along the inside of the tent, each chef assigned two for their dishes to be served from. The interior of the tent housed dozens of picnic-style benches, the tables covered with gingham red-and-white tablecloths.

"There's Stacy." Melora pointed across the crowded tent. She was speaking with several of her producers. Her notebook was open and she had a headset secured over her hair. That little electrical jolt sparking in his midsection every time he saw her was becoming a welcomed friend.

"See ya." Melora kissed him on the cheek and scurried off across the tent. The smile Stacy gave his daughter hit him higher up than the one a moment ago. This one pierced right through his heart, sending a seizing shudder up his spine.

The noisy tent grew silent around him, a dull, throbbing drum sounding in his head. His vision narrowed, then tunneled, so with a single blink, all he could see was her face and the brilliance of her smile. She lifted her gaze, staring off behind his daughter and connected with his. He swore he could hear her take in a breath, just like she always did right before he kissed her.

He was hard in a heartbeat. Fully, inconveniently, aroused.

Nikko had to will himself not to stomp across the tent, weave past the dozens of tables and people milling about, and pull Stacy into his arms, declaring for one and all how he felt about her. How he wanted her. How he wasn't going to let her out of his life now that he'd found her.

Melora pulled Stacy's attention from his. When Stacy broke eye contact and looked at his daughter, even from the distance he was from her, he could she was as overcome as he. She shook her head a few times as if she were coming out of a fugue and trying to refocus.

How long he stood there watching her, he didn't have a clue. He took several deep breaths and tried to quell his obvious desire from being witnessed.

Jesus.

He hadn't felt this horny this quick since he was fifteen and the mere thought of a girl would send him into a state of priapism.

Twenty-five years and a lifetime of sexual experience later and you'd think he'd be able to clamp it down.

When his name was called a few seconds later, he'd gotten himself back in order.

He had a finale to film. A show to conclude.

But later he and Stacy were going to have a long, long chat about the future.

* * * *

"You know who's winning so far, don't you?" Melora asked as they stood off to the side of the dining tent.

Dinner was done and all the chefs had been escorted to the portable kitchen tent—their own makeshift stew room—to await the announcement of a winner. Melora had just helped her pass out the voting cards and in a few moments they'd pick them up and bring them to Nikko.

"Yes. Your dad and I have been tallying them after every challenge. Plus, we've added up how each chef has done with the judges' votes."

Melora bit down on the corner of her bottom lip. "I know you can't, like, *tell me* who's won so far, but is it, like, close, between anybody?"

Stacy turned her head and tucked her chin to hide her grin. She knew Melora hoped Riley MacNeill would be named the contest winner. Melora's admission she'd snuck out to see the youngest chef after curfew still bounced around in her head. She'd debated with herself more times than not whether to tell Nikko. The moment she thought she should, as a responsible adult would, she'd remembered what she'd been like at the teen's age. A crush, even a first love, was something special and Stacy didn't want to spoil it for her.

"Well, I can tell you it's neck and neck between two chefs. In fact," she said, "it could go either way tonight with this group's"—she thrust her chin at the filled tent—"vote."

"I can't believe I'm, like, nervous." Her hands flittered up and out at her side. "This is the first time I've ever been with Daddy during one of his shoots. It's...exciting."

"And nerve-racking," Stacy added. "Looks like people are done. Let's go gather the votes."

When they had them all, Stacy pressed her earpiece and waited for Nikko to acknowledge her call.

"You got them?" he asked without preamble.

"Yes. Melora and I are headed your way."

While they walked back to the Stamps' RV, Stacy contacted her producers to keep them up to speed and coordinated with the set crew about what would happen once the winner was announced.

"Do you, like, *ever*, have a break?" Melora asked when they finally got to the camper.

Stacy chuckled. "All part of the job."

The air-conditioned interior cooled Stacy down as soon as they stepped into it.

"It's, like, a million degrees out there." Melora slumped down into a seat. She handed the canvas bag with the votes to Nikko, who shoved a bottled water across the table to her.

"Drink this." He offered another one to Stacy. "Mel, you need to go in the back for a few minutes while we count," Nikko told her. "I'm sorry, kid. Those are the rules."

She waved a hand in the air again. "'K. Get me when it's time to go."

"Will do."

"Thanks for your help," Stacy told her.

Once they were alone, Stacy's nerves returned. She took a gulp of her water, then sat across the table from Nikko. "Want to split the count up?" she asked. "It'll go faster. We can each tally our own, then pass them to one another to check."

She stopped when she realized he was staring at her, the groove between his eyebrows deepening.

"What's wrong?"

"You tell me," he said. "You've been quiet and a little out of it since lunch."

"I'm sorry." She rested her arms down on the table and clasped her hands together in front of her. A moment later, she unclasped them and rubbed them down her thighs. "I'm just tired and my mind's running in a million different directions. I just don't want to forget anything."

She knew she was babbling, but couldn't stop.

"Did something happen between you and Jade after I left her camper?"

She swallowed and kept her gaze trained on his face. She couldn't lie to him. Wouldn't. So she settled for the tactic she always used with her parents when she wanted to avoid unpleasant subjects: diversion.

Cocking her head to one side, she asked, "Did Jade say something happened?"

"No, but when you got back you were paler than usual and your hands wouldn't sit still. Kind of like right now." He dropped his gaze down to where she was twining and untwining her fingers together.

Immediately, she stopped. "Sorry."

"Stop apologizing, sweetheart, and tell me what's wrong." He reached across the table and grabbed her fidgeting hands with his own.

A lightning bolt of heat shot straight up her arm. Nikko leaned in, tugging her as he did. "Talk to me."

For a passing moment she considered confessing all. Just telling him about the stupid note, the reason why she'd forced Teddy to sign it; the doubts she'd been wracked with about working with Nikko after hearing about his volatile reputation, and how she'd ultimately lost her heart both to him and his daughter.

She wanted to confess she was in love with him, but knew if she said it, she'd have to tell him the rest as well, because she couldn't conceal it all from him. Not in good faith, anyway. In truth, she was afraid. Terrified that first, he didn't feel for her the same way she did him, and second, if he did feel anything for her it would all dissolve once he heard the truth about why she'd come to the ranch.

Never before had she been so torn about how to handle a situation. The heat from his touch couldn't warm the cold edge of sweat that slid down her spine.

Now wasn't the time to confess. They needed to finish the show, announce the winner, and deal with whatever was to come after that. Uppermost now was the finale.

"I will," she said, squeezing his hands. "But not now. We need to count these votes and get this show wrapped."

"But later on? You'll talk to me then? Tell me what's bothering you? What's going on?"

She shifted in her chair and let out a breath through her nose. "Yes. Yes. I will."

His eyes narrowed and he shook his head a few times while he continued to stare at her. She didn't think he believed her, so she pressed his hands again and said, "I promise."

Relenting, he let go.

Stacy's body quieted with relief. They hammered out a good rhythm between them as they counted, then recounted the final votes. Once they added the tally to the previous challenges, they knew the winner.

"It's close." Nikko glanced down at her tablet where the results were all stored. "But there's a clear-cut winner, so that's something."

"Are you two, like, *done* yet? I'm dying of boredom back here."

Stacy smiled when Nikko laughed and called out, "I forgot all about you."

Melora cracked the door open. "Ha-ha. You slay me, Nikko, you really do." She pulled it open wider and stepped out into the tiny hallway. "You done?"

"Yeah, kid, we are."

"Who won?" She bounced into the kitchen area and plopped down on the bench next to her father, glancing down at Stacy's tablet.

She'd had enough forethought to blank the screen before Melora sat, so the winner was still a secret.

"You'll find out the same time as everyone else," Nikko said, planting a kiss on top of her head.

"What do you think I'm gonna do if you tell me?" the girl asked, a peevish pout branching across her mouth. "Like, call TMZ and announce it? Why can't I know?"

Stacy gathered up the votes and shoved them back into the canvas bag. She knew Nikko would put them in the safe as he had every night of the competition, so if the vote was ever challenged, he had the physical proof they'd need. She handed the bag to him, watched as he locked it in a table drawer, then slid the key into his pants pocket.

"Because you can't." His tone put an end to the subject. "Now, come on. Let's get back and finish this."

His gaze found hers as he added, "I've got a list of items I need to see to once filming's done."

Stacy knew she was one of those items.

Chapter Twenty-three

"We'd like to thank our gracious hosts, Amos Dixon and his family, for allowing us the use of his magnificent ranch these past weeks." Nikko watched as Jade Quartermaine threw a million-dollar fake smile toward the rancher. She glanced down at the sealed envelope in her hand and then back up at the camera. Through half-closed eyes, she grinned coquettishly and said, "I've always had a little thing for tall, dark, rugged men. Add *cowboy* into the mix and, well…" She fanned herself with the envelope and rolled her eyes.

"Oh, *hurl*!" Melora said from behind Nikko.

Nikko bit down on his lips to keep his laugh contained. Several of the crew had no such compunction and twitters and chuckles surrounded him. He glanced over at his daughter to see her cheeks turn pink when one of the sound technicians high-fived her.

His gazed moved over to Stacy.

Her attention was settled off into the distance, her device open in her lap, but he could see the screen was blank. Her usually calm and serene face was pale, her mouth tight at the corners.

He wanted to drag her off and find out what was bothering her; what that bitch, Jade, had said or done to snuff out the light he was so used to seeing in her eyes. Then he wanted to fling her up in his arms and lose himself in her for the rest of the night…hell, the rest of his life, if he told himself the truth.

Laughter filtered in from the camera as Dan began listing the winners of the individual competitions and his attention was diverted back to the task at hand.

The chefs were all gathered in front of the head table as applause broke out for the two chefs who were tied with the most challenge votes, Clay Burbank and Riley MacNeill.

"Get ready," Nikko told Todd. "Jade's gonna announce the winner."

Since he already knew who it was, he wasn't as surprised as the other crew members when Riley's name was called.

The gathered audience broke out into whoops and shouts as the teen smiled and accepted the congratulations of the judges and crowd.

"That is too totally *amazeballs*," Melora said. From the corner of his eye he saw his daughter wrap herself into a side hug with Stacy.

The next hour was taken up with filming interviews—both Clay and Riley's—then a final filmed round of speeches by the judges.

Just as Riley's interview was complete and with the camera still recording, Nikko spotted Stacy etching her way to the chef's side and envelop him in a hug. Her smile was free and easy once again and she looked truly happy for the kid. The boom picked up her heartfelt congratulations as she told Riley how proud she was of him.

"This wasn't an easy competition in any sense," she said. "But you were able to hold your own against all the other chefs, and you should be uber-proud of yourself."

Melora and Burbank moved into the shot as Stacy spoke. For a moment, Nikko got an unfiltered look at his daughter's face and was simply stunned at what he saw there. The girl's smile was shy and childlike as she stared at MacNeill, but her eyes held something that shocked him to his core. His little girl had the look of a full-grown woman dancing in her gaze. A woman filled with desire.

What the fuck?

His gaze ping-ponged from Riley to Melora and then back again, registered the subtle, private glances the boy gave his daughter over Stacy's shoulder while he spoke and the realization hit him hard that his daughter and the chef had something going on between them.

Worry warred with resentment. Just yesterday he'd been the center of Melora's world; the only man on her radar. Today he knew that was no longer the case and it hurt his ego and his pride to know his baby girl was growing up and he couldn't do a damn thing to stop it.

Stacy's shout filtered through his musings and when he saw Burbank pick her up and spin her around, his emotions turned on a dime. Anger replaced the worry as a streak of selfish possessiveness flashed through his system. Before he could stop himself, he rose from the director's chair, bolted from the production canopy, and trotted as fast as he could back to the dining tent.

By the time he arrived, Stacy was nowhere to be seen. His gaze flicked around the still- crowded area and when he lighted on Melora, MacNeill, and Burbank, he beelined toward them.

"Daddy." It didn't escape his notice how close Melora stood to Riley, or how she took a few steps away from him when she spotted her father.

"Nikko." Burbank slid his hands into his pockets, his chef jacket unbuttoned almost to his waist. "Great competition. I don't even feel bad coming in second to the kid." His grin flashed when he turned his head toward Riley.

Ignoring the man, Nikko told his daughter, "We're gonna be leaving soon. Why don't you get back to the camper?"

She looked as if she was going to protest, but must have seen something in his eyes that told her now wasn't the time to argue. She bit down on her bottom lip, flicked a glance toward Riley, and then back to him and said, "'K."

Once she was out of hearing, Nikko continued to ignore Burbank, instead asking MacNeill, "Did you see where Stacy went?"

"She said she was heading back to the ranch. She had stuff to do."

Without another word, Nikko marched from the tent. He was stopped several times by crew and contestants congratulating him on a great finale. Just when he thought he'd be able to break free, Jade snagged his arm.

"Nikko, where are you flying off to on such a tear?"

He glanced down at her hand, then up to her heavily made-up face. The simpering smile plastered across it was as phony and vapid as the woman herself.

With more patience than he truly had, he slipped his hand over hers and pried it off his arm. "Jade, I don't have the time for you right now."

That said, he left the tent.

Daylight had carved into twilight and as he made his way to where the campers, vans, and cars were parked along the periphery of the valley, his eyes scanned the area for Stacy.

He spotted her just as she climbed into the production-crew vehicle. A moment later, he tugged open the door and followed her in.

"Stacy?"

She turned, surprise in her eyes. "What's wrong?"

He moved toward her and wound his hands around her upper arms. "That's what I want to know. What's going on?"

With a tiny head shake, she said, "I—I don't know what you mean."

"Don't." He gave her arms a squeeze, his gaze glued to hers. "You've been out of it all afternoon, ever since I took you to hear about Jade's project. Now I want to know what she said to make you so upset, because I know she did, or said, something after I left. Tell me."

"Yes, Stacy dear, tell him."

Nikko spun around to see Jade standing on the top riser.

Knowing her as he did, the expression he read on her face was pure malice. With a decided and calculated toss of her head, her hair not moving an iota out of its sprayed, perfect coif, she lowered her chin and stared at the two of them through half-slitted eyes, one eyebrow arched higher than the other, a very unattractive smirk across her lips.

He spun back around to Stacy. "Tell me. Please."

She swallowed. "I—I knew about the show concept for *Family Dinners* before Jade ever mentioned it to you."

He shrugged. "So? You knew before I did. Okay. Did you think I'd be mad?"

"No, it's not that."

"Then what? Come on, Stacy, you have to trust me."

She bit down on her bottom lip, her gaze flicking over his shoulder to Jade.

"Look at me, not her," he commanded.

Stacy's throat bobbled, the sound of her swallowing again loud in the small space between them.

"I knew about the concept of the show because...it's mine. I came up with it. Developed it."

"Really?"

She nodded.

"It's a good idea, I already told you that. There has to be something else that's making you so skittish, though. It feels like there is."

He could read the indecision in her eyes. And something else. Something that looked an awful lot like fear.

"If you don't tell him, I will," Jade said from behind them in a voice dripping with condescension. "Better to be honest now, don't you think?"

"Just shut up, Jade." He looked over his shoulder at her. She'd come into the camper and was leaning against the tabletop. "What are you even doing here? This doesn't concern you."

"You're wrong, Nikko. It does. More than you can ever guess."

He settled his attention back on Stacy.

"Tell me all of it," he said, his voice gentling.

With what looked like resignation, she nodded and slipped down onto one of the cushioned benches. Nikko sat down next to her and took one of her hands in his.

"I sent my idea for *Family Dinners* to Teddy Davis about a week before I came out here. He called me into his office and told me he was going to green-light the show, but he wanted me to do one favor for him before he did."

"That doesn't sound like Davis. He doesn't ask for favors. Ever. He usually shoots straight. Either approves an idea or doesn't."

"I know."

"What did he want you to do?"

She looked into his eyes and he swore he saw shame floating in them.

"He asked me to executive produce your show."

"*Beef Battles*? Why?"

"He said he needed someone he could trust to do a good job, and, well…."

"What?"

"Your reputation for not liking anyone to help manage your shows is a little legendary."

He lifted a shoulder again. "I can't argue with that because it's true. I don't like anyone but me calling the shots."

It was Stacy's turn to shrug. "He asked me to help keep a lid on spending and…"

"What?"

"Your temper." She bit down on her bottom lip.

"So, he asked you to come out here and help keep me from overspending and yelling? Is that it? Because from where I'm standing, that's not so bad."

"It's more," she said, casting her eyes downward again.

"Look at me."

She did. "What else?"

"I was afraid Teddy wouldn't keep his word about approving my show. That he was just agreeing in order to get me to come out here. So, I… that is—I—"

"She blackmailed him," Jade said.

"I did not!"

"What?" He spun around to Jade again. "What are you talking about?"

"She made him sign a document stating that she would get her own show *only* if she agreed to produce this one. You were just a means to an end, Nikko. Stacy produces your show, she gets her own as payment. Signed, sealed, delivered. Now, that sounds an awful lot like blackmail, doesn't it?"

The air in the room stilled; quieted.

His definition of blackmail and Jade's certainly weren't the same. But, still…

"Is this true?" he asked Stacy.

"It wasn't like that, I swear. I didn't blackmail him or push him into doing anything." She shot a nasty look at Jade over his shoulder. "I was only protecting myself, my idea. I couldn't just trust that Teddy'd keep his word and let me have my show after I was finished here. I didn't want to take the chance he'd renege, or change his mind about it. So I negotiated the terms for coming out here and doing what he wanted."

"To your advantage, apparently."

The hurt stung more than he expected it to. She'd used him as a means to an end.

Just as Flannery had.

"So you agreed to come out here if—and only if—he guaranteed you something in return."

Stacy's mouth pulled down at the corners. "It sounds horrible when you put it like that."

"But it's the truth, correct? You'd get rewarded if you kept me—what was it? Reined in, right?"

"Ultimately, yes. But—"

"So that's all this was?" He swiped a finger between their bodies. "You keeping me under control?"

"No, I—"

"That's all I was to you? A way for you to get what you wanted? A surefire way, it seems."

"Nikko, it wasn't like that—"

"Wasn't it? It seems to me it's obvious it was. While it may not be quite the blackmail scenario Jade paints, you did use me to get something you wanted."

With a violent shake of her head, she said, "I didn't use you. I wanted my show; Teddy wanted someone here. I only saw the end result, nothing else. But…" she reached back to try and take his hand again, but he snatched it away and stood.

"There are no *buts*." He looked down at her face and his stomach twisted into a knot so tight he could actually feel the pain of it pressing on his insides. "Nothing between us"—he snaked a quick glance at Jade, who was devouring every word—"was real. It was all an act. A way for you to appease Davis and get what you wanted in the bargain."

She shot up from her seat and tried to grab his arm. He pulled back.

"Don't say that. Please. Nikko, what you and I…what we have…it means something. It does. I—"

"No more lies."

"I'm not lying. Please—"

"I trusted you, Stacy. I thought you were one of the few genuine people I'd ever met in this business. Todd, the rest of the crew, they all like you, all turn to you with their problems. They rely on you, value your opinion. Trust you. I wonder how they'd feel knowing that you're just out for yourself? That you don't really give a damn about anyone else?"

Her head whipped back as if he'd slapped her. "Nikko, please. Please listen—"

"I'd done listening to you. Done with your lies. I'm just…done."

Shattered and angry, his heart broken and in tatters that he'd let another woman worm her way into it as a means to an end, he flew from the camper. Jade's sneer was the last thing he saw before leaping into the night.

* * * *

Stacy fell back onto the seat and dropped her head into her hands.

"You're better off without him," Jade said.

When she looked up, the woman was carelessly examining her perfect manicure. It took everything in her not to fly up and scratch the expertly made-up eyes out.

"Get out," she said, her voice a low rumble.

Jade's gaze took its time lifting up to meet hers.

What Stacy could only call triumph danced in their moist glaze.

"You really didn't think he was in love with you, did you? That he wanted to spend the rest of his life with you?"

Her caustic chortle made Stacy want to throw up.

"You really are a naïve little thing."

"I said get out. Now."

"Or what?" Jade tossed her shoulders back in an air of defiance. "You'll throw me out? Please." She waved a casual hand at her. "You don't have it in you, first of all. Secondly, you haven't come this far to do something that will permanently damage your career."

"You don't know me. At all. You have no idea what I'm capable of. Now. Get. Out."

Stacy liked to think it was the absolute coldhearted hatred she heard slip through her tone that finally got through to the bitch.

Jade's eyes widened, her mouth pulling open into a small circle. Just as quickly, she clamped it back shut. Without another word, shoulders square, chin high, she exited the camper.

As soon as the door shut behind her, Stacy slid to the floor, her legs losing the ability to keep her upright.

He wouldn't listen, wouldn't let her explain. His eyes had gone flat when he'd been speaking, the corners of his mouth pulling down to his chin. He looked...repulsed, furious, disgusted.

With her.

Through eyes clouded with tears, she pressed the number two on her cell phone.

A heartbeat later, Kandy's cheerful voice came through the cell.

"Hey, cuz. What's cooking in God's country?"

Stacy took a deep breath. "Leech."

Chapter Twenty-four

"You're getting out of this apartment today," Kandy said, hands on her hips as she glared at her cousin.

"And if we have to drag you out in your pj's, we will," her sister, Gemma, added. "You don't want two pregnant women to have to physically remove you from this place, do you?"

Kandy sat down on the edge of the bed and grabbed Stacy's hand. "You've been holed up here for two weeks. It's time to get out and be among the living again." The warmth that spread from her cousin's hand into her own icy one was a jolt to her senses.

"Two weeks is more than enough time to wallow," Gemma added, as she carefully lowered herself to the chair opposite the bed.

"I'm not wallowing," Stacy said. "I'm resting and recuperating after a very grueling assignment."

"Bullshit." Gemma pointed her index finger at her. "You're hiding out, playing the self-pity card. Over a *man*."

The word spat from between her lips.

Kandy shot an annoyed glare at her sister, then turned back to her cousin. "Gem's delivery may be a little harsh, but she's right, Stace. You have been hiding out. Avoiding the family, ducking phone calls and texts. And before you say you're tired and have needed the rest again," she added when Stacy opened her mouth, "we get that." She glanced back at her sister and nodded.

Gemma followed her lead and did as well.

"But there's resting and then there's isolating. That's really what you've been doing and it's just not good for you. It stops today."

Kandy squeezed Stacy's hand.

She didn't want to admit the truth, but her cousins were right. She *had* been isolating herself, shunning all contact with family, with work. She hadn't left her apartment since Kandy had driven her home from the airport. The moment she'd walked into the familiar, safe surroundings, the delicate thread she'd kept her emotions leashed together with since leaving the ranch at the crack of dawn the day after the finale, tore. Body-racking sobs flew from deep down inside her. She crossed her arms over her stomach and doubled over in the foyer, tears streaming down her cheeks like a plugged and congested dam had suddenly been unclogged.

Kandy had pushed her down onto the couch. Through a box-and-a-half of tissues Stacy had confessed everything, including how she'd fallen in love with Nikko Stamp and his daughter.

Kandy listened, as she always had, calmly and without interrupting once, until Stacy, talked and cried out, had been led into the bedroom and helped into bed.

Where she'd spent the majority of the past fourteen days.

Stacy knew if her parents had been there, they'd have descended on her the second she'd walked through the door and then camped out in her living room.

That she was thankful they were out of the country made her feel small and ungrateful, but she knew they'd have coddled and babied her with their version of loving and smothering affection.

Stacy neither wanted nor needed that. She wanted to be left alone and had gotten her wish.

Until the moment her pregnant cousins burst in on her solitude.

"I know," Stacy said with a sigh. "I know."

"Then if you know, get your skinny ass out of that bed and come to lunch with us," Gemma said. "This baby is starving"—she rubbed her hands across her burgeoning midsection—"and so am I. You look like you could use a good meal or two," she added. "And some sun. You're as pale as chalk."

Stacy couldn't help the twitch that pulled at her mouth. "You're such a boost to my fragile ego."

"Your ego is as hard as steel forged in iron," Kandy said, squeezing her hand again. "Grandma's backbone to a T."

Stacy remembered saying the same thing about her oldest cousin a time or two over the years.

"What do you think Grandma would say if she knew you were acting like this? If she walked in here and found you idling in bed with the covers pulled over your head, avoiding everything and everyone?" Kandy asked, one delicate eyebrow arched high on her forehead.

Stacy sighed again and sat up, adjusting the pillow behind her. "No thought needed. She'd glare at me through those all-knowing eyes of hers, fist her hands on her hips and ask, "Who you are? You not my Estella. Not my little *wojownik*."

The perfect imitation of their grandmother's thick Polish accent had her cousins grinning.

"She always called you her little warrior when you were in the hospital," Gemma said.

"I don't feel much like a warrior right now," Stacy said. The bone-sapping weariness of the past two weeks slowly wound through her. "I don't feel much like anything, except an idiot."

"You're not an idiot," Gemma said. "As far from it as a person can get."

"What do you call someone who falls for a guy who so obviously doesn't feel the same way about you, then? Who's so wrong for you on every level, but you still can't see anything else? Want anyone else but him? Smart? A genius, maybe?"

Kandy looked over at her sister and then back to Stacy.

"Normal?" she said, with a shrug.

Stacy's laugh had a sad edge to it. "If that's normal, then I want to be the polar opposite."

"Sweetie, correct me if I'm wrong," Kandy said, "but you've never really been in love before, have you? Total, consuming, devouring love?"

"The kind that knocks you on your ass and won't let you get up?" Gemma added.

"No." She shook her head. "I've never felt anything this powerful with any other man. It's…scary."

"You don't, exactly, have a history of getting too hung up on guys or letting them get hung up on you," Kandy said. "You pretty much shy away from strong relationships. Even before that whole disaster with Mark Begman, you held men at arm's length."

"Yeah. So?"

"I always thought it was because… well, you were afraid to let anyone get close."

Stacy shook her head. "Not so much afraid as cautious. I was always worried if I let a guy get to know me, get close… well, something bad would happen. Something tragic. Dumb, I know. But…"

"Oh, Stacy." Kandy leaned forward and hugged her. "You don't think the crash was your fault, do you? I mean, you can't."

"Not anymore, no. But I did. For a long time, especially when I was lying in the hospital with nothing but time to think. If I hadn't been so eager to rebel, that joyride would never have happened and Freddie Boxer would be alive today."

"Okay, so maybe you are a little bit of an idiot," Gemma said. "For thinking that," she qualified when her sister's head whipped around. "Nothing that happened was your fault. Nothing."

"I know that. Now. For the longest time, though, I protected myself from getting emotionally involved with any guy because I was worried it was. Keep it light. Keep it easy. Nikko was the first man I ever let get that close, let in. And I don't even think I let him in. He kind of just barreled in without any kind of warning."

She rubbed her eyes with the palms of her hands. "One minute he looked like he wanted to yell at me, the next he was holding me, his hand on my butt, his tongue down my throat, and all I could think was it felt so damn good. So…right. And it was wrong in so many ways. I was his assistant, and that whole workplace-romance thing bounced through my head. I was there to do a specific job, make sure it got done, and then leave. Not get caught up in a love affair with a guy who I didn't even think liked me. Who gave me no indication I was anything other than an annoyance at best."

Kandy's gaze slipped to her sister's. "You two have more things in common than you realize."

"What do you mean?" Stacy's gaze went from Kandy to Gemma. "That's what it was like for you and Ky?" Stacy asked, referring to her cousin's husband.

"Yup," Gemma said.

"I didn't know that."

Gemma flicked a hand in the air and pursed her lips into a very feminine pucker. "Only I was the one who was doing the yelling," she admitted. "The man made me crazy. In every way. He still does."

"But you two wound up together," Stacy said. "Ky loves you. Nikko doesn't love me. He thinks I'm untrustworthy and a liar. *A liar!* He wants nothing to do with me because he thinks I used him to advance my career. As a means to an end, according to him."

"You kinda did," Gemma said. When her sister shot her another annoyed glare, she added, "In the beginning and until you fell for him, that is."

"Okay," Stacy pointed her finger at her cousin much the way Gemma had just moments before. "I'll give you that. Maybe I did. Initially. But would he let me explain that? Would he let me tell him what I felt? Tell him how everything had changed? That he meant more to me than the show concept? That I wanted to be with him after the show wrapped? That I was totally in love with him and his daughter? No. He just looked at me like I was pond scum and stormed off like a big baby."

"The male ego has always been such a mystery to me," Kandy said.

"You've said that before." Her sister grinned. "A whole bunch of times."

"And it's still true."

Stacy raked her hands through her hair. "I can't believe he dismissed me outright, without even giving me a chance to explain what really happened," she said, ignoring her cousin's banter. "I never blackmailed Teddy. The offer was already on the table before he asked me to go to Montana. All I did was make him put it in writing."

"We know that," Kandy said.

It was as if she hadn't spoken. Stacy steamrolled along. "Sure, maybe I sweetened the pot a little by asking for full control, but Teddy agreed. He never said if I didn't go I wouldn't get my show. But Nikko never gave me the chance to tell him that. He just believed what Jade, that bitch, told him, that I had a quid pro quo agreement with Teddy. That I'd only agreed to produce the show if I was given my own when it was over as a repayment. Nikko never allowed me the courtesy to explain what really happened. Who does that? What kind of supposed grown man acts like that? It's no wonder people are scared of him. He's a megalomaniac whose only opinion he values is his own. The jerk." She kicked the covers off.

"Ah, and here's the Stacy we all know and love," Kandy stood. "Grandma's little warrior."

Stacy sprang up from the bed. "I'm done wallowing."

"I thought you weren't wallowing," Gemma said. Kandy shot daggers at her again. "Well, she said she wasn't."

"I did nothing wrong." She strode into her bathroom and turned the shower on. "I'm done wasting another second on regrets. Done mooning over a guy who doesn't want me. Who can't see me for the person I am. Who can't see I was willing to give him everything, every part of me."

The shower door slammed shut. "I need ten minutes," she called back to her bedroom.

"Take your time," Kandy called back.

"But not too long, because junior here is screaming for lunch!" Gemma added.

* * * *

Hearts, she realized as she plowed through her work emails and tried to de-clutter her desk, were both fragile and resilient. In the three days since she'd had her self-imposed banishment revoked and joined the living again, Stacy had learned this one very real fact. The heart she had never given to a man before had been battered and bruised, but still beat, still felt, and still went on.

After a lunch filled with family gossip and plans for the future, Stacy had kissed and thanked her cousins for forcing her ass into gear again. Then, she'd changed into workout clothes and put herself through an invigorating, exhausting yoga session, followed by a solid hour of meditation.

When she opened her eyes, the day had turned long and her spirits had turned light. She'd missed this during her emotional and physical exile. Missed the quiet contemplation; missed the rejuvenating bounce to her body and soul.

Wallowing, she'd found, did nothing but waste time. She realized that now, even though in the moment she'd needed the disconnection from everything in her life.

But not anymore. Her head was back on straight, her body was aligned, and her spirit was calmed. Grandma Sophie's little warrior was back.

Now all she had to do was clear her desk and see Teddy Davis. She'd arranged a meeting today, which he'd granted enthusiastically. She knew he'd grill her on the Montana production, but she was ready to answer any and all questions. When it came time to discuss her next project, she had an entire dialogue already constructed in her head. She was going to fight tooth and nail for her show.

A knock on her office door pulled her out of her musings. "Yes?"

Melora Stamp pushed her head through.

"Hey," the girl said.

A warm rush of pleased surprise ran through her. "Hey, yourself. Get in here."

Stacy rose and jogged around the desk, met Melora, and pulled her in for a tight hug.

When the girl wove her arms around Stacy's waist equally as body-huggingly snug, tears stung her eyes.

Stacy pulled back from the embrace and raked her gaze down the girl's frame.

"I'm so glad to see you. You look good," she said, meaning it. The subtle weight gain she'd noticed in Montana had started to fill in Melora's hollowed cheeks and neck. Now, the hollows were gone, her cheekbones high and round, her skin pink and tinged with a healthy glow.

"What are you doing here?"

The teen fell into the chair in front of the desk. "Nikko had a meeting, so I tagged."

Stacy had to will herself not to let out a sigh at the sound of his name. If he was in the building, there might be a slim chance she'd see him on her way to Teddy's office—a chance she didn't want to take. Seeing his daughter brought back the painful memory of the last time she'd spoken to him, the angry words he'd tossed at her, the heartbreaking way he'd left her. She took a mental breath and shut the feelings away.

"How've you been?" she asked. "Everything okay?"

"Cool. Things are getting back to, like, *normal,* after being away."

"School should be starting back up soon, right?"

Stacy hadn't realized until that moment how much she'd missed seeing that eye roll. "Ugh, yeah. I've got a few weeks, though, before it starts."

"Any plans? Or just having fun being back home?"

"Yeah, that's kinda the reason I'm here. I came with Nikko because I was hoping to catch you. Talk to you."

"Oh?" For a brief moment, Stacy was afraid it might have something to do with the way she'd abruptly left the ranch without saying good-bye.

"Gemma Laine called me," Melora said, her expressive eyes widening, a free and easy smile gracing her face.

"Oh. Oh, good." Relief washed through her. "I had lunch with her the other day and told her all about you and how much you like photography. I'm glad she reached out."

"She did, like, *way more* than reach out. I met with her yesterday, showed her some of my stuff. She offered me an intern job starting, like, *today, and* said if I can work it out, I can continue with it during school."

"Oh, Melora, that's great! Congratulations. I know how picky Gemma is with the people she lets intern for her. You must have really impressed her."

"She's so so so nice. I wanted to see you, to thank you for, like, telling her about me, and…"

"And?"

"Well." Melora dropped her chin.

"Sweetie, what is it?"

She watched as the girl took a deep breath, lifted her head, and stared at Stacy with such a look of pain in her eyes, she wanted to come around from behind the desk and gather her into her arms again.

"Did you and Daddy have a fight?"

Stacy's breath hissed in at the question.

"Because you left without saying good-bye and he was in such a grouch of a mood the night after the finale and the next day when he found out you'd left the ranch. He stomped around and grumbled like a rabid, starving bear when Mr. Dixon told us you'd bolted. You didn't even say good-bye."

She'd rushed it out all in one breath, the last word ending on a heartbreaking whine.

Before Stacy could respond, Melora went on. "I went looking for you the morning after. You weren't in your room. I needed to talk to you about, well...something. But you were already gone. I told Daddy and he went schizoid."

"What do you mean? What did he do?"

She sat forward in the chair and flipped her hand in the air. "Cursed. Threw his coffee mug. Then cursed again. I think he forgot I was in the room, 'cause he usually gets all batshit crazy if I so much as say 'damn.'"

Stacy was a little confused at his response. If he was so angry at her for "using him to advance her career" why, then, would he be mad she was gone?

"I know the two of you, like, *hooked up—*"

"*What?*"

"—and I thought you were, like, good for him. Daddy was happier than I'd seen him in a long, long time. I thought... well, I thought you'd, like, *be together* after the shoot was done. You know? Like a couple."

"Oh, Melora." Stacy sighed and shook her head. "Sweetie."

"Look, it was no secret, okay? I'm not two, you know. I could see how much Daddy changed when you were around. He was, like, calmer, and not such an ogre. I know some of that had to do with his leg pain getting better. But I think most of it had to do with you. How much he liked you. Depended on you. You were good for him."

Stacy sighed again.

"Plus, I saw him going into the main house one night when I was, you know, out talking with Riley."

"So much for keeping things a secret," Stacy mumbled. She wasn't sure if she was uncomfortable with Melora knowing about her and her father, or worried more people had found out about them.

"You did, didn't you? Have a fight? That's why you left before you were supposed to?"

"It was more of a misunderstanding," she told the girl after a moment. "But your father was very...angry at me and I thought leaving would be better all around. Production was done. He didn't really need me for anything any more." Not that he'd ever admit he had in the first place. "It seemed like the right thing to do at the time."

"It wasn't. It sucked. And it hurt. Big-time."

She could see that for herself. "Melora, for what it's worth, I never intended to hurt you. Especially you. I loved spending time with you. Getting to know you. I really did. You made what could have been a miserable two months so much better."

The girl nibbled on a thumbnail. With a quick nod, she said, "Okay. I, like, *forgive* you for bolting. Even though it was lame and shattering."

With a wry twist of her lips, she said, "Thanks. Are you—"

Her cell phone buzzed with a timed reminder for her meeting with Teddy Davis.

"Crap." She turned the reminder off. "Listen," she said, rising, "I have a thing I can't get out of. Are you going to stick around?"

"No. I've gotta get over to Gemma's studio by one. I don't want to be late my first day, you know?"

"No, of course not. When you've got a free afternoon, or even an hour sometime, text me. We can grab some lunch or go shopping. Do something fun, okay?"

The warmth from the smile that lit the teen's face seeped through her.

"Fab. Will do."

Stacy grabbed her notebook and phone, hugged Melora again, and said, "It was really good to see you. Really good. Thanks so much for stopping by."

"'K. I'll text."

Chapter Twenty-five

Stacy made her way up two flights to Teddy Davis's office.

When she'd called the day before requesting this meeting, he hadn't asked what it was about had he said anything about Montana or Jade Quartermaine. He'd simply named a time he was free and that he would see her then. He'd been polite and professional, and she'd been a little taken aback. She thought for sure he'd say something about *Family Dinners* or Jade. But he hadn't and she found herself a little uncertain of what was in store for her.

She pushed through the heavy glass doors to his office waiting room, bracing herself to see Teddy's horrible assistant.

Surprise jumped through her when she spotted someone she didn't know sitting behind the wide, cluttered desk.

A pleasant, open smile came her way. "Hi. I'm betting you're Stacy Peters."

Stacy nodded.

"It's nice to meet you. I'm Rebecca."

"Where's Althea?"

A smile she could only describe as *knowing* faced back at her. "Gone," was all she said. Stacy watched as she picked up the desk phone and punched one of the buttons. "Miss Peters is here…of course." She replaced the receiver. "You can go right on in. They're waiting for you in the conference room."

"They? I thought I was meeting with Teddy alone?"

The woman merely smiled and shook her head.

Stacy opened the door. Off to her right she saw another door, half open, to the area Teddy used for conference calls and project meetings. She crossed to it, rapped her knuckles across the frame, and then stepped in.

Davis was waiting for her. Despite the August heat swirling outside the thirty-story office building, melting the city dwellers and workers, he was clad from head to toe in a dark-blue three-piece, pinstriped, tailor-made suit with creases in the trousers so sharp she wondered how he didn't cut himself while getting dressed. An azure-blue button-down shirt, a bold paisley tie with matching pocket square and soft, hand-stitched Italian leather shoes completed his head-to-toe sartorial splendor.

When he grabbed her in for a full-body hug, the scent of Hugo Boss hit her senses full throttle.

"It's so good to have you home, Stace," he said, squeezing her, then pushing back to view her at arm's length.

His bushy brown brows beetled above his rimless eyeglasses as he peered at her through them. "Why did you wait so long to call me? You've been back, what? Two weeks?"

She nodded.

"Well," he said, taking her hand, "you probably just needed a rest. I hear the shoot was ridiculous busy and you were everywhere as usual, being your hyper-efficient self. Come on and sit down. We need to discuss a few things."

He turned, still holding on to her hand and just as she was about to ask who he'd heard from about the shoot, she got the shock of her life when she spotted Nikko Stamp sitting at the table.

She stopped short, yanking Teddy back a step when she did.

He looked...amazing. His hair was shorter and the tan that had started from the bright Montana sun had darkened to resemble tea with a splash of crème. The amber in his eyes seemed brighter, especially against his darker skin, and as his gaze stared across the room at her, her insides felt like a thousand butterflies were all flapping at once inside a lepidopterarium.

Teddy stared at her for a second, a ghost of a smile tugging at his lips. "I know you asked to speak to me in private, but I asked Nikko to join us because he's expressed an interest in directing your show."

Stacy's head shook side to side a few times before looking back to him. "My show?"

"Yeah, your show. *Family Dinners*? Remember? The one you pitched that I green-lighted before I sent you to Montana? The reason you're here today?"

"I—I—"

"Come on, Stace, sit down. Let's talk specifics."

He pulled her to a chair next to his and opposite from Nikko. She willed her eyes to settle anywhere in the room, on anything but at him, but they refused to heed her command. Drawn to him like light was to sunrise, her eyes found his. With a slight nod, he said, "Stacy."

Knowing her voice would shake with emotion, she stayed silent and nodded.

"So, kids," Teddy said as he leaned back in his chair and regarded the two of them. "I put *Family Dinners* on the winter-spring schedule for six replacement episodes, which means you'll need to start principle production pretty soon. If the show does well, it'll pick up for a fall starter. Stacy," he turned to her, "from the original proposal you sent me, you've already listed a dozen places that fit the bill for what you want. You'll need to pare that down to six by the end of business this week so we can get working on the travel logistics. Good?"

"Um, yeah. Fine. I can—I can do that. Sure."

Teddy turned to Nikko. "Just so we're all clear on this, Nikko, like I told you when you called, I gave Stacy carte blanche with crew choice. She decides who she wants to work with. I know you've expressed an interest in this show, but you still need to finish up the editing on *Beef Battles*. That's your primary concern."

It was Nikko's turn to nod. He leaned forward and placed his hands, clasped, on the table in front of him.

The urge to reach out, grab them, and press them all over her body was so quick and intense, she shuddered.

"I know, and editing is ninety-percent complete, just so you know." His gaze shifted to her. "I've been working on it around the clock since we got back so I could free up time."

"Great." Teddy grinned. "I love to hear that. Now, let's talk budget."

For the next half hour Stacy sat, dumbfounded for most of it, as the realization began to seep in that her show was still her show.

How had that happened?

Why had it happened? When she'd left the ranch, Stacy was certain the show idea had been stolen by Jade Quartermaine. That the woman all but had Teddy's blessing on hosting and taking over the production. During her self-imposed two-week banishment, Stacy had considered what her options were in regaining control. Apparently, she hadn't had to worry, because from everything the network programmer was saying, she was still at the helm. *Family Dinners* was hers—always had been—despite what Jade had said and done.

Now, as she listened to Teddy go on about production costs and time-slot choices, her body began to calm, then grow excited at the prospect that her dream was about to come true.

The one aspect that still confused and worried her was Nikko's presence. That huge stutter her heart kept experiencing every time he answered one of Teddy's questions or asked one of his own was becoming commonplace.

He was polite and sincere when he spoke, his gaze moving between her and Teddy, but always landing and staying on her face. Gone was the scowl she'd grown used to seeing those first weeks of production, replaced now by a relaxed and open expression. As she had been on site, she was once again impressed by how he was able to clearly see the big picture of the project and the tiny details inherent in bringing it to life.

Despite the way things had ended personally between them, Stacy appreciated what a marvelous leader he was.

Nikko's phone beeped and, as he rose, he said, "Sorry. Gotta take this." He moved from the room and Stacy took the opportunity to finally gear up the courage to ask Teddy the questions that had been drilling through her head.

Before she could, he preempted her.

"I know I ambushed you with Nikko, Stace, and you've probably got a ton of questions. But before you ask them, I need to tell you something first."

She took a breath. "Okay."

Teddy leaned forward and took one of her hands in his. "I know what happened in Montana."

She sucked in a breath, her face heating. How? Who had told him about her and Nikko? In the next instant, she answered her own question.

Jade Quartermaine.

Embarrassment shot through her.

"You—you do?"

"Yeah. I know Jade tried to hijack the show from you." He shook his head, his mouth pulling into a thin line.

"Oh. Well." Relief soared through her. "How did you? Find out, I mean?"

"Jade tipped her hand. Came waltzing in here the moment she got back from Montana, telling me how she'd heard about the project, had already gotten Nikko on board to direct, and was set to star. I asked her who she'd heard about it from, because"—he pointed a finger at her face—"I know you. Have for over eight years and I knew you'd never have mentioned a word about the show to anyone. Especially someone like Jade. When she said you'd been the one to seek her out, I knew she was lying."

"She was."

He nodded. "Yeah, well, it didn't take me too long to figure out who told her. Althea went ballistic when I signed that note for you—which, by the way, I only did to make you feel more secure. The show was yours the moment I read the proposal. Never a doubt." He squeezed her hand again. "When I confronted Althea, she confessed. I had no idea she was in cahoots with Jade. Believe me, if I had, I would have put a stop to their little spy ring the second I found out."

A quick grin shot from her lips as her stomach settled for the first time in an hour.

Hell, in two weeks.

"It's not every day you can use the words *cahoots* and *spy ring* in a normal conversation," she said.

"That's why I get paid the big bucks. Anyway, you'll notice Althea is gone. I fired her sorry ass on the spot and refused to give her a reference. As for Jade, well..." his pleasant smile turned just a shade nasty and Stacy remembered why his network nickname was Hitman. "Her contract is up for renewal and I can safely say her professional performance is being carefully evaluated with a fine-tooth legal comb."

"Teddy—"

He patted her hand. "Don't worry about anything, Stace. This is your show. Always was. Even before you agreed to go to Montana. Nikko—" he glanced up as the man came back into the room and lowered his voice—"knows that as well. I made sure of it when he called me. It's your decision who you want on your team, just like I agreed. If you want him, great. If not?" He shrugged. "We good, you and me?"

Overcome, Stacy leaned forward and kissed his cheek. "Better than good. Thank you. For everything."

His smile turned soft as he squeezed her hand a final time and sat back.

Nikko sat at the same time the table phone beeped.

Teddy answered it. "Yeah?"

While he listened, Stacy snuck a glance at Nikko. Her heart somersaulted when she found his eyes already trained on her face.

"Okay. Yeah," Teddy said into the phone. "Tell 'em I'll be up in five." As he hung up, he said, "I've gotta get to a meeting upstairs."

Upstairs, everyone at EBS knew, was the moniker for the offices of the television network heads.

"Stace, I'll need you to get me your specifics of crew and cast ASAP."

"Will do."

"You two keep the room. Talk. Nikko," he rose and turned to him, putting out his hand, "consider this your job interview. And remember, she has the final say."

Nikko rose as well, shook the man's hand, and said, "I know."

A quick kiss to Stacy's cheek and a pat on her shoulder and Teddy left, securing the conference door closed behind him.

Stacy was acutely aware she was now all alone with Nikko.

The urge to get up and run from the room was so strong she had to physically push herself down into the chair so she'd stay put.

She wouldn't let him see the hurt he'd caused her. She was better than that; stronger. Grandma's little warrior. She'd overcome far greater pain in her life than a battered and bruised heart and ego.

"Just be a professional," she whispered to herself. Keep it businesslike.

Nikko sat back down across from her. Neither of them spoke for a few moments.

"So. Since this is my official job interview," he said, after clearing his throat, "tell me how you envision the shoot."

Her head shot up at the slight hitch in his voice. One look at his eyes told her he was nervous.

Nervous.

"Well," she began, calling up all the calm she could from deep within her. Every meditative lesson she'd ever learned she willed forth.

She took a deep breath.

Keep emotions out of it. We're just two people discussing a project.

Stacy leaned forward and spread her palms flat on the table, mimicking Nikko.

Before she could blink, he reached across and grabbed them.

Waves of heat steeped into her, up her arms, settling in her chest, and knocking the breath from her.

"Nikko?"

On a moan, he shook his head. "I can't tell you what it does to me to hear you say my name again. I've missed hearing it. So much. I've missed…you."

"What?" She yanked back, but he tightened his grip.

"Don't, please," he said, impaling her with the emotions swimming in his eyes. "I need to say this before I chicken out."

Chicken out?

"Or you kick my ass to the curb. Which, by the way, I deserve."

He stood, never letting go of her hands, and came around to her side of the table. A gentle tug and he had her standing in front of him, the all-too-familiar heat of his body waving over her and making her…want. In one smooth move he let go of her hands and wound his own around her waist, pulling her against him.

Stacy laid her hands across his chest, intent on pushing away, but stood, paralyzed, when he said, "I'm so sorry."

His eyes darkened, deepened, as he stared down at her.

"Sorry?"

"For treating you the way I did. For being such a prick to you from day one." His grip tightened, pulling her even closer. They bodies touched from torso to knees. Under her satin bra her nipples hardened to two points as her breasts scraped against his granite-hewn chest.

His fingers slid back and forth across the small of her back, rubbing, pressing gently. Driving her insane.

"But especially for how I treated you after the finale."

When she bristled against him, he blew out a tired breath and shook his head. "I acted like a total moron."

"That's one word for it," she said before she could help herself, her desire to remain calm dissipating. "I can think of a few others."

"Nothing you can come up with I haven't already called myself. Or my daughter has."

"What?"

"When we found out you'd left, she lit into me. Held back nothing. She may be fifteen, but when she's on a tear she sounds an awful lot like my mother. I was so blown away by how mad she was it didn't even register she knew about us until much later."

Stacy nodded. "She came to see me before this meeting." Her face flushed from her neck, upward, at the memory. "She told me she knew we'd...hooked up, was the expression she used."

"*Christ.*" He shook his head and pulled her against him so her head lay across his pecs, her arms circled around his back. She could hear the steady thrumming of his heart and was calmed by it; soothed. She should pull away, she really should. But....

"It's humiliating to be called out by a teenager. Especially when everything she said was dead-on." His hands trailed up her back. "After she calmed down, Melora told me she knew you and I were involved, romantically. She was thrilled. Her word. Said it made her happy to see two people she loved happy."

Stacy smiled against his chest. She loved the girl too. How could she help falling for her snarky, honest, open personality?

"She didn't mince words, though, when she accused me of being the reason you left the ranch. She didn't even know about what went down with

Jade, just assumed you'd left and I was the cause. The kid is unbelievably intuitive, I'll give her that."

His knee snaked between her legs, opening them and finding a place to nestle against her. Stacy didn't think he even realized he'd made the move, it felt so natural.

"I went a little crazy after I found out you'd left," he continued. "It's a good thing the show was in the can because I can tell you, honestly, the crew would have mutinied. I was so angry."

"At me?"

"No, sweetheart, not you. Never you. Myself."

The endearment pushed her anger and hurt to the side as the word crept into her heart.

"I believed Jade even though I knew what a spiteful hag she is," he continued. "That was my first mistake. Not letting you explain was the second. I called Teddy the minute I calmed down."

"Teddy? Why?"

"I wanted to hear from his mouth the reason he'd sent you. I wanted proof that what Jade said was true. Before I could even ask, he mowed over me, wanting to know how you were doing. Told me he'd known sending you was a big risk—to you—but he was so confident you'd stick it out. That's when I asked him about Jade. I thought I was mad about the situation, but Ted went ballistic. Read me chapter, book, and verse about how he'd coerced you into going to Montana because he knew how beneficial you'd be for the production. And for me. Even if you'd refused, he told me, your project was still a go because it was that good of an idea. I told him I agreed."

He pulled back, cupped her cheeks in his hands. "I know you left because I hurt you," he said, rubbing his thumb across her bottom lip, "and I'm so sorry for that."

"I think you can share some of that hurt," she told him. Looking at his actions with a little distance had given her the ability to see that now. "You thought I'd used you. That everything we'd…shared together was just a means to an end. I can understand your anger."

He dropped his chin, closing his eyes for a moment. When he opened them, the piercing emotions swimming in them impaled her.

"No one likes to think they've been used. I've experienced it firsthand and believe me, it's soul-sucking."

It was her turn to take his face in her hands. "I know. Jade told me about your wife. She knew how it would look if you found out about the paper

I'd had Teddy sign. How my actions would seem to you." She shook her head. "She was right."

"I should have realized it was all Jade's doing, not yours. She's the one who uses people as stepping-stones. I should have known you'd never use anyone, never hurt anybody, just to get something you wanted. That's not you. It's not how you are."

"You really don't know who I am," she said, softly. "Or what I'm capable of."

"That's not true." He splayed his hands, the tips of his fingers spread over her butt. "I know you better than you think. You're smart, conscientious, kind." He slid his knee against her, and she realized right then and there he knew exactly what he was doing to her. "You're a born leader, even though you don't see yourself that way. You're warm and open and accepting. And you're the bravest woman I've ever known."

She huffed out a laugh. "I'm not brave."

His hands tightened around her again. "You are," he whispered as he bent his head, his lips hovering over hers. "And you're one more thing."

A gentle swipe of his mouth against hers had her knees softening. "W—what?"

"You're loved." He kissed her again. "I love you, Stacy. I swear to God I think I fell for you the second I stepped out of Dixon's truck. You were all professional and polished, strong and determined, with that take-no-prisoners attitude."

Stacy's body stilled, despite being engulfed in fire every time his lips pressed against hers. "Is that really how you see me?"

For an answer, his mouth took hers again, the soft insistence of his lips pressing, torturing, delighting.

"That, and so much more." A swipe of her bottom lip with his tongue and she opened for him. As he deepened the kiss, showing her the truth of his words, she let herself accept them.

He loved her.

Her.

He lifted his head and peered down at her, that familiar, furrowed glower she'd come to cherish covering his face again. "Tell me I haven't ruined us. Haven't ruined what was between us. I don't know how I'll get through the days if I have."

"Nikko." She sighed and closed her eyes. When she opened them again, she felt the sting of tears.

"Please, Stacy. Just tell me. I have to know."

Through a jagged breath, she told him what she'd never been able to tell any other man. What she'd never felt for any other man. What she felt only for him.

"I love you too."

Before she could tell him everything in her heart, he lifted her off her toes in a bone-rattling hug and rained kisses all over her face and jaw.

"Thank God," he said when he finally put her down again.

They stood, gazing at one another for a few seconds. Then, a heart-stopping grin split his face and it was all she could do to keep her balance steady.

"So." His eyes hooded as he dragged and flattened her up against him again. With one hand squeezing her butt, the other snaked around her neck, he asked, "Does this mean I got the job?"

He swallowed Stacy's laugh with his kiss.

Chapter Twenty-six

"What can I get you folks?"

Stacy smiled up at the buxom, middle-aged waitress waiting to take their order. A tinged-with-gray black-pixie haircut engulfed a plump face that had a sweet-eyed expression and a mouth that looked used to smiling.

Nikko ordered the meat loaf, while Stacy opted for a cheeseburger. When it was Melora's turn to order, the teen's lips pulled into a pout as she perused the broad menu. "I can't make up my mind. There's so many choices."

The waitress—or Maybelle, as her name tag read—smiled. "Sure are. Menu's been voted best in the state for the past three years. You like mac and cheese?" Her eyes roamed across Melora's face and torso. "Never met a teenager who didn't, and Earl's cheesy mac will spoil you for the rest of your life for anyone else's."

Melora's face split into a wide, open grin. "Sold."

Maybelle grinned, nodded, and said, "I'll be right back with your drinks."

"This place looks exactly like it was described," Nikko said, glancing around the crowded, noisy diner. "If the food is half as good as we've been told, the crew will never want to go home."

The research she'd done on Earl's Diner was extensive. Stacy knew all about their numerous dining and people's-choice awards from articles she'd read online. Today's stop at the diner was a preproduction go-see for her and Nikko to determine the logistics of filming the place. She hadn't contacted the owner yet, preferring to see the diner in its natural, everyday state, first.

So far, she hadn't been disappointed.

"So, this is like, the last one, right? Before you know if you're going to get renewed?" Melora asked.

Seated across from Stacy and next to her father, the teen's questioning gaze settled on Stacy.

"Yes. So far, the footage we've gotten on the others is good."

"Better than good," Nikko said. "But, yes, after this one is filmed, you're off the hook for following us around for a while."

To keep Melora in the mix and not home alone while he traveled, Nikko and Stacy had worked out a filming schedule that took them all across the country two weekends a month. Traveling with Nikko and his daughter to the various location shoots had been some of the happiest times in Stacy's life, compared only to the times she and Nikko spent alone.

From the moment they'd left Teddy's office, the two had spent every minute they could together. Nikko had asked Stacy to watch the edited footage from *Beef Battles*, wanting her opinion. He'd done an outstanding job and the show was guaranteed to be a ratings winner, of that she had no doubt.

Since declaring his feelings for her, Nikko's entire demeanor had changed; lightened. Melora had commented more than once about how much happier he was whenever Stacy was around. Privately, the girl had questioned Stacy about her own feelings. When Stacy admitted how much she loved Nikko, Melora had cried and thrown her arms around her. She was still so much like a little girl and her mother's death was still such a recent occurrence, that Stacy wouldn't have blamed Melora in the least if she'd resented her, or squawked at the amount of time she spent with the girl's father. But Stacy's heart had simply filled with the acceptance Melora had given her, and with her own love for the teen.

"It's been fun," Melora said, smiling at the waitress as she delivered their drinks.

"You folks just passing by or visiting?" Maybelle asked.

"Visiting," Nikko said.

"Well, if you're looking for things to do, sights to see, just let me know. My cousin, Donny, is the head of the Chamber of Commerce and I can have him give you a rundown on the area. We get a lotta nice families like yourselves passing through while vacationing. It's nice to stop a while and get the local flavor of a place, you know?"

With a wink, she ambled to the next table.

"She thinks we're, like, *a family* passing through town," Melora said, pointedly staring at her father.

Confused at the look, Stacy took a sip of her water, then said, "Makes sense she'd think that. Look around." She swiped a hand across the diner. The tables and booths were packed with people of all ages, from toddlers in infant seats to an elderly couple holding hands across a table.

"It's a family place."

"Yeah," Melora said, her eyes still settled on her father's face. "It is."

Nikko's ears turned a quick shade of pink under his daughter's scrutiny.

"What's going on?" Stacy asked, her gaze bouncing between the two of them.

"Yeah, *Dad*. What's going on?"

"You know," he said, laying his palms flat on the table, and addressing his daughter, "I've been giving serious consideration lately to enrolling you in a boarding school. Run by nuns. In Switzerland."

"Yeah, like that's ever gonna happen." She cocked her head toward Stacy and widened her eyes.

"Melora." There was a subtle warning in his voice Stacy couldn't fathom.

"*Nikko.*"

The scowl that had been missing for the past few months popped up on his face while they stared at one another.

"Okay, look." She rose from the booth. "I'm gonna go to the bathroom." Staring down at her father, she added, "Use the alone time wisely."

When she sauntered off, Stacy looked over at Nikko.

"Alone at last," he said with a sigh as he grabbed her hands across the table. "I'm serious about the boarding school."

"No, you're not. What was that all about?"

He shook his head and squeezed her hands. "I made the mistake of telling her something in confidence last week and she's like a tick. She won't let it go."

"What did you tell her?"

"Just something I was planning on doing." He stared out of the window to the parking lot.

When he didn't say anything further, she asked, "Care to share?"

He drew his gaze back to her and she was surprised to see the identical expression swimming in his eyes he'd had the day in Teddy's office.

He was nervous.

"Nikko?"

He dropped his gaze down to their joined hands and then back up to hers again.

"Stacy. Sweetheart."

When he went no further, she said, "You know, don't you, that I melt a little inside, every time you call me that, right?"

His mouth twitched at the corners. With a nod, he let go of one of her hands.

"I'd planned on doing this in a much more romantic setting. Not," he glanced around, "in the middle of a diner when we're working."

"Do what?"

He brought the hand he held to his lips, gently kissed her knuckles.

"I'm melting again." She chuckled. The laugh stopped cold when he drew his other hand back up to the table. In it was a small, blue, square box. The blue was so familiar, so iconic, she gasped when the meaning of it hit her.

"But Melora has a point. This is a family place, so it seems appropriate to ask you this here. Now."

With this thumb and index finger, he shot open the box to reveal an enormous emerald-cut diamond. Stacy's eyes started to burn and she couldn't decide if the tears were from joy or because the boulder staring back at her was so brilliant and bright.

"Stacy Peters, I love you. So much, there are times I can't breathe the feeling is so overwhelming."

She smiled at him.

"I know we had a rocky start. I was in bad place physically, emotionally. But if I've learned anything in the past year, it's that love can go a long way in healing a person. In making you feel whole again. So. I'm asking you to marry me. To take me, and my annoyingly perceptive daughter"—she laughed, her vision blurring through the tears—"as your own and making us a new family. One we can grow with. Love with. Spend together. For the rest of our lives."

Her hand squeezed his.

"Please don't say no," he added, his mouth quirking up at one corner. "There are at least fifty pair of eyes trained on us right now and I think I'd die of mortification if you said no."

She did a quick pan around them, saw the smiling, expectant faces of the diner's patrons all zeroed in on their table, and chuckled.

When she settled back on his handsome face, she said, "Well, I can't have your death on my conscience, so I'd better say yes."

When his grin split his lips in two, she repeated it so everyone could hear.

"I said yes."

Nikko slipped the ring on the appropriate finger on the hand he still held and when he leaned over to kiss her, through the sound of clapping, his baby girl's voice loud and clear called, "It's about, like, *freaking time!*"

RECIPES FROM THE DIXON RANCH

Sweet and Saucy Barbeque Sauce

This is the sauce recipe that Riley MacNeill used in the *Beef Battles* challenge that won him the first-place prize. He smothered his rack of ribs in it and the judges loved the sweet, juicy, and subtle tangy flavor profile.

2 cups ketchup
1 cup water
½ cup apple cider vinegar
6 tablespoons light brown sugar
6 tablespoons sugar
½ tablespoon black pepper
½ tablespoon minced onion
½ tablespoon ground mustard
1 tablespoon freshly squeezed lemon juice
1 tablespoon Worcestershire sauce

Combine the ketchup, water, vinegar, lemon juice, and Worcestershire sauce in a bowl. Set aside.

Mix together the brown sugar, white sugar, black pepper, minced onion, and mustard together.

Add liquid ingredients to dry ones. Mix thoroughly by hand—do not mix in a blender or with an electric mixer.

Cover and place in refrigerator for at least 2 hours. Can be left overnight.

Prior to using, remove from refrigerator and "paint" over meat, chicken, or pork prior to cooking. If possible, let "painted" protein marinate for 2–4 hours prior to cooking. Then baste at 5-minute intervals while cooking until protein is cooked to satisfaction.

Chicken Fried Steak
A cowboy favorite!

¾ cup breadcrumbs, unseasoned
1 ½ teaspoons fresh basil, chopped fine
½ teaspoon table salt
¼ teaspoon black pepper
1 large egg, beaten
1 tablespoon whole milk
plus
1 ⅓ cups whole milk
2 tablespoons oil (canola is best.)
1 small yellow onion, thinly sliced
2 tablespoons all-purpose white flour

The best cut of steak to use is top round steak, each individual steak cut at least ½ thick each, and 4 oz each. You can take a one-pound steak and cut it into fourths, if you want.

Pound each steak between two pieces of parchment paper with a cooking mallet until each is approximately ¼ inch thick. This not only tenderizes the meat, it makes it easier to cook.

In a small bowl, mix together the breadcrumbs, basil, ½ teaspoon salt, and ¼ teaspoon black pepper.

In another bowl, combine the beaten egg, and 1 tablespoon of the milk.

Dip each steak into the egg mixture, shaking off excess, and then roll in the breadcrumb mixture.

In a large skillet (12–14 inches) heat the oil over medium heat and cook each steak for 5–7 minutes, turning once, until both sides are brown.

Then, reduce heat to low-medium. Cover and let cook for 45–60 minutes, or until meat is tender. Transfer to a serving plate or platter and keep warm. Do not discard the skillet drippings.

To make the gravy, cook the onion in the reserved skillet drippings until tender, but do not overcook. If the onion turns brown, you have cooked it too long. Add in the flour and then slowly add in the milk (1 ⅓ cups) a little at a time, continually stirring until the gravy is thick and bubbling. If desired, add in a little extra salt and pepper to taste.

Pour over the steak and serve hot.

Spicy Short Ribs
Another ranch-hand favorite!

4 pounds beef short ribs cut into small, serving-sized pieces
⅓ cup ketchup
⅓ cup hot chili sauce
¼ cup molasses OR ½ cup brown sugar
3–4 tablespoons freshly squeezed lemon juice
3 tablespoons yellow, spicy mustard
⅓ teaspoon ground red pepper

Place the ribs in a 6-quart Dutch oven and add warm water to completely cover the meat. Bring it to boiling and then reduce the heat to a low simmer. Cover and simmer for 2 hours or until meat, when tested, is tender.

Drain the water.

Combine the ketchup, chili sauce, molasses (or brown sugar), the lemon juice, mustard, and the red pepper.

Brush the ribs with the sauce, then place the ribs in the broiler on a broiling sheet for 12–15 minutes, turning every 2–3 minutes and re-brushing with the sauce.

Once thoroughly heated and the sauce now resembles a glaze, serve.

Cheesy Corn Frittata
A hearty breakfast for the ranch workers

8 large eggs, beaten
1 tablespoon fresh, chopped basil
2 tablespoons extra-virgin olive oil
1 cup of freshly-cut corn—uncooked
⅓ cup sliced green onions
¾ cup freshly diced tomatoes, not canned
¾ cup shredded sharp cheddar cheese

In a bowl, combine the basil and the beaten eggs.

Heat the oil in a large cast-iron skillet and cook the corn and green onions for approximately 3 minutes. Add the tomatoes and cook for another 4–6 minutes, stirring often. The vegetables should be tender when speared with a fork. Don't overcook them to where they are mushy.

Pour the eggs and basil over the vegetables, stir everything together, and cook over medium heat until eggs begin to set—anywhere from 5–10 minutes depending on your stove-top settings. As the mixture begins to set, lift up the edges and tip the skillet so uncooked eggs slip under and cook directly against the heat.

When mixture is set, sprinkle with cheese and place into a broiler until the cheese is melted. This shouldn't take more than 2–3 minutes. Serve hot.

Acknowledgments

Research is important for any writer. You want to make sure if you're writing about a subject you give factual, constructive information to your readers. Writers can and do spend endless hours trolling the Internet, interviewing experts, and trying to corral every resource they can to make sure they get it right.

The character of Melora Stamp is probably the nearest and dearest to my heart of any character I've breathed life into. When I was plotting out *Can't Stand the Heat*, I knew she had to have some way of connecting with Stacy as more than just a likable, snarky, intelligent teen. Giving her an eating disorder was an idea I internally battled with myself about for weeks. But, in the long run, I knew it was the right way to go. Especially when I didn't have to go far to do any research. We all have certain issues in our lives that we'd rather not address and share with others. That's a normal human response. No one wants to look like they have serious problems in front of other people. For me, it's a decades-long battle with my own eating disorder and self-worth issues. The therapy instituted for Melora's anorexia was a familiar one to me, so I felt confident in presenting it the way I have. But it's not the only therapy that can be instituted. Therapy has to be individualized, because each person's eating issues are individual to them and them alone. If you know someone who has issues with food, or if you do, it's not too late to seek help and guidance. Remember: It's never about the food alone. There is always an underlying issue that leads to an eating disorder. For Melora, it was the unexpected death of her mother and being unable to control the events that came from that: Nikko's surgeries and hospitalizations; her thoughts that he didn't want her to live with him. It's never just about the food.

As always, I'd like to thank the staff at Kensignton/Lyrical Shine for making this story the best it could be, for you guidance, extreme patience, and professionalism along every step of the publishing process.

To my wonderful editor, Esi Sogah. Thanks for your brainstorming ideas about the title, your words of wisdom with plotting and editing, and your invaluable insights. You truly make my writing better with each and every book.

And, of course, to the two halves of my heart, my daughter and husband. You've put up with my ridiculousness for so many years that I can only assume it's because you love me unconditionally, fat or skinny, snarky or smiling. Without the two of you I would be no one.

Want to spice things up?
Then be sure to check out the other books in the
Will Cook for Love series
COOKING WITH KANDY
And
A SHOT AT LOVE
Available now from Lyrical Shine
Wherever ebooks are sold

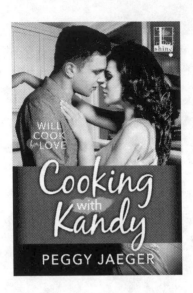

Sugar and spice and everything sexy make the perfect recipe for romance in this brand-new series by Peggy Jaeger. Look for exclusive recipes in each book!

Kandy Laine built her wildly popular food empire the old-fashioned way—starting with the basic ingredients of her grandmother's recipes and flavoring it all with her particular brand of sweet spice. From her cookbooks to her hit TV show, Kandy is a kitchen queen—and suddenly someone is determined to poison her cup. With odd accidents and threatening messages piling up, strong-willed Kandy can't protest when her team hires someone to keep her safe—but she can't deny that the man for the job looks delicious...

Josh Keane is a private investigator, not a bodyguard. But with one eyeful of Kandy's ebony curls and dimpled smile, he's signing on to uncover who's cooking up trouble for the gorgeous chef. As the attraction between them starts to simmer, it's not easy to keep his mind on the job, but when the strange distractions turn to true danger, he'll stop at nothing to keep Kandy safe—and show her that a future together is on the menu...

About the Author

Peggy Jaeger is a contemporary romance author who writes about strong women, the families who support them, and the men who can't live without them.

Peggy holds a master's degree in Nursing Administration and Geriatric Psychology and first found publication with several articles she authored on Alzheimer's disease during her time running an Alzheimer's inpatient care unit during the 1990s.

A lifelong and avid romance reader and writer, she is a member of RWA and her local New Hampshire RWA Chapter, where she was the 2016 Chapter Secretary.

Visit her at www.peggyjaeger.com.

Printed in the United States
by Baker & Taylor Publisher Services